Not Your Type

Elizabeth Jeannel

Cover design by Elizabeth Jeannel
ISBN 978-1-956037-00-5 (hardcover)
ISBN 978-1-956037-06-7 (paperback)
ISBN 978-1-956037-05-0 (ebook)
First Edition
First Edition: March 2022
This ebook edition first published in 2022

Published by Hansen House
www.hansenhousebooks.com

This book is dedicated all those who were somehow convinced love is pain.
To the generations of women in my family who suffered at the hands of those who claimed to love them.
But especially to a 20-year-old version of me who needed this book then, if only as a light in the darkness after everything that 'love' had given her.

We are breaking that cycle. That cycle ends here.

Dear Reader,

Firstly, thank you so much for your interest in *Not Your Type*. I cannot express enough how personal this story has become to me. This book started as a soft and fluffy romance about an ace woman who isn't out of the closet, and in the beginning, that's all I thought it would be. Unfortunately, I made the mistake of starting the writing process in the same month that I started therapy.

In therapy, I've worked on healing and learned better ways to cope with my traumas, so a lot of my personal experiences, particularly what I was feeling during the drafting stages, seeped into this book. My traumas became Ava and Parker's traumas.

While most of what happens in this story has been dramatized to better fit a fictional setting, some of these things did happen in real life to me, albeit in very different ways. I am a panromantic ace woman with an abusive ex (or two) who had to learn to accept love and believe that I deserve it.

I'm writing this to you so that you know what is in store. There are discussions of abuse, sexual assault, domestic violence, and stalking. There are on page discussions and scenes depicting alcoholism. I also feel there should be a warning that nearly every character works in the service industry.

For my Ace readers especially, you should know this book contains sexual scenes and scenes alluding to sexual activity. If you would like a more specific spoiler as to avoid these scenes, please check my website at www.elizabethjeannel.com.

Thank you again for your interest in *Not Your Type*. I can only hope that what you find in these pages is half as healing for you as writing them was for me.

All my love,

Elizabeth,

Prologue

Her name was Cam, and I didn't think I could ever love someone as much as her. By the time it was over, I didn't think someone would ever hurt me as much, either.

Cam and I met the summer before my twentieth birthday at the local mall. I'll never forget that day because it was the first time a girl had ever approached *me*. In public, not found me off a dating site. She knew I was gay because of my key chain, and she just casually came up and started flirting.

The attention was addicting. I had never had someone take so much interest in me, soak up every secret I had to share, explore every interest, ask about every person I'd ever loved. She learned so much about me, and showered me with a love so personal, I couldn't imagine it could be better than that. I later learned the term for that was love-bombing, and it was part of a vicious cycle I'd be trapped in for nearly three years.

She had this infectious laugh and a take charge attitude. At first, I liked that about her, the take charge attitude. It was nice to let someone else be in control, to let go and relax, but I guess I made it too easy for her. I made it far too easy for her to manipulate me, control me, change me.

Sometimes I think she chose me for a specific reason. She picked me out of a crowd and interviewed me that first day. How else would she have known I'd be so easy to control? I suppose people like her are good at spotting people like me, and the interview? I guess that didn't hurt either.

I was barely out of the closet, a one-month long girlfriend into a sexuality I wouldn't claim after Cam and I went our separate ways, and Cam? Well, I don't think she ever knew what the hell she wanted. It sure as hell wasn't me.

For some reason, I was hooked on her the moment I looked into her bright blue eyes, saw the flash of her perfect teeth, and I was always one blush away from saying 'I love you'. It was like she always knew just what to say, how to say it, to make me swoon for her.

The first six months were perfect, blissful even. I thought that's how it was when you're young and in love. I was exploring this whole thing, learning every inch of her body, and falling deeper for her with every wall she pretended to tear down for me.

Everything was perfect until she wanted to touch me, and she sensed my hesitation. It was the one thing I never gave her full control over.

Cam was patient about it at first. She told me we could take our time, even though I knew six months in was well past taking our time. She was patient. And then she wasn't.

Suddenly, my location had to be on. Or I could be cheating. She had to know who I was with all the time. She had to know my work schedule, my school schedule.

I should have known not to move in with her. When she was already controlling from 45 minutes away. But I'd already asked her to marry me. I'd gotten her dad's permission, too. Went to their place when she was working, and we had a long talk. I'd spent everything I had to get that stupid custom ring she wanted, and I was just as stubborn as I was clueless.

Because the moment she had me under her roof, I started losing grip on my identity. I lost contact with friends, family, anyone who could take me away from her. Until she was the only thing I had. I guess that's exactly how she wanted it.

Somehow, I convinced myself that's how it should be.

Sex became less about pleasing each other and more about her controlling me. The more she did that, the less I wanted to have sex with her, the less I wanted her to touch me, and the angrier she became. Because if I wasn't getting it from her, I had to be from someone else.

In a matter of months, our relationship shifted from "god how did I get lucky enough to call you mine, you're the most beautiful girl in the world." to "you're mine, and nobody else is ever going to love you like I do, so don't even think about leaving." Love turned into fear at the drop of a hat.

And it went on like that. Until she started going out more. She started seeing people I didn't know, leaving me home alone to wallow with the empty feelings she always left behind in her wake. Usually she'd yell before she left, so I'd be miserable without her.

She'd come home drunk and angry. Usually, she'd scream some more for a bit, try to force herself on me before passing out on the couch.

And any time I threatened to leave, it always ended the same.

She'd cry, beg, plead, promise to do better—be better. Then, for a short while, she would be. She'd be back to the Cam I fell in love with. She'd be home more, doting, kind, respectful. Once I thought... okay, it's fine again, she'd shift. And the cycle would begin again.

Still, I did everything I could to make it work. I bought lingerie and put it on before she came home with every intention of letting her do whatever she wanted to me once she got it off. I'd even pretend to like it—I was getting better at that.

When that didn't work, I'd clean the house, or I'd buy her gifts. But nothing was ever good enough. Because as much as she didn't want me to leave, she didn't want me anymore either, not really.

"Please." I asked as she got ready for a night out. I'd made dinner. I even did my makeup. There were tears forming in my eyes, and I tried to blink them back. I didn't need her calling me a little bitch today. "Stay home with me. I can—"

"There's nothing you can do for me that I can't find better from someone else."

I scoffed. "So, what, you don't want me anymore?"

She grabbed me before I could even blink, slamming my shoulders into the hallway wall. Her hand clinched around my jaw as she squeezed. It hurt. Just enough for my eyes to water, but we both knew it wouldn't leave a mark. Maybe it would be red for an hour or so, but by tomorrow, no one would know but me. Because Cam would forget about it by the time she got home.

That's how Cam was when she got physical. Painful, controlling, but secret.

"Listen carefully, of course I don't want you." She practically spat the words in my face. "You're lucky you have me. The only person who's ever going to love you is me. You think anyone could love you when you cry like a bitch every time, they touch you? When you lay there like a stiff board? Nobody is going to want you. Nobody. I'm all you've got."

She let my face go with a shove and stormed out the door, probably headed off to sleep with someone else.

She'd say those exact words to me every night for the next eight months before I would finally leave. By then, I was too damaged to think twice about the things she'd said to me. They became engrained in my brain like a mantra.

And even once I learned the word asexual, even when I knew there were other people out there just like me, I still didn't believe anybody would want me.

Parker

The tv was just background noise, as my eyes were glued to a random spot on the wall. I sat with a nearly icy mug of barely touched coffee in one hand, lost in my head, the train of thought having gone so far off track, I couldn't remember where I'd started. But mostly I was too tired to try.

"Okay, that's it." My best friend, Noah, snapped, snatching the mug from my hand. "It's late enough. Get out of here."

"Its nine am." I said back after a quick glance at the clock on our living room wall, surprised at how dry my throat was.

"Yeah, I don't care. Go get some breakfast, or go to the coffee shop." He said, dumping my mug in the sink rather dramatically, like he was making a huge point. "Hit the record store. I don't care, but you're not going to sit and dissociate on my couch. Not on my watch. A whole month of this, it's not healthy."

"I'm–"

"No, you're not. You can't just go to work, go to sleep, and fill your spare time separating from yourself. Jayde's gone. I know that hurts, and I know it's going to take you some time, but she's not coming back. And if she did, I wouldn't let her move back in anyway. Because you deserve better. Now get out."

"But I–"

"Nope, out." His normally sarcastic grin had turned into a fatherly-like scowl as he shoved a jacket in my hand and then shoved me out the front door.

He was right, as per usual. I was isolating. And dissociating. And as much as I knew it wasn't healthy, I had little motivation to do anything else.

I started walking and kept walking and walking. When you've been with someone for as long as I'd been off and on with Jayde, certain places are so emotionally draining, they're instantly off limits. Certain places sometimes feel like all places.

I stopped in front of a vintage style diner. It looked like someone had pulled it out of the past with baby blue booths and barstools inside. Jayde would have hated it. She would have called it tacky where I thought it was quaint. And just that thought made me step inside.

"Have a seat wherever you'd like, Honey!" A voice called from somewhere in the kitchen over the sizzling of fryers and grills.

"Thanks." I called back aimlessly, taking a seat at an empty baby blue booth.

The whole place was empty save for a one guy in the back who was hugging his mug of coffee like it might be his last. He gave me a soft, toothy smile and then turned his attention back to the window to his right. I must have come in just in time to miss any major rush.

An older woman came out of the swinging kitchen door with a steaming plate for the man in the corner. Her raspy voice said something to him with a wide smile before she made her way to me, the soles of her non slip shoes clicking ever so slightly on the black-and-white checkered floor.

She had one of those faces that just screamed, Mom, but you didn't dare guess her age. Her lips were painted a bright red, which was about the only color in her all-black uniform. And her mostly chestnut hair was on the top of her head in a curly bun woven with glistening grey hairs.

"Hey there, Sugar," she smiled, pulling out a small notepad. "Name's Meg. What can I get started for you to drink?"

"Um, an iced tea would be fine." I smiled back as she tapped her notepad and eyed me before turning away.

When Meg returned with a tea and a plate with a large piece of pie on it, I couldn't help but frown.

"You look like you could use one of these." She smiled, placing the pie in front of me.

I hadn't even gotten around to looking at the menu. I wasn't even really all that hungry.

"Thanks." I said as Meg slid into the booth across from me with a presumptuous flare that would normally annoy me.

"What brings you in here? And don't tell me it was the special."

A smile tugged at the corners of my mouth before I could stop it. "It was definitely the special."

Meg let out a sigh and leaned back against the booth, eyeing the door that hadn't opened once since I'd sat down. I wondered to myself how the place was open if they were always so slow. Or if she was so surprised to see someone new there that she sat down to chat with strangers.

"Bad breakup?" Meg asked suddenly, and just like that, my smile was gone. "Thought so." She added before I could respond.

"How'd you–"

"Nobody just stumbles into this place on a Thursday morning if they aren't avoiding their usual stomping ground, and with bags like those, I'd imagine you're up a little earlier than you're used to."

I set my fork down with a clank and eyed her for a second.

"Okay," I sighed. "You got me."

Meg gave me a sly grin, and before I even knew what I was doing, I was spilling my entire life story to her. I told her about my party-hard ex leaving me just months before I could pop the question, how I was starting completely over with a single, albeit my oldest, friend. How I had to do that in the very apartment I'd shared with her and said friend.

I told her how I was struggling to fill the voids that my ex had left behind, my time feeling empty now that I didn't know what to do with it. Or rather, I didn't have someone telling me what to do with it. I'd never been the best at making decisions of my own.

I told her about getting sober... ish. Because the mere taste of certain drinks made me ache for her. And even though I knew she'd be back, it wasn't like we hadn't been off and on before, I couldn't handle the inconsistency.

I told her how I felt like I had to become a completely different person because I'd tried so hard to be who Jayde had wanted me to be. I'd tried to fit myself into her mold, and even though it hurt like hell, I knew I had the chance to be more myself without her. I just didn't know who that was.

"What did you do before?" Meg asked when I'd finished spilling my guts. "Or what did you want to do but couldn't?"

I cleared my throat awkwardly. "I mean, I used to be a personal trainer. Jayde got jealous of all my clients, but I've long since let my license expire."

"You can't renew?"

That got me thinking. And then the front door dinged. Meg was on her feet before I could say anything else, bringing a check around not long after with nothing but the tea on it.

I left the diner with a plan.

The drone of my alarm echoed into my dreams, blending with the made-up sounds, and turning them into something else. I might have stayed asleep, running from an imaginary fire for another hour had Noah's grumbling not filled the otherwise silence.

"Parker, I swear to god, if you don't get up and shut off that alarm, I'm coming in there and forcibly removing you from that bed myself. And I promise you won't like my methods."

"I'm up." I groaned, reaching over to my alarm, careful to push the off button rather than the snooze. "I'm awake."

"You're late!" He called, his voice farther away like he was already down the hall toward the kitchen.

I looked at the clock, letting out a cross between a gasp and a hiss as I threw myself from the bed toward my closet. A year after Jayde left, and I still wasn't used to going to bed at a reasonable time or getting up before eleven am. I didn't know what I'd been thinking–booking clients at nine in the morning.

After yanking on two whole layers of clothing in under thirty seconds, I was out of my room and headed toward the door, shoving my feet into my running shoes while Noah shook his head from the little bar between our kitchen and dining area.

He wordlessly tossed a protein shake and a banana my way.

"Thank you." I grinned as I caught them both.

"Mhmm." He sighed into his steaming cup of coffee while he read the morning paper like my dad used to do.

I ran the entire way to the gym, which was across town nestled between a mattress store and a Dunkin Donuts. When I stepped inside, the yoga room was open and empty, which gave me a sinking feeling.

My client Katelin was still slipping her things into a locker near the reception area. She smiled over at me like she hadn't expected me to arrive any earlier than I had. Someone was getting used to my chronic morning tardiness.

"Looks like you've already gotten your workout in." She called over with a grin.

"Something like that." I laughed. "Ready to get started?"

She nodded, heading back toward the weights.

Katelin was honestly in decent shape. We'd only been working together for a few weeks, and I had a feeling she wouldn't need the sessions soon. I didn't mind. My goals as a trainer were more about building healthy relationships with food and exercise than distinct numbers.

When we'd finished, I headed off toward the coffee shop, where, like clockwork, a pretty brunette in a rush nearly dumped her coffee on us both.

"I'm so sorry." She said sheepishly, like she'd done two mornings before.

"It's fine." I let out a laugh, taking in the peony perfume she wore that filled the space between us.

Say something.

Before I could open my mouth, a hint of red dotted her cheeks. Her eyes darted toward the floor, and she ducked out of reach and into the sunlight. I let out a sigh and headed to the counter. My focus was mostly on the door, still thinking of Ava.

Bumping into her had started at the gym right after I'd begun training again. I'd opened the door for her every morning for a month. She'd say thank you as she clicked through what looked like a playlist and look up to about my chin before turning away. Not once did her eyes reach mine.

Then, I saw her at the coffee shop a few weeks later. She almost ran into me, nearly dumped her entire coffee down my shirt. I felt lucky it was iced as much as that was a crime in itself. But as soon as I saw her, as soon as the realization dawned on me, I didn't mind at all. She apologized, not even meeting my gaze before she slipped out the door and was gone. That was the first of many mornings I'd almost wear coffee home because of this woman.

I saw her at the grocery store just once, and I might not have even known it was her had it not been for the gym bag she was carrying as she purchased three items before darting out of the building in a rush. The gym bag I'd seen her with before, that so often dangled an emerald green yoga mat. The bag with my gym's logo on the side.

I was fairly certain we used the same vet. A week after the grocery store, I'd taken mine and Noah's cat, Samuel, in for his annual vaccines. And I could have sworn I saw a very familiar looking messy bun heading back to the exam rooms with the prettiest Siamese cat I'd ever seen over her shoulder.

A few weeks after that, she started working at the same diner where Meg worked, and where I'd become a regular since that first day. By which point, I couldn't ignore that I was seeing Ava pretty much everywhere, and I couldn't convince myself it was mere coincidence.

I'd asked Meg about Ava early on. I had a feeling she got to know everyone rather quickly like she had with me because in the weeks since I'd been coming to the diner, she'd had lengthy conversations with the majority of her customers like we were all old friends. Meg wouldn't say much about Ava, though. What she did say?

Ava had an ex-girlfriend. And it gave me far more hope than it should have.

She made me believe again. In fate, in destiny, in the decisions I had made since that nasty breakup. She motivated me to do better—be better. And I hadn't even spoken to her yet. But despite the good things I was doing, and despite believing the universe had put us on the same path, just the idea of her was terrifying to me.

Not terrifying as in I thought she was scary, but terrifying as in any game, any poise, any reasonable dignity I had went out the window the moment she was near me. Hearing her voice or seeing her face filled me with nerves like I'd never known.

I'd tried more than once to catch up with her at the gym, say something in line at the coffee shop, or even get her attention at the diner when she was working, but something always came up. Or she had her earbuds in. Or she was in a hurry to get somewhere. Or... I'd choked like the absolute chicken I am.

"So, how's the training going?" Meg asked later that day.

"Well, I'm doing it." I laughed, eyeing Ava as she slipped out of the kitchen and greeted a table without even a glance towards Meg's section. "I don't know that it's the best form of socialization, but I love it."

"That's a start–doing what you love." Meg's eyes followed mine, and she let out a sigh. "You know, if you're looking for socialization, I heard about an LGBT therapy group? It's at that coffee shop you go to every day."

"Therapy?"

She patted my arm. "You think you're too put together to use a little therapy?"

I scoffed playfully and gave her a smile. "I guess I'll think about it. You know when they're having it?"

Ava

"You will find love again." My mom had said at two in the morning when I'd shown up at her front door, everything I owned haphazardly shoved into the back of my Honda sedan.

It had been my sister, Willow, who opened the door before I even knocked. But her bedroom window was perfectly aligned with the driveway. I didn't know if it was because she was deaf, but she'd always been hypersensitive to light.

She had promptly gone back to bed, though, without so much as a word to me. Despite having not seen her in over a year, she hadn't seemed all that happy to see me. She hadn't been all that happy when I'd left, either. At the age of thirteen, I guess that felt like abandonment, especially since it had been mostly me raising her while my mom had practically worked herself to death.

"You'll find love again." My mom had repeated, as if she knew I was barely listening, instead staring at the mug of tea she'd practically shoved into my hands. "And it will change this entire experience for you."

This entire experience. As if Cam had just broken my heart. As if it had been nothing more than a simple breakup from a relationship that just wasn't right for me. But Mom didn't know the real story, and I wasn't about to tell her. At least... not yet. Not when it was so fresh and painful, and some of the darker details felt too raw to say out loud.

"You're young, babygirl." My mom had patted my cheek like she'd done when I was little. "You'll be over this before you know it."

I'd gone to bed after that. To my old room, which was mostly empty and bare. I felt like I belonged there because I, too, felt empty and bare.

I would never decorate that room again. Like it had been before. Before Cam. I'd never fill it with life, fill it with me. I'd never return it to its former glory. Partly because I couldn't.

We'd move a month later, and I'd never even completely unpack. That became so symbolic to me. Because I couldn't return to who I'd been, and just like all the stuff in my car, I wouldn't fully unpack what had happened to me, either.

I'd just move on, move forward, and choke it all down like that would make it as if it had never happened.

My light flicked on, and I jolted awake like I'd been smacked, my heart pounding. Willow was standing in the doorway with a mischievous grin on her face. I looked at the clock to my right. I'd overslept, and we were officially running late for our only day out a month.

"Hurry up, I'm hungry." Willow signed before slipping out of my doorway and into the living room.

I looked over to my dresser by the door where Willow had literally set out clothes for me across the open drawers, like I'd done for her when she was little. A slight laugh escaped my lips before it turned into a painful sigh. Lately her never ending kindness had begun to fill me with guilt.

I thought I'd have my life somewhat together by twenty-six. Instead, here I was shoving my achy limbs into clothes that were set out for me in the tiny apartment I shared with my little sister.

I didn't have my degree. I wasn't teaching elementary school, married, starting a family with a house in the suburbs. Theoretically, I could have had all that by now, but I didn't. And I was so sure, in reality, I never could. Too much had happened. I wasn't even sure that was still the life I wanted.

Instead, I was waiting tables at a tiny diner, scraping by most months even with a new second job added in, budgeting everything, and hoping like hell I didn't have to pick up and move or switch jobs again. While Willow, who had managed patience and grace I wasn't sure I could have throughout the last three years, stocked shelves at a local grocery store part time to cover what I couldn't. She somehow juggled her last semester of college into the mix. And the only thing about it that made me grateful was that she seemed happy, healthy, and functional.

One of us had to turn out okay.

Willow cleared her throat from the doorway as I hopped into my jeans. She eyed me for a second like I was taking far too long, so I grabbed a hair tie and threw my hair up, socks in hand.

"Sorry." I signed as I sat down on the bench near our front door. "I couldn't get to sleep last night."

Willow shrugged in response, grabbing her jacket and purse while I laced up my boots. She seemed used to my inability to get a regular night's sleep by now. I liked that she didn't ask why. I wasn't sure if I could tell her how often bedtime had come with trauma.

All her annoyance seemed to vanish the moment we stepped outside.

I stared at the new girl working the coffee shop counter for far longer than necessary. She gave me a dirty look in response while pulling a muffin out of their pastry display. I didn't know how to tell her that the cut and style of her fiery red hair was triggering, or that every time I walked into the shop to find her facing away from the door, I'd panic for a second before I remembered it wasn't her–it wasn't Cam. I shouldn't tell her. It was a me problem.

A part of me knew this was probably therapeutic in a messed-up way. Here I was, standing in a coffee shop I felt safe and comfortable in, mostly because Cam hated coffee, and every morning I faced someone who looked just like her. Hiding from redheads wasn't healthy.

Willow seemed oblivious, humming loudly next to me while we waited in line, twirling her strawberry blonde hair. She was swaying a little. If I didn't know better, I'd say she was doing it to the music. She was always so chipper in the morning, even if she'd been annoyed at me for oversleeping. I couldn't imagine being able to smile like that before eight am, or at least before I'd had my coffee. Maybe it was because she slept better than I did, not hearing sirens blaring at four am or being haunted by ghosts of her past.

The coffee shop was busy, as they always were before probably ten. Most of the two top tables were full, as were the worn black leather couches near the front window, and patrons on their way to work rushed past us like they hadn't just been standing where we were standing.

When our turn came up, Jane smiled widely and started taking Willow's order. She was one of the main reasons I enjoyed coming here, apart from the coffee. She made an effort to learn sign language for Willow.

"Good morning, Ava." She smiled once Willow was done, and I caught a glimpse of the new girl rolling her eyes.

I tried to smile at her, but she missed it.

“Good morning, Jane.” I said, turning my attention back to her with the best smile I could muster as I handed her my card. “I don’t know how you do it.”

“Some of us are built for sunrise, and some of us are built for sunset.”

I let out a laugh, making eye contact with the new girl, who was really getting tired of me already.

Willow had moved on and was admiring the flyers and posters that the shop let other local vendors hang. A twelve-by-twelve section of navy-blue wall near the long hallway that had led to the bathrooms and their more spacious back room was covered with various local business and event ads. Her hand waved to me as I grabbed my receipt, and I came to her side where she was pointing at a flyer for an LGBT therapy group.

“No, absolutely not.” I shook my head. “I don’t need therapy.”

“You need therapy more than anyone I know.” She signed back quickly. “You just told me you were ready to move on and get healthy. This is fate!”

I made a face at her fate comment and let out a sigh. “I’ll think about it.”

I’d been to therapy before, right after Cam and I split. My dad had pretty much insisted on it. He knew even less of what Cam had put me through than Mom or Willow, but even he noticed I was... different. More reserved, maybe. Something about taking control of my own life felt wrong when I’d had so little for so long.

Angela’s office had smelled like really old books and not in a good way. I’d always loved the smell of libraries. This was more like textbooks that had been kept in a musty basement. Her leather couch was hard and uncomfortable. And when she talked to me, it was like talking to a high school counselor.

It wasn't all that bad. She did give decent advice, even if I always felt like she was talking down her nose at me through her pointy teacher glasses. I actually think it helped in the beginning with just existing in a world where I no longer had to do what someone else told me to.

Then I got kicked off my dad's insurance and couldn't afford it. I might have been able to. If I'd been able to keep a job for more than a few months before having to quit abruptly and frantically find something new.

Near the therapy poster was another that caught my eye. It was an ad for a singing gig at a bar across town. It wasn't close to our apartment complex by any means, but neither was the diner or the department store where I worked, so what did it matter? There was no payment information, just a single phone number. And the whole ad was poorly done with bright colors that didn't work, and yet? It was a gig, something I'd been on the lookout for, for quite some time.

"Now this!" I pointed as I sighed to her. "This I could do."

"So do both. You act like you're *so* busy."

I let out a painful laugh at the thought of how rarely I was actually busy and looked back at the poster as our names were called, and Jane waved a rainbow flag to get our attention.

Willow turned and grabbed our drinks from the counter. I eyed the therapy poster again, checking the day and time the group was held. I wasn't off those days, but I had time between my job at the diner and the department store where I'd just started working. The coffee shop was basically a halfway point. I'd just have to change my normal route a bit.

I knew why Willow was pressing the issue. My depression had been getting worse, mostly because I hadn't actually seen Cam in months. It was making me paranoid, like watching a video that you know will be a jump scare.

Even I had noticed my own patterns. I was going out less, always looking over my shoulder, becoming hyperfixated on every redhead I saw.

Jumping from job to job every time Cam showed up had made it harder to make friends again. And there was very little connection I had to my old ones. They'd moved on with their lives. While I'd been picking up the pieces of mine. Cam really had destroyed so many of the beautiful things in my life. The only people who stuck around it seemed were the ones who felt they had to. Like Willow.

Sometimes, I thought she only stayed with me instead of moving across the country with Mom because she felt like she owed me. I'd taken care of her for so long, lost countless moments of my own childhood trying to make sure hers was good. It's not that Mom didn't also do that, but Mom was working three jobs, and I was the one braiding Willow's hair, tucking her in, helping with homework, and building science projects.

Other times, she made me feel like she was just grateful to have her sister back after those three years with Cam. She'd look at me sometimes like she thought I'd vanish again. Or like she thought my depression would hit like Mom's had when we were little. She worried so much; it reminded me she wasn't a kid anymore.

I'd consider the group at the very least, if only for Willow's sake. I did feel safe and comfortable every time I walked into that coffee shop, even with the new girl's red hair reminding me far too much of Cam. Those were my people, those specific coffee drinkers, even if they were normally in a bigger rush than me.

Willow came to my side, and I snapped a quick photo of the singing gig ad for later before we headed for the door.

"So, did you think about it?" Willow signed one handed, so it was almost hard to read, as we stepped outside into the early January sun.

"I don't know yet." I signed back. "I've only seen one therapist, and that was exclusive. I never share my problems with anyone—"

"That's why you should go!"

I made a face at her. "It just feels intimidating, meeting new people, and sharing my whole life story, the worst parts of it right away."

"So, don't. Share when you're ready. Go and listen. You're good at that."

She could tell I was ready for a change of topic, or maybe she was, because her attention was quickly drawn to one of the stalls for the riverside market that sold handmade bobbles from glass to wood, and everything in between. We came here a few times a month when she wanted certain ingredients for some fancy meal, she was planning that they sold on the farmer's side.

She made a little happy noise and took off, and as she did, my line of sight was drawn to a familiar figure, with a hairstyle I recognized, and I froze, heart pounding furiously in my ears. For a second, I contemplated running, leaving Willow behind, and not saying a word.

It had been nearly eight months since I'd seen her. Cam. Before that, it had been more frequent. Once a month, it seemed, she'd show up at my work, beg for a little of my time *to talk*. And I'd quit, sometimes on the spot, find a new job on a different side of town, start over.

Willow and I had moved twice, once when I'd found a note from Cam taped to our door, the other when she'd actually gotten inside and ransacked my room.

It was part of why I had to work two jobs. Deposits weren't cheap, and neither was that two-to-four-week gap in pay every time Cam weaseled my new place of employment out of... whoever she got her information from. And it was also why I didn't talk to anyone but Willow. Who else could I trust?

I was never ready for it, though. Never ready for the powerlessness that came from looking her in the eye. Never ready for the panic that swelled through every inch of my body the moment her voice echoed in my ears. Every time I felt safe, there she was again, reminding me how powerless she could make me feel.

"Are you okay?" Willow signed, appearing in my line of sight with her face all twisted with concern.

I glanced around her to where the woman had been standing, and she'd turned. It wasn't Cam, but I was in tears, anyway. And I decided then that I would be going to that therapy group after all.

Parker

"I still can't believe you're going to go to *therapy*." Noah shuddered from our dark grey sectional as he switched the tv to say yes to the dress, the brown curls on the top of his head bouncing as he did it. "Ever since Jayde left, you're the most well-rounded person I know."

"And yet I still bottle my feelings and have not a single regularly sober person besides you in my social circle." I scoffed as I sat on the bench next to the door and tied my shoes.

"You're right. It's far better than isolating and dissociating on my couch for weeks on end. I approve."

"Thank you. I think it'll be good for me. It's being held at my favorite coffee shop, and who knows, maybe I'll meet my *soulmate* there?"

"Right. I don't think most people use group therapy as a dating service."

"It was a joke, Noah. I highly doubt I'll meet anyone who doesn't have as much baggage as I do. Not exactly a great way to start a relationship. How do I look?"

"Like a walking lesbian stereotype as per usual." He said without turning around.

"Gee thanks. Want me to grab you anything while I'm on that side of town?"

"Please get me one of their double chocolate muffins, thank you!" He grinned over the couch like a giddy child, revealing dimples on each side of his mouth. Then he eyed me, his blue eyes scrunching up as he raised an eyebrow. "I was right. You do look like a walking lesbian stereotype."

I scoffed. "Okay, I'll be back in a bit."

"Yeah, yeah, love you. Have so much fun talking about your feelings with complete strangers." Under his breath, he muttered. "Extroverts, I swear."

I sighed as I shut the door behind me. He was also an extrovert. He just couldn't stand most people.

I made my way to the coffee shop as the sun was setting over the city skyline, leaving everything in an orange glow. I found myself shivering about halfway. I probably should have just taken the car, but if Noah wanted to leave, I knew he'd be annoyed. I was in better shape, and he was a baby about the cold. Besides, technically, the car was in his name, even if we did go 50/50 on literally everything.

I was only slightly winded as I walked up to the dimly lit windows and stepped inside. It was always so warm and welcoming there, with local art for sale on the walls, local ads up for display, and couches for lounging spaced out everywhere. As I stepped into the line, a familiar name echoed in my ears.

"Ava!" I looked over to find a familiar figure reaching across the counter.

"Thank you." She smiled, her voice carrying to me only barely, before she slipped down the hall.

Toward the backroom, where the therapy group was held.

Suddenly it was much warmer in that coffee shop than usual. I placed my order quickly, even more nervous than I'd already been about sharing dark parts of myself with strangers.

When I stepped into the backroom, everyone had already taken seats in a circle of chairs that looked unnerving. There were only a couple empty of seats, but no one seemed to be talking yet. I made it, just barely.

"Well, hello!" A tall blonde woman stood from her seat and gestured to the empty chairs. "Two new faces today. Go ahead and have a seat. My name is Carmen, she/her, and I lead the group. Do you want to introduce yourself now or as we make the rounds?"

"Um," I felt my cheeks flush. "Now works. Hi, everyone, I'm Parker." I paused because I didn't know what else to say.

"What's your pronoun preference?"

"Uh, She/her."

Carmen's smile was warm as she wrote down my name and pronouns on her clipboard and retook her seat. I'd only just settled when I looked to Carmen's left and saw... *Ava*. That Ava. My Ava.

Not my *Ava.*

She was hunched over so that her brown hair covered most of her face, and she was chewing absentmindedly on the edge of her thumbnail. Though, her black sweater sleeve was pretty much covering that, too. But I knew it was her. I'd recognize that face anywhere at this point.

No way was this not a sign.

Was it a sign, though? Or was it Meg? Because Meg had definitely been the one who'd told me about this thing. Out of the blue, when I'd just been eyeing Ava and talking about struggling to connect. I suppressed a huff.

"Anything else you want to add, Parker?" Carmen asked, pulling me from my thoughts. I looked at her just as Ava looked up from the floor.

I shook my head, feeling my face flush as Ava's attention briefly fell on me, and then away again before I could meet her gaze.

"I am a licensed therapist, so if there is anything private you need to discuss, I do offer one-on-one sessions with everyone in the group. Let's get started. Ava, why don't you start?"

When I looked at Ava as she began to share, her attention was back on the floor.

"Um." Ava sighed, not meeting anyone's eyes. "I don't really know... what I'm doing—"

"The group is new." Carmen smiled. "So, that's okay."

Ava nodded, but there was a red tint to her cheeks.

"Why don't you start with what brought you in?"

Ava sucked in a shuddery breath and looked down at her hands as she tugged at her sweater sleeves.

"Well, my sister pushed me to go. She's kind of been hassling me about it." Ava laughed nervously, and a little round of laughs filled the room. "I think she's worried about me. I went through...a lot with my ex, and I know I've not dealt with all of it. We thought maybe...maybe this would help."

"That's a great place to start. It's okay to take this slow. How are you handling things now?"

"I mostly just work, eat, sleep, repeat."

I felt my chest clinch as I thought back to the time when that was exactly how I lived, too. How I'd been living for a while because Noah was still one of my only friends. I was friend... ly with everyone. Or I tried to be, anyway.

Carmen's head tilted. "It sounds to me like you're going through the motions."

Ava nodded, looking up at Carmen only briefly.

"How about, this week as you're going through the cycle, take a minute out of every day to note something you enjoy?" Carmen suggested. Her smile was soft, but Ava didn't see it. Her eyes were back on the floor.

"And then next week, we'd love to hear more about the things in your life that make you feel something. I want to open up the door for one-on-one sessions if you'd be comfortable. I know sometimes the big group can be intimidating, especially when there are more personal things you need to work through."

"Thank you." Ava smiled, meeting Carmen's eyes for only a second.

"Did you have anything else you want to share?"

Ava shook her head, going back to chewing on her fingernails, and Carmen turned to the next person in the circle as if she hadn't expected Ava to say more.

I was hung on the idea that Ava had just as much to deal with as I did. Somehow, through the months that I'd been bumping into her all over town, I'd never once considered what she might be going through, or what she might have been through. I'd put her on some pedestal, and now that she was real... realizing she was *real* was a shock to the system.

As we went around the circle, and each person in the room told us a little piece of themselves, I was surprised to find just how open these people were. The way they talked reminded me of slumber party talk in movies. Not that I knew much about that. I'd never been invited to one of those. But the group interacted like they were all long-lost friends, and I couldn't imagine going into that much detail with a group of strangers.

Ava's attention rarely strayed from the floor. Carmen occasionally offered to let someone give suggestions. I didn't, but Ava did. She seemed much more confident than when sharing, her voice carrying across the room, like giving advice was easy, but speaking her own peace was not. I'd never related to something more.

"Parker, did you want to share now that everyone has gone?" My throat went dry. "Is there anything in particular that brought you in?"

I didn't want to share anymore. Because what I said to Noah was echoing in my ears. This wasn't the place to meet someone. The people in this room did have baggage. I had baggage... and Ava had baggage, too.

Freaking universe. No, *freaking Meg.*

Carmen was still looking at me, and I cleared my throat, ready to say no when I remembered why I'd really come to the group. Sure, Meg had made the suggestion, but there wasn't pressure there. I thought coming here would help me work through the last of my issues with Jayde.

"I'm struggling a bit after getting out of my last relationship." I chose my words very carefully. The last thing I wanted was to come off damaged, and that made me feel worse because I didn't come to the group to be fake. I'd spent far too long doing that with Jayde. "It was... really unhealthy. I thought coming here might help me... learn some better habits."

"I hope it does." Carmen smiled.

"I think that's all for now. I kinda want to get a feel for things first."

"Okay," Carmen nodded, turning her attention to the rest of the group.

I'd hoped, if only a small part of me, that sharing would catch Ava's attention. Because despite what I'd said to Noah, I couldn't deny what I felt. I couldn't deny the way I'd become so captivated by her, or the way I'd wanted to hug her since she'd shared with the group.

But her eyes were on the clock. The session concluded and before anyone else could even make their way to the refreshment table, Ava was out the door.

And before I could think about following after her, Carmen stopped me.

"Parker, I make a note to exchange numbers with members of the group." Carmen smiled up at me in a motherly fashion, though she couldn't have been more than five years older than me at most. "Only if you're comfortable with that, but it's come in handy. You never know when you'll have a mental health emergency."

"Oh, right." I nodded, thinking I definitely needed Carmen in my life when Jayde left. Talk about mental health emergency. "Sure, I'm fine with that."

She handed me a clipboard where I could write down my number next to my name, and I tried hard not to let my eyes stray to the line above where Ava's name had been scrawled out in a swirly cursive that didn't match up with the rest of the form. I was not going to look at her number. That's weird.

"We'll see you next week, then?"

I nodded.

"Wonderful. Thank you for joining us. I really do hope it helps."

"Thank you, Carmen." I replied.

"Please, help yourself to the refreshments." Carmen smiled before she made her way toward a door that was marked 'employees only.'

There was a short brunette woman standing halfway in and halfway out of it, dressed in the most business casual blazer I'd ever seen. They talked for a second before Carmen kissed her, and just like that, this would never not be my favorite coffee shop.

I turned away from that private moment and gave a few goodbyes as everyone grabbed some snacks. Then I purchased Noah's muffin and headed home, trying hard to force myself to face the fact that Ava wasn't perfect and put together. She was real. But maybe I was okay with that.

"She's in the therapy group!" I practically yelled as I tossed a double chocolate muffin on the couch next to Noah.

He didn't catch it, but he did just about jump out of his skin. I was fairly certain he hadn't moved a single inch since I'd left. Though the smell of dinner carrying from the kitchen said otherwise.

"*She,* she?" He asked, as he looked between me and the paper bag like he'd forgotten he'd even asked for the muffin.

"Yes! She, she."

"Damn, Parker." He rubbed the bridge of his narrow but long nose. "I didn't mean use the therapy group as a dating service *literally*."

I flopped on the couch, causing Samuel to stir and meow at me.

"I have to ask her out. It's fate." I said, as I scratched between Samuel's ears.

"No, it's not. That waitress from the diner told you about it. I bet she knew Ava was going."

"Always a skeptic." I gave him a playful glare.

"Skeptic or not, I'm just glad I'm not the only one pushing to *make a move* already." His mouth was full of muffin, but that did not stop his cheap shots to my ego. "What is it with this girl? Didn't you used to have... I don't know, an ounce of game?"

"Cruel." I let out a sigh. "I just have to plan it out right." I said firmly, trying to imagine all the best scenarios in which 'Hi, I know we go to therapy together, but do you want to date someone you know has a massive amount of baggage anyway?' would blow over smoothly.

"You should have plenty of opportunity. Tomorrow, the day after that, the day after—"

"Okay, Noah, I get it." I let out a sigh, and he laughed as he switched the channels. "I'll ask her the first chance I get."

And then I didn't see Ava for a week.

Ava

The moment I got home from the group; I knew Willow was coming down with something. She was curled up on the couch, wrapped up in a blanket, shivering between sniffles while she tried desperately to work on her homework. That's just how it starts.

She'd had the flu a handful of times when we were younger. For some reason, she always got it worse than I did, and I was pretty certain it was because she was rail thin and five foot eight. I had no clue where she got her metabolism, but I wished Mom had passed some of it on to me. Until we were sick, that is.

"Are you sick?" I signed.

She shook her head, but her teeth chattered.

I took one look at her trembling hands and turned back around to hit the late-night convenience store down the road. I knew better than to let her try to fight it off without at least the cheap stuff.

When I got back, I made her take the night time version and sent her to bed. She was far worse the next day, and I had to basically force her to text her manager. She was fine missing school, but missing work made her feel guilty. I had a feeling it was because I already paid most of the rent.

So, I spent the next week juggling extra shifts at the diner to make up for it, telling Willow they just needed me. I wasn't sure if she bought it, but she didn't need to feel guilty. She took care of me enough.

And when I wasn't at work, I was serving up soup and tea for Willow. I barely had time to practice for this singing audition, but I got a few hours in while Willow slept.

I didn't even have time to get coffee. Not that we really needed to be spending those five dollars a day, anyway.

I felt lucky I was a decent waitress, or that week might have set us back. That's what happens when your financial situation is hanging on by a thread.

"I'll just take this last table—" I started, headed out the kitchen door as three teenagers tucked themselves into one of my booths.

"No, you will not." Meg reached out and took my notepad from me. "You've got that group therapy to get to. Get out of here. I've got this one."

"Are you sure? I still have ten minutes."

"They'll be here at least thirty. Go on, get out of here. I can handle this."

I hesitated for a moment. I had officially reached my quota, and the bills would be paid at the very least. But Meg gave me a motherly glare, so I gave her a one-armed hug and dashed toward the back, where we had a tiny nook for the staff. I slipped out of my non-slip shoes, tucked them in my cubby, and grabbed my purse.

Less than five minutes, and I was out the door and headed across town at a brisk walk. I basically had power walking down to a science.

I still had forty-five minutes to get to the coffee shop. But the walk took at least thirty, and the long way around with a trip around a block and through a couple of alleys added time. I didn't think Meg knew that. Or maybe she did. The woman was far too smart to be waiting tables.

By the time I reached the coffee shop, the cold had seeped into my bones, and I'd never been more grateful for a warm cup of coffee, even if I did hesitate about spending the money. I hugged the cup as I slipped down the hall where voices from the group were carrying and filling me with nerves.

When I entered the back room, ignoring the sign marked "private" on the door, everyone was huddled together in smaller groups having general conversations like friends do. There was a redhead in the group named Tate, and I remembered it was Tate because she'd tried to talk to me the week before. She seemed not only unsuspecting but sweet, but it didn't stop me from being apprehensive either time I walked in the room. She seemed friendly. Chatting with everyone like socializing was easy for her. It had been a long time since I'd made friends like that. I didn't know how to connect with people anymore. I'd just grown... detached.

I could probably use a friend like Tate. If I had the nerve and could get past how much she reminded me of Cam at first glance.

The circle of chairs where everyone would sit in only a few minutes were empty, save for one. The woman who'd started attending the group the same week I had was sitting alone, scrolling on her phone, ignoring the rest of the group like I intended to do until I could determine whether they could be trusted. Maybe she was also a little detached. It was somewhat comforting to not feel like the only in that respect. Even if it was a little sad to think about.

I took a seat, two chairs down, and she looked up. We made eye contact for a brief moment, and I was enticed. I hadn't gotten a good look at her the week before. Then again, I hadn't gotten a good look at anyone the week before.

She was ridiculously beautiful, one of those people with seemingly perfect facial symmetry and a jawline that could cut glass. Her brown hair was shaved on the sides, but the top came down to her shoulders in untamed waves in a just-ran-my-fingers-through-it kind of way. It was barely covering a tattoo that crept from the back of her neck to her ear. The way most of it was hidden made me want to ask about it.

She caught me staring and looked back down without a word. Was she blushing? No, she wasn't blushing. Why would she be?

Then she gave an awkward shift in her seat in my direction and cleared her throat just as Carmen walked through the door with her singsong voice echoing across the room.

"Sorry I'm late, my lovelies!" She grinned, wiggling her fingers as if to pull everyone in while her shoulder-length blonde hair bounced with each step. "Let's all get comfortable and we can get started, shall we?"

I looked over at the woman again, the beautiful one who I couldn't remember the name of. Why was I always the worst with names? She had settled back in her chair and shoved her phone in her pocket, but I could see her eyeing me from the corner of her eye while the rest of the group took their seats.

"How was everyone's week? Anyone have any important news to share before we begin the circle?" Carmen asked as she took the seat to my right.

Why did she sit next to me again? It made me nervous, like I was on the spot or being watched. Like she *knew*. A small part of me wanted that to be true, so I didn't have to go through this process. Or maybe she could be clearer about just how accepting this group was before I risked being kicked out.

Because I should have spoken up. I knew I should have spoken up. This was supposed to be the week. I was supposed to come out, tell them I was asexual, and pray they didn't ask me to leave the group. But I choked on my nerve as others shook their heads and kept quiet instead.

"Great, Marcy, why don't we start with you?" Carmen continued.

I felt a sigh escape my lips before I could stop it, but Carmen and *that* woman were the only ones who appeared to notice. I gave Carmen a sheepish smile. I wasn't sighing about Marcy. I was sighing about me.

I was afraid of really unloading on these people. I knew I shouldn't have been. The whole point was to give us a safe place to talk about our problems, to feel accepted, to get advice. I just didn't know how to talk about my problems or trust anyone enough to feel like I could be accepted.

I was trying hard to hold out hope. This was only week two, and while so far, I'd only given advice I couldn't follow, there was a chance I'd grow more comfortable with time. I just wanted some sense of community, even if I wasn't sure I was welcome in it.

Because I knew there were other asexuals out there—somewhere. I knew that. I'd found a group of them online. The problem was, I hadn't met any of them in person, and being the only is very lonely.

As we made it around the circle, I could feel my heart begin to race. I braced myself as the woman next to me told Carmen she was done.

"What about you, Ava?" Carmen asked. "What happy things happened this week?"

I took a deep breath. I'd had this whole speech planned out. I was going to open up. I had to. But I shifted in my seat, and my throat went dry. I had to clear it three times before I couldn't speak.

"Um," I shrugged, angry at myself as the words flowed out of my mouth, but I had thought about happy things at the very least. "My cat was being a weirdo early in the week, and that was nice. It made me laugh. My sister was sick with the flu, so I had to take a few extra shifts at work. Mostly, I spent the week working, so more of the work, eat, sleep, repeat."

"That's good, though!" Carmen smiled. "Even small things make big progress."

Open your mouth and come out of the closet, dammit.

"You're not seeing anyone, right?" Carmen asked suddenly, and it was like she'd shone a spotlight on me.

But she'd probably know the answer to that if I was out of the dang closet. Why did it matter anyway?

"Still a single Pringle." I uttered flatly, all too aware that I was casting a glare her way.

"Is there anyone in your life who might be able to help you note memories as they come and go?" Carmen smiled at me warmly, and I realized I was taking my anger at myself out on her.

"Yeah." I nodded, letting out a shaky sigh. This woman was getting worried about me. "I have... people. I think that's all for now. Someone else can go."

I said it too quickly, too dismissively. Carmen noticed.

"It seems like that might not be the case." She frowned at me. "There's no pressure, but are you sure you don't have anything you want to tell us? This is a safe place. You can talk about anything."

I'm Asexual, and I'm afraid you'll kick me out because of it.

I was instantly on the verge of tears, and Carmen eyed me with a knowing look, her facial features softening in that way that people do when they feel sorry for them. I thought she was going to press when I shook my head in response. Instead, Carmen moved on to someone else, still eyeing me to the point that I had to look down at my hands. A single tear fell down my cheek, and I wiped it so fast, I practically slapped myself.

She let out a sigh.

It wasn't an angry sigh. At least she didn't seem irritated, and I knew what that looked like. If anything, she seemed worried, almost motherly. It reminded me of Meg, and that should have made me feel safer talking to her. But after everything Cam had put me through, trust just didn't come easy. I kept everyone at arm's length, even Meg.

I knew Carmen was trained to work with people just like me, but I still felt like at this rate, she might've asked me not to come back just for lack of contribution.

I glanced over at the clock. If the meeting ran over again, I'd be late for work. We only had ten more minutes, and five more people who had yet to speak. My anxiety typically took over before I could walk out of anything before it was over, but I thought I just might have the courage. Especially if Autumn started talking about her cats again. I couldn't really judge her, though. I'd talked about mine.

But, she didn't. She passed, moving on to *that* woman, and my attention was held, if only for a moment. She'd been short with her share the week before, just like I'd been, and a part of me was curious. I felt like I was the only one taking things slow here. Everyone else seemed to jump right in. Everyone but her.

"I'm actually feeling really good this week." The woman said, rubbing her hands on her black jeans. "Life's been pretty bleak for a while, but I think it's starting to look up."

Carmen smiled widely, eyeing her. "Any particular reason?"

We shared a brief moment of eye contact. Her mouth turned up in a slight smile, and I felt my stomach tie in knots.

"Yeah, I think I'm finally ready to move on."

I looked down quickly, my cheeks burning. Why was she looking at me when she said that?

"That's great, Parker!" Carmen said cheerily. "How is it going with forming healthier habits?"

She let out a laugh. "I guess I could be doing better on that front, but I've not reverted to old unhealthy ones."

The group laughed a bit.

"That is definitely a positive." Carmen beamed with pride like there was some sort of breakthrough with this woman that all of us had met a week before. "Did you have anything else you wanted to share?"

The woman shook her head, her eyes wandering back to me. I looked at the floor. Looking at her made my stomach tie up, and I did not need that.

Jax went next, starting off with "this is probably going to be a long rant," and just with that, I knew it was best to leave rather than be late.

So, even though I felt ridiculously rude, and I was shaking as I apologized six times before scurrying out of the room, I still did it. I'd probably explain my situation next week. Maybe then no one would be offended when I left early. Or maybe they'd give me an excuse not to delve into my problems and ask me not to come back.

I apparently needed an excuse. Maybe for more than myself. Willow, for some reason, thought this group was good for me. I thought if I stopped coming, she'd probably smack me.

I let out a sigh when I stepped outside, and then I had to catch my breath. It felt like a whole different world from that circle of chairs. I was just picking my walking music when I felt a hand on my shoulder. I jumped at the touch, only relaxing slightly as I turned to find *the* woman from the group staring back at me.

God, she was even prettier up close. Who had skin that perfect? Did she even have pores? I could feel myself staring, so I looked down, trying to busy myself with my glove. I couldn't fight the urge to look back up when she spoke.

"Sorry, I didn't mean to scare you." She smiled, a flash of bright white, perfect teeth. "It's Ava, right?"

I nodded. "And you're..." I felt myself frown. Fuck. I still couldn't remember. I was sure Carmen had said it in the group. But I pondered too long, and she told me instead.

"Parker."

Her cheeks flushed a bright red that I couldn't ignore this time, and she did that adorable head scratching thing people do when they're nervous. But her nervous was still powerful. She had these bulging biceps that pushed against the sleeves of the plain flannel button down she had rolled up. Teamed up with the black men's pants she was wearing, she looked like a total stereotype.

I remembered when I'd tried to dress gay.

"So," Parker breathed nervously, tucking her hands deep in her pockets. "This is probably going to sound weird, leaving therapy and all, but I was wondering if maybe you'd want to—"

I felt a chuckle escape my lips before I could stop it as I looked down. "I'm not your type."

"How would you know what my type is?" She was smirking at me when I looked back up. Cocky and beautiful and infuriating.

"I mean, I guess I don't... but—"

"So, what you mean is that I'm not *your* type?"

"I didn't say that." I said breathily, unthinking, and I felt my cheeks grow hot, which annoyed me. "I just... know this wouldn't work."

"Because—"

"*We* are definitely not compatible."

"Well, I know you don't talk much in the group." She shrugged, frowning like she was piecing together a puzzle. "You're not interested in women?"

I let out a breath. It was far more complicated than that. "It's not...that. It's just I'm..."

I swallowed hard, eyeing the people around us, scanning the crowd for Cam.

"But—but you come to the meetings?"

"Yeah, I'm lucky I get to come to the meetings." I sighed, looking back at the shop, like the rest of the group might overhear. But none of them had come back out yet, which meant they were probably still chatting.

"Lucky? Are you...are you an ally?"

"The A doesn't stand for Ally." I bit my lip. I shouldn't have said that. I sighed, looking down at my watch.

"So, then—"

"I promise I'm not trying to be an ass, but I can assure you that I am not what you're looking for."

I looked up at her. God, her eyes were beautiful. This dark brown that just gleamed in the street light and made me want to write songs about. It had been a long time since someone had taken an interest in me. I never gave anyone the chance. But she seemed so determined to figure me out, and for some reason, it reminded me of Cam's interview.

I felt a familiar sting, and my eyes got all watery, so I looked back down again. It was ridiculous to assume everyone was out to get me. Not everyone was Cam. Not everyone got to know people for their own gain. But I didn't know how to tell the difference.

I sucked in a deep breath and started walking away.

"Hey, wait up." She called after me, shoving her arms in her coat.

"I can't." I grinned despite myself as I rolled my eyes. She was so... peppy. "I'm already late."

"Hot date?"

"Work actually." I sighed, still smiling as she fell in step with me.

"Didn't you just get off work?" She asked.

I frowned at her in response and then checked over my shoulder to make sure we weren't being followed. She was still looking at me when I turned back around.

How did she know that?

She pointed down at my apron. How had I forgotten to take that off? I had straws nearly falling on the street.

"Second job." I shrugged as I untied the apron and shoved it into my bag.

"You know... it's getting kind of late. Maybe I could walk you."

"I'm okay." I swallowed, checking behind us again, as I contemplated whether I wanted this perfect stranger to know where I worked.

Think of an excuse.

"Then you'll be out late."

"I can handle myself." She shrugged, biting her bottom lip as she smiled with a ridiculous sense of confidence.

Not good enough.

"I'm sure you can." I nodded, unable to stop myself from looking at her arms again. They looked even bigger in a coat. I got this strange urge to reach out and touch them.

Why was I like this?

Her cheeks flushed, and she looked up at the road ahead. No snow on the sidewalks, but plenty of salt crunching under our feet.

"You're not some kind of stalker, are you?" I squinted at her playfully. It would be my luck I'd end up with two of them.

Her eyes grew wide. "What? No, I—"

"I'm kidding." I laughed before she could freak out for real as I cast another glance behind us. "Kind of."

"That's not funny."

"I mean..." I laughed again, feeling more nervous the more I talked about it. Like the very allusion to Cam would make her materialize. "Logically, you could totally be a stalker, so it's a reasonable question."

"But wouldn't a stalker just lie and say no?" she asked, raising an eyebrow.

"Probably." I nodded, feeling a smile coming on. "You said no, so—"

"Oh my god, I'm not a stalker!"

I laughed again, if only because laughing about my situation was the only way to keep from crying about it sometimes. I glanced over my shoulder once more. And she let out an exasperated huff.

We were quiet for a few minutes before I realized she was staring at me.

"What?" I asked, eyeing her out of the corner of my eye.

She sighed. "Why don't you think you're my type?"

"Why are you so convinced I am? Compatibility has more to it than looks, you know."

Parker opened her mouth and then shut it again, letting out another sigh before letting silence take over for a few more moments. She already sounded out of breath, keeping up with the brisk pace I had to have in order to make it on time because of the constant zigzags and circles. Clearly, power walking wasn't her preferred choice of cardio.

"Didn't we pass this street already?" She asked, looking up at the street sign, and I wondered how she hadn't noticed the four left turns we'd just made.

The only response I could muster was a weak, 'mhmm' and a tense nod. I hadn't even considered how odd my varying route would be to someone who didn't know. Willow seemed used to it. I'd never had to think about how bizarre this behavior was. It was so rare that there was someone new in my life. It had kept me safe, but that didn't mean it was normal.

"Are you trying to get me lost? Because I've lived here my whole life, so good luck." She was grinning, and it almost settled my nerves. That or her sheer confidence and size.

Maybe if Cam was following us, she'd keep her distance.

"No." I smiled back, though I was sure she knew it was forced. "I'm not trying to get you lost. I'm just... this is part of my process."

I glanced over my shoulder for probably the fifth time since we'd left the coffee shop, and I felt Parker's eyes on me. My cheeks and neck grew hot, and I looked down. But Parker didn't look away.

"Is everything okay?" Parker asked, glancing behind us to where the street was mostly empty, as it usually was at this time of night.

I nodded, risking a glance at her face. There was concern there, and her shoulders were squarer, like even she was sure we'd been followed.

"Are you sure? Because you've checked behind us like eight times now."

Eight times. I was getting paranoid.

I let out a sigh, saying, "It's fine." Even though I knew it wasn't, and that definitely wasn't an explanation.

I wasn't sure I owed her one.

She sucked in a breath like she might say something, and then let it back out, taking another gander behind us. She thought I was crazy. And suddenly, even if there was a chance I'd change my mind, let her in, not keep her at an arm's length, it didn't matter.

"What's on your playlist there?" She asked, surprising me as she gestured to the earbud, I'd thrown over my shoulder so I could actually hear her.

I hadn't realized my music was loud enough for her to hear.

"Oh, um..."

She reached her hand out for it, pausing for a second, just inches from my shoulder, as she said, "May I?"

I felt my throat go dry, thinking for a second of all the things Cam had used as a weapon that she'd learned about me early on. But I nodded, trying desperately to ignore the feeling in my stomach when her hand brushed my shoulder. Or the way my heart started beating faster as her face inched closer to mine. I turned forward.

The Canadian pop band that was echoing through both our ears was one of my comfort bands. I could play all of their music without skipping a single song. I eyed her as her head bobbed for a second, and then she let the earbud drop back on my shoulder.

"I like it." She smiled. "I've never heard it before—"

"They're Canadian." I said awkwardly, feeling defensive for no reason and several reasons all at once. "So, you probably wouldn't have."

"Makes sense. I honestly don't listen to music all that much anymore." She let out a sigh. "So, I probably would have just assumed it was me."

"You don't listen to music?"

I felt myself frowning at her rather intensely, but I, for one, could not imagine living life without *music*. Music was emotion. How do you even express yourself without—oops.

"How do you even express yourself?" I blurted before I could stop myself. "Music is emotion."

I just barely caught a hint of a blush creep up her cheeks and she ran her fingers through her hair.

"Honestly, I don't." She shrugged. "I haven't been great at expressing myself for a long time."

That was a bit too personal for me, and I slowed as we approached the department store.

"Sorry." She said, slowing down to match my pace. "Too much?"

I shrugged, my eyes wandering to the tattoo on her neck. She tilted her head, eyeing me, and I met her eyes.

I gave the street behind us another glance. It was empty, as it had been for a few months. I let out a sigh.

"Look, I have to get inside." I said, taking a step back.

"Isn't this place closed?" She frowned, eyeing the large glass doors.

"Yeah, I dress the mannequins a few nights a week."

"What? People do that?"

"Did you think they dress themselves?" I laughed, doing a little finger wiggle.

She gave a playful shudder.

"I'd hope not." She forced a laugh. "I bet it's creepy, though."

"I've seen worse." I rolled my eyes. "Thank you for walking me."

She nodded, smiling. "So—"

"I'll see you next week?" I asked, backing up the steps to the door.

She sucked in a breath, holding it like she might have said something else before nodding. "Yeah, I'll see you next week."

I offered a smile before heading inside. Through the tinted doors, I caught her standing idle on the sidewalk for a moment, looking around with the biggest frown.

Parker

The entire walk home, I was reeling, and for some reason, I found myself looking over my shoulder every so often. I'd never met someone who could smile like that while simultaneously looking like they were scared for their life. The whole walk, Ava had this fearful look in her eye, and a tenseness in her shoulder that only relaxed once we'd reached her work. It made me feel protective, which even I knew was ridiculous.

What was I supposed to do now? How was I supposed to go back to seeing her on the street and saying... nothing?

It's not that I thought highly of myself, or I thought I should automatically get a girl's number because I asked for it. Because I didn't think that way. I could take no for an answer. It's just... she didn't say no. If I knew better, I'd have thought she was flirting with me. She just... thought I wouldn't be interested in her for some reason.

I stepped inside my apartment and kicked my shoes off next to the door.

"How'd it go?" Noah called over the couch as I hung up my coat.

He'd been hyping me up the last couple of days. I needed the hyping. Talking to women was hard. Talking to anyone was hard, but especially women.

I sighed and shook my head before coming around the couch and plopping down, leaving a little space between us for Samuel, who gave me a soft meow as I scratched between his ears.

"What did she say?" He asked, more disappointed than I expected him to be. "What did *you* say?"

I gave him the side eye. "I barely got to *try* to ask her out before she told me she wasn't *my* type."

He grinned, as perplexed as I was. "How would she know what your type is?"

"That's what I asked!"

"Maybe you're not her type?"

"I also suggested that, and she said, and I quote 'I didn't say that.' She was blushing when she said it, Noah, *blushing*. I don't know." I threw my forearms over my eyes. "I can't figure her out. I just can't."

"Is she seeing someone?" He asked.

"Actually." I laughed. "One of the only things she said during group was that she's a single Pringle. And she has a cat. She's a cat person, Noah. There's another box on my perfect girl list."

He grinned and then sighed like he had to ponder. "Maybe she only dates femmes."

I laughed. That would be my luck. "I don't know. She did say we aren't compatible, and that she's lucky she gets to come to the meetings."

"Is she an ally?"

It's like he was reading my mind. We were pretty much the same person half the time despite all the ways we were not. Brain twins, as I liked to say.

"She said the 'A doesn't stand for ally.' I still don't—"

"She's asexual!" He clapped like he'd won bingo. "... Or Aromantic."

"She's what now?"

"Asexual or aromantic. It means she either doesn't experience sexual attraction or doesn't experience romantic attraction. Or both?"

"Okay." I nodded, staring off into space for a moment before Noah's voice pulled me back.

"So, are you going to try again?" He asked, changing the channel from Say Yes to the Dress to something we'd both enjoy. He knew I'd never ask, but he did it anyway.

"Absolutely not." I let out a soft laugh. "She didn't say no, but...she didn't say yes either. Even if she seemed...flirty, that doesn't mean I should press my luck."

"Does this mean you're giving up on the universe?"

"If the universe wants us to be together, it's going to have to try a little harder because I'm not about to be one of those pushy people who can't take a not yes for an answer. I feel like I did that enough already."

"There's my girl." He grinned. "You still going to therapy?"

I sighed. I didn't know the answer to that. "I don't know. With Ava there, it's harder for me to share honestly, and that kinda takes away the point, doesn't it?"

Maybe I could try to attend something else with the local community. Carmen did offer one-on-one sessions, and I wasn't exactly opposed. She seemed connected. Maybe she could help me find something.

"I'll go with you." Noah said, not meeting my eyes, after a few minutes of watching CSI. "If that would help."

"You hate therapy." I grinned, looking at him from the corner of my eye.

"Yeah, but I love you."

We spent the rest of the evening watching tv before heading to bed.

That night, I looked up asexuality online. I stayed up far too late reading articles and threads from other asexual people as they talked about their experiences. And after reading people's stories, studies, and blogs, I still didn't understand why being asexual meant she wasn't my type.

And as the thought crossed my mind, I realized being asexual might not have as much to do with it as whatever baggage came along with the number of times, she looked over her shoulder.

The next morning, I groggily slipped into my workout clothes, and grabbed a water and my bag like usual. I waved to Noah, who was seated at the bar in our kitchen eating fruit loops, before I raced out the door and headed straight to the gym. I had to jog to make it on time, but at least it wasn't a run.

I was only a block away when I passed Ava on the street, the shock in her voice pulling me from the hyperfocus I had on the doors.

"Parker?" Ava frowned at me when I looked down at her.

I almost missed her completely.

"Oh, hey!" I smiled, a little out of breath. "Good morning."

"Hey." She grinned as I rushed by. "Are you—"

"Just headed to the gym." I shrugged, eyeing my watch because now I was pushing it.

"This gym?"

I nodded. "I'm a personal trainer so—"

"Have you been doing that long? Like... here?"

I could practically see the cogs turning in her mind.

"About eight months, give or take." I checked my watch again. "I'm really sorry. I have a client waiting. Good to see you, though."

Yeah, that was casual. That was cool. My ego was not shot.

I could still see her standing stunned on the sidewalk when I opened the doors

"Good morning, Parker." Maddi, the receptionist smiled, as she did most mornings. "Katelin's already checked in."

"Great, thank you, Maddi!" I said in response, doing a little drum on the table as I walked by.

"Only five minutes late today, Parker. I think you're getting the hang of mornings." Katelin grinned at me. "Isn't there some rule that gym rats are supposed to be up at the crack of dawn?"

She was always so flirty. Flirty and straight. And married. Happily, she claimed. Even if her husband was an asshole. I got a sense of pride knowing how much Jayde would have hated that I was working with her.

"Okay, first off, I've already told you, I'm not a gym rat." I said, tossing her a set of elastic bands from the shelf near the lockers.

"Have you seen yourself?"

"You've earned an extra set."

Her jaw dropped.

"I said what I said, go get to stretching."

Katelin laughed, but didn't argue.

"So," I said as we both sat down in the empty area near some of the cardio machines. "How do you feel about the meal plan? Do you think intuitive eating could work for you?"

Katelin sighed. "I mean, it feels nice? Not stressing over good foods or bad foods, just balancing what I eat. I feel like I'm eating more foods I actually like."

"That's a great start. What seems to be the problem?"

"My husband thinks eating Oreos, even just a few a couple days a week, is hindering my progress."

"Screw him–not literally."

Katelin snorted.

"What I mean is," I grinned. "You can't keep depending on diet foods. You have to figure out how to work with your goals in a way that's sustainable. Two Oreos a couple days a week is far better than binging the whole package in one sitting. And you're far more likely to stay on track if you're not being pestered by cravings or feeling guilty over breaking your diet."

Katelin nodded. "He just doesn't get it."

"Next time, tell him all that beer is hindering his progress. That'll shut him up."

"I don't want to be divorced." She laughed. "I just want him to see that I'm breaking a cycle here."

"He will." I nodded encouragingly. "You're already doing so well. Even if he's not proud of you yet, I am."

"Thanks."

There was a sadness behind the smile she gave me. This guy did not deserve her. But that was absolutely none of my business. I made a habit of not getting too attached to my clients. Normally, they didn't keep in touch.

But normally, they didn't joke around and chat like Katelin did either.

"Hey, did you ever ask that girl out?" Katelin asked as we headed over to the pull-up bar.

"What girl?" I frowned at her, feeling my cheeks burn as I instantly thought of Ava.

"The one you practically pine over when you hold her door open every morning? Maddi said you were going to ask her out."

"Of course, she did." I let out a sigh as I helped her get the elastic band set up. "And, yes. I did indeed. I don't think it's going to work out."

"That sucks, I'm sorry." She said as she did her first chin-up. "Your perfect girl is out there; I just know it."

"I know. I think she's just taking too long."

"She must be chronically tardy like you."

Katelin smirked at me.

"Five more." I glared, and she let out a loud laugh that caught the attention of some real gym rats.

By the time we finished with our session, it was already past ten. I slipped into the coffee shop and grabbed one for me and Noah. Normally, I'd pass Ava on my way in or out, but I didn't that day. So, I knew I must have been really late. I rushed out of the shop, taking the shortcut to my apartment, and made it home in time to shower.

Ava

I could not get Parker's ridiculously beautiful face out of my head. I thought about her through my entire shift and the twenty-five blocks home, and not just because walking alone again felt much less safe. But that bugged me every time I checked over my shoulder.

When I finally got home, the house was quiet in a way that always made me tired. Everything was clean and put away. I could hear the soft tic of our cheap clock. Willow had already gone to bed, having left a plate of food in the fridge for me. I didn't even bother reheating it. The extra time was too much.

Milo, our Siamese cat, greeted me, meowing softly until I left a green bean on the tiny bar between the galley kitchen and our tiny dining area before heading toward my room. I'd only just reached my door when I heard a noise coming from Willow's room.

She flipped on her lamp as I stepped in the open door. She smiled sleepily, signing to me. "How was work?"

I set the plate down on the end of her bed before signing back. "It was good. My coworkers are quiet, though. You'd fit right in."

She glared at me playfully before a smirk spread across her lips. "Do you like it?"

I nodded. Dressing mannequins at night alone in a department store was still new, but the acoustics were perfect for testing lyrics I wasn't ready for anyone else to hear yet, if ever. Playing covers of other people's songs was one thing, but my own was different.

"What about therapy?"

I shrugged. "Same as last week." I forced a smile, thinking about Parker. I wasn't ready to tell Willow about her just yet. "Why are you still up?"

"Waiting for you." She signed back. "I worry about you being out so late. And I miss you. I feel like I barely see you now that you have this new job."

I couldn't help but frown at that. "Why don't you come with me to my audition tomorrow?"

"Really?" she asked.

I hadn't ever asked her along for an audition before. It didn't feel like the most professional thing ever. But it wasn't like the ad had been either, so my hopes weren't ridiculously high, regardless.

"Yeah, what time is your test?"

"Early." She grumbled.

I laughed. "So, maybe we should go to bed."

Willow grinned. "I'd like to come... if that's okay."

"I wouldn't have offered if it wasn't. I love you. Thank you for dinner."

She nodded before reaching toward the lamp. "Don't stay up too late." She signed before turning her lamp back off.

I yawned as I flopped onto my unmade bed, feeling suddenly exhausted. It was just past one, which wasn't as late as I was sure it could have been, but an entire day on my feet plus walking between jobs would do that.

When I finished my food, I slipped into the bathroom and started getting ready for bed, pausing with my toothbrush hanging out of my mouth at the dark circles under my eyes and the acne scars on my cheeks. I'd all but grown out of my old cystic acne, and the vitamin E oil I'd been using was helping, but I could still see it. What the hell did Parker see in me?

What had Cam seen in me?

No, I wasn't doing that to myself.

I practically stormed off to bed, curling up my beat-up quilt. I'd been so exhausted moments before, but as I lay there staring up at my nearly dark ceiling, all I could think about was Parker's stupidly perfect smile.

I was amused by how much of a cliché she was. The men's clothes, the button down specifically, even the cologne she wore. Everything about her was a walking lesbian stereotype. And being the sucker that I was, I loved every bit of it. But women like Parker were like forbidden fruit for women like me. She'd walk away the moment she knew I was asexual, and I knew it.

And just that thought had tears in my eyes. Why couldn't I just...

I let out a sigh and rolled over. It was stupid to even think about. I never should have gone to that stupid group therapy in the first place.

After bumping into Parker outside the gym, *my gym*, I could have sworn I saw her leaving the coffee shop as I headed up the block. She was practically sprinting down the sidewalk, though, so I couldn't be certain, but I thought I recognized a certain neck tattoo.

Willow met up with me there, literally jumping for joy as she flashed her phone screen at me. She'd not only passed her test, she'd aced it.

"That was quick!" I signed as I handed her a coffee.

"She graded them while we were finishing up." She sighed, handing me my guitar. "This class was so hard. I'm glad it's over."

Benefits of accelerated learning. I wished that had been available seven years ago.

"Only one semester left. How do you feel?"

"So ready. I hate college."

I let out a laugh. Willow was smart, ridiculously so. She picked up everything rather quickly, if she had the urge to do so and a teacher willing to explain it to her. She'd not always been so lucky in that respect. Even the most accommodating places seemed to be out of touch with disabilities.

"We should celebrate!" I looped my free arm in hers, lugging my guitar as we headed toward the bar where I'd be auditioning.

I had a rough idea where we were headed when I'd looked the place up online. It was just a few blocks from the department store. Not exactly on my way, but not so far that I'd be back tracking if I got the gig. I needed this, maybe more than therapy. Okay, a stretch, but didn't all therapists advocate for self-care? Music was my self-care.

"Are you sure?" Willow asked. "We only just got everything figured out after I was sick."

"You passed a whole class. That's worth celebrating."

She made a noise. "Only if you get the gig."

I sighed, smiling. "Okay, fine."

The street was quiet when I knocked on the back door of the restaurant like the manager, Nathan, had instructed me to do. A couple minutes later, I knocked again. I probably waited a solid ten minutes before he opened it with an angry huff. Not sure which one of us was running late, but I was pretty sure it wasn't me.

"I didn't realize you were a duo." He grumbled as he eyed Willow standing next to me.

"I'm not, this is my sister, Wi—"

"I don't really care." He sighed, waving us inside. "I'm a little pressed for time. I was expecting you ten minutes ago."

"I was here." I said back, giving him my best fake smile when he sneered back at me.

"Well, let's see what you've got. We are taking serious musicians only."

He didn't give me time to respond before he disappeared into the sound booth a few feet from the small stage. I expected him to turn on the lights, but he didn't. The entire stage area stayed dark, only lit by the sunlight coming in the front windows. The restaurant was eerily quiet. I could just barely make out the sounds of the kitchen. I caught a glimpse of the bartender like a silhouette, darting around, filling the cooler with what looked like beer.

"Whenever you're ready." Nathan called, poking his abnormally long neck out of the booth.

I quickly pulled my guitar out of the case and took a seat on the small stool in the center of the stage. Willow had taken a seat closest to one of the large speakers, and had a hand on it, which gave me a sense of resolve. I gave it a couple strums to test the sound and let out a sigh.

Then I played my heart out.

Somewhere in the middle, I realized Nathan had ventured out of the sound booth and was watching with a weird look on his face. I didn't think anyone had ever looked at me like that. Like I was some mystical being—a unicorn. Is that what awe looked like? Maybe.

He clapped at the end of the song and came to the stage.

"So, listen, I wasn't offering a paid gig, just a tip jar, but—" He let out a sigh and looked me firmly in the eye. "What do you say to Friday and Saturday nights, two, maybe three hours, minimum wage?"

He was lucky I wasn't looking for a paid gig because any musician who was would know that was such a shit offer.

"Can I still leave out the tip jar?" I grinned, hopping off the stool and setting my guitar back in the case.

"I—uh, yes... yes, I think we could do that."

"Great, I'll be here Friday." I smiled. "I do have another job, so it might be closer to six, but that should work for dinner rush."

Nathan nodded numbly, like he didn't actually believe I'd accepted as the bell on the door rang and customers began streaming in.

"Mind if we stick around? Maybe have lunch?" I asked.

"Sure, that's fine."

Nathan disappeared into the sound booth again, and I waved Willow over. She was beaming like she might have been able to read his lips in the dark, or maybe she was just feeding off my energy. I left my guitar on the stage as we slipped into a booth across from the bar.

Parker

Noah was waiting for me when I came out of my room. He was dressed, too, which was unlike him. He was normally happy to wait to get ready until we were rushing out the door for work. Of the times we'd been late to the bar, it had been my fault a total of no times, a miracle that may have been.

"You look ready to go." I sighed as he sipped what was left of the coffee, I'd brought home.

"That's because I am." He groaned. "Nathan called us in early."

"Us?" I raised an eyebrow. We were supposed to be getting lunch.

"Yeah, both Karlee and Ellis called in, so he needs openers for the bar and the kitchen."

"Ever since they got together—" I rolled my eyes, taking my cup of coffee back into my room so I could get dressed. "He's still expecting us to close, isn't he?"

"Sure is!" He sighed, and even from the hall I could hear him pouring food for Samuel.

"At least we don't have to worry about rent."

He laughed, loud and sarcastically. "There is that. How long do you need? He's asked me twice how soon we can be there."

"Give me five."

It was closer to ten minutes before I was dressed, still braiding my hair as we made our way to the car. Since the bar was across town, we always drove. It was typically the only place we drove, as our apartment was within walking distance of nearly anything we could want. There were plenty of places to work that were closer, maybe, but none that paid so well. And paying rent was more important, as was saving.

I had dreams.

Nathan was bouncing on the heels of his Vans when we walked through the door. "Finally, we open in fifteen!"

"You're welcome, Nathan!" I called, suppressing the urge to flip him off as I set my things behind the bar, and checked the coolers for what needed stocked. I could not wait to find a bar of my own to buy and quit this place with dignity.

There was still an unfocused fog in my head, as usual, within thirty minutes of drinking my first cup of coffee in the morning. Normally, I'd have another one before coming in. Nathan was damn lucky, and he should have been grateful Noah kept a closer eye on his phone than I did.

Or that we weren't reasonable people with lives and things to do four hours before we were scheduled for work. Otherwise, he would have been high and dry.

Noah silently made his way to the kitchen, which was absent of its normal chatter and clatter. When I ducked through the doors to grab lemons from the walk-in cooler, I saw him turning on ovens, cooktops and fryers with a frantic but somehow methodic flare. Behind him, there was a large box of uncut vegetables needing prepped. I'd thought I had a lot to do.

It was unlikely the printer for the bar would go off before my shift was actually supposed to start. But I knew once the doors opened, the printer in the kitchen wouldn't stop for most of the afternoon. He'd probably be sweating through his shirt before four o'clock even came around.

When I stepped back out of the already warm kitchen, Nathan had disappeared into the sound area. *Typical.* He'd rather sit in the office watching us on camera than in person. Is that how businesses were supposed to be run? No, absolutely not.

Much to my surprise, not long after, I heard music echoing through the bar—live music. Without a doubt, the woman singing had to have the most amazing voice I'd ever heard outside of competition tv shows Noah watched when he thought I wasn't paying attention. She was playing the guitar along a soft and tame cover of a Paramore song. I hadn't listened to their music in years.

"Hear that?" Noah asked before I could make my way back to the front with a case of beer for the bar. "Nathan finally found someone to audition! I can't imagine why anyone would want to play here."

"She's good, though." I shrugged.

"Better than good! Too good for this place is all I'm saying."

I let out a laugh and headed back to the bar. I couldn't really see the performance from the beer cooler, with the stage lights off, but she was only better out there with the acoustics right.

Nathan wasn't the best person. He'd been cutting off anyone who auditioned for weeks before they could finish, like this place was some exclusive location, so I was shocked to hear her actually make it all the way through the song. He even clapped. Maybe he'd actually hire her if he knew what was best for him.

I shook my head as I headed back into the back for more beer for the bar. The familiar ding of the door flowed into the kitchen, which marked our first customers of the day. I was still stocking, but that wasn't really a problem for me. I might make a total of two drinks before four when happy hour started, which meant Nathan would probably bark at me to do some serving or bussing or both.

Before I could even finish cutting lemons, I heard the familiar sound of the kitchen receipts printing, and Noah got started. Within minutes, the kitchen was too hot for the black button-down Nathan liked for me to wear. I hurried to finish with the lemons, feeling sweat forming at the nape of my neck.

I had just slipped back out of the kitchen when I caught a glimpse of Ava's shiny brown hair. She was already seated at a booth near the bar, talking with her hands. Wait, no, she was *legitimately* talking with her hands. Speaking fluent sign language. I recognized a few of the simpler signs from high school. I sucked in a shallow breath and ducked back into the kitchen to where Noah was flipping chicken on the grill.

"She's here." I said, feeling a wave of shock and numbness completely consume me.

"Who's—" He started. "Wait, *she,* she?"

I nodded frantically.

"Oh! Well, that's a good sign, isn't it? Did you invite her, or is this more of the universe?"

"No, I was too busy trying to get to know her. I never thought to really tell her anything about myself?"

"So, she's just here, out of pure coincidence?" He raised an incredulous eyebrow. "I mean, you did say the universe needed to work a little harder."

I shot him a glare. “We don’t even use last names in the group, so I don’t know how she would have even found my socials.”

“Which one?”

“Darker hair in the red sweater.”

“Oh, she’s cute.” He grinned. “You going to say hi?”

“Absolutely not.” I scoffed as he made his way back to the grill before something burned. “What would I even say?”

“*Hi*?”

I rolled my eyes.

“Well, it’s not like you can stand in the kitchen the whole time.” Noah said, passing a plate of food my way for me to run. “Nathan would have both our heads.”

I let out a sigh, glancing back to where one of our servers was getting Ava’s drink order. She looked in a good mood at least, smiling far more than I’d seen in a while.

“See if her friend is single, too, while you’re at it.” Noah called before I could slip out.

“I thought you were *exclusively* seeing guys this month.” I grinned.

He shrugged. “She’s cute enough I’ll make an exception.”

I let out a laugh as I slipped out the kitchen door, setting the bowl of lemons on the bar on my way to the dining area. I ran the plate of food to one of our waiting customers, just a few tables down from where Ava was sitting.

My hands were sweaty as I tried to hype myself up in my head. *She’s just a woman. No big deal. Just say hi.*

“Hey there.” I breathed, feeling my cheeks burn as I reached the table.

“Hey,” Ava frowned, looking up at me and then around the restaurant. “Are you—?”

"Please, this is my place of employment, so if anyone is stalking someone..."

She let out a laugh before turning toward the girl in front of her and signing so fast I couldn't keep up. Luckily, she spoke aloud while she did it. "This is Parker. She's in the group. This is my sister, Willow."

Willow smiled wide and said aloud, "Nice to meet you."

I sucked in a shallow breath, trying my best to remember what little sign language I knew as I fumbled through, saying it was nice to meet her, too.

"Sorry," I sighed. "My sign language is a little rusty."

Ava looked surprised. "No, that was... almost perfect, actually."

"Well, I guess I remember something from school then."

Callie, their waitress, came back with drinks. "Parker, you're not jacking my table, are you?"

I laughed, "No, just saying hi to a... friend."

Ava met my eyes, her cheeks turning a bright red.

"They're all yours." I said to Callie, looking at Ava, when I added, "I'll see you next Monday?"

"Yeah," Ava nodded, smiling, before I turned away.

I was all the way back in the kitchen with Noah before I realized I was about to be in trouble for not asking if her sister was single.

Ava

I got the gig. Even if it was painstakingly clear, working with the manager would be rough, we were celebrating. Well, celebrating as best as two girls hanging onto their financial situation by a few threads could celebrate. But I was trying my best. I wanted her to feel like each class she passed was a big deal, and it was.

Willow was only one more semester away from her degree, and then maybe she could become a vet tech and stop apologizing because I paid most of the rent. And I? Well, I was just happy I could start performing again, even if it was a minimum wage, part-time thing.

I never would have thought, given the sheer number of people in this city, that I would get hired in the same restaurant where *Parker* worked. And yet, there we were, sitting in the restaurant Parker worked, having just been hired. She'd find out eventually, but that didn't mean I had to tell her today. Especially not when I was pretty sure I'd already bumped into her twice that morning.

That, and I didn't want to know what she thought of my singing.

"You like her." Willow signed the moment Parker and our waitress left the table. She was smiling as she did it, a smug little grin like she knew everything.

“That obvious?” I signed back, taking a large sip of my drink. I knew better than to argue. Willow knew me better than anyone, and she was good at reading the room.

Willow nodded. “Why didn’t you tell me about her? She seems nice.”

“Because I don’t want you getting big ideas. It won’t go anywhere.”

“How do you know?” She raised an eyebrow at me.

“Because I’m not her type.” I felt myself slouch.

“How do you know?”

“Because I’m me.” I signed back quickly. “Can we talk about something else?”

Willow sighed. “You deserve to be happy.”

I jumped as Parker’s voice echoed next to me.

“One seafood salad,” Parker grinned, as she set the plate down in front of Willow. I wondered just how much sign language she knew, and how much of that conversation she’d picked up on. “And one cheeseburger. Can I get you ladies anything else while your waitress is with another table?”

“Yeah,” Willow said out loud, signing along as she did. “Your number?”

I nearly choked on soda. Oh god, I was going to be sick. Immediately, both of my hands were shading my face like the sun was in my eyes. Or maybe I was dying of embarrassment and could not stand the thought of making eye contact with Parker again. Ever again.

“Uhm.” Parker cleared her throat. “I’m technically not allowed to give it out to customers. Um, but—”

“That’s okay.” I said through gritted teeth as I made a gesture across my throat at Willow. “My sister is being silly.”

Parker let out a laugh. "W-well, if there's anything food related, I can get you, don't hesitate to ask."

I didn't look up until I heard the swing of the kitchen door close.

"Why would you do that?!" I signed.

"Because you wouldn't." She was grinning slyly, and I let out a deep sigh.

I looked down at my cheeseburger, which I wasn't sure I was still hungry enough to eat. Willow, on the other hand, was digging into a bowl full of seaweed and fish. Looking at it made me almost as ill as the previous conversation.

Just as I had mustered the courage to try and eat, Parker was out at the bar. I know she was just doing her job; making drinks, cleaning cups, lugging around large boxes of beer, cutting lemons with a flare I knew I'd never muster clumsy as I was.

But watching her work was so distracting. I don't think I really got around to touching my burger before Willow was halfway finished with her nasty salad.

"You're welcome." Willow said, pulling my attention from Parker's biceps.

"For what?" I signed back.

Willow pointed to where Parker was smiling back at us. It was innocent and dazzling and beautiful, and I felt a stupid flutter in my stomach. I let out a sigh, looking down before Parker could see me blush. I was not in the headspace for this. So much for celebrating.

"Can we go, please?" I asked.

"You didn't even eat." Willow crossed her arms.

So, I took two bites of my burger and asked for a box.

Parker

I'd been staring at the ten digits left on a napkin with my name for over thirty minutes when my first customer sat down at the bar, and I had to actually work. I was pretty sure Ava hadn't left the number. I was pretty sure it had been Willow. So, the likelihood of me sending her a message was slim.

But knowing Willow thought Ava liked me enough to leave it got me through the rest of the day and into the night when it was time to close up.

Noah was still annoyed that I'd forgotten to ask if Willow was seeing anyone twice, but not quite so annoyed that he wasn't happy for me. He was the best kind of friend. Maybe one day I'd step up my wing woman game a notch and deserve him.

It was as we were headed home that I realized we passed that dark department store almost every day; the one where Ava worked. And sure enough, just three blocks down, I saw a familiar silhouette trudging along in a fresh patch of snowy sidewalk.

"Hey, slow down." I said to Noah, who noticed immediately and pulled closer to the curb.

Ava jumped as I rolled down my window, pulling a headphone out of her ear while she reached into her purse. There was a look of fire in her eyes that dissipated when I spoke.

"Want a ride?" I asked.

Ava was still walking, but Noah was going at a snail's pace to keep up with her.

"My mom taught me not to take rides from strangers." Ava smirked over at me.

"Come on, Ava. It's freezing out tonight, and this isn't the best neighborhood."

She let out a sigh, but she was shivering, and I had a feeling she was going to say yes before she even stopped. "I guess we're lucky you're not technically a stranger."

She climbed into the back seat. Noah was shaking his head like he couldn't believe my luck. His track record with meeting new people was horrible. He gave me a look, a look only Noah could give, with pointed eyes and raised eyebrows, a slight shake of the head, that basically conveyed I still had wing woman duties before pulling away from the curb.

"So—"

"You know, if we keep meeting like this, I might actually just need to get your number, so it's not such a surprise." Ava had leaned forward in the tiny back seat, and had her arms up on the back of our headrests. "What is this? Three times today?"

"Something like that." I grinned over my shoulder at her. "It's okay, though. Your sister was kind enough to give me yours."

Her face fell. "She did not."

I nodded, holding up the napkin that I'd carefully stuffed into my apron.

She breathed in and let out a deliberate sigh. "I hate her." She grinned.

Noah cleared his throat.

"Speaking of your sister." I said before Noah could throw something at me. "My incredibly awesome best friend Noah here was wondering if she was seeing anyone."

"Oh, yeah?" Ava let out a little laugh, and her attention went to Noah, almost like a switch had been flipped. "You know she's my *baby* sister, right? I can be incredibly protective. Parker told you we met in therapy, yes? Has she told you I'm *unhinged*?"

I felt Noah get a little tense as they made eye contact in the rearview mirror. He was terrible with confrontation, and even I wasn't completely used to how serious Ava was with her sarcasm. When Noah said nothing, Ava shrugged, like his reaction wasn't fun enough.

"Nah, she's not seeing anyone." Ava sighed. "And since she's going around passing out numbers, and you're *incredibly* awesome, I feel no shame in giving her number to you."

I could see Noah turning bright red even in what little light came from the streetlights we were passing.

"Well, thank you." Noah cleared his throat, this time out of nervousness.

"On one condition." Ava said before I could even pass her Noah's phone. "You have to take her on a real date. All that upstanding gentleman bull. Because if I give her number out and you're not ridiculously like her dad was, then I have to hear about it—hey pull over at the next block. That's me."

"I think you're in luck." I smiled, passing Noah's phone into the back seat. "Noah actually *is* an upstanding gentleman."

Ava rolled her eyes and smiled as she typed into Noah's phone, finished adding the contact and passed it back to me just as Noah was pulling up to the curb.

"You need me to—" I started, but Ava pulled out a rather expensive looking taser.

I felt my eyes go wide. That was rather formidable.

"I got it." She smiled, letting out a small, awkward sigh. "Thank you for the ride. I really appreciate it. Willow hates when I walk home."

"Any time." I nodded back. "I mean, this is pretty much our route home anyway, so—um. No big deal."

She did a little drum against the safe edge of her taser with her fingertips, but there was a smile on her face. And then she reached for the door, but not before leaning forward and kissing my cheek.

It sent a wave of chills—the good kind—down my spine.

"Goodnight, Parker." She said as she slipped out of the car and into a rather depressing looking apartment building.

There was a beat before I could even realize she'd already gotten out of the car. My cheeks were hot. Hell, my whole body was hot. It was just really warm in that car.

"You okay over there?" Noah asked, having not moved.

It was then that I realized I hadn't either.

"Y-yeah." I nodded.

"You have it so bad for her." Noah laughed, pulling away from the curb.

I was basically a robot the rest of the way home.

Ava

Why did I kiss Parker's cheek? *Why* did I *kiss* Parker's *cheek?*

What the hell was I thinking?

I was thinking she was being sweet in a genuine way, and I hadn't seen that in a while. I was thinking she was cute, and I *wasn't thinking*.

Willow was still up doing homework when I walked in the door. Her books and notebooks and notes were all strung out all over the living room. She was such a mess, but a determined mess. I knew it would all be back in order before she went to bed.

She looked up, rather surprised to see me.

"You're home early." She signed over her work, frowning at me slightly.

I nodded, realizing I was out of breath from panicking all the way up the stairs. "Parker gave me a ride."

Willow grinned rather big.

"Why would you give her my number?"

"Because I knew you wouldn't." Willow shrugged. "I know you like her. It's okay."

I sighed. "Well, I gave your number to her friend."

"What?" She frowned at me like I was some kind of alien. "Why would you do that?"

"Because he's awesome." I grinned. I really didn't know that much about him, but he seemed alright. He had a job at least, which was better than any of the guys she'd dated recently. She had a thing for toxic men. Got it from our mom. I guess that's why Mom seemed better off with women. It's too bad that wasn't the case with me.

"You don't even know him, do you?" She signed, her face turning a deep shade of red. Oh, she was angry.

I shrugged. "You don't even know Parker, either."

She let out a huff, and looked back down at the notebook she'd been writing in, signing, "Dinner is in the microwave," without even looking up at me.

A laugh escaped my lips, and I felt my phone buzz as I made my way to the kitchen. Willow was already annoyed with me; I wasn't going to make it worse by not eating her food. It was still warm, and Milo came chirping in, yawning as he did. I really was home early.

Text Message
Tuesday 12:38AM

If you ever need a ride, don't hesitate to ask. -Parker.

I was trying not to smile when I heard Willow clear her throat.

"Is that her?" Willow asked.

I rolled my eyes and nodded.

"You're welcome."

I swear if Noah isn't just the greatest guy in history, my sister is going to kill me.

Read 12:39AM

I typed back to Parker, pressing send before I could think better of it.

And then I'll just have to come after you.

Read 12:40AM

Then, luckily for both of us, he's the best person I've met in my entire life.

Better be. She's so mad at me.

Read 12:40AM

Parker sent back a laughing emoji, and I felt something hit my head. I looked down to where a bright green skittle was rolling across the floor. Shit, she had great aim. Milo went after it, pouncing. I knew he wouldn't eat it, but it was likely I'd never see it again, regardless.

"What was that for?" I signed.

"He texted me! What do I say?" Willow was holding up her phone like it was a foreign object.

"Hi?" I suggested with a grin, and she reached for another skittle, so I ducked under the counter.

She's now throwing skittles at my head.

Delivered

There was a beat in which I thought Parker might have gone to bed.

What a waste of skittles.

I laughed as another skittle came across the counter, falling at my feet.

You're telling me. I paid for them.

Read 12:42AM

Oh, so thievery and assault by skittle.
I think that's a federal offense.

Wait, we've reached a ceasefire.

Read 12:43AM

Told you, Noah is amazing.

I poked my head over the counter to look where my sister was texting, slouching on the couch, and smiling like she had a schoolgirl crush. I let out a little laugh. Willow looked up at me as if she'd sensed she was being watched and rolled her eyes.

"He is nice." She signed. "Thank you."

"You're welcome." I said, looking down at my phone.

"Ava." Willow said aloud, mostly for emphasis because she was signing, too. "It's okay to like her."

I let out a sigh, nodding. And then I bit my lip as my eyes started to well up because it really wasn't okay to like her. Because I'd liked Cam, too, and look where that got me?

Goodnight, Parker.

Read 12:47AM

Sweet Dreams ♡

A heart. *A freaking heart.*

Parker

Noah didn't stop texting Willow the rest of the night. It had been a while since I'd seen him like that–probably high school. He hadn't been all that serious about anyone since we'd graduated, and on one occasion, he'd told me he was holding out for something... extraordinary.

Me, too.

"Look who's got it bad, now?" I teased, poking my head into the living room.

It was well past when he was normally sawing logs, disrupting any of my attempts at going to bed at a usual hour, and instead, he was lounging on the couch with the most childlike grin I'd ever seen on him.

"Okay, but I'm not afraid to admit it." He sighed, letting his phone hit his chest. "She's great."

"Oh, yeah?" I smiled back. "Well, you're going to regret your life choices in the morning if you don't go to bed soon, and I don't like playing dad like you do, so–"

"Please never refer to yourself as a dad again. You're inching on ew territory. We don't discuss... that part of our lives, m'kay?"

I smirked back at him. "Oh, you're policing my kinks now?"

He squirmed his way off the couch. "You're not allowed to have a Daddy kink, and if you did..." He got really close to my face. "I don't want to hear about it."

There was a serious sass to his walk as he headed to his room that reminded me just how rooted he was with his masculinity. It was not fragile. Not one bit.

"You better not start referring to yourself in the third person, either!" He called over his shoulder.

"Daddy's heading to bed now." I laughed, shutting off the living room light.

I heard a fake retch from his room before his door shut with a loud thud.

I eyed my phone as I slipped back into my own room, looking at the message from Ava, probably reading too far into it. Over-analyzing every single word had become such a habit–one I didn't know how to break.

The next morning was more of... that. Noah walking around the house grinning and giggling, barely looking up from his phone as I raced around to get ready. I was happy for him, but also jealous. I had a feeling I wouldn't be hearing from Ava. I just didn't know why.

When I got to the gym, she plowed right into me on my way in, her face in her phone.

"Oh, I'm–" she sputtered, lingering closer than usual as she let out a laugh when the realization set in. "Hey."

"Good morning to you, too." I smiled, feeling my cheeks burn. I'd imagined her finally looking up at my face so many mornings. I didn't think I'd ever gotten to see her eyes up this close. They were somewhere between emerald green and sage.

"Is this what it's gonna be like every day?" She raised an eyebrow at me as she fiddled with her phone again.

"Pretty much." I nodded, letting myself laugh.

She let out a hesitant laugh in return, and I caught Kaitlin eyeing us from the lockers.

Ava sighed, following my line of sight, and when she looked back up at me, there was a shift in her mood. Her smile was gone, replaced with an expression I had no way of deciphering.

"Well, I'll let you get to work." She smiled, forced. "I should probably go before I'm late, anyway."

"Right, yeah," I nodded. "I'll see you later."

I stepped out of her way, feeling both Maddi and Kaitlin watching me closely as Ava slipped out the doors. No game. I had no game.

"So, what was that about?" Kaitlin asked. "I thought you said it wasn't going to work out? Sure, seems like there's something, something."

"Oh hush, grab your gear." I sighed, looking at the door. "It's awkward is what it is."

"Because she's obviously in to you." Kaitlin said as she grabbed the elastic bands she's been using.

"What?" I frowned at her.

"Oh, yeah, definitely."

Why'd she turn me down, then?

Ava

"Meg, your regular is here!" August called through the kitchen door. "And Ava, you've got one, too."

"Thank you." I nodded, sending off an order to the kitchen before slipping back out the swinging door into the dining room.

I felt my heart race at the sight of Parker across the room, sitting casually like she belonged there. When she said she'd see me later–

I let out a short breath, bypassing my own section as I made my way over to the table where she was sitting.

"What are you doing here?" I asked, barely above a whisper.

"What do you mean?" She frowned.

"Look, me showing up at the bar the other day, that was coincidence. You can't just... Parker, I *work* here."

"Ava, you're not trying to jack my regular, are you?" Meg said in a teasing voice as she came up to my side with a drink in hand.

"Your regular." I repeated, looking between Meg and Parker, who was smiling sheepishly.

"Yeah, every Tuesday and Thursday." Meg frowned like she was thinking deep when she looked down at Parker. "For what? The last year now?"

I felt the blood drain from my face. I hadn't even worked there for a year. I swallowed hard, looking down at my apron. Just how many places did Parker see me?

"You okay, honey?" Meg asked, her hand touching my upper arm in a motherly way.

I nodded, looking over to the new table I hadn't greeted yet. "Yeah, I'm good."

I couldn't look at Parker before scurrying away.

Meg's regular. MEG'S REGULAR? The good-tipping, overly polite regular. The one she sat down with every week and chatted with. The one Meg said needed her 'motherly guidance' the most.

I knew Parker had looked familiar in the therapy group that first week, but I would have remembered her face.

Wouldn't I?

My table left before Parker finished her food. She stuck around; I knew that. Meg was always chatting with her, even if I'd never realized it was her. When I went on break, I hesitantly slipped into the booth across from Parker. I watched as she ran a hand through her dark hair and eyed me.

"I'm sorry." I said with a sigh. "I shouldn't have assumed—"

"It's okay," she shifted. "Remember that first week in the group? We both talked about exes? I have baggage, too. I get it... kind of."

A laugh escaped my lips before I could stop it.

"I mean, I've never had a stalker–"

I felt myself stiffen.

"We don't have to talk about it."

"Thank you." I sighed. "You're not... you're not following me, are you?"

"No." She smiled. "I'm not."

"Then, how do you explain..." I waved around the air. "All this? The therapy group, the gym, the coffee shop, here?"

"Well, the therapy group was Meg. But, honestly?" She let out a soft laugh. "I thought you were following me at first."

"Really?"

She nodded.

"And then I thought it was some sign from the universe."

A scoff slipped out. "The universe? What, you believe in fate and all that?"

She nodded, "Yeah, I really do."

I said nothing, so she continued.

"I thought it was kind of cool." Parker shrugged. "I just saw you everywhere for a while. A long while."

I looked up to meet her eyes as Meg walked out and right back into the kitchen. "Just seems like a whole lot of coincidence to me. You've been seeing me everywhere, but I don't remember you."

"I mean, I feel like you never really... saw me," Parker shrugged. "Like when you nearly dumped coffee on me–"

"Oh, my god that was you." I covered my face as my cheeks burned. "Of course, that was you."

"You never meet my eyes."

"Because I'm embarrassed... and I kind of thought you were a guy... so."

Parker let out a loud laugh and then hushed herself quickly. "That's fair."

I sighed, trying to think back to all the times I might have seen Parker, but coming up short. I knew my head was always on a swivel, always scouring my surroundings... but looking for Cam. Looking for red hair and blue eyes, someone nearly three inches shorter than Parker.

I looked back up at Parker's dark hair and dark eyes. Of course, I looked right past her. Because I wasn't looking for her.

"It wasn't until therapy that I decided to actually pick up the nerve to talk to you." Parker said after a minute.

"*You*... were nervous about talking to *me*?" I raised an eyebrow, and she did that head scratching thing again.

"Yeah, I really was." She brushed a stray piece of hair from her face, and for some reason, I imagined doing it for her.

Stop that.

"Maybe you don't realize it, but you're really beautiful, like *intimidatingly* beautiful."

I scoffed again.

"I'm serious, Ava."

"Well, I'm not—"

"'My type,' I know." Parker smirked.

I let out a sigh.

"You know—"

"My break's over." I breathed. "Guess I'll see you on the way to the gym tomorrow?"

"Maybe if I'm not late."

I felt a smile coming on. I almost told her I'd be performing, too. Almost.

Parker was actually early, weird as that seemed at first. She didn't notice me come out of the yoga room. Her headphones were in, rather contradictory to her claim that she didn't listen to music. Her eyes were straight ahead while she pushed against a contraption loaded up with what looked like a ridiculous amount of weight to me. It seemed effortless to her, and extremely difficult at the same time. And for some reason, I couldn't stop watching.

She pushed through a set or two while I leaned against the hallway door. A logical person who'd been through what I had might have been nervous just seeing that much strength... and power. She could probably throw me and not even struggle. But the more I got to know Parker, the more watching her train muscles I was constantly refraining from giving a good poke... made me feel calmer–safer.

My phone buzzed, and I pulled it out of my bag. I was probably running late. Or Willow wanted a coffee.

I felt my cheeks burn as I looked up to where Parker was now guzzling water from her water bottle and eyeing me with a smug grin.

I walked over to her despite the bubbling embarrassment resting in the pit of my stomach.

"You're early." I said breathily, trying hard to be nonchalant.

"And you're fixing to be late gawking at me like a picture show."

My cheeks burned even more.

"How much weight is that?" I asked.

Maybe her ego would derail the subject.

"That is two hundred pounds."

"So, what you're saying is you could bench me without any problems?"

She eyed me up and down, making me wish I'd kept my mouth shut, as she muttered 'no way' under her breath.

"187, baby. These thunder thighs come at a price." I instantly regretted the word 'baby' slipping out of my mouth.

It was her turn to blush, and she bit her bottom lip, looking down at her phone to hide it.

"I thought you didn't listen to music." I said, hoping to derail the subject yet again.

"Peer pressure." Parker shrugged. "Some girl I like said music is emotion or something like that."

I let out a soft laugh. "Well, this has been awkward, but I am now late."

"Yeah, gawking will do that to you."

"You'd know."

Her jaw dropped, and she promptly shut it like she'd been called out.

"See you later, Parker."

Parker

So, Ava and I were friends. Sort of. Acquaintances? We were walking this fine line between friendly and flirty, and it all felt so muddy. It was confusing in all the ways I'd never had to be confused before.

Admittedly, Jayde was my first serious relationship, but even the casual flings I'd had... things were clear. At the very least, I knew if they were interested, and I couldn't say that for Ava.

After that day in the gym, she'd say hi to me a couple times a day, and we'd go about our routines. There was tension there. She seemed unsure about the weird way our lives overlapped. Much less confident in the power of the universe than I was, and while that sucked? Well, at least I was able to get to know her.

I felt better just being seen.

Maybe what the universe knew that I didn't was that we weren't meant to be together. Maybe we were just meant to set up Willow and Noah because they seemed to be hitting it off swimmingly.

Noah spent at least an hour a day just texting Willow. And every now and again I'd catch him on video chat struggling to sign to her. He'd been watching a bunch of videos online on sign language, but they weren't helping him all that much, even if he could sign the ABC's really fast.

He thought I had it bad.

At least one of us was on their way to a happy, healthy relationship. Some days, I just hoped Ava and I could at the very least get to a point of friends, if only for two of the most important people in our lives. Maybe then I could let go of whatever I'd thought this would be, move on to something... real.

Other days, I couldn't get past the warm feeling I got when she was around. Like I was home. I hadn't felt that in a long time, and there wasn't much that felt more real than that.

Despite the hesitation, I was slowly learning more about her, finally letting myself actually listen into the subtleties that made her... Ava. I learned we liked at least two of the same bands from the band tees she wore to the gym. I found out she was lactose intolerant as she ordered her coffee one morning, and seeing her interact with customers at the diner, members at the gym, the people who worked at the coffee shop. She had all the vibes I wanted more of in my life.

She was just... kind.

Where were the unforgivable flaws? Where were the dark clouds, the doomsday music, the Earthshattering kaboom? Because... Ava was my type. And I had no clue how to get her to believe it.

Ava

The rest of the week felt like an endless cycle of bumping into Parker. I hadn't changed anything about my schedule, but there she was nearly every day. If she wasn't working at the gym, she was working out in it. It seemed we had the same days off, and for the most part, the same sleep schedule. So, between Tuesday and Friday, I saw her almost twelve times in passing.

I still hadn't told her about the gig at the bar where she worked. I was surprised she hadn't brought it up. I was surprised Nathan hadn't said something. Or Noah, though I'd asked Willow to tell him not to blab. Which was smart.

I was nervous enough that Friday. It was my first live performance in years. I didn't need Parker making a huge deal about it, and I just had a feeling she would have. She was so... hype. I felt like that would have made my nerves even worse.

Willow tagged along, and when I walked into the back door where the stage area was to set up, I couldn't even see Parker. She must have been off cutting fruit or something. On a Friday, that wasn't surprising. But it was good. Seeing her, her seeing me, *before* I went on, that would have just made it impossible to sing.

I needed this. I needed to perform again.

Nathan walked up to me, practically beaming. "I thought you might not show."

"Why wouldn't I?" I shrugged.

"Tiny place, tiny crowd."

I nodded. "That's not so bad. Anything I should know before I get started?"

"Play some soft stuff." He shrugged, already turning away from me. "They're here to eat and drink. You're supposed to be background noise."

Cool. I rolled my eyes. Why not just set up a playlist then? Having live performance doesn't make you cool if you don't make a big deal about it. Nathan was clearly just trying to get with the hipster crowd by bringing in a soft-spoken cover artist. At nearly fifty, he was way too old to be dressing like a twenty-year-old fuck boy. Which meant that his whole aesthetic was kind of sad.

I bit my lip. I still needed this. Performing made me happy. So, even though my new boss had all but ruined this gig of mine, I set up and started playing.

All the nerves dissipated the moment I started the first song, an acoustic version of one of those pop songs you don't expect to work as acoustic. I'd expected performing again to feel overwhelming, but it was like with each breath, I relaxed. I felt at home. I felt more myself than I had in a long time. As if a little part of me was unpacked and put in the right place.

Nathan had been right. The crowd wasn't large, so I was surprised by the volume of the applause. I risked a single look at the bar where Parker was struggling to focus on drink orders.

And when I started the next song, I realized people were moving toward the back tables to be closer to the stage, and small crowd or not, that was all I really wanted from performing. I just wanted people to hear me play.

My set wasn't super long. I had a shift at the department store that night, anyway. But I played every cover I'd ever done from 90s hits all the way up to the current stuff. Nathan came by twice with his own personal requests, which annoyed me. My music wasn't drawing a crowd from the streets, but I could tell people were sitting toward the stage a little more than they had been the other day, and that at least made me happy by the time I was packing up.

"Wow." I heard a familiar voice say behind me as I was locking up my guitar. "I had no idea that was you the other day."

When I turned around, Parker was standing behind me, leaning against the wall next to the tiny sound box. She still had a towel over her shoulder and hadn't taken off her apron, so I figured she wasn't off work yet. Taking a break, maybe. Things had slowed down after the dinner rush, and even with the bar, this wasn't quite the Friday nightclub scene.

"Yeah," I nodded. "I would have said something, but I was already nervous."

"First gig?" She asked. Her eyebrows were raised like she found that hard to believe.

"No, it's just... been a while. I used to perform a lot before—just before."

I sucked in a shallow breath, feeling her eye me curiously, and suddenly, I had word vomit.

"I started at my old church before we left it. I've managed some national anthem singings over the years, a few open mics." I rambled. "I used to be a regular at a bar downtown on Thursday nights. I had to be gone by ten since I was still underage, but I made enough money to buy my first car."

"That's impressive. Why'd you stop?" Parker asked.

I couldn't answer that, the words were caught in my throat because a part of me did want to tell Parker. All of it stopped when I met Cam. I put away my guitar for almost three years. She said it was stupid, and I wasn't that good. I needed a real job. It took me a while to play again after we'd split. It took even longer to get back to where I'd been, and I'd only just started improving. Once you stop a skill... sometimes you lose it.

"I just didn't have the time." I shrugged, eyeing the stage. "So, I guess we'll be seeing more of each other. More than on the street, anyway."

"Guess so," she grinned. There was a drink in her hand, which she reached out to me. "Figured after dealing with Nathan all evening, you could use one of these. I saw him suggesting songs to you a couple times. Your sister said you like rum."

"Oh, thanks." I took it, feeling my stomach get all fluttery when our fingers brushed. "Is she still here? Willow, I mean."

Parker nodded, turning slightly so I could see where Willow and Noah were seated in a booth. "Yeah, she was waiting for you. Noah doesn't get off for a couple more hours."

I let out a sigh, unable to keep from smiling at them as I took a drink. Noah was speaking sign language, though not super well. It looked like he was making some of it up as he went along when he got stuck. He blushed when she corrected him, but he didn't seem annoyed. It was nice enough that he was trying. Her last boyfriend had tried to convince her she just needed hearing aids. As if he knew more about her own disability than she did.

"I tried to tell him you could teach him." Parker scoffed, shaking her head. "But he's been watching videos online instead."

"Pride's a funny thing." I sighed. "Besides, it's better if she teaches him. I don't need to speak for her. She's more than capable."

Parker smiled and sighed, looking back at me. Something about the way she was looking at me, her posture maybe, made me uncomfortable in that oddly good way. It was that way you always dream someone will look at you. That way I knew she couldn't look at me because once she started looking at me like that, it just might kill me when she stopped.

I took a long drink, looking away from Parker and back at the stage.

"You're really good, you know." She said, like she was trying to reassure me. "Noah said you're too good for this place."

A laugh escaped my lips. "Yeah, well, nowhere else will hire me, so."

"You should put up videos online or something."

"I do."

Parker looked surprised.

"It's just..." I sighed. "There are thousands of other people doing the exact same thing, and I love it, but it doesn't pay the bills."

"I get that." She laughed, but it was more of a sigh; painful almost. "I mean, I have a business degree, and I'm a bartender."

"Wait, what?" I found myself grinning.

"Yeah, I was going to run some multimillion-dollar company one day." She did that nervous head scratch thing. "But as it turns out, that's not as fun as it sounds. And I'm not the only one. Noah has a culinary arts degree, and he makes grilled chicken from someone else's recipe."

"Those two are going to fight over the kitchen like no one's business."

Parker looked over her shoulder. "You think?"

"Oh yeah, Willow almost went to culinary school." I grinned.

"No way."

I nodded.

"Do you think they know yet?" Parker laughed.

"Probably not." I shrugged. "I bet they'll figure it out when they're both picky about food on their first date. How come Noah's not working in some fancy kitchen somewhere?"

"Same as me, I think." Parker turned back to me, sighing. "He knows what he wants."

"What do you mean?"

"I want to run my own bar someday. And he wants to run a kitchen. This is just a placeholder until we get there."

Her voice dropped into a whisper. "Between you and me, we both hate it here. Nathan's a dick."

"So, why do you stay?" I asked, and she eyed the sound booth.

"Pays the bills."

She gave a defeated shrug like that was that. But after jumping from job to job, I knew that wasn't the case. There were hundreds of other things she could be doing rather than working for him. Pot? Kettle.

"Couldn't you make more money training?" I asked. I'd considered a personal trainer exactly no times because I knew how expensive they could be.

"I'm sure I could." She nodded. "But I don't want to. That's not why I do it."

I felt myself smile as I eyed her. "Why do you do it?"

"I like helping people, and there's no one better to help than someone who's working their way up a mountain you've already conquered."

I stared at her for a moment, really taking in her face. I'd misjudged her.

"Well, I appreciate the drink and the conversation, but I have another job to get to."

Parker nodded. "Be careful."

I smiled, "You be careful. There are girls with expensive tasers out there."

Parker let out a deep laugh as I headed over to the table where Noah and Willow were sitting.

Willow looked up at me and grinned.

"I guess that's my cue." Noah laughed, sliding out of the booth. "You did really great, by the way."

I felt my cheeks burn. "Thank you."

Noah gave a wave to both Willow and me before heading back to the kitchen. Parker was already behind the bar again, making drinks for another table. I could feel Willow's eyes on me, watching her.

"You look so happy on stage." Willow smiled, but it was sad.

She'd told me once before music was the only thing that had ever made her want a hearing aid. She'd tested them out once, but she said she didn't like them. I wasn't sure if that was because of the cost. But she'd said it wasn't a cure, and that she could be perfectly happy without them.

I squeezed her shoulder. "Thank you for coming. I don't think I could have done this without you."

She brushed me off. "Of course. I wouldn't miss it."

"So, Noah, huh?"

A blush crept up her neck and cheeks. "He tried to sign along with one of your songs."

"No, he didn't."

She nodded.

That made me feel good, at least. Even if I was sure he'd messed it up.

"You're not walking home, are you?" I asked.

She shook her head. "Noah said he'd drive me once he gets off."

I nodded slowly, looking back over at the bar. Parker flashed me a perfect smile and my stomach got all fluttery again. I forced one back, but I had a feeling it was less than beautiful.

Get yourself together.

"Parker said they'd pick you up, too. If you get off the same time." Willow signed to me when I'd pulled my attention away from Parker again.

"Okay," I smiled. "I better get going then. Otherwise, I'll be there all night."

I kissed the top of her head and made for the door, waving to Parker as I did.

Parker

Watching Noah struggle his way through sign language was painful, but it was the happiest I'd seen him in a while. Willow didn't seem to mind, as she corrected him over and over, and he blushed his way through their conversation. She seemed happy, too, though I didn't know her all that well. She didn't seem like the type to fake a smile or a laugh. And she was doing a lot of laughing.

I'd never been more grateful to be in the backseat. It had been a while since I'd been a third wheel. Seeing Ava make her way down the stairs of the department store gave me a wave of relief.

She climbed in next to me, and the relief was replaced with nervousness.

Her guitar rested between us for the duration of the drive, which was a clear picture to me of where we stood. No longer a third wheel, it was more like the two of us were now third wheels as Noah tried to figure out how to continue talking to Willow while driving safely. It wasn't exactly working, but it was making Willow laugh, so he had that going for him.

I caught Ava smiling at them a few times, and then she'd smile at me. We could do this. We could be friends for Noah and Willow.

When we pulled in front of their apartment, Willow asked if we wanted to come inside.

"I'm down." Noah smiled, pulling forward toward the parking area before I could even respond.

Ava and eye met eyes, and an awkward tension filled the back seat.

Noah pulled into a poorly lit parking garage, following Ava's instructions to go around to the second level. She said there was a designated parking space there.

"We never use it." Ava said in an off tone I hadn't heard her use before, but her shoulders were rigid. "We don't have a car, but it's closer to the doors."

As we made our way to the parking section for her floor, I noted massive blobs of mismatched paint covering graffiti, and a part of me thought a little artwork just might do the place some good. The poor lighting left the corners of the garage completely dark and mysterious in a way that even unnerved me.

When we got out, Ava led us through a metal wire door with a thick broken number pad lock and down a musty hallway with a flickering light. I didn't know how old the building was, but the owners sure weren't doing their part with maintenance.

"Welcome to Casa de Us." Ava sighed as she opened the door, gesturing to the living area.

I was more occupied with the front door. The knob was loose, and I was willing to bet the screws holding everything in place were only an inch long at most. For someone who looked over her shoulder and carried quite literally the most expensive taser I'd ever seen, Ava didn't seem all that concerned with security in her apartment.

At least, that's what I thought until I saw four chain locks at my shoulders that were shiny and silver.

"What?" Ava asked, frowning at me.

"Knob's loose." I shrugged, and I watched as her weight shifted like she was about to get defensive.

"Yeah, the maintenance guy was supposed to come around and fix it, but... clearly, they don't do a lot of fixing around here. You want something to drink?"

"Sure." I nodded, shutting the door behind me.

Ava disappeared into the galley kitchen, while Noah and Willow were scanning a large rack of movies next to their little tv.

The living room was fairly small, probably the size of a large bedroom, with a little couch that took up the largest wall. Between the couch and the coffee table, the room was pretty full as it was.

The walls, though, were covered in pictures, artwork, tapestries. It was far more decorated and homier than what Noah and I had done with our place. The most we had was a clock on the wall and a hook for our coats.

I rounded the corner to the kitchen to find Ava grabbing cans of soda from the pantry cabinet and cracking ice out of little trays in a frenzy.

"You know, I could fix that for you." I said, making her jump.

"What? The ice tray?" She laughed.

"The doorknob. It just needs a new screw."

"Oh, I mean it's really–"

"It's no big deal to me, and I'd feel better knowing it shut right." I offered a smile.

"Okay." She nodded. "Yeah, sure. It's been... bugging me."

She fiddled with the ice tray again, seeming to have little luck. I held out a hand, and she passed the tray over with a sigh.

"I get the feeling you're not used to hosting guests." I smirked at her as I passed back the tray, all the cubes loosened.

"Did the basket of laundry in the hallway give it away or the sink full of dishes?" She eyed me as she put ice in the mismatched reusable restaurant cups she'd laid out.

"I honestly didn't notice either. You just seem a little... on edge. We can just go, if you're–"

"No, it's okay." She shook her head, offering a choice between grape and orange soda, and I let out a laugh.

"I'll take grape, please."

"Good, I need to get rid of the stuff. What are they doing in there?"

"Picking out a movie."

"Oh, nice." Ava let out a soft huff and pulled a couple of bags of popcorn and a large bowl out of the cabinets. "Do you mind taking those in there to them?"

She motioned to the drinks, and I took them to the living room without another word.

I set the drinks on the coffee table, where white, hand-crocheted coasters were laid out in the middle. Willow told Noah and I to have a seat, so we sat on opposite ends of the couch, though opposite was used lightly as we were still pretty close together. I found myself wondering how we'd all fit on that little couch.

When Ava came back into the room, she let a weird noise loose from her throat at the sight of us before setting the popcorn down on the table and taking a seat next to me. With the three of us, there wasn't much room for Willow, and I had a feeling Ava wasn't all that comfortable making it work.

The most awkward not first date in history.

Ava

Willow put on a movie and promptly fell asleep. Noah followed soon after, and that left me and Parker awake on my couch, scrunched up together, with Milo somehow napping on the cushion above our shoulders. Despite how awkward that felt at first, Parker's arm had somehow made its way over my shoulders, maybe because that was the easiest way for all four of us to fit on our little couch. Or maybe because she was trying to make a move. I couldn't be sure, but even so, it was oddly comforting.

Maybe I was just touch starved.

I couldn't tell if this was a ploy. Had the three of them cooked this up together, or was my sister really just out to get some innocent arm cuddles out of this goof of a man? It was kind of working, regardless. Having Parker and Noah on my couch felt oddly... right. I hated it. Because I didn't want it to feel right.

Parker shifted after a few minutes, and leaned closer to me.

"You wanna take a walk with me?" Parker whispered.

"Isn't it kind of late for that?" I grinned.

"You've got an expensive taser. I have muscles. Besides, you'd normally be halfway home right about now, wouldn't you?"

"Good point."

I eyed Noah and Willow before nodding. A little cool, winter air might do me some good. Sitting next to Parker was making me feel warm and gooey.

They didn't even stir as we slipped out the front door.

"It's not too bad for February." I breathed, watching as my breath dissipated into nothingness.

"The weather?" Parker chuckled softly. "You wanna talk about the weather?"

"Guess not." I laughed. "They'll be okay, right? I mean...Willow really is my baby sister, so I worry."

"What? With Noah?" Parker raised both eyebrows. "Yeah, she will absolutely be safe with Noah. I meant what I said. He's a good guy. One of the few."

"Have you known him long? I guess if my sister is going to be into him, maybe I should know more about him. Backwards timing, I guess."

She laughed, "Maybe. I mean, Noah and I have been friends since the sixth grade. He's pretty much the only family I have now. We came out together—I"

"Wait, Noah's—"

"Bi, yeah."

"You know Willow's pan, right?"

"What? Really?" Parker raised an eyebrow.

I nodded, "Yeah, she's not exactly quiet about it. You didn't see her lanyard? Or the buttons on her backpack? She's got this one with a frying pan on it."

Parker let out a loud laugh, and then eyed the street, which made me laugh just thinking about when Willow bought that button. She'd laughed about it nearly the whole way home.

"So, you've known him a long time, then." I sighed.

Parker nodded.

"Noah's just... good people." She smiled, looking at the road ahead. "He's funny and decent. His moral compass never fails him. Most of the time, he's just a genuine pleasure to be around.

He really has his head on straight, he always has. We sort of gravitated to each other as kids, like we knew we'd be safe with this person. He's gotten me out of a dark place more than once. And he's been my rock through some of the hardest times of my life, so maybe I have a biased opinion."

"Yeah, well. I think my sister is pretty much the purest thing on the planet, so. I can't say I'm unbiased, either."

"Is it wrong of me to ask what happened to her?"

"Normally, yes." I nodded. "It's typically pretty frowned upon to ask anyone who's disabled what happened to them."

Parker's cheeks turned a bright red. "I'm sorry, I didn't mean—"

"I know, it's idle curiosity, just—you probably wouldn't know much about ableism." I sighed. "Willow was born deaf, so nothing happened to her. When I was seven, it was the most fascinating thing on the planet. I asked tons of questions, which no doubt exhausted my already exhausted mother."

Parker laughed.

"But my mom explained that people can hear because of tiny hairs in their ears, and Willow was born without them." I continued. "It changed all of our lives. She became my whole world. I learned sign language when I was eight, and since the noisy baby toys didn't really speak to her, she mostly liked watching me play my handheld video game. I'd lay on the floor with her for hours, making her giggle."

Parker looked at me, and I felt myself blush.

"I guess it's established that we love the two of them a shit ton." Parker sighed. "And from the looks of things, it's going well. Sounds like we are going to be seeing more of each other, so tell me something about you."

"Like what?"

"What's your middle name?"

"I'm not telling you my middle name." I scoffed. "That sounds like a trap."

"I'll tell you mine." She shrugged like it was somehow a logical and fair trade.

"And what would I do with your middle name?"

"You definitely come off as the kind of person who uses full names to scold their friends like a mom."

"Oh, we're friends now?" I grinned at her.

"Aren't we?" There was a soft, almost pleading look in her eye, like she might actually be hurt if I said no.

"Yeah, I guess we are." I let out a sigh. "It's Grace."

"Ava Grace. It's pretty."

"Your turn." I looked at her through the corner of my eye. I most definitely did scold my friends like a mom. Or I used to, anyway. When I had friends.

"Rae."

"Parker Rae...?"

"Watson." She rolled her eyes.

"Like Sherlock and Watson."

"This is going to be a running joke, isn't it?"

I nodded as I smiled at her. "Yeah, probably."

It was Parker who glanced behind us first, like I normally did. I followed her gaze, realizing I hadn't done it yet. Because I felt... safe with Parker. For the first time in months, I genuinely wasn't worried about Cam.

"Why do you want to own a bar?" I asked.

"Oh," she let out a big breath, and a cloud of vapor swirled around us. "I mean, I don't really want to own a bar. I want to have something like Brickhouse, just LGBT friendly. I remember when I first came out, we didn't really have a place, you know?

And a lot of people have sort of made their own here and there. We've got the one club. I don't know. I guess, I just want a more chill place. A place anyone in the community can feel comfortable bringing a date. Especially if the club scene isn't their thing. I never really had that."

I nodded slowly.

"What about you?" She asked. "What's your dream?"

"What? With my music?" I sighed. "I don't know. I don't think I want to be a touring artist or anything. That sounds exhausting."

"What, you don't want to go platinum?"

I scoffed. "And be a paparazzi-stalked rockstar? I don't think I have it in me. I'd settle for being able to sell just enough songs to pay rent. I guess that's my dream."

I felt my cheeks grow hot as she eyed me.

"Sounds like a good dream to me."

"Really?"

"Yeah," she nodded. "I mean, you know what you can handle, and you know this is what you want to do. You're just not itching to be the next biggest thing. Mid-grade fame."

I let out a laugh, but I felt the weight of her eyes on me as we rounded a corner.

"What?" I asked finally.

"Nothing." She smiled back, but I knew it was something.

I had lied when we'd stepped outside. It was not warm for February. Or, if it was, the cold was finally settling into my bones, and this walk was starting to make me stiff. A shiver escaped my lips, and I flexed my fingers.

"Here." Parker reached for my hands.

Hers were oddly warm, almost like the cold air hadn't touched them at all. She was radiating heat, actually. I wondered to myself what kind of coat she had and where could I get one? She brought my icy fingers up to her face, and I thought for a second she'd kiss them. Instead, she blew on them. A weird mixture of relief and nerves washed over me.

I met her eyes, which were just a few inches from mine. God, we were so close, and I was suddenly reminded of how beautiful she was. Under different circumstances, I'd be tempted to kiss her.

Oh no, I looked at her lips. *Run.*

"We should get back." I whispered, slipping my fingers out of her grasp, and feeling two different kinds of cold set over me.

I wanted to kiss Parker, but I didn't want to want to. I couldn't.

Parker

Noah and I slipped out of Ava and Willow's apartment not long after Ava and I got back. He didn't notice we'd left, and I had no intention of telling him. Not yet. He was too happy, living in his own little moment of bliss.

He grinned from ear to ear from the time he wormed his way out from under Willow on the couch, miraculously not waking her, until we were all the way home.

"Sisters." He said halfway home. "How'd we manage sisters? I thought...friends at best? We'd both meet someone that the other could get along with eventually. You know... hypothetically—"

"Here we go." I laughed.

"—if we got married, we'd legally be family."

"You're already my family, Noah."

"Okay, but legally would be pretty cool."

"You're not wrong." I sighed.

"What's got you down, bro? I figured you'd love being squished on the couch next to Ava."

"Love? That's a stretch. I like being around Ava more, it's just... I don't know. She doesn't seem so sure about me."

"Have you tried asking again?" Noah asked, eyeing me at a red light. "I mean, I know we both agreed a not no isn't a yes, and I'm not normally one to tell someone to keep asking, but now you're telling me you didn't get *any* vibes on that little walk you guys took?"

"How did you—"

"Come on, you didn't think I was actually asleep, did you? On that tiny couch? You know I need a king sized bed or I'm not even dozing."

I laughed. "You did that on purpose."

He gave me a wry grin as the light turned green.

"Was Willow in on this, too?"

"Oh, heck no. That's why I'm so happy."

I sighed. "Okay. Okay, we had...a moment. But Noah, Ava doesn't seem so sure about me, and maybe that's my cue to just...back off?"

"You're the worst about assuming things. Why don't you just *ask* her? Ask her what she wants. You never once did that with Jayde. Maybe it's time you make a change. And you know what? If she's up to that back-and-forth nonsense, then bail. You deserve better than that. You deserve someone who knows what they want and knows that something is you. I hope you realize that by now."

I let out a sigh and nodded as we pulled into the parking garage of our apartment complex. I couldn't argue with anything he'd said, but I wasn't going to give him a big head about it. He was far too cocky as it was.

It wasn't until I'd gotten upstairs and settled in bed that I could really process... that moment. I'd seen the face a few times over the years enough to know when someone is thinking about kissing you. Ava made the face, and that face on Ava about me? Made me feel all kinds of ways.

Knowing she'd thought about it only made me wonder why she'd chosen to walk away. And I had a feeling it was the same reason she'd turned me down in the first place.

Ava

Parker was waiting for me when I got to the shop. No, she wasn't waiting for me; she was just waiting in line. But she noticed me the moment I walked in the door and her face went from neutral to a wide smile in almost no time.

"Hey, Ava." She said, making room for me inside the small lobby.

"Watson." I nodded back.

She made a face somewhere between a smirk and a frown, and it made me grin.

We were nearly shoulder to shoulder. I'd seen her three times since our little walk, and somehow the awkward tension still hadn't dissipated. It was all I could think about since Friday night. Every time I looked at her face now, all I wanted to do was kiss it.

"How have you been?"

I let out a sigh. "Isn't that what we're supposed to talk about in there?"

Parker grinned, "Yeah, but you never do."

I shook my head, but couldn't help but smile. "I'm fine. How are you?"

She shrugged. "My roommate won't stop talking about this *amazing* girl he met the other day. He's getting annoying, but other than that, it's been great."

I rolled my eyes as the person in front of us finished with their order.

"You should go ahead." Parker said rather quickly.

"What?" I stammered. "No, you were here first."

"I don't even know what I want yet."

I let out a huff, but didn't protest because there were more people coming inside behind us, and I wasn't about to hold up the line. So, I quickly asked for my lactose free peppermint mocha. I'd barely finished answering the barista's questions when Parker spoke up again.

"And I'll have one of the Lucky Leprechauns. She's on my ticket."

"No, I'm—"

Parker passed over a twenty before I could even finish grabbing my card from my wallet. I stood there as she finished giving her name, in disbelief at what had just happened.

"I could have paid for myself." I groaned through my teeth as we made our way to the receiving area.

"I know." She smirked. God, I hated when she did that. I stared a little too long because she said, "What? Do I have something on my face?"

I felt my cheeks burn, and I looked down. "Thank you. For the coffee."

"Any time."

"Why do you keep doing this?"

"Doing what?" She frowned. It was so genuine I thought she actually had no clue what I was talking about. I knew better.

"You know what I mean." I swallowed hard. "Just—flirting and... and—" I let out a breath.

"It's just coffee, Ava. No big deal. I'd do the same for a number of my friends. Besides, if I was really flirting, you'd know. I'm just trying to get to know you."

"Why? I told you I'm not—"

"Not my type, I know. But we're friends, right?" She sighed as they called our names and handed my coffee to me.

I had to fight hard not to jump when her fingers brushed mine. I did not need this right now. I didn't need any of this right now.

"I don't know why you're so convinced of that anyway," She continued as we stepped out of the way. We still had ten minutes until the group was supposed to start. "Just because you're—" She lowered her voice. "Asexual?"

I felt my whole body stiffen. I was going to kill my sister. That was not her business to go around telling whoever she wanted. Especially not someone she knew I liked.

Parker was still looking at me expectantly. Like maybe she wanted me to confirm or deny it. Or maybe she wanted me to explain why I thought being asexual was a reason she wouldn't like me. I didn't get why, if she *knew,* we were even having this conversation. Somehow, I couldn't grasp yet why that wasn't a deal-breaker.

Because for Cam, it was.

So, I turned around and practically ran out of the coffee shop. My eyes were getting blurry as I made my way outside. Screw therapy. Screw this conversation. I was not doing this. I had almost two hours before I had to be at work. There were so many things I could do with my time.

"Ava, wait." Parker called after me. But I didn't wait. I didn't stop. I didn't even breathe another breath of that air.

We were on the sidewalk, and a way down the block before she caught me by the wrist, sending a flutter through my stomach. *Stupid stomach.*

"Please, just leave me alone." I breathed, trying desperately to make myself stop crying. She did not need to see me crying.

"Hey," she breathed, releasing my wrist almost instantly. "I'm sorry. I didn't mean to upset you like that."

"I really can't do this right now, and I have a sister to yell at, so."

"Your sister didn't do anything, Ava. I figured it out."

I scoffed.

"Okay, Noah helped me figure it out." She sighed. "It was that thing you said about the 'A not standing for Ally?'"

I let out a nervous breath, wiping my cheek. "Of course, it was."

"I don't really get why that matters, though."

I looked up at her. Her eyes were so full of concern.

She really didn't get it.

"Ava?" she whispered. "I really am sorry. I—"

"Forget it." I shook my head, walking around her toward home.

She kept up with me. "Ava, you're one hundred percent my type. Everything about you is my type. So, whatever wall you've built up about this, it's not a problem for me. If you tell me right now with complete honesty that you have no interest in me what so ever, I'll walk away. You'll never have to hear from me again. Not until Noah and Willow's eventual wedding."

I choked back a laugh and stopped walking. "You really don't get it."

My eyes were getting misty again, so I looked down at the ground.

"What don't I get?"

"I can't give you what you want." I looked up at her, and her whole face softened.

"Not everything is about sex, Ava." She gave me a soft smile. "Maybe, just maybe, I like you. And I don't care that you're asexual. I like you anyway. And I want to get to know you better. But if you don't see me that way—"

I felt a sigh escape my lips before I could stop it. I was biting my bottom lip.

"Ava," she whispered. I looked up. "You want to go somewhere? Maybe get some food? I'm not feeling therapy today."

I nodded, forcing myself not to think better of it.

Parker

We stepped into a tiny sandwich place just a few blocks from the coffee shop, and a few more from the department store where Ava worked. I figured sandwiches were a safe bet at keeping her from being late. And even safer at keeping this from being a date. If I was going to take Ava on a date, I could do better than this.

"You ever been here before?" I asked.

Ava shook her head, but didn't say anything.

"Anything sound good?" I pointed at the menu.

"Why don't *you* go first?" She smirked.

I guess I deserved that.

So, I ordered and paid for myself, and then Ava did the same. Yeah, definitely not a date. That was probably best, given that I had already pressed my luck with coffee, and getting her into a restaurant with me was a miracle, anyway.

"I just want to say," Ava sighed as we sat down, and she sipped what was left of her coffee. "This is not a date. I'm only here because I'm hungry."

"Okay." I nodded.

"Why are we here?"

"Because we're hungry."

"No," she scoffed, smiling. "Why do you keep... why do you keep talking to me? I—"

"Do you want me to be rude and ignore you?" I grinned as her eyes met mine. "Because I can do that."

She bit the inside of her cheek.

"For your information, you initiate conversation, too."

"I know, but... I feel like it isn't the same."

"Isn't it?"

She looked down. "I don't know... I would have thought you'd have given up by now."

"There's no end goal here, Ava. I mean, yeah, I like you. I'd love to get to know you, but we do work together, kind of. I'd be happy to just be your friend."

"Why?"

"Why not?"

She let out a big sigh and leaned back in her chair.

"If you don't want to be friends, that's fine." I smiled. "I can take no for an answer. I can leave you alone, if that's what you want. We don't have to talk, ever. But you've never said that. You insisted I wasn't your type, which isn't true. You seemingly agreed that *I* might be *your* type, and you had to rush off to work. And then Friday... but not once have you ever looked at me and said 'Parker, I'm just not into you, and I don't want to date you.' Or 'Parker, I don't like you. I don't want to talk to you.' All you've really done is try to give me reasons why *I* might not want *you*."

She took a deep breath and looked down at her food.

"I get the feeling we are kind of stuck seeing each other at this point."

Ava met my eyes again, absentmindedly fiddling with wax paper around our sandwiches, but there was a hint of a smile at the corners of her mouth.

I sucked in a shallow breath. "I'm not intimidated by your sexuality."

"You say that now—"

"And I'll say every day if I have to."

"Why?" she breathed, her bottom lip quivering.

"Because I think you're worth it." I reached over and touched the back of her hand. "And I think it's time someone made you believe you're worth it."

She didn't pull away. She just looked down at my hand touching hers. And then I saw a tear falling down her cheek.

"I'm sorry—"

"No, it's okay." She sniffed, taking back her hand so she could wipe her cheek. "But, um. If we don't eat and go soon, I'll be late."

"Yeah," I nodded. "Okay."

Ava

After we finished our sandwiches, Parker walked me to the department store, mostly in silence. Because I think she'd said everything she wanted to say already, and I had yet to find the words to push her away. Maybe because a part of me didn't want to. A part of me wanted that fairytale, even if I knew I'd never get it.

People don't... stay this good. They change. The hurt is inevitable.

The space between us felt like miles. As we meandered and zigzagged, albeit far less than usual for me, toward the department store, we were mostly silent. I felt far too safe next to her, far too protected from Cam, or anyone else, for that matter.

"Well, I guess I'll see you later." I sighed, not meeting her eyes as I aimed to start up the steps.

"Ava wait" I felt Parker's hand on my wrist. It slid down slowly as I turned until her fingers were brushing my callouses.

I looked down at them, and she started to pull away, but I held on as I stepped back down to her level.

"What you said earlier—at the coffee shop." She sucked in a breath and looked down at our hands for a minute. "I can—I will knock it off. Just see you around and be casual. If that's what you want. But I—I just need to know. For sure, one way or another. Because I can't stop thinking about you, so... I need a no. I need you to tell me no. Tell me to leave you the hell alone, or that I'm not what you're looking for."

My heart was pounding loudly in my ears. Parker wasn't looking at me, her eyes on the street behind me somewhere. She had this look in her eye like she couldn't get the words out if she was looking at my face.

"I can't."

"Why?"

"Because I'm bad at lying."

She bit the inside of her lip. And then she just looked down at me for a few seconds, eying me. There was a new tension between us now. Why did I want to touch her? But more importantly, why couldn't I walk away?

"What do you want, Ava?"

"I wish I knew." I said breathlessly, feeling exactly what I'd felt on Friday when we'd been just a hair closer than this.

Parker let out a shuddery sigh that made my chest ache. Suddenly, the distance was back. She was miles away again. If she needed a concrete decision from me, she wasn't going to get it. Because the internal battle about her was far too strong to just *know*.

When she met my eyes, there was a hint of fear there. I didn't think it was possible to see Parker... scared.

"I think." I bit the inside of my lip. "I think we should be friends."

I squeezed Parker's hand, and she pulled away, leaving my fingers suddenly icy.

"Okay." She nodded, meeting my gaze with an achingly neutral expression I had a feeling she was fighting hard to maintain. "I can do that. Goodnight, Ava. Be careful."

She offered me a faint smile and stuck her hands in her pockets, already backing away.

"Goodnight." I muttered, painfully aware of how small my voice sounded.

She turned around, and I started up the steps with a serious ache in my chest. I only made it up two whole steps before I looked over to where her silhouette was growing smaller, realizing I didn't want her to ask me what I wanted. I'd wanted her to kiss me.

Or maybe I wanted to kiss her.

I shot down the steps before I could give it a second thought. If I second guessed myself, I'd lose the nerve. My willpower would kick in. That nasty voice would talk me out of it, remind me I wasn't good enough for her. That nasty voice that wasn't even mine.

"Parker." I called out just a few feet behind her, and she stopped and turned, eyebrows raised.

Don't think, just do it.

I practically threw myself at her. Our lips crashed together in that unfamiliar way that always came with kissing someone new. A soft noise escaped her throat, and I felt her simultaneously stiffen and relax when her ridiculously warm hands wrapped around my waist. The unfamiliar feeling faded so quickly I almost didn't notice. She pulled me closer to her, and it felt like my entire body was on fire.

The thought occurred to me that Parker knew what she was doing. Maybe not with me, but in general, with women as a whole. It was something about the way she kissed me, an unmistakable confidence, from the moment my lips touched hers.

For me, it was just Cam. And I'd be damned if I was going to give a single person, much less Parker, anything Cam had ever asked of me. So, I was hesitant, unsure, like Parker was the first person I'd ever kissed.

I don't know how long it lasted; a second, a minute, longer. What I do know is when she pulled away, both of us breathless, she still stood close, brushing the stray hairs from my face. And she was looking at me. She was looking at me in that dangerous way that meant I was already too deep in this to back out now.

Parker

"Doesn't this ever creep you out?" I asked Ava while I sat on the corner of an empty clothing display in the back room of the store.

She was carefully dressing a fifth mannequin according to a specific list she was following. The whole job seemed fairly odd to me, but I guess having someone dress the mannequins when the store was closed looked better than while customers were inside. All the ones she was dressing, though, weren't out where anyone could see them.

"Should it?" She smirked, looking at me over her shoulder.

"I don't know. Empty store, all by yourself?"

"I kind of like it. The doors are locked with a keypad and a silent alarm. I have a lot of time to think, and the acoustics in here are fantastic."

"Oh, yeah?" I smiled.

"Please don't ask me to sing something." She laughed, grabbing the paper and scanning it. "I'll be right back."

I nodded, eyeing her as she walked away.

I know I was supposed to feel confident and cool. I'd gotten what I wanted, right? But I was losing my mind. How does a person go from saying we should be friends to kissing me like I held all the air she needed to survive? And how was I supposed to walk away now, when I officially knew what kissing her felt like?

This wasn't supposed to happen. I wasn't supposed to be in this deep. I barely knew her. And somehow... somehow, she was already the center of ninety percent of my thoughts.

If she was so against me and her being... well, I didn't know what we'd ever be, but why...? Why what? Why did she kiss me? Why had she said we should just be friends and then chased me down the street? Why was she so convinced we weren't compatible in the first place?

"I'm almost done, I swear." She sighed as she walked back up.

I wondered why the store changed the mannequins so often when Ava spoke again.

"I think once they finish getting their spring line up out, I'll probably be out of a job." She sighed. "I haven't been given anything other than this one list of seasonal displays, and I'm almost completely done."

"What will you do then?"

She shrugged. "I was hired as kind of an everything person? It was general product display in the job ad, so I might be rearranging the tie display next. Who knows?"

She fumbled with the shirt a bit longer before putting the mannequin back together. Then she let out a sigh and stepped back.

"What do you think?" She flashed me a sarcastic grin, like she was holding back a laugh.

I looked up at the short-sleeved plaid shirt, the khaki cargo shorts, and squinted, realizing after only a moment this was a female presenting mannequin.

"Oh, you think you're funny?"

Ava laughed, grabbed her things and headed for the door, with me trailing after. Our laughs and footsteps were echoing through the store. I caught up to her as she reached the back door, grabbed her around the middle and spun her around.

It made her laugh even louder. I wished I could have bottled that sound.

I set her down, and she continued to giggle, but she was out of breath.

She eyed me for a moment before she turned and clocked out at the computer near the exit. As reached for the door, she entered a code, and we stepped out into the cold air.

"Can I walk you home?" The words hung in the air between us, but after all the checking over her shoulder she did, I felt better making sure she was safe.

She bit her lip and nodded, and then we were off.

"Why me?" Ava asked after a moment of walking in silence.

"What do you mean?" I asked, eyeing the way she was fiddling with her coat zipper.

"I mean... out of all the pretty girls you could have asked out, why did you decide to ask me?"

"Because I felt like the universe put us on the same path."

"There you go with the universe again."

I grinned.

"I'm serious." She sighed. "Between the group and the clubs around here, you could have asked anyone. Why me, why... therapy of all places?"

"I don't go to clubs anymore." I swallowed hard, avoiding her curious gaze. "I don't know. Therapy made me feel like we had something in common. I don't feel like I fit in that group, and it seemed like you felt the same way." I shrugged if for no other reason but to give me a moment to think. "But the way you listened to everyone and tried to give them advice made it pretty clear you care."

"Why don't you feel like you fit in?" She asked.

"Everyone's just so... confident about who they are with their pronouns and stuff. All this is kind of... new to me, I guess? I never really had a chance to connect with the community."

"But you're sure you're a lesbian."

It wasn't a question. It was more of a clarification that I didn't even know I needed.

"I mean." I swallowed. "I think so?"

"You think so?" She grinned, looking up at me.

I could feel this odd sense of pressure building up because I knew she was waiting on an answer, but the truth was that as much as I liked women, I didn't know. Not after the rabbit hole I'd taken looking into asexuality just to understand her better. That was never something you wanted to hear. Did you ever really *know,* though? Or were we all just living a lifelong experiment to figure out who we were?

"It's fine." She said after a moment of my hesitation. "Sexuality is a funny thing."

"Yeah," I let out a sigh.

And then we were quiet, the silence setting in, but still feeling loud.

When we reached her house, she did the thing. The, fiddle with the keys, unsure what to say or do, thing. The, I might want to kiss you, but I won't say that, thing.

I reached my hand for hers. She eyed it for a second, hanging in the air, before smirking at me. She slowly put her hand in mine, and I pulled her to me, wrapping my arm around her waist. She sucked in a quick breath, meeting my eyes for a second before she looked down.

She didn't move, though. Her eyes met mine again, and I reached a hand up to her face before I leaned in.

It wasn't ridiculously long. I pulled away, putting my forehead to hers.

"Goodnight, Ava." I whispered, letting go of her waist.

"Goodnight, Parker." She smiled, but there was a bit of sadness there.

I wanted to ask about it, but I didn't. I just let her walk inside and up the stairs.

Let me know when you get home safe.

I smiled as I read the message before I'd even reached the end of her block.

Ava

The house was quiet, and Willow was asleep when I walked into the apartment, which was a relief. I didn't want to talk about kissing Parker. At least, not yet.

I slipped off my jacket, realizing it smelled like her. Some tie between the cologne she wore and bourbon, maybe a little bit of spiced rum, too, I couldn't be sure. Something about it, though, was very... Parker. She often smelled like a bar, but not in a bad way.

Why was I smiling like that?

Milo wove between my feet, pulling me from the weird trance I was in, standing at the door, smelling my jacket. I slipped it on the hook and made for the kitchen, feeding Milo, handing him a couple peas, and heading toward my room.

I heard a familiar sound. I froze, fork halfway to my mouth. Willow's light turned on.

So close.

"You're late." She signed when I peeked into her room.

"Busy night." I signed back after setting my plate on the foot of her bed, shrugging.

Was I still smiling?

"How was therapy?"

I didn't go. "It was good."

"How's Parker?" Willow raised an eyebrow at me.

Oh shit, I was blushing. I looked down at my plate.

"What happened?" She signed the words so fast I almost missed them, but she was grinning. "Parker told Noah you both skipped therapy."

I felt the color drain from my face.

"Why would you lie?" Willow added.

I let out a sigh. "I didn't want to talk about it yet."

She raised her eyebrow again.

"Okay, okay... I kissed Parker."

She gasped, I grimaced. I wasn't ready for this conversation yet. I wasn't ready to go through the steps of figuring out what it all means. Because that meant it was *something*. And I liked the grey space, where it wasn't anything.

The grey space was safe.

"So?" Willow asked, giving me an incredulous frown.

"So, nothing." I shrugged, biting my lip to keep from smiling.

"Do you like her or not?"

I nodded, looking down at my feet. And then I felt my eyes well up because I didn't want to like her. A part of me wanted to. A big part of me wanted to jump into everything head first. But that's what gets you hurt, so the more rational part of my brain just wanted to run away.

Willow got up and wrapped me in a tight hug. I let myself cry on her shoulder for a minute. I didn't know why I was crying, really. Over Cam, maybe. Over the way she made me feel like I didn't deserve someone like Parker. The way she'd convinced me someone like Parker would never want me.

Willow didn't say anything. She just let me cry. Because she already knew. The short, less gruesome version, but that was bad enough.

I'd been afraid of this exact thing for a long time. Ever since Cam. It's why I self-isolated, why I became detached and reclusive. Being lonely was safe. Being lonely at least meant I couldn't be hurt again.

I pulled away, and she kissed my forehead like I used to do to her when she was little, and still did on occasion. It made me laugh.

"It's okay to like her." Willow said again, like she had that day in the bar. "It's okay to love someone again."

"Whoa slow down speed racer." I laughed. "I said I kissed Parker. I didn't say anything about love."

"Yeah, but I know that's what you're afraid of."

I sucked in a breath, nodding.

"Maybe she won't hurt you and leave." Willow smiled. God, she looked so much like our mom. "Maybe she'll love you no matter what."

"And maybe she won't. Maybe she can't."

"Maybe you're letting fear keep you from a good thing. You're letting Cam control your life, and she's not even here."

I winced when I saw her sign for Cam's name, but she was right. A single tear fell down my cheek, and she reached up to wipe it away. I was the big sister. I was supposed to take care of her. Give her a good example. And here she was, taking care of me instead. When did she become such a grown-up?

"Just see what happens." She smiled, yawning. "And if it doesn't work out, I'll always be here to pick up the pieces."

I scoffed at that. "Alright, enough mushy, go to bed."

"I love you."

"I love you, too."

I grabbed my plate as she turned off her lamp. My phone buzzed when I reached my door.

Safe and sound.

I sighed, flopping on my bed as Milo came trotting in. I let him have a bite of chicken this time, too.

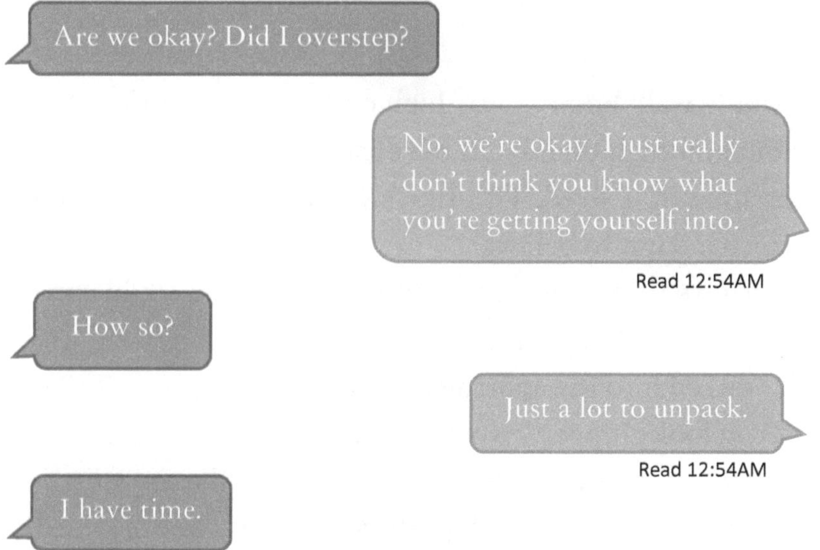

I didn't know how to respond to that, so I just stared at the message while I ate my chicken.

Goodnight, Ava. Sweet dreams.

Parker

The whole walk home, I was high on life. I was confused as hell, too, but still high on life. I'd never stop believing in the universe for as long as I lived. I'd always be a believer. Nothing could convince me not to believe.

Because there was no way someone like Ava could come into my life by mere happenstance.

I walked into the apartment, beaming.

"You look chipper." Noah laughed.

Why was he awake? It was nearly one in the morning.

"I kissed Ava." I sighed, putting my arms over my head.

He tossed the magazine he'd been flipping through over his shoulder rather dramatically. He'd been waiting for me.

"Twice."

"Okay, okay. Tell me everything."

"Well, I already told you we skipped therapy." I breathed. "And then we went to the sandwich place on 6th, and we talked. She told me I wasn't her type again. And then I walked her to work, and we talked some more... and she said we should be friends, and I was headed home—"

"Wait what?"

"And then she chased after me, so I guess technically the first time she kissed me."

Noah frowned at me. "Go back to the part where she said you should be friends and then changed her mind in mere minutes?"

I took a deep breath and fell backwards over the back of the couch, so my legs hung off the top, causing Samuel to stir from where he was napping on the arm. "Noah, you ever just...felt the spark?"

He nodded.

"It was the spark."

"Which is great and all, but you know the spark doesn't last forever. You have to build on chemistry for it to mean anything."

I nodded, letting out a sigh. "Shit, I told her I'd let her know when I got home."

"Oh, checking on you, is she?" He smirked at me.

"Well, it is late, you know."

"Right, that's it."

He continued to eye me, hanging upside down on the couch while I texted Ava. We made eye contact, and he was giving me his dad look.

"What?" I asked.

"Did you actually ask her?" Noah asked, finally. "Did she say 'Yes, Parker, I want you.' Or did you just skip that part and kiss her?"

"We're figuring it out."

He let out a long sigh and squeezed the bridge of his nose. "Do you listen to me... ever, you love-struck buffoon?"

"We officially met in therapy." I said, sitting up correctly and nearly kicking him. "There's... baggage to unpack."

"That doesn't answer the question. Does Ava *want* you, or is she just confused?"

I wasn't sure I wanted to answer that question. Whether or not Ava knew just what she wanted, didn't make her just like

Jayde, and I knew that's where Noah was going. I wasn't ready to ruin this night with critical thinking.

"That's what I thought." Noah said when I didn't respond.

"It's fine, Noah." I insisted. "I think she's just—just scared. She's been through something, maybe even worse than what Jayde put me through."

"You can't fix people. Stop trying to fix people."

"I'm not!"

"I've got my eye on her, that's all I'm saying."

Ava

I was dreaming about Parker again.

I should have known the kiss was a bad idea. No, I did know, and Willow couldn't convince me otherwise. I shouldn't have skipped therapy. I should have muscled up, and gone in, and came out of the damn closet to someone other than my mom and sister, and I should have acted like an adult and admitted I needed those one-on-one sessions Carmen had offered at a discount rate three times already.

She knew I needed it. Maybe she had super therapist Spidey senses, but somehow, she knew. And she wasn't wrong.

I wasn't ready for Parker. I wasn't ready to be dreaming about Parker and kissing Parker. And there was no way Parker was ready for all of this... So, I didn't respond to her message when I woke up. She hadn't overstepped. She hadn't done anything wrong, but this... wasn't right, and I knew it.

I just needed to pick up the nerve to end things, whatever things were. I wasn't ready for that yet either.

Tuesday was my me day. Normally, Willow had class. I was off work. So, I spent every Tuesday sleeping in, working on covers, doing the most minor of house work which normally consisted of picking up empty plates from my bedroom, doing some bathroom tidying, and tossing an unsorted load of laundry into the washer.

Typically, Willow stopped by in the afternoon to say hi before she headed off to see a friend or whatever it was she did. That day, she and Noah had a big date.

Willow was already gone when I woke up, pancakes left in the microwave and a note that said she'd be gone for the rest of the day. *Text me if you need me. Don't wait up.*

The audacity.

"Stop moming me, Willow, that's my job." I mumbled to myself as set the note to the side and lathered a breakfast I didn't cook in syrup.

So, I had the whole house to myself from early in the morning until later that night, and I couldn't focus. I couldn't focus on my music. I couldn't focus on writing music. I briefly considered watching tv, but I knew it would just be background noise.

I was normally pretty good about not messing with my phone. It hurt my flow, but I had no flow. My brain kept wandering to the unanswered message from Parker.

Just before lunch, my mom called.

"Hey, Mom." I sighed, setting my guitar aside.

I wasn't really playing it anyway, and my mom could go on for hours.

"Hey, Sweetie." She was always so cheerful. Sometimes I wondered if she used her customer service voice on me. "How are you? You never call me anymore. I just get updates from Willow."

"I've just been busy lately." I sighed, flopping back on my bed.

I didn't want to tell her I never called anyone.

It was true, though. I was busy. Busy paying rent. Busy paying off debt, some of which I had acquired with the help of a certain ex who refused to repay a dime of it. I knew my mom cared, and she loved me and Willow, but she wasn't here. She decided to move across the country. And some of us couldn't afford to go with her. I'd tried hard not to be resentful.

Maybe couldn't afford it was the wrong way of putting it. I probably could have saved a ton living with my mom forever, but I had a feeling her offer to take us along was only halfhearted to begin with. She liked the idea, but maybe liked the idea of finally living out some of her own dreams, too.

Besides, I liked the city. The small town my mom moved to didn't exactly sound appealing to me or to Willow. And while a cross-country move might have been a great change after Cam and I split, leaving my dad behind to work himself into oblivion wasn't an option for me.

"Willow told me you started a new singing job! And you've met someone?"

I felt my cheeks burn as I thought of the text from Parker that had gone unread and unanswered for nearly three hours. *Willpower. I had so much willpower.*

"Willow is exaggerating." I let out a laugh. "I have a new... friend."

"Whatever you're calling it these days. Have you—"

"What's up with you, Mom? How's the new job?"

"Oh, it's good. Keeping me busy, paying the bills. Mae finished in the house finally. We can start moving in soon."

Mae. My mom's girlfriend. Nothing has ever been as weird or cool as my mom coming out at the same time I did. I remember being so hesitant about it. I planned out exactly what I'd say, when, where. I rehearsed for days. I was terrified.

And this woman had the audacity to look at me, laugh, and say "Me, too."

"That's exciting." I sighed. "What color did you go with?"

"Red, you know me."

I laughed. "Mae let you paint the whole house red?"

"She'd probably let me paint the grass if she thought it would make me happy. You deserve that, too. Willow tells me you're still having trouble. Are you still seeing that therapist? The one your dad found?"

"No, I told you. I couldn't afford it after I got kicked off his insurance."

"Ah, that's why Willow's so big on you going to this group therapy thing. Is this woman licensed?"

"Yes, Mom." I groaned. "But I don't know if... I don't know if I'm going to keep going. I don't feel like it's helping."

"Well, you need something, Babygirl. You can't keep going on like this. You took care of Cam—"

I winced at the sound of her name.

"You took care of me when I was still in town. And you're taking care of Willow. When does Ava take care of Ava?"

Great, now I was crying. She must have heard me sniffle, because she sighed.

"Oh, sweetie. I wish I was there. You can get through this. I know you can. What's the harm in giving this new girl a try? After everything Cam put you through..."

There it was again.

"You deserve a little bit of something good."

"What if it doesn't work out?" I sighed, wiping my cheeks.

"But baby, what if it does?"

"I just let..." I paused, still unable to say Cam's name out loud. "Her in so easily. And it got me hurt."

"That doesn't mean you never let anyone in ever again. What if she doesn't hurt you?"

"There's too many what ifs."

"I know." She sighed. "You remember how I was after James?"

"Yeah, I remember."

I probably remembered better than she did.

My mom married James when I was six. Barely a year later, along came Willow. He was as good as far as step dads go. A little awkward in the beginning, I remember that, but once we had willow, and we were all learning sign language, it felt like we really came together as a family.

James had passed away when I was thirteen. It sent my mom into a depression spell like I'd never known. She'd say in bed for days on end, for a while she didn't have a job, and if I remember correctly, it drained all her savings.

Willow didn't understand, not really. I think for a while she was waiting for him to come home, and he just didn't. And I didn't know how to explain it to her either.

My dad was over a lot more. Willow started coming with me when I went to his house. And it wasn't long before she was teaching him sign language. He started treating her like she was his, too. He'd buy her Christmas and birthday gifts. He took her along when we went on fun outings to the fair or the zoo. I think that's the only thing that got Willow through it.

Mom, though, wasn't okay until much later. She held onto that grief for years. I think I got it from her. Love deeply, so deeply you lose yourself.

"Don't let one bad love ruin love for you entirely." My mom said after a moment.

I got her to change the subject, move on to something safer. We talked for a few more minutes about Mae and their dogs. I told her more about the singing gig and the smallest details about Parker I could muster. And then I hung up.

The red text notification was mocking me. I let out a sigh.

The silence in the apartment setting in, along with the words my mom had said, echoing in my ear. *What if it does?*

Hey yourself.

Are you working today?

Parker

When I finally got up and around, I made my way to the gym. I didn't see Ava. I never saw her on Tuesdays, though, so I wasn't surprised. I'd never questioned it much before, but now I was curious. Not that she had to tell me, but I could ask what she was up to every Tuesday, right?

I sent it as I was leaving the gym. It was unread when I reached the coffee shop. And still unread when I got home and handed Noah his coffee. But I didn't send anything else. I wasn't about to press my luck any more than I already had. If she wanted to talk to me, she would, and if she didn't, well then, I'd just have to get over it and try to be a friend.

I knew that would be hard because all I'd thought about was her all morning. Sometimes you meet someone, and maybe it's just a vibe, maybe it's just a hunch, a feeling, but you know this could be your person. Maybe Ava wasn't my person, but she was supposed to be in my life, and I'd just have to make that work. Especially if things between Noah and Willow kept going the way they were.

The two of them were basically in constant contact now. Which mostly took the form of texting, as Noah was still struggling with sign language. He'd gotten serious learning it though, mostly through videos online and Willow's patient corrections, which were probably helping more than the videos.

Either way, he was planning some big first date with this paycheck. More power to him. From what he'd told me, she was pretty great, even if they would have a minor communication issue for a while. Texting seemed to work just fine.

Noah and I spent most of the day on the couch watching Halloween movies while he waited for Willow to get out of class, and I cuddled with Samuel. Apparently, the big date was going to last all afternoon and evening.

Just before lunch, I got a ping.

Hey, yourself.

I grinned. I knew it was a stupid grin from the look Noah gave me—a cross between a smirk and a frown.

"Don't even," I said, tossing a couch pillow his way. "You've had a cheesy smile on your face for three days."

She sent another message before I could respond.

Are you working today?

I am not.

Read 1:23PM

Want to come over?

I could feel Noah eyeing me from the other side of the couch, so I slid Samuel onto the middle cushion, and headed to my room. I could still feel him eyeing me until I was all the way down the hall with my door shut.

"Don't forget to ask the hard questions!" He called after me.

Is this a trick question?

Read 1:24PM

I wasn't sure if she was serious, but I was already changing out of my post-workout pajama pants and into real clothes.

I'll be there in fifteen.

Read 1:25PM

I came back out of my room less than a minute later dressed except for my shoes, which we kept by the door. Noah looked up and squinted at me, and I looked down at my ripped jeans and sweater.

"Where are you headed, looking so snazzy?" Noah smirked at me, already getting ready to change the channel. "And why do you have your tool bag?"

"Ava asked me to come over." I shrugged. "I said I'd fix the handle on her front door. I figured if I'm headed over there anyway, I can do that, too."

Yes, so casual. We were casual.

"You sure that's a good idea? Hanging out, not fixing the door."

He didn't look at me when he said it. I knew that meant he wasn't making conversation; he was trying to make me think.

"Why wouldn't it be?" I asked as I sat down on the bench next to the door and started lacing up my boots.

I let out a sigh. "Did Willow say something?"

"No, no." I heard him suck in a deep breath. I was pretty sure Willow had said something. "I just think... you know what? Never mind."

"No, what is it?"

"Nothing."

"Noah."

"I just think she's a little... hesitant." He sighed. "That's all. You haven't asked the hard questions, so you don't have the big answers. Don't you want someone who... *wants* you? Don't you want to *know* she wants you?"

He turned around to look at me with his last statement.

"Is this because she's asexual or because she has a past?" I asked as I started lacing up my other boot. "Because I don't think she can control either, and I have a past, too, Noah."

"Neither! That's not what I—I just—" He sighed again, rubbing his hand over his face. "It just doesn't seem like she's as into you as you are into her. I don't want you to get hurt again, okay? You fall fast and hard, and you're not always the best at letting other people catch up. You just started seeming like yourself again. I just don't want you to lose yourself in someone who isn't ready for you."

"Well, thank you for the concern." I nodded, grabbing my jacket from the coat rack. "Have fun on your date."

"I love you, Parker!" He called as I slipped out the door.

I flashed the "I love you" sign back at him and headed toward Ava's apartment.

Ava

It was closer to thirty minutes after her text when I heard a soft tap on my door. When was Parker not late?

I smiled when I opened the door, feeling it turn to a frown when I found her holding coffee, a paper sack, and a tool bag. It was the first time I'd seen her in anything other than a button down and dress pants or workout clothes, too. Seeing her in jeans was weird.

"Refreshments?" She smirked as she stepped inside.

"You're so cheesy." I laughed as I shut the door. "What's the tool bag for?"

"I told you I'd fix the handle? I figured since I was already here...unless you want me to make a special trip–"

"No, that's okay. I didn't... I didn't think you'd actually–"

"If I say I'll do something, I mean it." She offered me a smile, reaching out one arm.

I took the coffee she had outstretched to me, letting that sink in. "You can hang up your coat if you want. I'd take off your shoes, too, if you don't want Willow hunting you down."

"God, her and Noah are perfect for each other."

"He have a thing against shoes in the house, too?"

"You have no idea." Parker rolled her eyes as she set down her coffee and the bag while she unlaced her boots. "Neat freak that guy."

I smiled. "Yeah, I guess they are perfect for each other. You should know I absolutely do not clean this place. I mean, as clean the stained carpets get. I try... to keep *my* room clean, but that's about it."

"And you should know I'm absolutely okay with that."

I took a sip of the coffee, smiling because how did she remember I liked peppermint? The smile faded as a lump formed in my throat. I thought of all the things Cam had learned about me immediately, too. My favorite foods, my favorite drinks, my favorite movies, so she could use them against me.

Parker's not Cam. Parker's not Cam. Parker's not Cam.

"So, I was thinking." Parker said, standing up and grabbing her coffee. "I'll fix this door, if you want to go heat this up? It's better warm."

She reached the bag out to me, and I eyed it. "What is it?"

"Cinnamon roll." She smiled widely, pulling a couple of tools out of her bag.

"You know, I don't really have any screws or—"

"I got it."

She gave a small box a shake, rattling the screws inside.

"Right." I nodded, turning toward my kitchen as the sound of her small drill filled my apartment.

What was I thinking?

I shouldn't have told Parker she could fix the knob in the first place. Now I felt like I owed her something. I did. Didn't I?

The microwave beeped, and I ignored it, thinking for too long of all the favors I'd had to return to Cam.

"So, did you have a master plan?" Parker said from the doorway of the kitchen, causing me to jump. "Sorry, you okay?"

Oh shit, I was crying.

I gave her a nod as I turned back toward the microwave, giving my cheek a good wipe. As I grabbed the little plate I'd set the cinnamon rolls on, I felt Parker's warm presence... in my space. I looked up at her, her face all twisted with concern.

She took the plate from me and set it on the counter, and then she eyed me, closer than anyone had really looked at me in a while.

"You really... didn't have to—"

"Are you really crying because I fixed your loose doorknob?" There was a hint of a smile on her face. "That took me two minutes, and I already had the screws lying around. It's no big deal."

I let out a breath. "I don't like feeling... like I owe people..."

"Ava this isn't the stock exchange. I fixed your doorknob because I want you to be safe, and to feel safe. You don't owe me a thing. Except for one of those cinnamon rolls, I definitely bought one of those for me."

I smiled despite myself, a little laugh slipping out, as she took the plate to our two-seater cafe table. I followed her out of the kitchen hesitantly, coffee and two forks in hand. The silence in the house made me hyperaware of just how bad of an idea this had been–me and her, alone in my apartment, after she'd just done something nice for me.

"Thank you." She said, taking one of the forks as I sat down.

We almost never used this table. I felt like Willow had wanted it more to fill the space than anything else. I'd always expected her to use it for her homework, but I had a feeling there just wasn't enough space for all her books.

"So," Parker said, her mouth halfway full. "What's your master plan?"

I raised an eyebrow, eyeing her for a second as I took a bite of the cinnamon roll, which was, admittedly, extremely good.

"I just... because you invited me over? What... do you want to do?"

I grinned as she glanced around the silent house, almost like the realization that we were completely alone had just set in. And she was clearly confused because we both knew what we wouldn't do.

"Do you ever get skin hungry?" I asked before I could talk myself out of it. I took another bite, if only to keep myself cool and collected.

She looked at me like I'd opened a third eye. "Do I ever get what now?"

I let out a laugh. "Skin hungry... it's where you just like... really need to hug, or to touch... someone?"

A smile was tugging at the corners of her mouth. "Did you invite me over here to cuddle?"

"Maybe." I could feel my cheeks growing hot. "We could watch a movie or something, if you don't—"

"Okay," she smiled.

"Okay." I breathed.

We sat there awkwardly for a minute before Parker went back to her cinnamon roll. I could barely keep up; she ate so fast.

"Are you in a rush?" I laughed.

She grinned. "When I was in school, we had twenty minutes from the time the lunch bell rang until we had to go back to class, and I've never recovered from the speed eating."

"That sounds exceptionally unhealthy."

She nodded, "Oh, yeah, I'm aware." She took another bite, slowly. "Thank you for pointing it out, though."

I couldn't tell if that was sarcasm or if she was seriously thanking me, so I went back to my plate.

We sat mostly in silence, the tic of the clock making me even more nervous as Parker eyed me in that dangerous way over her coffee. And when the little plate was empty, she just looked at me, leaning back in her chair with a confident grin.

I let out a sigh, grabbing the plate and taking it to the kitchen, and when I turned around, she was standing in the doorway, coffee in hand.

"Shall we?" she asked, reaching her hand out to mine.

I eyed it, and my stomach tied in knots. Maybe this wasn't such a good idea.

I reached out and took her hand anyway, biting my lip hard as I took her to my room. No way was I going to let Willow forget something, walk in, and find me curled up on the couch with Parker.

Parker

Ava slipped a movie into her DVD player. I leaned against the door frame, sipping what was left of my coffee as I eyed the contents of her small room. Her queen-sized bed was pushed against the far corner and took up the majority of the room, leaving about four feet of space to walk through. Her headboard was old and rustic, with wear and tear people were going for on purpose these days, but I had a feeling she'd had the set forever. She had a single nightstand and a dresser that seemed to match the headboard, albeit with less wear and tear. And every flat surface in the room was covered with a vast array of things from, chap stick to notebooks to receipts and loose change.

She looked up from the tv stand and stood at the foot of her bed, also scanning the room, eyeing everything like she was seeing it for the first time. I watched as her cheeks flushed, and she pretty much looked at anything but me. I'd never felt awkward tension like that before. We'd never even hugged, just went straight to the kissing thing. How was this supposed to work?

When she finally met my eyes, she shrugged, rubbing her palms against her sweats, and I let out a laugh.

I sat my coffee on her nightstand and held my hand out to her. "Come here."

She smiled sheepishly and took my hand.

I pulled her closer to me, wrapping my arms around her shoulders. She was hesitant as her hands went around my waist, but the moment she was tucked fully in my arms, I felt her relax. She let out a ridiculously deep sigh, her cheek resting against my chest, and all the awkward tension was gone, just like that.

"Better?" I asked as I leaned my cheek against her hair.

"Mhmm." she mumbled, nodding softly against my shoulder.

I tried hard not to get too caught up, but Ava fit perfectly under my chin like a little puzzle piece. This was one of those times when I knew I was in the right place at the right time. The universe most definitely wanted me to be here. Because holding Ava just felt *right*.

The hug was supposed to make her feel better, but I was relaxing, too. I couldn't remember the last time I'd just *hugged* someone. Sure, I gave half-hearted hugs to my friends, even exes I was amicable with. But this? When was the last time I'd just held someone like that? I didn't want to let go.

Ava lifted her head after a minute and looked up at me.

"What?" I asked.

She let go of my waist and reached for my jaw instead, and then her lips met mine in a rush. I sucked in a breath of air as my hands instinctively went to her waist. My stomach was in a whirl, realizing Ava had an almost magical spell on me. And then, as quickly as it began, Ava pulled away, looking up at me for a moment, before she was out of my arms.

"We're missing the movie." She whispered, taking a seat on her bed.

I ran my fingers through my hair. I'd forgotten there even was a movie.

Ava eyed me out of the corner of her eye as I slowly took a seat next to her. I knew there was an undefined line that I most definitely didn't want to cross, but I was too nervous to ask outright. She grabbed my wrist, and I thought for a minute she was going to hold my hand. Instead, she threw my forearm over her shoulder and curled up against my chest.

I laughed, resting against her headboard. "Comfy?"

She nodded wordlessly, wrapping her arm around my stomach. I turned my attention to the screen for the first time. I knew this movie. God, I'd watched it a hundred times at least. My dad had a thing for 80's movies.

"What was that line?" I whispered along. "'You have no power over me.'"

Ava looked up at me, frowning.

"What?" I asked, grinning. "Sorry, should I not—I'll be quiet."

I looked back at the tv, but I could still feel her eyeing me.

"What?" I asked again.

She leaned in and kissed me again, timid, soft, and somehow growing familiar. Kissing Ava shouldn't feel that familiar.

"What was that for?" I grinned when she pulled away.

She shrugged, letting her head rest against my chest again.

"Is this your favorite movie?" I asked after a few minutes of silence.

She nodded.

And then, after a few seconds, she looked up at me with a playful glare. "What's your favorite movie?"

I took a deep breath, thinking. "I don't know. I like Halloween movies, I guess."

"You mean horror movies?"

"I mean, yeah, but I like the happy ones, too." I felt myself blushing.

"A genre isn't a favorite movie." She grumbled.

"I don't know." I sighed. "I've never had to pick before."

She scoffed, letting her head fall back to my chest.

"What? I could tell you my top five, but picking just one?"

"Okay," she laughed. "If we were in the zombie apocalypse, and you could only watch one movie for the rest of your life, what movie would it be?"

I tried not to hang on to her use of the word "we," but I sucked in a deep breath, and sighed, shaking my head.

"What is it?"

"No, you're going to judge me." I laughed, trying to focus on the tv.

"Oh my gosh, just tell me."

I eyed her out of the corner of my eye and shook my head.

"Parker..." she sang. "I'll find where you're ticklish."

"Oh, no you won't." I raised my eyebrows as I tried to get up, but she grabbed my waist before I could, and was wiggling her fingers along my sides.

First try?

I nearly fell off her bed. The only means of saving myself was grabbing onto the sheet and sliding further over, further under her. The next thing I knew, she was completely on top of me, arms crossed over my collarbone, her chin resting on them only inches from mine while she looked up at me expectantly.

"Now that I have you right where I want you." She nodded triumphantly and glared again.

I let out a laugh.

"What is your favorite movie?"

"Nope." I smirked, and she tried tickling me again, but I caught her wrist and slid my fingers between hers.

She eyed our hands for a moment, and I contemplated letting go. But she didn't pull away. She just let out a sigh and looked back at me.

"I promise not to judge you."

I raised an eyebrow.

"Come on, Parker."

"The Fast and Furious," I sighed, finally. "Hands down."

"Why?" she asked, what looked like idle curiosity on her face.

I could feel one of her feet brushing against mine. I couldn't tell if she was trying to tickle me or not, but it was working.

"Ummm." I bit the inside of my lip, feeling my pulse rise in speed, but I couldn't tell if it was the topic at hand or just Ava on top of me. "It was one my dad watched a lot, I guess. It reminds me of him."

She nodded slowly, maybe sensing my tension. She didn't ask anything else. Instead, she rolled to the side, curling up against my chest where she could see the movie again. She didn't let go of my hand, though, leaving our fingers entwined across my stomach.

After a few minutes, she was asleep.

Ava

I had to give Parker credit. Coming over to my house and letting me nap on her shoulder was probably one of the best things someone had done for me... ever. Did I snore? I don't know. Did I drool? Well, her sweater wasn't soaked, so I'd hope not. How long was her arm numb? No clue. She didn't tell me. She didn't even seem annoyed that I'd fallen asleep.

She didn't act like I'd wasted her time or like she regretted coming over, which I half expected the moment I told her I just wanted her to cuddle with me. Instead, she seemed... happy about it, and almost sad to be leaving. There wasn't an ounce of pep to her step as she walked toward the door.

Despite knowing I shouldn't keep giving in to whatever was drawing me to her, I let her kiss me before she left, long and slow. It took my breath away. I knew that wasn't good. I knew that meant I was growing some sort of attachment to her, and I definitely didn't need that.

"I'll see you tomorrow?" She asked, her hand on the no longer loose doorknob.

I nodded, and she opened the door just as Willow was walking in.

Willow gave me a look, and then looked to Parker, who turned a rather obvious shade of red before darting out our front door and heading toward the stairs.

Willow waited until the door was shut before she signed a thing.

“What have you been up to?” She gave me another pointed look.

“We watched a movie.” I shrugged.

“And?”

“And nothing.” I turned, headed for the kitchen.

She followed.

“Are you—”

“We aren’t anything.” I signed quickly. “I’m hanging out with Parker. That’s it. How was your date with Noah?”

She blushed bright red. “It was really nice. We went to a sushi place, and our sushi came out on fire! He bought me flowers and opened the door for me.”

“Yeah? Did he kiss you goodnight?”

“Did Parker?”

And then it was my turn to blush, so I turned and grabbed some lactose free ice cream from the freezer.

“That’s what I thought.” She signed when I turned back around, taking the ice cream out of my hand and heading for her room.

Rude.

“You were gone for a long time just for sushi.” I signed, bringing the spoon she forgot to grab into her room.

“Parker was here a long time for one movie.” She smarted back.

I sat down on her bed next to her, and we spent the rest of the evening chatting about her perfect date while she fished for more info on Parker that I refused to give.

It was weird going to sleep that night by myself. I hated that feeling. The feeling that I needed Parker for something—that I needed anyone for something. But as I lay there, staring up at my ceiling, all I could think about was her. It had been a long time since I'd slept as well as I had curled up in her arms.

I was trying. I was trying to listen to Willow, trying to listen to my mom, trying to listen to the tiny voice of hope in my head that wanted nothing more than to be around Parker all the time where I felt safe and wanted. Maybe I could work around my own issues.

Parker and I didn't have to talk about what this meant. She didn't have to ask me to be her girlfriend. We could just... be. And that could be okay.

Everything was grey between me and Parker. I needed that grey area. That's the only way I could convince myself this wouldn't end in disaster.

But there was that inner voice telling me it would still end in disaster. There was that voice comparing her to Cam. The voice of doubt that hung on every change in tone, every misspoken word. And that voice didn't think even the grey area would work. That voice, that part of me that was scared and hiding behind walls, knew the only way I was going to get out of this safely was by pushing Parker away before she could hurt me in the first place.

Parker

I'd never forget the words 'skin hungry' for as long as I lived. I'd heard of touch starved or craving affection. Funnily enough, I realized that's exactly what I'd been for a long time. Jayde didn't hug. She didn't cuddle. She wasn't interested in real intimacy unless she was a whiny, hungover mess. And I felt like I could handle having nothing but intimacy from Ava.

It was weird. I'd never known how much I'd needed that until I got it.

After narrowly avoiding Willow's looks, I met Noah on the stairs of Ava and Willow's apartment. He looked up at me in sheer disbelief before shaking his head.

"You're still here?" He scoffed.

I grinned. "You kissed her."

He flushed, looking away. "What did you do all day?"

"We cuddled."

"You cuddled?"

"Yeah, she took a nap." I shrugged as we reached the car. "And I watched *The Labyrinth* on repeat for five hours."

He stopped with his hand hovering over the door handle. "Why do you seem so happy about that?"

"Because it was fantastic! When was the last time you just... hugged someone? Just hugged them to hug them?"

Noah shrugged.

"There wasn't anything else waiting, Noah. No expectations. I got to just... cuddle with Ava. I didn't have to do anything else... why are you looking at me like that? Doesn't that sound amazing?"

"I don't know." He laughed as he climbed into the car. "Maybe we just want different things."

"And that is why we aren't together."

He scoffed at me before turning the key in the ignition.

"Yeah, *that's* the only reason."

I smirked back at him, letting out a sigh as we headed home.

"I'm guessing you didn't ask her what she wants and get a concrete answer before this cuddle sesh?" Noah sighed about halfway home.

"You just had a big date you've been talking about all week, and you want to talk about *my* love life?"

"My date went well because Willow and I actually communicated early about preferences, wants, goals and needs."

I scoffed, looking out the window.

"Look, if you don't wanna talk about it—"

"I don't."

"That's fine." He sighed in that fatherly way he did. Dude was going to make one hell of a dad one day. "I'm just trying to look out for you."

"I know." I met his eyes only briefly before they were safely back on the road. "I just... I have a good feeling about her, Noah. I know it's not as simple as what you and Willow started, but in my gut, I know something's right."

"What did your gut say about Jayde?"

"I never asked it, to be honest. We were always too drunk or hungover for my gut to have a say."

"Right." He groaned.

"This is different. Surely you can see that." I insisted as we pulled into the parking garage.

"Yes, I can see that this is not a mirror situation, but that doesn't mean that I think things are off to a healthy start."

He didn't say anything else as he gathered his things and we headed inside, and I didn't want to argue, so I didn't either.

Things would be tough with Ava. I knew that. We'd have our share of challenges, and she was guarded, most likely for good reason. But I had been too for a long time. If I could bring down my walls after everything Jayde put me through, I knew I could show Ava it was okay for her to do it, too.

Ava

When I woke up the next morning, there were trace amounts of Parker's cologne on my pillow, giving me ghost feelings of her. And there was a 'Good morning, beautiful' text waiting for me that Parker had sent the night before. God, I had a cheesy grin on my face. I just knew it. *What was I doing?*

Inviting Parker over to *cuddle?* In what way was that smart?

I'd dreamed about her, too, to add insult to injury. That probably wasn't good, but I didn't know what I could do about that. I couldn't control my dreams.

As I eyed the text, I felt my eyes well up. This really would end in disaster. There was no way it couldn't. She was already acting couple-y, or at least like she wanted to be.

Then, I realized I still had to figure out just how I was to scare Parker off before this became something I couldn't run away from.

I met Willow in the living room. She was packing up her books for school, and gave me a wave. She seemed in an even better mood than usual, walking around smiling at her phone. She was almost late texting Noah.

I headed out for the gym a few minutes later, hoping some soothing yoga would ease my newly found tension.

"Parker, are you actually on time?" I asked as I tucked my yoga mat into my bag and slipped on my shoes.

"Looks like it." She smirked, leaning in to kiss me. It was weird that she wasn't afraid to do that in front of people. Even weirder that I wasn't, either. "Good workout? Looks like you broke a sweat."

I rolled my eyes. "Not everyone lifts weights for a living, but yes."

"Spending money. I have a big girl job, too." Parker's grin was infectious and infuriating. "I still can't believe you come to the gym just for yoga."

"I'm a closeted extrovert." I laughed. "This way, I can be around people and refill my energy without them actually talking to me."

"You sound like Noah. You really are not a morning person, are you?"

I shook my head, and she gave me another infectious smile.

"So, what are you doing tonight? There's this movie that just dropped. I was thinking maybe we could rent."

"I can't." I sighed, grabbing my bag.

"Getting tired of my cuddles already?"

I let out a laugh. "No, once a month, I go over to my dad's... we get a pizza and watch Star Trek."

"Wow, you really aren't afraid to scare me off."

Perfect choice of words.

"I keep trying, but apparently you like horror or something." A felt a sly grin spread across my face as an idea struck me. "You should come, I mean, if you want."

"To—to your dad's?" She frowned. "Like, to meet your dad? Shouldn't we—"

"Nope, we shouldn't. It's cool. He's probably too scary for you, anyway."

"Right, well, in that case, I'd love to."

"Great, I'll meet you at the coffee shop around seven?"

She did the head scratch thing and nodded. "Yep, seven sounds great."

"Wear your brown pants." I laughed, kissing her cheek before I made my way to the door.

"Real funny." She snapped back, but there was a splash of crimson on her cheeks and a look of panic in her eyes.

This could work.

Parker

"So much for things not working out." Kaitlin said sarcastically the moment Ava was out of the gym doors and out of earshot. "How'd you go from 'definitely not' to kissing her? I don't get it."

I let out a laugh, tossing the elastic bands she was needing less and less her way.

"Clearly you don't know how lesbians work." I smirked.

"Clearly. Why do you look like you're on the brink of a nervous breakdown?"

"She just asked me to meet her dad. Tonight."

Kaitlin raised her eyebrows at me.

"Right. I think it was just a joke at first, but... I shouldn't go, right? I should text her and tell her we should wait for all that. We haven't even been on a real date yet."

"I don't think I'm the right person to ask for relationship advice." Kaitlin laughed as she started her stretches.

I let out a sigh. Yeah, I should have been talking to Noah. But I knew exactly what he'd say. He'd say absolutely not, do not go to meet her dad before you've even been on a date. That's a terrible idea.

You haven't even asked the hard questions.

And he'd be right, and I'd hate that he was right. But more importantly, I was stubborn. I wanted to do whatever would make Ava happy. Oddly enough, I'd said the same thing about Jayde.

"Hey, what's the name of that coffee shop you go to? Maddi said something about it being your religion or something?"

I laugh out a deep laugh. "She said what?"

"I don't know. I was talking about a bad experience next door, and she said you went on a tangent once about only drinking coffee from some place on Jasper Avenue?"

"Oh, yeah, that's because she's a hipster who only shops brand names."

"Hey!" Maddi called across the room.

"I meant it!" I grinned at her.

Maddi flashed me her middle finger, but she had a grin on her face as she answered the phone. I loved this place. I'd never switch gyms again.

"Jasper Avenue Coffee Company." I said, turning my attention back to Kaitlin. "It is the best coffee shop in town."

"You headed there after this?" Kaitlin asked. "Or did you already go today?"

"Oh, yeah, I'll head over there before I head home."

"Cool, you mind if I join you? I hate going new places by myself. And Brandon hates coffee."

And that's how I ended up standing in a coffee shop that most definitely felt like mine and Ava's place with my client.

"So, this is the place, huh?" Kaitlin asked as we slipped into the coffee shop. "Look, it better be worth the walk, and the calor–"

"Nope, we aren't doing that." I shot her a look. "What did we say?"

She sighed. "'Food isn't a reward, and coffee feeds the soul.'"

"Damn straight."

Kaitlin smacked my arm and then turned her attention back to the board. "So, what's good here?"

"Everything." I laughed, eyeing the handwritten menu with its chalk art. "I'm partial to the Lucky Leprechaun. The Irish Cream is soul satisfying."

"Hey." I heard Ava's voice.

"Hey, you." I said as she joined me in line, looking nervously between me and Kaitlin. "Kaitlin, this is Ava. Ava, this is my client, Kaitlin."

"Hi, it's nice to meet you." Kaitlin smiled. "What do you get here? I'm super indecisive."

"The peppermint mocha." Ava said, and I felt her loop her arm with mine.

A smile crept at the corners of my mouth when Kaitlin looked between us.

Kaitlin stepped up to the counter and ordered, and then casually dipped out the moment her coffee was up, giving both of us a wave as we waited in the receiving area.

"Kaitlin seems... nice." Ava said as she watched the espresso machine intensely. "And really... pretty."

"Oh, yeah, she's great." I nodded, following her gaze. "Super motivated. I wish her husband could see it, though. He's an ass."

"Husband. Oh."

I heard a soft sigh, and I looked down where Ava was beet red.

"Yeah... Ava Grace, are you jealous?"

"What?" Her voice went up an octave. "No, that's–"

"You seem a little—"

"Should I be?"

When she looked up at me, I knew for sure there was some sort of past issue coming up.

"No," I said, pulling her close to me and kissing the side of her head. "Kaitlin is my client. I have a big no dating clients rule to begin with. It's hard to work with someone you're dating, and it doesn't seem healthy giving someone you're into weight loss or fitness advice."

She nodded, looking down at her thumbs and picking at her cuticles.

"Hey, you don't have to worry about that, okay?" I said, trying to offer the most reassuring smile I could. "I have a one-track mind, and it's on the Ava train."

She let out a laugh, and gave me a shove, but I could see a nervous look in her eye that didn't dissipate even when I was kissing her goodbye and heading to one of the comic stores across town for a shirt.

I was definitely going to meet her dad.

Ava

I almost expected Parker to bail. Meeting the parents? That was definitely girlfriend territory. Serious relationship stuff. Pressure. And after that morning with Kaitlin... Kaitlin who really was super pretty, even if she was married. Women left their husbands all the time. I couldn't relate, but getting trapped in heteronormativity was a thing.

I couldn't help but notice how similar we looked. Same brown hair, similar skin tone, similar body type. She was just in better shape. They'd be a power couple. I didn't know if Parker had a type at all, but I was sure just looking at her, Kaitlin was probably a better fit for the mold.

No matter what Parker said about her one-track mind.

I was surprised as I approached the coffee shop to find Parker waiting for me, leaning against the brick wall near the door, looking like whatever the female version of tall, dark and handsome was. She was such a beautiful human being.

And she was wearing a Star Trek shirt.

"You're here." I said, and she smiled back.

"I said I would be, didn't I?"

"Yeah, well. It's my dad, so."

"I'll have you know; parents love me."

"Of course, they do." I grinned. "Nice shirt. I'm guessing it's part of your master plan?"

"Thank you, and yes, wearing the right attire is a quintessential part of making the parents love me." She said as she threw her arm over my shoulder. "So, where are we headed?"

"Twenty-first and Pennsylvania." I grimaced, thinking briefly of the nearly thirty block walk.

"Oof. Why didn't you have me snatch the car from Noah?"

"I didn't think about it honestly."

"We can take a cab."

"What? No, it's really not—"

But she was already hailing a passing car before I could even get the words out of my mouth.

"Parker, it's—"

"No, you just got off work, working on your feet. We can take a cab, I got it. Are we picking up the pizza, or does your dad tackle that?"

"Um, I usually do. There's a place about halfway there I usually stop."

"Okay, after you." She gestured to the open taxi door.

I realized that was the first time someone had opened the car door for me. Like chivalrous gentlemen did for women, old-fashioned and cute if you're into that sort of thing. I never really was before. Cam wasn't the take care of you type, not unless it was in front of my mom for appearances. But something about Parker wanting to take care of me, even as simple as paying for a cab so I didn't have to walk, hit me right in the feels.

And sent a wave of guilt washing over me at the conniving way I'd set this up.

I climbed into the car and gave the name of the pizzeria I typically stopped every fourth Tuesday of the month. And we were off, Parker's arm over my shoulder, her chatting up the cab driver like they were close friends.

"Dad?" I called as I closed the door behind me and slipped my coat on the rack.

"Well, hey there, baby bear, you're early." My dad came around the corner with his reading glasses on and pulled me into a hug. "And you've brought a friend."

I looked at Parker, who was half frozen, cheeks burning. She gave a soft wave as she placed her coat on the rack, balancing the pizza she'd insisted on carrying for me in her other hand.

"Yeah, we took a cab." I said with a forced smile. "Dad, this is Parker."

"Parker?" He asked, reaching out his hand. "Your parents must have known early."

"Dad!"

"Nah, that's funny." Parker grinned. "At least I know where you get your sense of humor from."

"She certainly doesn't get it from her mother." My dad smiled to himself as he took the pizza from Parker and led us into the den. "Love the shirt, by the way, nothing like the original series. I think Ava's starting to figure that out."

"Oh yeah, I agree." Parker nodded, and I looked at her skeptically.

"Have you even watched Star Trek before?" I whispered as my dad went to grab plates.

"Probably." She shrugged. "We watched a lot of sci-fi when I was a kid."

I eyed her, realizing she was completely unfazed and unafraid. In fact, as he returned, she took a seat on one of my dad's worn leather couches and accepted a plate full of pizza. They started chatting about comics and fiction novels like they were pals.

My dad had never done that with Cam. Then again, Cam had never made an effort to be truly liked by my parents, and Parker... Parker was opening up more and more, proving to me she wasn't just full of surprises, but she actually did somehow fit into my life.

It only terrified me more.

Parker

"So, that went... well, right?" I asked, Ava's hand in mine as we walked most of the way back to her side of town.

She'd said she needed to walk off all those extra carbs, but I had a feeling she just didn't want me covering a taxi again. I'd decided I was okay with that. I'd had to insist three times she didn't have to pay me back for the first one.

"Yeah," she nodded, but she was staring off down the road and chewing on her nails like her mind was a thousand miles away. "My dad really seems to love you."

"So, why do you seem upset?"

She let out a sigh. "I feel like maybe this was a bad idea. I mean... it's too soon to meet the parents, isn't it? We aren't even dating."

Ouch.

"Yeah," I said through a fresh lump in my throat.

I pulled my hand away as a reflex, and Ava's demeanor changed. She was suddenly fully present, eyes wide, mouth agape.

"Parker, I didn't mean it like that."

"I know how you meant it, Ava." I whispered, trying my best not to show how I actually felt, which was mostly confused, and a hint of hurt. "You don't want to date me."

She let out a shaky sigh in response. I swallowed hard, feeling my heart begin to race.

"Look, if this is about the whole, 'not your type' thing—"

"It's not." she said breathily. "I mean, yeah, it's that, but it's also—it's—it's just me... I'm not—"

I could see her cheeks glisten in the moonlight, and I wrapped my arms around her shoulders, but she didn't relax. She pulled away, giving me a slight shove.

"Don't be nice to me when I'm being cruel to you." She sobbed, turning to walk away.

"I don't think you're being cruel, Ava. I think it's hard to open up to someone if you've been—"

"But you don't know what I've been through. You don't have the first clue." She snapped back at me. There was so much hurt in her eyes when she faced me. "I'm not trying to get closer to you. Tonight—tonight was supposed to scare you away. Who wants to meet the parents after two weeks of... God, whatever this is? We barely know each other."

How can someone break your heart without even being yours?

"We don't have to do this." I said calmly, far more calmly than I felt.

I wasn't angry with Ava. I knew whatever had her hurting like this had nothing to do with me and everything to do with whoever had hurt her so badly she felt like the only way to keep herself safe was to push away anyone who tried to get close. And I couldn't make that better. Not like this.

"I'm not going to push you." I continued, hailing a cab, feeling Ava's eyes on me as I did. "I'm not going to pressure you into opening up to me, or make you feel like this is something you have to do. But I do have a clue. Because I have a feeling you and

I have been through some of the same things. Maybe you don't see it, but I do."

I opened the door of the waiting car, and she sniffled before climbing in. She looked up at me, surprised, when I shut the door behind her. I handed enough cash to get her home and a decent tip to the driver through the front window. Ava met my eyes just before the car pulled away, and I let out a sigh.

The universe sucked.

Ava

The house was quiet and clean when I walked in. A hint of whatever Willow insisted on putting on the carpets every time she vacuumed filling the air. I ducked into Willow's room to find it empty, her bed made. I let out a sigh. She was probably with Noah. Which meant she'd hear all about it when Parker got home.

I'd been thinking about what Parker had said the entire way home, even as I climbed into bed, and eyed my empty text messages. I wanted to scare her off, and I had. Just not in the way I originally intended.

There was an aching in the pit of my stomach, somehow not from the pizza. Trying to scare Parker away... that was wrong. I should have just been honest. Because this... this was Cam level immaturity. I was better than that. The last thing I wanted to do was act like Cam.

For some reason, all I wanted was to talk to Parker about it. I wanted to know what she meant by 'we'd been through similar things'. I wanted to know what she'd been through because maybe if she understood... maybe I wouldn't have to talk about what had happened.

But talking about what had happened was exactly what I needed to do. Because what I needed to do was to work through it. I knew that. I shouldn't have skipped therapy.

Did you make it home okay?

Read 10:58PM

Yeah.

I eyed the message, typing up several responses and deleting them. None of what I had to say felt good enough. How do you make up for treating someone the same way your literal abuser treated you?

I can't do this back-and-forth stuff, Ava. I'll be here for you if you need someone, and I'm always here as a friend, but it's clear you don't know what you want. So, maybe it's best we are just amicable for now. I think we are stuck with each other with these two. Goodnight.

The message came with a photo of Noah and Willow curled up on what I assumed was Parker's oversized couch. I had a feeling she wouldn't be coming home that night, and suddenly the silence in the house was overwhelming. A wave of loneliness washed over me because I could still smell Parker's cologne on my pillow.

Parker was right. I didn't know what I wanted. No, I did, but I didn't think I could have it. I didn't think it would last, and I didn't think I'd be able to pick up the pieces again if it all fell apart.

Parker

"Alright, kid, what's up with you two?" Meg asked, gesturing to Ava, who was taking an order with a smile only a few of us would know was completely fake. "Last week she's surprised to find you here like she knows you. Now you're avoiding even looking at each other."

"I thought we'd be good together." I shrugged. "She doesn't seem to agree with me. She doesn't know what she wants just like—"

"She say that, or are you inferring like you do with everyone else in your life?"

Ouch.

"The latter."

"Thought so." Meg cleared her throat and pulled a tube of ruby red lipstick out of her apron to reapply. "I think it's probably a bit more complicated than that, isn't it? You have a history. I know she has a history, and maybe neither of you have really figured out how to get over your past, have you?"

I swallowed hard.

"She tell you her whole life story like I did?" I asked.

"I know a thing or two that I won't be telling *you*. That's all I've got to say about that." Meg closed the tube and tucked it back into her apron pocket. "But that girl? She's about as genuine and incapable of true malice as they come, so if you're comparing her to your cold-hearted ex, you better just stop."

I nodded, meeting Meg's eyes.

"I just..." I let out a sigh. "I don't think I can be with someone who doesn't know they want me again. And Noah's—"

"Noah seems like a good guy." Meg gave the table a little tap with her thick red nails. "But he isn't you. This isn't his life. As much as he seems like a well-meaning friend, he doesn't know the whole story."

"But you do." I grinned.

She smiled back, eyeing Ava. "I know enough. I know what you've both been through. Give or take a few of the rougher details. So, when I tell you not to give up on her just yet, you should know, I'm giving you advice from a big picture view."

I nodded, looking back at Ava again. She let out a genuine laugh and leaned over to talk to a little girl wearing cat ears. She was different with kids. I'd noticed that before. I wondered if maybe she was more herself.

"Now, I'm going to go get you some pie." Meg said, pulling my attention back to her.

Meg was gone in a flash, leaving me to think about all the times I had already compared Ava to Jayde. It made me wonder... if Ava really had been through something like what I had, maybe all of her back-and-forth was just her comparing me to someone else, too.

I looked back at Ava, who had left her table and was collecting dirty dishes from another one in her section. She glanced around like she'd forgotten something, and her eyes found me. She gave me a hesitant smile before heading into the kitchen.

"Hey." Ava said, pulling me out of my thoughts. "Mind if I join you?"

She bit the inside of her lip, and I let out a sigh, gesturing to the empty booth across from me before I could think better of it. I'd said we could be friends. I'd meant that, but I was still mulling over my conversation with Meg.

"My feet hurt." She let out a deep sigh.

She laughed when I raised an eyebrow at her.

"Want me to rub them for you?" I smirked, hating how easy it was with her that much more.

"Uh no, but thanks."

"Long day already?" I asked.

She shrugged. "Sometimes I love it here, and sometimes I just... don't want to be here."

I nodded. "I feel that."

"So, why do you come here two days a week? And don't tell me it's for the pie."

I sucked in a deep breath, feeling my shoulders get a little tense.

"It's okay, you don't..." She bit her thumbnail. "You don't have to tell me."

I let out a sigh, thinking about what Meg had said. I told her the truth the night before. I did think we'd been through some of the same things. I did think we had a lot in common, and I didn't want to do this back-and-forth thing with her like Jayde had done to me one too many times. There I was, comparing the two again. How could Ava open up to me, or even know all of that, if I didn't open up first?

"I was self-isolating." I said finally.

Ava looked back at me.

"I'd just been dumped, rather harshly. And for the first month, all I did was work, sleep, and sit on the couch, doing nothing. Apart from Noah, everyone I knew was friends with her. She liked it that way. They basically reported back to her, so it felt like nowhere was safe."

"So, one day after Noah basically kicked me out of the apartment, I was out walking, and I stopped here." I let out another sigh, looking over to where Meg was talking with another customer. "Meg sat down and talked to me for a good hour. Maybe she knew I needed somebody. She's got a mom brain, I think."

Ava laughed and nodded.

"I just kept coming back." I looked down, pushing pie around my plate. "It gave me a reason to get out of bed on my day off, and forced me to talk to someone, anyone who could be objective. I think it helped me out of a dark place."

I heard Ava suck in a shudder of a breath, and when I looked back up, she was looking away, but I could tell she was on the verge of tears.

"You okay?" I asked.

She nodded, but she didn't look at me.

"What is it?"

Ava looked back at me and shook her head before grabbing my fork and stealing a bite of my pie. I gave her a playful glare, and she laughed. The tears dried up almost instantly. I thought about all the times I'd had to do that. Dry up my tears like they'd never been there just to avoid the pain that came with talking about the pain.

"I have to get back to work." She sighed as she got up. "See you tomorrow?"

"You work tonight?" I asked.

She nodded softly.

"You want a ride home?"

She bit the inside of her lip. "Sure."

"Okay, I'll see you tonight."

She smiled at me before disappearing into the kitchen.

I let out a sigh. I'd pined after this girl for months. I could at the very least wait it out a bit more.

Ava

I half expected Parker not to show again. I wasn't sure why, really. She didn't seem like the type, but I was so used to being let down. And after how we'd ended the night before, I couldn't figure out why she'd want to be nice to me, anyway. I didn't know why she was being nice to me at the diner either, but I had a feeling Meg had something to do with it.

Seeing Noah drumming furiously against the steering wheel to the music he was playing was surprising. He seemed in an oddly good mood despite how much I knew he was starting to not like me. I hated that thought–not being liked.

"You're here." I sputtered as Parker rolled down her window, the black button down she wore to work in the bar already unbuttoned a couple notches.

"I said I'd be." She smiled back, almost an ounce of shock on her face. "Did... you think I'd forget?"

I shrugged in response and crawled into the back seat. We were quiet most of the ride to my apartment, and I was pretty sure Noah was only being nice to me for Willow as he kept eyeing me in the rearview mirror with a look of pure distaste. It was probably the same look I'd have for him if he wasn't treating Willow like a princess, so I couldn't blame him.

I deserved that. I wasn't exactly acting like girlfriend material, and I had a feeling he felt like Parker deserved exactly that. She did. I knew she did. But I didn't know how to be what she deserved. I didn't know if I could. Every time I tried to picture me and Parker together, there was Cam's voice in my head telling me all the ways it wouldn't work.

I wondered what my inner voice sounded like. It had been so long since I'd heard anything but hers.

When we pulled up to the curb, I muttered a soft thank you and hopped out of the car. I made it all the way to the complex doors before I felt Parker's hand on my wrist. She slowly let go, sending chills up my arm.

"Hey, I had a question for you." She shivered in the late February air in that button down, but she didn't seem to care.

"Oh, yeah?" I smiled despite myself.

"Will you go on a date with me?" She asked.

That was not the question I was expecting after the last twenty-four hours. The fact that she was talking to me at all felt pretty miraculous to begin with.

I let out a little gasp, and I felt a lump rise in my throat when I met her eyes. Again, I was reminded how beautiful they were, dark and deep, such a contrast to Cam. Her eyes were bright and piercing. Polar opposites. That should have been a sign. If I'd believed in the universe and all that.

"Parker..." I let out a sigh. "After last night..."

"Okay, not a date." Parker let out a breath, somewhere between a sigh and a huff, but she was smiling. "No expectations. No rules. Just us, being ourselves, maybe for the first time in a long time?"

I met her eyes again, thinking about how true that was. I couldn't remember the last time I'd been able to really be myself around anyone but Willow. I was always putting up a little bit of a front.

"A dinner between friends." She continued, basically rambling. She had a nervous bounce in her legs. "I want to know you. And if we go Dutch, it's not a *date,* date. Like getting sandwiches."

I felt myself smirk. "You know that's not how it works."

I looked down at my keys for a moment. I wanted to say yes. Because I wanted to somehow undo this ridiculous scheme to scare her away, go back to that grey space before I'd admitted what I was doing, and stay there for a while. Because I couldn't deny how much better I felt when she was around.

"It's okay." She smiled, almost looking like it was genuine. "You don't have to say yes. We can still be friends either way."

"It's just—"

"You don't have to justify it, Ava. It's okay, really. I'm not gonna push you... any more than I already have."

We both let out a soft laugh, and then I sighed.

"I'll think about it." I forced a smile. "Goodnight."

I stood on my toes to kiss her cheek before darting for the door, hearing the softest 'goodnight' echo behind me. I glanced back before opening the doors and watched as Parker climbed back into the car. Parker didn't notice, but Noah did.

His glare was so painstakingly evident. He was shooting some serious daggers my way. It was going to be a long time before he and I were okay.

The next morning, as I waited for the manager to arrive and unlock the doors, I leaned against the back wall of the diner. I must have been staring off into the distance for a hot minute because Meg had to snap her fingers to get my attention.

"You okay, sugar?" She asked, eyeing me closely. "You've got one serious thinking face on this morning."

"Yeah," I sighed, considering whether I should tell her what was really on my mind or not, but Meg knew when I was lying. "Parker... asked me on a date."

"That's great!"

The manager arrived, and I shifted my face away from her.

"I told her I'd think about it." I said over my shoulder as we shuffled inside.

"Well, what would you go and do a thing like that for?" Meg asked, blocking the doorway out of our small little break room as I switched out my shoes and pulled my apron from a cubby.

"What do you mean?" I frowned back at her.

"That woman's had her eye on you for months."

I let out a shaky breath, and Meg toned down her aggressive approach.

"Your ex is long gone, honey." Meg sighed, taking a seat on the small bench next to me. "You said before when you were training that you might only last a month here, and it's been eight. No sign of her. She can't hurt you anymore, not unless you let her, and seems to me that's exactly what you're doing."

I sighed and nodded in response, hearing the familiar clicks as the stove tops got heated for the lunch rush. Meg grabbed her things and slipped out, leaving me to think about Parker and our friend date, and how I'd wanted to say yes.

So, what was stopping me besides me?

Parker

The next night, Ava played in the bar again. Seeing her play was so much better than seeing her in passing. She was captivating, and not just to me. I mean, I loved watching her play, but the entire room did, too.

She was different on stage. It felt like all the walls she built up came down for a while. She smiled more, and not in a customer service sort of way. It was almost like she was glowing in the stage light, and she seemed so at peace.

When she finally put down her guitar and called it a night, the dinner crowd was already dwindling. I'm pretty sure it was getting late for her to head to the department store, but she didn't seem concerned. At least, she didn't seem in a rush to me.

Meanwhile, I had a number of glasses to wash and an entire bar in disarray. I hated the way Friday nights always went by in a blur. Sometimes I'd get FOMO just thinking about where I could be instead. But it was the best paying night of the week. And I knew better than to think there was anything for me anywhere else on a Friday. Nothing out there but trouble.

I heard the familiar sound of a bar stool moving and turned to find Ava leaning on it.

"So, where would we go on this *friend* date?"

My heart was pounding immediately, but I tried to keep it cool.

"Wherever you want, I guess." I cleared my throat as I slid a wine glass back into the overhead holder.

"You don't even have a plan?" She did an overdramatic gasp.

I felt my cheeks burn.

"I just figured... we'd figure it out together." I murmured, seeing Nathan eye us from the sound booth.

"So, you're trying to play it safe by having me help you plan it out so you don't overstep?"

"That..." I breathed, feeling my cheeks puff out. "How do you do that? Is Meg giving you lessons or something?"

She laughed and then took a deep breath. "I'm going to be big and brave, so let's go wherever you originally had in mind."

"Right, okay, um." I swallowed hard. "See, that was sort of a fancier—"

"Wherever it is, it's fine. I can do fancy. You think I can't do fancy? That sounds like a challenge."

I bit my lip to keep from laughing and drawing more of Nathan's attention.

"Okay, fancy it is, but I'll have you know, this will be the best friend date you've ever been on." I smirked, grabbing more glasses to wash.

"I've never been on a friend date." She laughed, watching me work. "So, I don't really have anything to compare it to."

"Great. Perfect. That's good because... then we don't have any rules about it, right?"

"Right, that's what you said. No rules. Just us."

I took a deep breath, and set down the glass I'd been washing, just embracing the word 'us' coming out of her mouth. And we just looked at each other, the lull of the bar turning into a hum.

"I gotta go." She sighed. "Let me know when you're ready to plan this epic adventure."

And then she slipped out the back, waving to Nathan, who shook his head at me before heading back into the sound booth. I'd wager he was getting really tired of his restaurant playing matchmaker with his employees.

It took some convincing to get Noah to let me borrow the car that Tuesday. He was not quiet about his disdain for the idea. But after some careful explanation, he and Willow worked out something for the two of them at Ava and Willow's place. I should have known driving him over there was going to earn me a hard time.

"So, you're really going on a date with this girl." He sighed. It wasn't a question.

"I told you. It's just a friend thing." I insisted as we made our way across town to Ava and Willow's apartment.

I'd tried my best not to dress up despite the fact that I was taking her uptown. This wasn't a *date,* date. This was a friend date.

"Right." Noah chuckled, mostly to himself. "Which is why you're in a button down."

"Okay, firstly this is a flannel, it just so happens to be mostly black. Second, I wear button downs five days a week."

"For work. This is a date." He pointed to my pants. "You're wearing slacks. And aren't those your dress shoes?"

"A *friend,* date." I insisted.

"I don't think there is such a thing. Not when there's all this... tension between you two." He sighed. "Besides, how many friends kiss their friends?"

He had me there.

"I'm still not sure about her." He said after a minute. "I mean, I know what you said about this being a process. I know you like her, and she doesn't seem... she seems like a decent person, but even Willow has noticed Ava's doing this back-and-forth thing."

"We're figuring it out." I sighed.

"You're getting in deep; you mean. Look, just don't ask me to pick sides because I really like this girl, Parker. I've got a good feeling about her."

"Yeah, me too."

We met eyes for a brief moment, and then we laughed. All the tension went out the window. Noah wasn't good at serious, and I hated when things got tense. Lately, it felt like there was a lot of both. I wasn't willing to pin all that on Ava. I was getting in deep, and I couldn't stop it.

I was surprised when Willow opened the door and not Ava. I was normally the one running late. She looked upset. I wasn't sure if it was with me, with Ava, or maybe both. This thing with us really did have her and Noah on edge.

"She's not ready yet." Willow signed, but stood in the doorway like I wasn't welcome to wait inside.

I nodded slowly. "Okay, you want me to wait in the car?" I tried my best to sign along, but it was pretty rusty.

Willow thought about it for a second, eyeing me, and then nodded. "Where's Noah?"

I liked that he had his own name sign now. Instead of spelling it out, she'd mixed his name with the sign for 'boyfriend,' which was pretty adorable in my opinion. I didn't want to know what her sign for me would be.

"He's still getting his stuff out of the car." I smiled. "He planned some really special dinner for you guys to make together."

She beamed and then glanced back at their bathroom door.

"I'm sorry." she said. "I don't think she should be dating and skipping therapy. It was good for her. If you care about her, you'll tell her to keep going."

Willow started to shut the door, and I backed away. I hadn't even realized Ava had skipped therapy. But, then again, I'd probably know if I'd gone myself.

I just didn't trust myself to be honest with Ava sitting right there. I realized as I headed back downstairs that I didn't have to worry about that after all. But I wondered if maybe Ava had skipped it for the same reason.

Ava

"I don't get it." Willow signed from the tiny doorway of the bathroom, making me feel rather closed in to the already cramped space.

I hated when she did that. She left me no room to escape, and I had a feeling she did it on purpose. It just didn't help that our apartment made it so easy.

"You keep going back and forth." Willow continued. "Do you like Parker or don't you?"

I let out a sigh and put down my makeup brush. "I do. It's just... I'm scared, Willow. I haven't felt this way about anyone since—"

Since, Cam.

"I don't want to get hurt again." I bit the inside of my cheek hard. "I don't think I'm capable of dealing with another broken heart. You know better than I do that I barely got through the last one."

"Maybe you should be in therapy, then." She signed so fast I almost missed it.

I had a feeling that was entirely related to my skipping the group the day before. I didn't want to talk about Parker in front of Parker. And I didn't think I'd have the courage to just talk about myself. So, I just didn't go.

"I probably should, and maybe I will." I lied.

"So, why are you going on a date with her if you aren't ready?" Willow was getting red in the face, which was fairly easy for her, as she was so pasty as it was.

I let out another sigh as I grabbed my mascara and fiddled with the cap.

"It's a friend date. It doesn't count."

"Does she know that?" Willow raised her eyebrows, and I heard a knock at the door.

Leave it to Parker to be on time when I'm running behind. I had a feeling Noah had something to do with that. Parker had mentioned he and Willow were doing something.

"It was her idea." I sighed, gesturing to the front door. "Will you get that?"

I shut the bathroom and hurried to finish my makeup, careful not to smudge mascara all over my nose like I normally did when I was in a hurry.

I heard Parker talking for a second, and then the door shut, and there was silence again.

Shit.

I opened the door, probably as ready as I was going to be to find Parker not in my living room. Dammit, Willow.

"What did you say?" I asked, feeling myself begin to fume as I ran toward the door, stumbling into my shoes.

"I told her you'd be out in a second." Willow signed as she took a seat on the couch, careful not to squish Milo. "You look beautiful. Please don't hurt her. I really like Noah."

She had a childlike look in her eye, and I was suddenly reminded that I was the big sister again. And I'd gotten her tangled in the middle of my problems.

I let out a sigh and walked over to the couch despite my sister's rules about shoes in the house. I pulled her off the couch into a hug, and I heard her sigh.

When she pulled away, I signed, "I don't think Noah is going anywhere, and I'm going to do my best not to hurt Parker, okay?"

"I just want you to be sure." Willow was almost tearful. "Because he and I will have to pick sides, and that's not fair."

I nodded, eyeing the door.

"I love you." She said, when I looked at her again. "You deserve to be happy, too."

I gave her a kiss on the forehead and headed out the door. I found Parker and Noah by their car out front. Noah had what looked to be an overnight bag, but I couldn't be sure, and a giant bouquet of flowers in his hands.

"Need any help there, Romeo?" I asked, causing both of them to jump.

Noah shook his head, "I'm good, thank you."

"I asked twice." Parker sighed, turning to me. "Wow, you do fancy."

I looked down at the black and green dress I'd slipped on. I'd mostly worn it out of spite for the little voice in my head because Cam had hated this dress. She'd never said it didn't look good on me. In fact, she'd said the opposite. It was flashy. It drew attention. It made her friends ogle at me.

I felt my cheeks burn, realizing Parker was doing just that.

"Not a date. Right." Noah called over his shoulder as he headed for the doors, struggling the entire way. "Sure, looks like a date to me."

"Not looking so bad yourself, Watson." I grinned at her after Noah had made his way inside. "If you're Parker Watson, does that mean I can be Sherlock?"

"You have the detective skills of a noseless dog. You didn't recognize me at therapy when I'd been coming into the diner the entire time you'd worked there."

"Ouch. But you're not wrong."

Parker opened the door for me in a very this-is-a-date way, and I eyed her before climbing in.

"No rules." She grinned as she shut the door.

And I realized suddenly, this was a date, and maybe I was okay with that.

Parker hadn't been kidding. This place was fancy. A high-rise restaurant overlooking the city. They had a koi pond inside with a running waterfall, a jazz band playing on a massive stage, and an actual dance floor where people were actually dancing.

Worse though, it was fancy in the no-prices-on-the-menu way. Which made me nervous for my bank account. Suddenly, I didn't want to eat anything. I should have asked to help pick the place, but at the very least, I was glad I'd dressed up.

We'd just gotten seated and asked for drinks from the waiter when Parker got right into very date-like territory.

"So, how'd you know you were asexual?" She asked as I eyed the menu.

I looked up at her with nothing less than a scowl I couldn't keep from making.

"What? I'm just curious. I've been doing my own research."

I sighed, still eyeing the menu for something I thought might be safe. "I guess sex has always been... not my thing. It actually makes me kind of uncomfortable. And, like... I don't need it, you know? But if I'm in a relationship, and they're into it... I guess. I don't mind. It's different now. After my last relationship, I don't really know."

"Where does the whole attraction thing fall in?"

"You know how people just see someone and go 'I'd tap that?'"

She nodded.

"Well, I never feel that way. I mean, I can tell when someone's... pleasing to the eye. It's more like their aesthetic. I don't ever take a look at someone and think about having sex with them."

"So, what about me?" She smirked. "Am I... aesthetically pleasing?"

I rolled my eyes. "Yes."

"Ava Grace, did you just call me pretty?"

"Shut up, Parker."

"So, are you ready to tell me why you don't think you're anyone's type?" She said as she took a sip of her drink. "Because I'm not seeing any red flags here."

"Nope." I kept my eyes on the menu. "But take your rose-colored glasses off and they'll be a lot clearer."

She sighed. "Okay, what do you want for dessert?"

I let out a laugh.

"What?" She frowned.

"We haven't even ordered dinner yet."

"I'm sure that's unrelated to the price of bananas," she said with a straight face. "But I'll have you know I am an adult, and I can eat in whatever order I please."

I laughed again and eyed the dessert menu carefully placed with large pictures in the middle of our table. Also, with no prices.

"The brownie thing looks good." I shrugged, turning back to the menu.

Everything looked dangerous. And expensive.

"Brownie thing it is." Parker nodded. "You want to share one of these big pasta bowls with me? They're huge."

"You've been here before?" I asked, raising an eyebrow. For some reason, Parker didn't seem like the wine and dine type.

"Unfortunately. But newer, better memories can make things you once hated... seem better. And I thought you'd like the music."

"I do." I smiled, eyeing the band again with their shiny instruments. I thought of my beat-up guitar for a minute and sighed. "If I split a pasta bowl with you, how do we go Dutch?"

"We don't actually have to go Dutch." She shrugged, not meeting my eyes. "I mean, officially we said no rules, so—"

"Parker."

"What?" She looked up at me. "Listen, this place is expensive. And originally, when I'd planned on bringing you here, it was... when I imagined this was a *date*, date. And then... well we changed things—"

"And now you're worried about it?"

She nodded.

"Okay," I sighed. "This feels like a date, date already. Lowkey. So, *if* I let you pay for dinner, I get to take you somewhere... *not* expensive for dessert."

"But—"

"You don't want that brownie thing, trust me."

Parker eyed me skeptically, but nodded. And by the time we'd finished sharing that pasta bowl, it was already the best date I'd ever been on. Friend date, real date, it didn't matter. It had been a long time since I'd laughed that much, even if it got some scowls from the other, more well-off patrons around us.

Somehow, she convinced me to go to the dance floor.

"You're far too dressed up to eat pasta and go home."

There was a gleam in her eye that I couldn't fight against because, more than anything, I wanted to see more of it. I put that gleam there. Parker was happy because of me. That was something I never felt like I'd done for Cam, or anyone else, really. I felt like I tended to just disappoint people.

I made Parker happy.

Without rules. Without defined expectations. Just me being me, I made her happy. And I wanted to cling to that.

So, we swayed on that dance floor for at least three songs. It was hard to gauge as they flowed so well together. She spun me around a bit to the faster ones. Neither of us were great dancers, not the jazzy kind, anyway, but we were having fun, and I felt like that's what mattered.

And for those few songs, everything felt okay. Better than okay, but it had been a long time since I'd been able to even reach 'okay' at all. It felt right, her hand on my waist, the other carefully holding mine.

She was so much bigger than me. Four inches taller, muscles for days. Whereas Cam had been right at my height, had never even been to the gym, especially not for strength training. But I felt safe with Parker. I knew she could have, but she wasn't going to hurt me.

Parker

Ava was right. I didn't want that brownie thing. The handmade churros she got from a local food truck downtown, just a few blocks from her apartment? So much better. Handmade soul food over chef pastries any day. I'd just never admit that to Noah.

We looked odd. All dressed up, just walking down the sidewalk. But there wasn't any parking near the food trucks, so we'd left the car at her apartment.

"This is so good." I said with my mouth full. Classy, Parker.

"Right?" Ava grinned; mouth also full.

"Do you go to the food trucks a lot?"

She shrugged. "Only when Willow is busy. She's not a huge fan. I bet her and Noah would have loved that restaurant, though. I think it's way more their speed than ours."

I let out a laugh. "You're right."

"Who'd you go there with that made you hate it so much, though? I mean, the food was okay, and the band was nice. Probably not worth the price tag you wouldn't let me see."

I let out a whispery groan.

"Oh, that bad, huh?"

"I think you're probably the only one who knows just how bad."

"Yikes."

"Yeah, that's about the only word that describes my ex accurately. Just one big human yike."

She laughed, tossing the empty paper in her hand in a nearby trash can. And then turned to me and let out another laugh.

"You have cinnamon and chocolate all over your face."

I felt my cheeks burn as I struggled to decide if I should wipe it on my sleeve like an animal.

"Here." She grinned, pulling a napkin from the food truck out of her tiny purse.

I'd always wondered what it felt like when I watched this stuff in the movies. I couldn't decide if it was more or less embarrassing than I expected. Ava's concentration left a crease between her eyebrows as she proceeded to clean my face in a motherly way that I was sure she pretty much only used on Willow. I wondered where that big sister mojo went when they were grown.

"There." She smiled, looking up at my eyes, and the crease faded, but the tension in the air between us did not.

"So much for a friend thing." She whispered, and then she reached up and kissed me, and not in the timid way she had in her room.

Her hands went to the collar of my shirt, and mine went to her waist. I imagine it was quite the show for anyone walking by, but the street was pretty quiet, and maybe that's why Ava was so confident. When she pulled away, I was basically gasping for air.

"So much for a friend thing." I repeated, and we both laughed. "What does this mean?"

"Does it have to mean anything?" She looked down at her hands, which were resting on my collarbone. "Right now? Can we just—not define it—not label it? I do want you, Parker. I know that. I just need time to figure the rest out."

"I can do that." I nodded, brushing the hair from her face.

"Okay," she sighed, fiddling absentmindedly with one of the buttons on my shirt, not meeting my eyes. "And I'm sorry. For the other night with my dad—"

"You're scared, I get it."

She nodded. "But I should have just been honest about it. I'd never want to treat you like—like I've been treated."

"We all do things we normally wouldn't when we're scared or when we've been through rough times." I swallowed hard, thinking of all the not-so-great things I'd done after Jayde and I split, which mostly started and ended with getting drunk and hooking up with her friends. "How about we agree to just be honest from now on? If we aren't ready to talk about something, we can say that."

Ava looked up at me and smiled, nodding slightly. "I can do that."

Ava

The next morning after our date, I didn't hear from Parker, which I knew was probably normal. She clearly wasn't up yet. So, despite how different I felt, I tried to go about my day, thoughts of her buzzing in my head as they were.

I made it to the gym, worked through a yoga session, and headed home. I was a block from my apartment building when I saw her. Which meant she was really late. She jogged right up to me, anyway.

"Good morning, beautiful." She smiled, leaning in to kiss me.

"You know you're late, right?" I said with a grin as I pulled away.

"Eh," she shrugged, kissing me again before she jogged off.

I shook my head as she rounded the corner toward the gym. Was this a thing now? Kissing Parker on the street just a block from my house? I couldn't decide if I loved it or hated it. The attention I loved. The contact, also great. The girlfriend feel of it though... I wasn't so sure about that.

It was okay... so long as we were still in the grey area, right?

I let out a sigh, trying to choke down all the ways this could go wrong in my head. We had time to figure it out. We didn't have to do it right now.

"Hello again," I heard Parker's voice in my ear as I stood near the receiving area of the coffee shop.

She wrapped her arms around my waist from behind. I eyed the people in the lobby around us, but nobody seemed to be paying any attention, except maybe the less than new girl behind the counter who still glared at me from time to time.

Benefits of being one of the few LGBT friendly spaces in town, maybe. Nobody cared what we were doing.

Why were Parker's arms so damn soothing?

"You're late." I sighed, reaching up to touch her cheek. "Like really, really late. And sweaty, oh my god."

She laughed and rubbed her cheek against mine.

"Gross, Parker, I *just* showered!"

"Ava and Parker!" Jane called, giving me a knowing grin over the counter before she returned to her work.

Parker gasped. "Did you get me coffee?"

"Yes," I rolled my eyes, passing the one I'd gotten for Noah as a peace offering as we slipped out of the tiny lobby and onto the street. "Because you're late, now get your sweaty butt out of here."

She kissed me, and I pushed her away after only a second. "Go, Parker!"

"Okay, okay." She grumbled, somehow managing to grab my waist coffee in hand and kiss me again before she dashed off.

"You taste like salt!" I called after her. "And not the good kind."

She turned, walking backwards. "What's the good kind?"

"You're a bartender, you tell me."

She smirked, facing the other end of the street before taking off at a jog.

I knew I'd see her again at the diner in an hour. But I knew she'd likely be late getting there, and she'd probably linger, and then she'd be late for work. I had a feeling Noah would have something to say about that. Even if it wasn't really my fault.

Parker

"So, how was the date?" Noah asked as I raced to slip on my shoes the next morning, nearly half an hour late. "You barely said anything last night."

"Good." I nodded. "Great, actually. We're figuring things out, I think."

"So, it was a date!"

I rolled my eyes. "I'm late, Noah, but... yes."

"Great, just great. I'm calling Willow. We need a game plan."

I slipped out the door and took off toward Ava's apartment at a full run.

I almost expected her to change her mind again, ask to take it all back, and pretend whatever happened at the end of that date hadn't happened. Maybe for her to avoid me completely. I braced myself for her to pull away when I tried to kiss her, or tell me she hadn't meant what she said. She didn't want me.

But she didn't. Everything was...normal.

She embraced me like this was okay. We were okay.

"Alright, so what's going on with you two?" Meg sighed, looking between me and Ava, who'd taken her break at my booth. "Spill the beans."

Ava blushed a little as she made room for Meg in the booth.

The diner was mostly empty. Just me and one other table.

"We had a... date." I looked at Ava as I said it, nervous about saying that aloud.

We decided not to define things, but that didn't mean that wasn't a date.

"Oh, good, then I can invite you both." Meg let out a sigh of relief, and Ava and I both frowned at her. "I've got a friend who's throwing me a birthday party, and I love you kids, so I wanted you to come, but I was not about to have some awkward tension and eye making from across the room."

Ava laughed. "We are not that bad."

"Honey, I could feel the awkward between you two from in the kitchen, and the only thing you should be able to feel near that cooktop is hot."

"Okay, that's fair." I grinned, pushing my pie around. "I'd love to be there. When and where's the party?"

"It's next Monday at this place on 5th and Cunningham—"

"The Taphouse?" I felt myself tense up.

"That's the place." Meg eyed me for a second before looking at Ava. "Should be starting around seven if you want to stop by."

"We'll be there." Ava smiled, looking between the two of us.

I wasn't so sure about it, though.

The Taphouse was Jayde's favorite bar. I couldn't begin to count the number of times I'd been dragged there so she could karaoke with her friends. It was nice enough, decent drinks, good staff, but I had avoided the place since she and I split, and I had no intention of going back, even for Meg. Which hurt me to even think about.

"Right, well, I'm going to go grab myself something to eat. You let me know if you need anything." Meg smiled, giving me a once over before she got up from the table. “And no presents. I’m too old for bows and all that nonsense.”

Once she was on the other side of the kitchen doors, Ava grabbed my fork and asked. “What’s wrong with The Taphouse?”

“Nothing.” I said, taking a sip of my drink. She wasn’t having it.

“Something. As soon as she said it, you went pale.”

“It’s just... another one of those places.”

“Don’t want to talk about it yet, got it.” Ava nodded. “Well, it’s for Meg, who has been there for us both, and last night you said that thing about making new memories in old places, so let’s do that.”

“Ava, it’s not—”

“I’ll be there with you. It’ll be great. And we’re gonna have to go shopping. I don’t care how old she thinks she is; I’m getting her a bow the size of her face.”

I smirked despite how sick I suddenly felt inside as Ava slid out of the booth and leaned in to kiss me.

“I really...” I sighed. “I really don’t think this is a good idea.”

“It’s Meg, though.”

And I nodded, thinking of all the times Meg had been there for me. What was the worst that could happen? I ran into my ex? That had happened a few times already.

Ava

Despite what we'd said, the look on Parker's face made me want to ask about The Taphouse. I just wasn't ready to pry if the expectation was that I had to spill all the painful truth about the places Cam had made me avoid, too.

I probably would have gone to one of those for Meg, though.

That weekend, performing felt different. I didn't feel like I was singing for a crowd. I felt like I was singing to Parker. And something about that felt dangerous. Even if the looks she gave me made me want to melt.

Those were dangerous, too.

By the time Monday came around, we were on a whole new schedule, which involved kisses each time I saw her, and Parker and Noah picking me up from work each night to drive me home. Noah seemed to have finally stopped glaring at me like I was the enemy, which was nice.

Parker and I went to the mall to find something for Meg, which turned out to be a lot more fun than I expected. The two of us knew Meg fairly differently, and that meant we couldn't even try to agree on what to get her. We ultimately settled on a gift card to the beauty store that I knew carried her brand of lipstick. But I still got the biggest bow I could find to put on the box.

Parker thought it was funny. I knew Meg would, too, even if she'd have a smartass comment to make about it.

I was shocked when Parker and Noah both showed up at my door Monday night, Noah with another bag in hand. I wondered what massive dinner he had planned with Willow because we had just thrown out the leftovers from the last one. Good as it was, they made way too much.

“Have fun.” Willow smiled at me after taking the bag from Noah so he could slip out of his coat and shoes.

“You, too.” I said back, taking Parker’s hand as we headed down to the car.

“How are you feeling?” I asked, giving her hand a little squeeze about halfway out of the building. We still hadn’t talked about The Taphouse or why she didn’t want to go.

“I’m fine.” She sighed, rubbing my knuckle with her thumb. “Just... promise we won’t stay too long?”

“We can leave whenever you want.” I smiled. “As long as I get to watch Meg open this box and find out there’s a gift card in here.”

Parker grinned. “Okay deal.”

Parker

When we got to The Taphouse, it was fairly empty. No sign of Jayde or her parade of pals. Just a very oddly gathered group of vastly different people ranging from Meg's age all the way down to a handful of little kids. I knew I couldn't have been the only person Meg had helped over the years.

I instantly felt better about coming.

"Oh, I'm so glad you girls made it." Meg came over to give us both a hug. She looked different out of her all-black uniform and into a dress with bright butterflies all over it, which was clearly more... Meg.

"Me, too." I smiled, meeting her knowing gaze.

"Here, I got you the biggest bow I could find." Ava gave Meg a sly grin.

Meg let out a huff, and wordlessly pointed to a table overflowing with gifts garnished with equally large bows. Next to it was a pinata in the shape of a woman, that had clearly been custom made a distinct bun on the top of the head and bright red lips.

"Looks like you're never too old for bows, huh?" I said, earning a smack to the arm.

Ava placed the gift on the table, and we went to the bar for drinks.

The evening started harmless enough. We had some cake; someone I didn't know smashed a plate full of whipped cream in Meg's face. Which made Ava laugh loudly enough that Meg threw some of it at her.

Everyone insisted Meg open her mountain of presents, all with large bows, the contents of which varied almost as much as the gifts Ava and I almost got her before settling on the gift card.

There was a single round of drinks. Then, before Ava and I even noticed, everyone was signing up for karaoke, singing wildly off key, whether because of the alcohol in their system or just because they couldn't sing.

Meg headed out around then, muttering something about valuing her ears, arms full of gifts that I helped her load up in her car. And then Ava and I waited for her turn at the mic.

Surprisingly, I was having a great time. Even with how familiar some of it was, it was still new. Because it didn't involve Jayde or her awful friends. And Ava was giving me far too many reasons to smile. Maybe just because she was having a good time herself.

I knew she wasn't much for parties, the club kind I was used to, but this was fairly tame by my standards. It was tame. It was fun. It was good.

And then.

"Parker?" a familiar voice called across the bar. "Oh, my god! It's so good to see you."

Ava

Parker went stiff as a board and ghostly pale as a woman called out to her from the doors. She was way too dressed up for a bar, even on this side of town. She'd fit right in at a club, maybe.

I didn't go to clubs, but that looked like something you'd wear clubbing. Bright green and sparkly, short with matching green heels I'd probably break something in.

Everything about her looked expensive. From her shiny hair extensions to her hand painted, rhinestone studded, inch long acrylic nails to the name brand handbag she had dangling from her elbow.

I watched as this woman wrapped her arms around Parker's shoulders, and even though I could see Parker not hugging her back, it bothered me. It bothered me like seeing Kaitlin with her in the coffee shop had bothered me, but this felt different somehow.

"I never see you out anymore." The woman grumbled, stomping her heeled foot like a toddler.

"Yeah, there's a reason for that." Parker rolled her eyes and took a long swig of her beer, not even looking in the woman's direction.

"Well, I miss you." She trailed her index finger up and down Parker's arm, and I watched the muscles in Parker's neck bulge. "Everyone does..."

The woman's eyes drifted to me, giving me a distasteful once over. "Who's your pretty friend?"

"Jayde, this is Ava. Ava, this is Jayde." Parker let out a sigh. "My ex."

Parker met my eyes for only a second before she looked ahead again.

This was Parker's ex? This woman whose current outfit probably cost more than every article of clothing in my closet combined? This snobby, stuck up, clearly two-faced party girl... that's... who Parker was into.

I knew I wasn't her type.

"Oh, don't say it like that." She stuck out her bottom lip at Parker, then turned to me as she said. "You know you can visit me anytime. I know how needy you are."

"What's that supposed to—"

"Actually, Ava," Jayde continued before Parker could finish. "I've heard a lot about you. A little birdy told me Parker had a new... project. I heard all about how... well, *not* needy you are."

I felt my cheeks burn, and my mouth fell open before I could stop it. I looked to Parker to say or do *something*. Because if there was something I was not good with, it was ex drama. Clearly, since I just ran from mine.

"Jayde!" Parker snapped, turning on her with gritted teeth.

Jayde smiled a sly grin as she took a step back. "Well, listen, it looks like the karaoke list is full, so we're gonna go. It was so good to see you. And Ava, nice to meet you."

Jayde touched my hand, and I yanked it away.

"Yeah, I wish I could say the same." I snapped back.

"Aww, well, don't worry. I have a feeling we won't be seeing each other again." The look she gave me should have scared me, but I was too angry for that. "Parker, really, don't be a stranger."

She gave us a wave and was gone, the little parade of her equally snobby looking friends following after.

I looked at Parker, inching closer so the rest of the bar wouldn't hear us. "When did you tell your ex about me?"

"Ava, I swear I didn't." She grabbed my hand. "Jayde knows literally everyone, so who knows who she heard about you from?"

"I don't just go around telling people I'm—" I sighed, shaking my head and taking a sip of my drink.

"I don't talk to her. Not if I can help it. I haven't seen her in months, but this is why I didn't want to come here. She's always here."

"It just bothers me."

"I'm sorry. Jayde's... well, there's a reason we aren't together."

"What is it?" I raised an eyebrow at her. "Because she doesn't seem to realize it's over."

She winced, letting go of my hand. She turned toward the bar and took a long drink from her beer. After a second, she let out a sigh.

"Jayde doesn't know what she wants." Parker said flatly. "That's the reason. Whatever she wants, it sure as hell hasn't ever been me."

I swallowed hard. How many times had I thought that same thing about Cam?

"Parker—"

"You know what?" She snapped. "You don't get to be mad at me over the things my ex does. Whatever Jayde does or doesn't think, that's on her. I said it's over, and that should be enough. I've made myself crystal clear to her more than once."

"I'm sorry."

She sighed, and I could feel my heart beginning to race. Suddenly, I didn't want to go home with Parker. I knew that was a stupid thought, but my brain couldn't stop from thinking about how this would go if I were still with Cam. I couldn't help but think about how this fight would escalate the moment we were behind closed doors.

Parker's not Cam. Parker's not Cam. Parker's not Cam.

I watched Parker pull out her wallet and toss a few bills on the bar between our drinks. Her arm was so close to me, just inches from my face. I didn't even realize I'd flinched until it had already happened, until the realization washed over Parker's face. Until I watched her anger dissipate the moment her eyes met mine.

My chest hurt. I felt my eyes swell. My sense of fight or flight kicked in, and I bolted from that barstool at a run.

"Ava—" I heard Parker call, but I wasn't stopping.

I was only a block down the street when I heard Parker running after me. I shouldn't have been surprised. I did yoga. She went for a jog every morning. And I was on the verge of a full panic attack.

She ran in front of me, and I stopped, nearly crashing into her chest. There was only a brief pause in which she looked at me, probably saw I was about to lose it completely, and wrapped her arms around my shoulders.

"Ava." she whispered into my hair. "Ava, no matter what happened... I'd never hurt you, okay? I'd never do that."

Parker's not Cam. Parker's not Cam. Parker's not Cam.

"You're safe." She said, rubbing my back. "You're safe with me."

And with one hand practically holding me upright, and the other cradling the back of my head, I felt safe. To cry into her chest in the middle of a busy sidewalk. To let her take me home and curl up with me. And to not make me talk about what had just happened.

After that, Parker and I started spending nearly all of our free time together. We started nearly every morning bumping into each other on the street. Normally Parker was late. She'd kiss me even though I was sweaty and gross, and then I'd see her again at the coffee shop, where I'd kiss her even though she was sweaty and gross. Then we both headed to work. She started to fill every spare minute I had.

I even started sacrificing some of my alone time on Tuesdays. I'd spend my breaks at the café on Thursdays at her normal booth. Sometimes I'd walk to Brickhouse with her, practice a few songs on the afternoon crown, *unpaid of course,* as Nathan had a fit the first time I did it.

This was so different. From Cam, or any of the relationships I'd had before her. Parker didn't demand anything, ever. She'd ask. And she'd listen. I found that really refreshing because I wasn't used to being in control. I wasn't used to having the option of control.

It was like Parker was taking everything at my pace, something I hadn't known I needed. We settled into the grey area of whatever this was. Jumped headfirst, really. We were in a sea of grey area, and the shore was black and white. I just didn't know how long we could tread.

Parker

Whatever this undefined thing was, it was pretty great for me. Jayde had been very public about the two of us, parading me around like some kind of puppet. She told me what to wear, how to act, who to be around. She was even bossy in the bedroom. I had to be present for all of her family events, all her friend's events, but she was never present for mine.

With Ava, she just seemed happy when I was around, as I was. It was like every day was that first date. No expectations, just us. Come as we are, be ourselves, and enjoy the time we had together. And we did enjoy our time. I'd never laughed as much with anyone as I had with Ava. But there were times... times it was clear we were walking a fine line between great and catastrophic.

I was a little rocky with the asexual side of things. I was okay with it, and understanding it more the more time I spent with Ava. But like everything else about her, the boundaries and where she fell on the asexual spectrum was new to me. We didn't talk about it, so the lines were unclear.

A couple months in, we were curled up on her bed watching movies. It wasn't the first time she'd taken a screen time break to kiss me instead of paying attention to the movie. I'd learned she had a thing for running her fingers over the sides of my hair where it was shaved. I... didn't always know what to do with my hands.

"Hey," she whispered, her lips meeting mine the moment I turned even the slightest bit in her direction.

Her hands went to my hair, and she giggled at me softly. My hand went to her waist—her bare waist, where her shirt had ridden up only a few inches. She was out of my arms so fast I didn't even have time to blink.

"I'm sorry." I stammered.

"Me too." She whispered, tugging at her clothes just out of my reach.

"You have nothing to apologize for."

"I shouldn't have—"

"No," I reached my hand out to her. "You draw the line, and I won't cross it."

She eyed me skeptically for a moment before she nodded and curled back up in my arms. Like it hadn't happened. Like everything was fine. She didn't kiss me again until I was leaving, though.

Everything was pretty different after that. There were rules, boundaries, lines we agreed to keep, but I thought maybe that was a good thing.

We agreed not to talk about things we weren't ready for. We agreed sexual things were off limits. We had to come to an agreement on what that really meant. It felt pretty normal to me, setting boundaries. Even though with Jayde, we'd had none.

Except those rules, those boundaries, they kept me from knowing her better. Sometimes, I felt like no one had known me better, and yet there were so many unanswered questions about her. When I tried to ask them, she'd pull away completely. And she stopped asking about my past, too. In fact, after a while, we stopped talking about anything that wasn't present and superficial.

All the while, I… did nothing. As Winter turned into Spring, we took more walks, spent more time outside, and I started actually enjoying that Ava walked literally everywhere. Because it just meant more time I got with her. And before I knew it, the summer was almost over. But as much as the seasons had changed, very little about us had.

We were still miles apart, using telephones and telescopes, playing make believe.

Ava

"So, do you actually know how to cook?" Parker asked one Tuesday, slipping her arms around my waist from behind.

I sucked in a shaky breath. I could feel her lips inches from my neck, breathing over me. I'd hated when Cam held me like that because I felt like I couldn't get away, but with Parker it was soothing. Because I knew there were no expectations. She was just holding me to hold me.

"Actually, yes." I laughed, reaching up to touch her face. "I taught Willow if you can believe it."

"What? No way."

I nodded, grinning.

"Growing up, my mom worked three jobs, so most of the time it was just me and Willow. Latch key kids."

Parker let out a soft laugh. I could feel her thumb absentmindedly caressing my ribcage.

"But," I continued. "I couldn't do everything, so I let Willow help. And she just fell in love with cooking."

"Why didn't she go to culinary school?"

"She realized as much as she loves to cook, she also loves animals. And being a vet pays better. She can still cook and be happy about it. She just claims Thanksgivings now."

"Her and Noah are going to fight so hard."

"Oh, I know." I said. "I have no idea how they've managed these massive cooking sessions in this tiny kitchen, to be honest."

"Maybe that's why Noah's starting bringing her to our place more." Parker said.

"Yeah, maybe. I just miss coming home to her cooking from time to time."

I heard a soft laugh, and Parker sighed, almost contented. "So, where's your mom now?"

"Oh," I sighed, unsure how I felt about getting into details. "She and her girlfriend live in—"

"Wait, she has a girlfriend?"

Her arms loosened for a second before she pulled me back in again, and I giggled.

"Yeah, they live in South Dakota. It was pretty cool. I came out of the closet, and instead of getting mad, she said 'lol me too.'"

Parker snorted. "Is anyone in your family straight?"

"My dad. My dad is definitely straight."

"Speaking of. How'd your dad take that? Your mom coming out, I mean."

The two of them were getting oddly close.

"Oh," I shrugged, which was hard with her chin resting on my shoulder. "He and my mom split when I was a baby. So, he didn't really seem all that surprised."

"I'm sorry. I bet that was hard."

"It's okay. I mean, he was still around, clearly. They just weren't good together."

Parker nodded.

"What about you?" I asked.

I felt her stiffen, and I reached a hand up to touch her face. She kissed my palm and let out a sigh.

"My mom left when I was little." She whispered. "Like really little. I don't even really remember her. Just flashes of her figure here and there. And my dad... he—he passed away a few years back."

I set down the spoon in my hand and turned around. She had this glassy look in her eye.

"My dad's actually the reason I believe in fate and the universe." Parker sighed, not really meeting my eyes. She was glued to our shopping list on the fridge. "He was always talking about faith. Not religion or anything like that. Just having faith that there was something. Something out there worth believing in."

"Sounds like he was a good guy."

"He was." Parker nodded. "He didn't care that I was gay. He told me soulmates come in all colors, shapes and sizes."

I felt a painful laugh slip out of my throat. I didn't know if I believed in soulmates.

"Did he think your mom was his soulmate?" I asked, wishing immediately I'd thought better of it.

"What? No." She laughed, looking back at me. "He said she gave him me. He always said my stepmom was, though."

"What happened to her?"

"She moved." Parker shrugged like it wasn't a big deal, but I could tell she was hurting just talking about it. "They met when I was in high school, so we weren't really that close. But I know she loved him. She comes back to town every now and again, and we have lunch, but I think she's mostly moved on."

"Thank you for sharing that with me." I smiled. I kissed her quickly before turning around. "I really don't want to burn this, though."

Parker let out a painful laugh. I couldn't tell if talking about her dad made her feel better or worse. But her attitude was different for the rest of the day, and then I realized I'd need to take things at her pace, too.

Parker

"So, I've been talking to Willow about Ava." Noah started from my doorway.

We were about five months in to the undefined thing.

"That sounds a little gossipesque, but go on." I nodded as I put away the laundry I was wildly behind on since I'd been spending so much time with Ava.

"Look, I just want you to be... careful."

I met his eyes, and I felt a swell of anger that I tried to choke down.

"What's that supposed to mean?"

"Willow... is worried about Ava." He sighed. "She doesn't think she's worked through all this stuff with her ex, and the way she talks about it—it's got me worried, too. But, about you."

"I'm fine, Noah, really. But thank you for the concern."

He scoffed. "Look, you have a habit of falling for women you think you can save, and it gets you hurt. I'm not saying Ava is Jayde—"

"She's not."

"I know that, but I think some of these things you're a little underqualified to help her through."

"I'm not trying to help her through anything. I'm just seeing where the road takes us."

Noah nodded; his frustration evident on his face. "So, what are you going to do when the band aid wears off, and you both realize she needs to actually work through trauma? Or... that you do?"

I let out a sigh. "I guess we'll cross that bridge when we get to it. But for the record, I'm not opposed to her going to therapy, and I've never not encouraged that. She chose to stop going, and so did I. And not because of each other."

"Right, the extra whole evening together has *nothing* to do with it."

"It doesn't. And even if it did, we could go to therapy together."

"Do you not see how codependent that is?" He scoffed. "At all?"

"Like you're not spending all your free time with Willow?" I tossed my laundry aside. I was too annoyed for chores.

"Willow has friends she spends time with besides me. Willow is desperate to see more of her sister, who she misses. She takes time to call her mom, and she takes time for *herself.* Ava doesn't even see her *dad* without you. What's the last thing you did by yourself? Besides work."

I let out a sigh and took a seat on the bed. Because I couldn't deny...he was right.

"That's what I thought." He let out a sigh, and the tension in his shoulders dissipated. "This isn't healthy, Parker. I just... I want you to be healthy, and, yeah, maybe I wasn't so sure about Ava at first, but at least for Willow's sake, I want her to be healthy, too."

I nodded. "Okay, I'll work on... some separation. I—I need to go visit my dad's grave anyway. I haven't really talked to Ava much about it."

"That's perfect. Maybe spend a night off... somewhere besides Ava's house, too, while you're at it."

"Okay." I sighed.

"I'm sorry, I just—"

"No, don't be. I—I want us to be healthy, too. I just. I didn't realize we weren't."

"Therapy might have helped with that."

I soft laugh escaped my throat. "Maybe."

"You should think about going back." He sighed, tapping slightly on my doorframe before edging his way out. "Or maybe...I don't know, going by yourself?"

I nodded, and he was gone, leaving me with no motivation to do my laundry.

That evening, I was supposed to spend it with Ava. We had an unspoken plan, but that had become fairly normal every day. And I was taking my conversation with Noah to heart, but I wasn't ready to talk about my dad any more than I already had. So, I headed to the diner on my way to the cemetery.

I was nervous, to say the least. How was I supposed to cancel plans with Ava without telling her what I was doing? I'd been trying my best since our first date not to compare her to Jayde, but I knew if I'd told Jayde I had something to do without her, and wouldn't say exactly what it was, she'd have thrown a fit.

"Hey, you." Ava smiled at me, sneaking a kiss near the front door where the rest of the diner wasn't fully visible. "I don't get off for another hour."

"Yeah, that's." I sighed. "That's why I'm here. I was wondering. Do you think we could maybe watch a movie another night? I have something I need to do. And I just... um..."

"Need to do it without me?"

I met her eyes, and she didn't seem angry, not even annoyed. In fact, she was almost smiling.

"Yeah, I know we—"

"Hey, you don't have to explain it." She smiled, squeezing my hand gently. "We agreed we'd be honest with each other, but we also agreed not to cross lines, right? So, if this is a line for you—"

"I don't know if it's a line, I just—"

"Ava, your order's up!" Autumn called from the kitchen.

"On it!" Ava said back, turning back to me in a lower tone. "Do whatever you need to. It's fine. Willow's been wanting a night just the two of us, anyway."

She snuck another quick kiss, and then backed away, slipping into the kitchen and leaving me wondering why I ever compared her to Jayde in the first place. Or why Noah thought we couldn't be healthy.

Ava

When I walked into the apartment, Willow basically had a four-course meal prepared and strung out across the small bar between the kitchen and our dining area. I didn't know how to tell her that after an entire day around food, I wasn't all that hungry. So, of course I ate it with a smile on my face.

And like I knew it would be, it was delicious.

She'd rented a movie, some romantic comedy I hadn't heard of, but knew the plot to the moment it started. Guy and girl meet, they both have problems, they deny any and all attraction to one another until they can't anymore. Then disaster strikes, they break up, and in one big magical moment, they end up together again.

We didn't watch the movie.

"I'm worried about you." She signed two minutes in.

I should have known this wasn't just a girls' night in. I let out a sigh, shifting, so that I was facing her.

"You need to be in therapy." She continued. "And Mom agrees. Do I need to stage an intervention?"

I laughed. Wasn't that what this was?

"No," I said. "I'm okay, really. I've... been a lot better lately."

"You're spending time with Parker to avoid your problems. That isn't better."

When did she get so insightful?

I eyed her for a second, my focus catching on the worry line between her eyebrows. The worry line she'd developed about the time Mom moved and she got a clearer picture of just how messed up I was. Because when it was just me and her, it was much harder to hide.

"Okay." I set my drink down. "I have been spending a lot of time with Parker lately, but she makes me feel better."

"Of course, she does. She's giving you affection and making you go out more, but you can't cover up your pain with Parker's love."

I cringed. "Whoa, nobody said anything about love."

"That's the problem!" She was turning red. "Why are you so afraid for her to love you?"

"We just... started seeing each other. We aren't even official yet. It's a bit early for that."

"It's been almost six months of her here almost every day, and you're not official yet?"

I let out a sigh. "I'm not ready for labels."

Willow nodded tersely. "Noah is my boyfriend; we see each other half as much as you and Parker do."

"Good for you."

Willow threw a piece of the kettle corn she'd made at me, and I glared back.

"You deserve a healthy relationship... for once."

She actually thought me and Parker weren't healthy. Which meant Noah probably thought so, too. And if my mom was involved... then my dad was probably involved. And that meant I really was just one misstep away from an intervention. But I wasn't even sure what I was doing wrong.

I let out a sigh and grabbed my drink again, turning toward the movie I'd missed the beginning of and was no longer interested in finishing, not that I'd been all that interested to begin with.

If Parker and I weren't healthy, then maybe I didn't know what a healthy relationship looked like.

Parker

After visiting my dad's grave, replacing the flowers, and chatting with his headstone about Ava for nearly forty-five minutes, I realized Noah was right. I did need time to myself. I needed time away from Ava that wasn't just for work.

I liked to think he could hear me, my dad. I liked to think he was listening and watching over me. And I often wondered if he'd be proud of how I turned out and what I was doing with my life. He'd probably be telling me exactly what Noah was, and that ate at me.

I took the long way back. The sun had been set for a while, so there wasn't much to see, but the extra fresh air gave me more time to think. I had no idea how I was going to talk to Ava about this. We'd never gotten around to getting serious about anything. We'd settled for easy.

When I got back home, Noah was on the couch watching tv. Samuel was playing with a bottle cap in the dining area. Seeing them there, so casual, made it seem if for a moment, that not much had changed. He still had the same haircut, his brown ringlets resting on the top of his head, and watched the same reality tv shows. But despite how similar everything looked, I felt different now.

I plopped down on the couch next to him and let out a deep sigh.

"You can say it, it's okay." He grinned, but he didn't look at me.

"You were right." I groaned, knowing I was making his already big head even bigger. He was too smart to be a chef. "I do need time for myself."

"Thank you. I'm glad you agree. How'd Ava take it?"

"Fine, actually. She seemed excited about spending time with Willow."

"Really?" He asked, glancing over at me.

"Yeah, why are you so surprised?" I raised an eyebrow at him, and he gave me an over-exaggerated shrug in return.

"No reason."

"I told you, she's not Jayde."

"I never said she was!" He said, raising his voice slightly, and then mumbled. "I think she acts like her sometimes."

"She doesn't though." I snapped, eyeing the smug look on his face. "Jayde was spoiled, entitled, and controlling. I did everything for her, and I never got a single thing in return besides constant criticism of everything I did. She had everything handed to her, her whole childhood, and she still had to live with me rent free."

"Ava is hard-working, she cares about people, and she fights me on paying for anything. She's never once tried to control me. And personally? I think she's been traumatized by someone in her past she's not ready to tell me about. The two are not the same."

Noah stared at me for a minute before letting out a sigh and turning back to the tv.

"She still hasn't told you about her ex?" He asked, his eyes still on the screen. It dawned on me that maybe he knew more about Ava's ex than I did.

"No," I sighed. "But honestly, that's fine because she doesn't know much about Jayde yet, either. We've been—"

"Not even covering your bases. You know talking about your past should happen by like the fourth date, right?"

"We've been taking things slow."

"No, you've been avoiding dealing with your problems, which might not have happened if you both had therapists. Separate therapists."

"You hate therapists." I said flatly, looking at the screen where some desperate housewives were arguing over something.

"Yes, yes, I do because therapy and working on myself is *hard,* Parker." He flipped off the tv. "Not because I don't think it's important. I hate being called out on my negative behavior, but that doesn't mean I don't think that's sometimes exactly what I need. If you told me right now that I should be in therapy, I'd at least consider it. But I'm not the one who was in a toxic relationship with someone who forced me to be someone else. I've never dated an overt narcissist. I consider myself lucky. I don't have your trauma."

I eyed him for a minute, and he let out a sigh.

"You're my best friend. I love you. I stand by what I said earlier. I want you to be healthy and happy, not blissfully ignoring the elephant in the room that is all of your trauma and hers."

I nodded. "Okay."

"Okay."

He got up and headed toward his room.

"I love you, too, Noah." I called as I slouched low on the couch.

I spent the rest of the night reading about overt narcissists, realizing all this time I thought Jayde and I weren't compatible. I hadn't realized she was actually abusive. Or that the back and forth was really... a cycle.

Ava

Parker started acting weird for the next week–distant. I wondered if Noah and Willow had something to do with it. Maybe they had staged an intervention after all.

First with the skipped plans for her... whatever it was she had to do. Which really wasn't a problem, but I didn't appreciate being bombarded by Willow instead. I hated being told she wanted to spend time with me only for her to turn around and parent me.

Then a few days later, Parker stayed over at the gym, something about her last day with Kaitlin. I didn't see her again until the next day.

She told me once she and Noah were going to have a "dude's night" which was hilarious but fitting to me. There was some speech about 'dude' being gender neutral. I said I didn't want to know any more about whatever it was they were up to.

I was trying not to be upset. Parker could have plans without me. She could do things without me, but... the vague way she was going about it reminded me a little too much of the way Cam just started going out and spending time with new people out of the blue. No warning, no communication.

I just couldn't tell her any of that. Parker didn't know about Cam. I couldn't tell her why I felt that way without sounding jealous and possessive unless I told her about Cam, and I was definitely not ready to unpack that load of baggage. Which only made me think about what Willow had said even more.

I felt lonely again.

So, I started trying to fill my time instead, mostly with music. All the extra time gave me room to practice chord progressions I hadn't taken the time for with Parker over every day. I'd been practicing, just not progressing.

I couldn't think of what else I was supposed to do. It wasn't like I had friends to call up. And I felt like I didn't always know when Parker would be free, so it was easier that way. To just... wait at home until she called or texted. Willow was right, that wasn't healthy either.

Meanwhile, Parker was always doing something. Maybe that was normal, but I'd just grown so used to Parker... always being around. I was sure there was a word for that. And maybe Carmen could have helped me, but I wasn't ready to go back to therapy either.

Things had just started feeling okay again. *I* had just started feeling okay again.

Parker

"Are we okay?" Ava asked that Tuesday at the diner.

I looked up to where she was standing next to my usual booth. She was fiddling with her pen and not meeting my eyes.

"Yeah, why?" I scooted further into the booth. "Come here. I know your last table left."

She flopped into the booth with a soft huff. "I just... feel like you've been really busy lately, and I didn't... I just wanted to know if it was something I did—"

"Ava, no."

I kissed her forehead, and she gave me a sad smile.

"I just—" I let out a sigh. "Noah and I had this long talk—"

"I knew it." She bit the inside of her cheek and slouched. "Those two are the nosiest—"

"They're right, Ava."

She glared at me, a tie between playful and serious.

"What?" I laughed. "We've been spending every waking minute together, and in all this time, we've never talked about the hard stuff."

"We agreed..." I saw her lip quiver and she bit it.

"I know." I said softly. Why was this so hard? "We agreed not to talk about something we weren't ready for, but it's been almost six months, and we hardly know each other."

"You know me better than anyone."

"Yeah, that's what I thought, too, but you don't know what I've been through, and some of that has made me who I am. That's important. It's hard to talk about, but it's important."

She let out a sigh and sat up straighter. "Willow said the same thing. Sort of."

"Okay, so how about we work on that?"

She eyed me and scrunched up her face.

"Don't look at me like that." I grinned. "I'm being serious. Come over tonight. We can... talk."

"Come over as in... your place?" She asked, her voice going up an octave.

I nodded. "Noah's got some family thing. Probably won't be back until tomorrow, and he said something about Willow studying for a big test. So, I probably shouldn't come over to your place. Why not?"

"I don't know." She said as the bell to the door rang, and she stood up.

"You don't have to answer right now." I shrugged. "You think about it and let me know."

"Okay."

She leaned in and gave me a quick kiss before disappearing into her section.

Ava

I hadn't been to Parker's apartment before. I didn't know why that made me nervous. She'd been at mine probably hundreds of times. But I'd been avoiding it for several reasons, the main one being I felt safer in my own room, where I could ask Parker to leave any time. Rather than feeling stuck across town. It reminded me too much of being stuck in the suburbs with Cam.

But I was also avoiding seeing or hearing anything Willow and Noah were up to. Ew.

"Hey you." Parker grinned as she opened the door.

"Hey." I smiled, kicking off my shoes. I did not want to have this talk. "So, you gonna give me the tour?"

She let out a soft laugh and nodded.

Parker's apartment was easily twice the size of mine. Their living room fit a giant sectional that I remembered briefly from photos, and had a balcony off to the side that they could actually put furniture on. She had an actual dining room with an actual dining set, and a kitchen with space for more than one person to cook. It had an island and these really pretty oak cabinets. It made more sense now why Willow was always there.

But it was their *bathroom* that made my jaw drop. It was about the size of my bedroom, with two matching sinks, what looked like actual stone countertops, and a massive soaker bathtub you never see in apartments.

"Oh my god, your tub!" I gasped. "It's huge."

"Oh, yeah, it's pretty great." She sighed, doing the neck rub thing. "Especially when I've gone too hard at the gym. It was one of the deciding factors on this place."

"I literally can't remember the last time I took a bath. Must be nice."

"Well, you're more than welcome to it."

I scoffed.

"I'm serious, Ava. Do you want to take a bath?" Parker raised an eyebrow at me.

"Uh no... I—I came here to hang out with you."

She shrugged. "I'll still be here."

I let out a laugh.

"Really, if you want to take a bath, feel free. I don't mind, and Noah is already gone."

I could feel a smile coming on, along with an idea. I could take a bath *and* hang out with Parker.

"What?" she asked, studying my face. "Why are you looking at me like that?"

"Do you want to take a bath with me?"

Her cheeks turned bright red, and she narrowed her eyes.

"Is this a trick question?" She whispered. "Nope, I'm not falling for it."

"It's not a trick question," I laughed. "Cross my heart. Take a bath with me."

She eyed me a moment longer.

"Please?"

"You can't just... 'please' something like that!"

I shrugged. "I just... did?"

She sucked a breath between her teeth. "Why?"

"Why not? You said you wanted to talk about the hard stuff. That's vulnerability. What better time than when we're stuck in a tub together?"

"I..."

"What are you afraid of?" I teased, grabbing her hips and watching her blush even more. "You guys have bubble bath, right?"

I didn't let go of her hips as I started backing through the bathroom door.

"Ava—" I heard her breath hitch.

I let go if her hips, my arms falling to my sides. I felt my own cheeks burn.

"I'm sorry." I said quickly, looking down at the floor because I couldn't bring myself to look back up at her.

She grabbed my chin. Nobody had ever done that before, not like that. It was this gentle, almost pleading thing. And when I met her eyes, she had this soft smile.

"You're so fucking confusing." She smirked.

Gah, I loved when she did that.

She kissed me quickly, and then stepped around me toward the tub. She didn't say a word as she flipped the fossette on and took off her shirt.

When she turned around, the only thing I could think about was abs. Holy abs. Tattoos on her hips that looked something like a zodiac sign. And a massive scar along her left ribcage.

Parker normally wore large flannels or bulky sweaters, or baggy hoodies. During the summer, I saw her in a few cut off tank tops, which did little for all the urges I had to poke and squeeze her biceps. But I'd never seen that much of her. I was too afraid to move that far. And Parker... never asked.

I'd never have known she was hiding rows of perfectly chiseled muscles, especially given how soft she was to cuddle with. And if I thought she had massive biceps before... whew.

"Everything okay?" Parker asked.

I wished then that I had a single solitary ounce of her confidence. She had this smug grin on her face when my eyes flashed back up to hers like she was enjoying this—being seen by me. And maybe she was.

I thoroughly enjoyed looking at her.

"Mhmm." I nodded, feeling my cheeks burn.

"Okay," Parker smirked, unzipping her pants as she walked over to the cabinet under the sink.

I watched as she dumped a ridiculous amount of bubble bath into the tub and then dropped her pants to the floor. You'd never know under the somewhat baggy men's jeans she wore, but Parker had a cute butt, too.

When she turned back around, she leaned against the tub, her arms crossed in front of her somehow in the least threatening way possible, looking at me rather expectantly. "You just gonna stand there gawking or what?"

I felt my cheeks burn again, and I bit my bottom lip. Her arms looked even more bulgy like that, and I wanted to touch them.

"Turn around." I grinned.

"Seriously?" She raised an eyebrow, but she was smiling.

I nodded.

"Okay," she said with a laugh.

I could see her in the mirror, which meant if she tried, she'd be able to see me, too, but she put her attention to the water temperature instead. That made me feel a little better, at least.

Parker had never seen me naked. She'd seen my morning hair too many times to count. She'd seen me asleep and snoring. She'd seen me briefly in a one-piece swimsuit. But there was something very specifically vulnerable about being completely naked in front of someone.

Mostly, I just hated my body. It was my biggest insecurity. I couldn't remember anyone else admiring me, either. And Parker? Well, I'd never met someone who put so much effort into sculpting their own muscles.

I felt like I'd just be a massive let down.

Originally, I'd thought this was a brilliant idea, but standing naked in Parker's bathroom was pretty nerve-wracking. It reminded me a little bit of the high school locker room, having to change in front of nearly all the girls in my class. I'd always opted for changing in the stinky bathroom stalls.

She was still just standing there, feeling the water, not even turning her head toward the mirror. It was weird because I'd never felt that respected.

I let out a deep breath and reached out to her. She took a shuddery breath when I touched her back, kissed her shoulder, and I saw her head turn towards the mirror.

"Eh," I pushed her chin back toward the tub.

She let out a chuckle. "What now?"

I didn't say anything. Instead, I ran my hands up her back to her sports bra, hooking my index finger under the band. I felt her stiffen and relax again as her breath hitched, but she lifted her arms as I slipped the bra over her head.

I could hear her breathing. It was faster now. Why did that give me so much satisfaction? Because I was completely in control of the situation, and I couldn't remember a single time I'd been naked and in control.

My hands slid back down her sides, and Parker caught them at her hips.

"Ava, you're going to kill me." She whispered.

When I glanced in the mirror, her eyes were closed, and it looked like she was doing a breathing exercise. I didn't quite get what that meant, but I knew she wasn't comfortable, and that most definitely wasn't part of the plan.

I let go, and she slid her boxers off herself.

Yeah, she had a cute butt.

"Get in." I said.

I heard her let out a laugh, but she climbed in the tub, and I got in behind her.

Parker

Why did I open up my big mouth? We could have cuddled, watched a movie, talked for a bit. Instead, I had Ava naked in my bathroom, taking my clothes off. Maybe that wouldn't have been a problem if I knew it wouldn't go anywhere. But I knew it wouldn't go anywhere, and I was okay with that. But something about knowing the boundaries even as her hands removed my clothes felt torturous.

I was surprised by how relaxed I was once we were settled in the tub. All the tense, nervous energy was gone. She was leaned against the back of the tub with me resting on her shoulder. Her hands were going through my hair in this soothing rhythm that made everything slow down. Or maybe it was the temperature of the water, a fine line just under scalding.

We were supposed to be talking, but when I was curled up in any way with Ava, I felt at peace just existing.

"What's this tattoo mean?" She asked after a few minutes, brushing a finger along my neck.

I felt a chill where her finger had been.

A laugh escaped my lips. "It's a rune."

"What's it mean?"

"It literally means I'm a lesbian."

"What?" She laughed.

"Mhmm." I nodded. "It means woman for a woman. It's a rune for love."

"Mmm." She sighed.

"What?" I asked.

"Nothing."

I turned my head to look at her, and she gave me a tired smile.

"Switch me."

"What?" She grinned.

"Switch me spots."

"Umm."

I didn't really give her a chance to answer. I just got out and waited for her to scoot up. But I noticed the way she pulled her knees up to her chest, like she was shielding herself from me.

When I slipped back into the tub, she was looking at me over her shoulder, but she hadn't moved.

"Ava, are you okay?" I asked.

She shook her head.

"Do you want to get out?"

"No," she whispered.

"What's wrong?"

She let out a big sigh. "All the bubbles are gone."

"Mhmm." I nodded. "That tends to happen."

She bit her lip. "I don't know if you've noticed, but water is see-through."

I let out a laugh. "I noticed that, yes. Are you afraid of me seeing you? Does that make you nervous?"

She nodded, looking ahead again.

"I have bad news for you." I whispered, wrapping my arms around her waist.

I felt a little hesitant about it, thinking back to that day in her room, but she let her knees drop slightly and leaned into me.

"You wear yoga pants five days a week. They leave very little to the imagination."

She turned her head slightly, and I saw her grinning.

"I'm serious, Parker." She sighed. "Have you seen yourself?"

"Once or twice." I shrugged, planting a kiss on her shoulder. "Have you seen yourself? Ava, you're beautiful."

She scoffed.

"I mean it."

I felt her relax, albeit slightly, and we leaned back against the tub again. She wove fingers through mine, and let out a sigh.

"What?" I asked.

She shook her head.

"You know, I wasn't always a gym rat." I sighed; I could do hard. "I used to... I used to have really bad body image issues."

She turned and looked up at me with a frown.

"Oh yeah, all through school I—I skipped meals, exercised a little too much—all cardio. I had myself convinced I had to be a certain size to be happy. It got... pretty bad." I let out a deep sigh. "My dad, he got me some help, and I discovered strength training. I eventually developed a healthier relationship with food. That's why I became a personal trainer."

"I thought you trained to show off your muscles, to be honest." I could see her grinning.

"You know I'm not going to look this good forever, right?" I gave her sides a poke, and she wiggled.

"Knowing you?" She looked up at me. "You'll probably still be going to the gym when you're sixty."

"You're probably right."

"And when I'm sixty, going to the coffee shop will be my daily exercise."

"Not if I bring it home for you on my way back from the gym." I poked her side again, and she let out a soft squeal, but she didn't stiffen at my insinuation like I expected her to. "I have goals."

"Oh yeah? What are they?" She grinned.

"To make you blissfully happy. I think it's working."

"You're so smug."

I let out a sigh. "Yeah, I know I seem smug, but deep down, I'm scared I won't get what I want like everyone else."

"And what do you want?" She asked, as she pulled one of my hands out of the water to place kisses on my fingers.

"A family."

She let out a sigh, both of our hands going back under the water.

"Who knew you could be so deep, Parker Watson?" She said it like a joke, but I felt my whole body go rigid.

"Don't call me that." I muttered quickly. Too quickly. God, that was harsh.

"Okay."

"I'm sorry, it's just—"

"No, I get it." She said, adjusting her whole body so she could look up at me. "Sometimes you associate something with someone else. Sometimes it's good, and others not so much."

Ava gave me a sad smile before she leaned in to kiss me. And then she settled back against my chest.

"Can we just stay here forever?" She sighed.

"Absolutely." I nodded. "We can barricade the door. Only open it for takeout."

She started giggling. "Oh, Noah would be so mad. How would he pee?"

"He lives at your house now, but we have a balcony, and we hate our downstairs neighbors."

She was giggling louder as she said, “That’s so gross. What’s wrong with them? Are they rude or something?”

“No, they just have really loud sex at weird times.”

“Oh god.”

“It’s horrific. We have to turn the tv on full blast. They sound like they’re trying to make a cheap porno.”

That did it. She was laughing loudly for a good minute before she settled down and let out a sigh.

“What’s wrong?” I asked.

“My fingers are all pruney and the water is getting cold.” It came out as a grumble.

“So, what you’re saying is that you want to get out, but you don’t want to get out?”

She nodded before letting out a sigh as she leaned forward.

“Parker!” I heard my name come out of her throat in a whine.

“What?” I sat up.

“Look what you did!”

I looked over to where her clothes were sitting on the floor, in a puddle, probably from when I got out to switch places.

I let out a laugh.

“Parker, that’s not funny!” She grumbled again. “What am I supposed to wear? I don’t know if you’ve noticed, but—”

“You have a butt?” I grinned. “Oh, I noticed.”

Her cheeks flushed, and I got out, feeling her eye me while I grabbed a towel and wrapped it around my waist.

“I have clothes you can wear.” I leaned in, pausing inches from her face. “Unless you’d rather stay like this.”

She frowned, and I kissed her fast.

“I’ll be right back.”

“Okay,” she sighed.

Ava

We had to have been in that tub for an hour at least. I was completely naked in a tub with Parker for an hour, and not once did she try to make a move, or make me uncomfortable. If anyone was doing that, it was me.

Why did this feel so right and so wrong at the same time?

Parker gave me this dangerous feeling every time she touched me. It was this comfort that I couldn't remember ever feeling with anyone, especially Cam. Like I was home. Like I was safe. Like nothing could hurt me.

And I couldn't shake the question of why.

Why did Parker do that? Why did she let me curl up against her chest, between her legs, completely exposed and vulnerable, and not even... ask?

I felt like I was waiting for Parker. Waiting for her to change. Waiting for whatever cover she had to drop. She couldn't just be this *good*, right? She couldn't just be this okay going... without? That's not how it works. I was waiting for her to change her mind and just admit that she needed something from me. That eventually, we'd have to cross that line for this to work.

I sat in the tub after she'd gotten out for a minute with a sense of resolve setting in. Because why couldn't I give her something she needed? It felt like she was always doing that for me, always going out of her way to make sure I was okay.

I grabbed a towel and followed her down the hall. When I stepped into her room, Parker still had the towel around her waist, and I could see all the muscles in her back. It was like she was all muscle. Hard as a rock. So how was she so freaking soft?

There was a part of my brain that went to this dark place I hadn't been in for a long time. There were expectations here. Weren't there? We'd never been this vulnerable before, but now that we were, I couldn't ignore it. Two people, alone and naked together? Two people who'd been... in an undefined thing for nearly half a year, and hadn't moved past kissing?

I knew what Cam would say. Parker would get tired of waiting. She'd leave. Because I wasn't good enough as I was. And if I wanted to keep her, I needed prove that I wanted her. Or she'd just get it from someone else. Just like Cam.

I swallowed a golf ball sized lump in my throat and wrapped my arms around her waist.

Cam was wrong. I could make Parker happy. I could be enough.

Parker

I felt Ava's hands slip around my waist, slow enough it gave me chills. It brought with it that feeling I'd had when she'd taken off my bra.

"Hey you." I grinned as she planted kisses on my shoulder blades.

"Hey," she replied.

Everything had seemed fine just a few minutes ago. We were laughing and happy, and I thought it might actually be okay to talk about some of the tough stuff. Why did Ava suddenly sound sad? Or maybe nervous. I couldn't be sure.

I turned around, and her hands went to my hair before I could ask. Her lips met mine in a rush, and by instinct, I grabbed her waist. There was always a warm feeling that filled my entire body when I was kissing Ava. This felt different, and I became hyperaware of the fact that the only thing between us was towels.

Why did being naked around Ava feel so different in that tub?

A part of me could feel her pushing me backwards, toward my bed. But my head was in such a whirl, I couldn't focus on anything but her lips. And her tongue. And her teeth.

She shoved me down, playfully, and I had a split second of coherent thoughts before she was on top of me, lips on mine, straddling me.

My brain was screaming because I knew what she was doing. Ava didn't kiss me like this. She didn't kiss me like she was building me up. And as much as a tiny part of me wanted Ava in that way—it was hard not to. The rest of me knew we'd drawn lines for a reason. And I couldn't think of a good enough reason for her to want to cross them now.

Her lips made their way to my jaw.

"Ava..." I whispered. Shit, my throat was dry.

Once she started kissing my neck and biting along my collarbone, the words wait and stop got lost in my throat. Because her hands had now made their way to my hips. She was holding them with this intense pressure that made the whole room feel warm. My heart beat was pounding furiously against my eardrums.

The urge to pick her up, turn this around, climb on top of her washed over me. Because I knew that's what Jayde would have wanted. That's all Jayde ever wanted. But Ava wasn't Jayde. Ava wasn't anything like Jayde. Maybe I didn't know what Ava wanted, but I had a feeling... this wasn't it.

"Ava, stop." I breathed, and she pulled away instantly. "What are you doing?"

"I thought it was obvious." She murmured, and a blush crept its way up her neck.

"I thought... you said sex makes you uncomfortable. You said you weren't sure about it."

"I also said, if I'm with someone and they're into it, it's different." She paused. "And you're into it. Right? Into... me?"

"Yeah, but—"

"Then I don't see the problem."

"The problem is—I—" I let out a shaky breath, realizing her towel had mostly come loose, and I could see far more of her now than I could in the bathroom.

I looked back up at her eyes. *"You're* not into it."

"But you are?" She frowned at me like I was being ridiculous. Like this was simple, and she had no clue why I could possibly feel any different.

"Just because I am doesn't mean we have to—you don't have to do that. Who told you that you have to do that?"

"What if I want to?"

I let out a breath. "Do you?"

She eyed me for a second, her confidence wavering. "I don't know."

"Okay." I pushed the damp hair out of her face. "Well, if and when you figure that out and decide, we can talk about it. But you don't have to do something you're not one hundred percent sure about. Not for me. Hell, not for anybody else either."

She nodded slowly.

"I'm fine with things exactly as they are, okay?"

Her eyes started to glisten.

"Come here." I wrapped my arms around her and picked her up.

The tiniest, most adorable squeal came out of her throat, and then we were resting against my headboard. She curled up under my arm, and I felt a little shudder run through me. I still didn't have a shirt on, but I wasn't about to get up.

"Do me a favor?" Ava asked. She had a sly grin.

"What?"

"Don't shave this. I like it."

She ran a finger along the thin patch of hair that ran from my belly button down under the towel.

She really was going to kill me.

Ava

Parker and I never got around to talking that night. I knew that's exactly what we needed, and I did plan on getting there. The more Parker proved to be nothing like Cam, the more I wanted to trust her. It just never felt like the right time to tell her everything I needed to say. As much as I believed her when she said we'd been through similar things, I didn't think she was quite prepared for just how bad things had been with Cam.

On Saturday, I'd only just put my guitar away when I saw Nathan coming my way. He didn't talk to me much on the nights I played, other than to suggest songs for me to play. And he'd never come up to me when I was leaving. He had his hand behind his back all awkwardly, and he didn't make eye contact with me until he was three feet away.

"So," He sighed. "You've done pretty well the last few months, bringing in a bit of a crowd on the nights you sing, and I never miss anyone's birthday, so here."

He passed the card over without looking at my face, which I didn't necessarily mind. It wasn't like we'd spent a ton of time getting to know each other over the last few months. From the way Parker talked about him, Nathan was like that with everyone.

"Thanks, Nathan." I nodded, forcing a smile.

He nodded back, and then he was gone. I eyed the lavender envelope and tucked it into my guitar case.

"I didn't know your birthday was coming up." Parker said from behind me, making me jump.

"Yeah," I sighed. "That's because I don't celebrate it."

"What? Why not?"

I sucked a breath of air through my teeth, the memories of all the ruined birthdays I'd spent with Cam flashing through my mind. The words *'birthday sex'* echoed through my head.

"I don't really like birthdays." I shrugged, but I could tell Parker wasn't buying it.

"Is this one of those things?" She asked.

I eyed her for a second before nodding.

"Well, you know what that means, right?"

"No." I groaned. "This isn't one of those—"

"Oh, yeah, we are making new memories." She grinned.

"Parker... I don't know."

"It's your birthday. Let me at least try to make that a good thing. Nothing big, just you and me."

She was looking at me with a hopeful grin, that playful glimmer in her eye that I'd noticed she got when she really wanted to make me happy. Cam had never wanted to make my birthday good. My birthday wasn't about me. It was always a gift for her with my name on it.

"Fine, but if you throw a surprise party, I will walk out."

"That's fair." She nodded, a wide smile spreading across her whole face.

"I gotta go."

"Be careful. We'll pick you up in a bit?"

"Yeah," I sighed, stepping back toward the doorway so Nathan couldn't see us from the sound booth window.

Parker gave me a quick kiss, taking my guitar like she'd started doing, so I didn't have to carry it from Brickhouse to the department store.

"Thank you." I whispered, giving her hand a squeeze before ducking out the back door.

I could do birthdays again. Maybe with Parker it wouldn't be so bad.

Parker's best friend dating my sister was turning out to be a real problem. There were no secrets anymore. Between Noah and Willow, Parker and I could not do anything without it going around to the entire family like a gossip chain. Nosey Nellie's the both of them.

Sunday afternoon, I got a call from my mom.

"Hey, baby girl!" My mom said cheerily. "I heard you're going out for your birthday."

"Dammit, Willow." I sighed, taking a seat on my bed. "Yes, Parker and I are going out for my birthday."

"Aww, that's great, sweetie."

"It's really not that big of a deal."

"Of course, it is. You've been anti birthday since—"

"I know." I bit the edge of my thumbnail.

"I've got something coming in the mail for you. Should be there on time."

"No, Mom! You didn't have to... I didn't need anything."

"You need a lot of things, but that's beside the point." There was a beat where my mom was oddly quiet. "I can't wait to meet this girl. I know Willow thinks you're spending an awful lot of time together, maybe too much, but I think that's just the lesbian way."

I let out a loud laugh. Whether I was a lesbian or not, she was right.

"Am I wrong? Me and Mae moved in together in what... six months? When you know, you know."

A lump rose in my throat. I didn't have the heart to tell her why Willow thought what she did. Willow didn't think we were moving too fast. She thought we weren't moving at all, and she was right. For all the time Parker and I spent together, we were still practically strangers. We knew each other's mannerisms to the T, but when it came to the inner workings, both of us were walking on eggshells.

"I think this will be healing for you." My mom said softly. I think the last time she'd used that tone was when I'd shown up on her doorstep after I'd left Cam. "You've been so afraid to embrace the things Cam screwed up for you."

I winced at the sound of her name. Just hearing about her still made me shake.

"Yeah." I whispered. My eyes were getting misty, and I couldn't stop myself from sniffling.

"I'm sorry, sweetie. I didn't mean to upset you."

"No, it's okay."

I looked over at the photo on my dresser of me, my mom and Willow. I was in the center, wearing my cap and gown. Who was that girl? Because I didn't recognize her anymore. That wasn't me, not anymore. Cam had ruined that girl. She'd taken every beautiful thing about her life and twisted it into something ugly. Until that girl became me—someone who struggled enjoying anything Cam had tarnished, which was everything.

"It's okay to move on." My mom whispered. "It took me a long time to admit it after I lost James. I know that's not the same, but grief and trauma, they both change us. They both make it hard to enjoy things or embrace new, happy things."

Now I was crying.

Parker

I'd never met someone who was this against birthdays. I tried to ask the person with the most intel, so I knew what to get her, and apparently, we were all on a present ban. No gifts. No parties. No decorating. No telling anyone when her birthday was. According to Noah, who got the information from Willow, Ava hadn't celebrated her birthday in four years. She stopped celebrating before she and her ex split, and had been anti-birthday ever since.

I'd thought Jayde was bad.

I was really struggling to plan out something so simple for someone who was normally great at gifts and planning. I'd never struggled with birthdays before. But I wanted to make Ava's birthday great. I wanted to make new birthday memories for her. I just didn't want to go too far.

"So, where do you want to go?" I caved Sunday morning when I saw her at the coffee shop. "For your birthday."

"I don't know." Ava shrugged, eying Jane, who was busy making coffee and didn't seem to be paying attention to our conversation. "But I don't like cake, so maybe somewhere with good pie."

"You ate cake at Meg's party." I pointed out.

"Because it was Meg, and I wasn't about to be rude."

"Alright, no cake."

"Thank you." She smiled, but there was a sad look in her eye.

"Hey, we don't have to do this if you really don't want to." I said quietly, as I pulled her closer to me and kissed the side of her head.

"I know." She sighed, leaning into me, her arms wrapping around my waist. "My mom thinks it'll be good for me."

"You told your mom?" I raised an eyebrow and tried to crane my neck to look at her.

"Oh no, Willow did."

I let out a laugh. "Right, that makes more sense."

"Those two gossip so much." She grumbled. "I can't tell her anything without knowing what Noah thinks about it."

"I think that's how it's supposed to be, actually." She frowned up at me. "I mean, sure, have privacy from whoever you're... with. When it comes to... private things? But secrets... I think it's normal for Willow to tell her boyfriend everything, or to want to."

Our names were called, and Ava pulled away. But it felt like more than a few feet between us all of a sudden. I was painfully reminded of all the secrets I'd had to keep with Jayde to maintain peace. All the little lies I'd told just to avoid a fight that sometimes bubbled up, anyway. Every time I'd avoided saying what was on my mind so she didn't threaten to leave.

If Cam had been anything like Jayde, and I had a feeling she'd been worse, maybe Ava was keeping secrets and holding back because she thought it was keeping her safe. From me.

The thought made my chest ache.

Ava had gotten serious about this whole new memory thing. She was far more dressed up than me. I was trying to keep it casual, but I kind of liked seeing her in a dress, looking fancy for her birthday, and me wearing jeans. It meant she got to be the center of attention on her own birthday, maybe for the first time in a long time.

But I'd had to talk her into not going back upstairs to change. We were already late, big surprise.

I handed her a tiny box with a big bow, and she glared at me playfully. "I said no presents."

"Yeah, well." I smirked back at her. "This one was Meg's idea, so I think the two of you might be even for the very big bow you got her."

Ava let out a laugh and climbed into the car. She waited until I was in the driver's seat to open the box, saying several times that she didn't need anything. But she was beaming when she pulled the necklace out of the box. It was a tiny gold guitar pick, personalized by a small jewelry shop midtown.

"Oh, my god. Okay, I actually love it."

"Read the back."

"Through dangers untold and hardships unnumbered." She looked up at me, her eyes glistening.

"I know that's your favorite movie, but I kinda felt like that particular quote fit you pretty well." I smiled. "I may not know all of it yet, but I know enough to know you've been through a lot."

"Parker that's—probably one of the best gifts I've ever gotten." She whispered, leaning over the console to kiss me. "Okay, let's go before I change my mind. Something bad always happens on my birthday."

I let out a laugh and started the car. "Not tonight."

The place I settled on was oddly one of the few places I'd been to with Jayde that was more my vibe than hers. It was strikingly similar to Brickhouse in design, but was set up with food as the focus instead of alcohol.

Noah had loved that about it, so we'd both been a few times. As much as the memory of bringing Jayde there still stumbled through the back of my mind, I'd already rewritten that memory.

And bringing Ava only made that rewrite stronger.

"Isn't this place your competition?" She smirked over the menu. It was on the same side of town and had a similar vibe.

"I'm a bartender," I laughed. "And I feel no deep sense of loyalty to Brickhouse, anyway."

Ava nodded sarcastically.

"Do you want to go somewhere else?" I asked, raising an eyebrow at her. "Because I do know this place across the Boulevard that doesn't even have the prices on the—"

"This is fine." Ava's eyes went wide. "It's really nice, actually."

"Well, this place has the best chocolate cream pie I've ever tasted, so I hope you like it." I let out a big sigh.

"You've been here before?"

We locked eyes over the menu for a second, and I nodded tersely.

"Two memories, one date, got it." She smiled, looking back down.

"I thought it might... make you feel better if you weren't rewriting memories alone."

"It does, actually."

She bit her lip and let out a sigh. I caught a glimpse of the necklace I'd gotten her sparkling against her collarbone, and even though I knew Ava and I had a long way to go, I felt like everything was going to be okay.

Ava

Something bad always happened on my birthday. Always. At sixteen, my cake caught the kitchen on fire. Seventeen, I sprained my ankle as we left for a restaurant. At eighteen, Cam "lost" the gift she'd gotten me, and after a huge fight, I let her use my debit card to buy a new one. At nineteen, the neighbor heard Cam screaming at me and called the cops. I had to lie and pretend we were watching a movie.

That was the last birthday I'd celebrated. Because my story wasn't convincing. It was my fault the cops were called. I made her look bad. And I had to make it up to her.

As Cam and I went to bed that night, I promised myself I'd never celebrate another birthday again. Because I couldn't handle the disappointment, the disasters, or reliving that night in my mind.

Somehow, Parker was making all of that seem like a distant memory. Rewriting was working. I was having fun. Her gift wasn't just meaningful, I hadn't had to pay for it. The chocolate cream pie was really good. And nothing had gone wrong.

I knew when we left that restaurant, there wouldn't be any expectations waiting for me back at her apartment. We'd curl up, watch a movie, and fall asleep. The end. Roll the credits. I didn't owe her anything.

Or so I thought.

"Parker?" a woman called across the room.

"Lexi?"

The woman came up at full speed, and I watched Parker get up and give her a one-armed hug. Her arm lingered on Parker's for a moment as she shifted so her back was mostly to me. Sure, that wasn't obvious at all.

Was I jealous?

"I haven't seen you in like forever!" The woman practically groaned, reminding me an awful lot of Jayde. "You don't go to the clubs anymore?"

"Nah, I pretty much left that scene." Parker shrugged, looking to me with a sheepish smile.

"That's a shame. We miss you. Jayde's been a bore as per usual."

I swallowed hard, pushing my pie around with my fork.

"What have you been up to?"

Parker stuffed her hands in her pockets. "Just working mostly."

"You always were such a hard worker."

Blech.

Parker smiled awkwardly in response, her eyes flashing back to me only briefly.

"So, what are you doing here?" The woman asked, still having not acknowledged my existence.

"Oh, it's my girlfriend's birthday," Parker smiled over at me. "So, we're celebrating."

The woman turned back to me, and I gave a less than enthusiastic wave. Her entire attitude changed. Her hand finally dropped from Parker's arm. I would have been relieved, but my mind was still lingering on one word in that sentence.

Girlfriend.

"Guess we know why you left the club scene." She gave me a stink eye that Parker couldn't see.

Parker blushed. "Yeah, but I left before—it just didn't feel like me anymore."

The woman scoffed. "Well, when you come back, hit me up."

She ran a hand down Parker's arm again–*why was that a thing*–as she walked away, and it made me rage.

Parker took her seat again, sighing while she shook her head. When she looked up at me, her lighthearted expression fell.

"What?" she asked. "What's wrong?"

"Can we go?" I felt my eyes drifting three tables over to where Lexi and her friend had sat in full view of us.

"Look, Lexi can be pretty—"

"Can we go?"

She took a sharp breath and nodded, waving down our waiter.

I didn't care what Lexi was like because I didn't care to know her. Sure, it annoyed me seeing her flirt with Parker right in front of me, but I could handle that. It was apparently a thing amongst Jayde and her people. And Parker didn't seem willing to set any clear boundaries with her ex, but I didn't feel I was in the right to say anything about it again.

I was more upset that she was telling people I was her girlfriend. We had agreed, no labels. We'd agreed on undefined. That was the beauty of the grey space. That's how I worked around my rules. That's the only way Parker and I were okay.

And here Parker had gone around and fucked it all up.

Because suddenly me and Parker were black and white, crystal clear. And that terrified me.

Parker

"You can't just go throwing words around without talking to me about it." Ava snapped as we stepped into my room, tossing her little purse on my bed with an unmistakable fury.

"You're right. I should have talked to you about it." I let out a sigh and ran my fingers through my hair. "I just... we've been doing—this. Whatever this is. Ava, it's been six months."

"I don't care. We agreed, no labels."

I nodded. "I know. I'm sorry."

"What if I'm not ready to be someone's girlfriend?" She raised an eyebrow.

God, she was so mad. She'd never yelled at me before. We'd never had a fight; we'd barely even had a disagreement. We'd always breezed over everything, laughed it off. We didn't take much of anything seriously. But I could tell this was a serious, genuine fight. And all over a single word.

I felt a lump rising in my throat. I'd never once thought Ava was just like Jayde, but at that moment, that's exactly how it felt. I'd said the wrong thing, a tiny little slip up, and now it was a full-blown fight, fuming and passive-aggressively ignoring me the whole ride home. Making me wait until I asked what I'd done wrong, stewing about it, until she was screaming instead of just talking about it calmly.

And because it reminded me of Jayde, there I was retreating back to those old habits—do whatever it took to de-escalate—say whatever it took to keep the peace.

"Okay, so you're not my girlfriend." I said slowly. "That's fine."

"Is it?"

I rubbed the back of my neck. Of course, that wasn't good enough. "I don't know, Ava. I really don't."

She let out a soft laugh, looking away, out the window at the city lights, like she'd rather be anywhere but here.

"Be honest with me. You'd be hurt if I started seeing someone else, wouldn't you?"

Her eyes snapped back to me, and I could see them pooling up. "Is that what you want?"

"No! I don't—fuck..." I let out a sigh. "I don't want to see anybody else. That's not what I meant. I just—we don't see anyone else, right? We are exclusively seeing each other. I don't know what else to call you. It's easier—"

"So, you want to call me your girlfriend because it's easy?"

I closed my eyes and let out a breath. "Stop twisting my words. You know that's not what I meant."

She was chewing on the inside of her cheek when I looked at her again.

"Ava," I swallowed hard. "What is this? You and me, spending every free minute together? We've spent six months getting to know each other, opening up, albeit slowly. What do you call that?"

She started chewing on her thumbnail, and didn't respond.

"I don't have a problem with not using labels, or I didn't when this all started because I thought eventually, we'd grow into it. But if that's not the case, I'd just like to know why."

"Because I'm not ready! Because the last time—" She stopped, catching herself like she did anytime she almost told me something about Cam.

I only knew it was Cam because of Willow. I only knew what little I knew because of Willow. Because Ava didn't tell me anything. She was afraid of telling me anything, afraid of getting too close, and I knew that because this was a fight response.

"Last time, what?" I asked slowly, calmly. There was no way she was opening up to me if I couldn't chill out.

She shook her head, and a single tear fell down her cheek.

"Ava, you can tell me, it's okay."

She shook her head harder, taking a step back as she covered her face with her hands. I wrapped my arms around her. For a second, I thought she'd push me away, but she cried into my chest instead.

"I'm not her." I whispered into her hair.

"I know." She mumbled into my chest before pulling away.

"Then why don't you trust me?"

"Because you're going to change your mind."

Her words hung in the air for a minute, and I felt my heart racing in my chest.

"Maybe not today." She said, barely over a whisper. She was shaking. "Maybe not tomorrow, or next week, or next month, or even next year. But eventually, you'll realize that I'm not enough."

Her bottom lip was quivering. I'd never seen her hurt like that. She'd had all these walls up this whole time, and after six months, this was the most vulnerable and honest she'd ever been with me.

"What if I don't? Ava, what if I want to keep fighting for you every day for the rest of my life?"

That did it. She started sobbing and fell back against my chest. I could feel her knees going weak, so I walked her to my bed, and I just let her cry. Back when I was going through ED recovery, a therapist had told me you have to feel it. It doesn't just go away. If you bottle things up, eventually, they spill out.

I had a feeling that's what this was. I hadn't seen Ava cry quite like this before. We'd never touched the hard topics. We always stayed on safe discussion, small talk. We were biding time and staying blissful for as long as possible, but this was real, whether we liked it or not. This was the consequence of all that bottling.

We laid there, her head on my chest, sobbing until my shirt was soaked for just under an hour before she settled into sniffles, and eventually went quiet all together. I thought she might have fallen asleep.

"Her name was Cam." she whispered, and she immediately had my attention. "And I didn't think I could ever love someone as much as her. But by the time it was over, I didn't think someone could ever hurt me as much either."

Ava told me all about Cam. How they'd met, and all that Cam put her through. She cried, I cried. But I didn't interrupt her. I didn't say a word; I didn't dare. She was finally spilling. It felt like she might have been telling me things even Willow didn't know.

Because Willow didn't say Cam was abusive. She didn't say Cam had isolated her from everyone she loved. She didn't say anything about Cam being manipulative. But suddenly all the things Ava had said to me, especially in the beginning, made sense. The way she'd flinched that day at the Taphouse made sense.

I hated Cam.

I'd never realized I could hate someone so much without even knowing what they looked like. And I'd never been much of a hateful person. Jayde had all but ruined my life, and I didn't hate her. But if there was ever anyone I'd like to punch on sight, it was Cam.

How can you hurt someone you claim to love like that? Especially someone like Ava?

I knew one thing was absolutely certain: I'd never do that to her. I didn't care how many therapists I had to get, how much growth I had to do—and I knew I had at least a little—I would never be like Cam.

Ava

I was alone in Parker's bed when I woke up the next morning, the smell of her cologne lingering on the pillow. My head was throbbing, which happened when I ugly cried, but it had been a long time since I'd let myself do that, much less in front of someone else.

I could hear voices carrying from the other room. I got up, hoping Parker might have a Tylenol. When I heard my name, I froze.

"So, what happened with Ava last night?"

Parker sighed. "We just... had a lot to talk about, I guess. I'm not going into detail. It's not my story to tell, but she's been through a lot."

I let out a sigh. I was grateful Parker didn't gossip like my sister.

"Well, these walls aren't soundproof, you know?" I heard Noah set something on the counter with a clang. "Are you two okay?"

Parker was quiet for a minute, and I could hear my heart racing in my ears. I'd never told anyone about Cam. I thought for sure if there was anything that would make someone reconsider a relationship, surely it was emotional baggage the size of Texas.

"I think so." Parker said finally. "I think we've got a long way to go, though."

"Oh, no need to tell me. Don't think I didn't hear that bit about 'the rest of my life.' But as long as you're willing to do the work, I support."

I heard Parker let out a soft laugh. "It doesn't feel like work, though. None of this has ever felt like work. I mean, I know it's not perfect, but I know it's right. She's just–she's my person, Noah."

"Your person?" Noah said. "What does that even mean?"

I felt a lump rising in my throat. *Please don't say love. Please don't say love.*

"I think she's it for me." Parker sighed. "She's *that* person. When my dad used to talk about true love and soulmates, this is exactly what he was talking about."

Fuck.

"You gonna tell her that?"

"Eventually, when the time's right." Parker cleared her throat. "I don't think she's ready for that yet."

Nope. Nope, nope, nope. I could not do this.

This was too black and white. Too crystal clear too soon. To go from undefined to girlfriend, to vulnerable and in love and soulmates in twenty-four hours was way too much for me, and suddenly, I was in a full panic.

This is why I didn't come to Parker's place. I had to get out.

I turned around and started grabbing my stuff. I had a whole bag at this point of laundry and random crap strung around Parker's room.

Six months. I'd been tiptoeing around this grey, undefined thing with Parker for six months. This is what I got.

I shouldn't have told her about Cam. We shouldn't have started this in the first place. I should have trusted my gut instincts and stayed as far away from Parker as I could.

"Whoa," I heard Parker from the doorway, and I froze. "Everything okay?"

Parker

Ava was sleeping soundly when I woke up the next morning, which seemed pretty odd to me because she was always the first one up. But her eyes were still puffy, and I remembered crying like that once or twice. It took a lot out of you.

I could just barely hear Noah in the kitchen making breakfast, and the fear that he'd overheard our fight set in. But he smiled at me when I slipped into one of the barstools, and he passed me a cup of coffee.

After all the negative things he'd said about Ava, it was weird seeing him approve again. He'd amped me up so much in the beginning, then taken all of that back when Ava wasn't... well, Willow. I knew he just wanted me to be happy, but I couldn't help but feel hurt not having his support throughout this whole thing. I knew what I wanted, and I didn't care that it wasn't easy going.

Good things are work sometimes.

I heard a shuffle from my room. Noah gave me a knowing nod and passed me a coffee for Ava. I figured she might need it. The last time I'd cried like that, it left me with a headache from hell.

There was a sniffle when I reached the hallway, and I stepped in to find her frantically shoving a t-shirt into her duffle bag. It wasn't the t-shirt that painted a clear picture, though. It was that

I couldn't see anything else of hers around the room anymore. There had been tiny traces of her strung about for a couple of weeks, and suddenly my room looked much cleaner.

"Whoa." I mumbled, setting her coffee on my dresser. "Everything okay?"

I knew it wasn't. Something was wrong. Because I'd definitely seen this frantic packing method before. Just once.

"Yeah," she wiped her eyes and gave me this painted on smile, and I knew. "Just have to go."

My heart sank deep into the pit of my stomach, where it only goes when I know something bad is about to happen.

She bit the inside of her lip and fumbled with the zipper of the duffle bag for a second. I knew I was blocking the exit. Maybe if I hadn't been, she'd have already been gone.

"You don't." I whispered, my eyes welling up instantly.

I knew that look. I knew the look she was giving me. Because it was the same look Jayde had given me the last time she'd left. I'd always hated comparing the two of them because Ava wasn't Jayde, and if she wanted to leave, it wasn't for the same reasons, but that didn't make it hurt any less.

"I can't do this." She shook her head. "I'm not–"

"You can't do what?" I mumbled back. For once, I wanted her to stop beating around the bush and be honest with me.

"Please don't make me say it."

She zipped the bag, looking away from me, and I tried to pull myself together. I needed to be rational and collected. Because I could fix this. Whatever I'd said or done, I could make it better.

"Whatever it is we can—"

"No, we can't." Ava sighed, grabbing the duffle bag strap and slinging it over her shoulder.

"Please don't do this."

"I have to go."

"Ava..." I sucked in a shaky breath. "Please, stay... stay with me."

She shook her head slowly and looked down at her hands. "I can't."

"What can I do to—"

"Nothing, Parker." She was crying now, too. "There's nothing you can do. It's not... it's not you."

"Right, 'it's not you, it's me.'" I let out a bitter laugh. I didn't even mean to, but I couldn't help it.

She closed her eyes for a second and took a deep breath. "Please, just let me go."

I stepped inside the room, giving her space to leave. I felt my throat go dry. A numbness set over me as I took a seat on the bed. But Ava hadn't moved yet. She was standing there, eyeing me.

She walked over to me, wrapping her hand around the back of my neck like she might kiss me, and for a split second, I thought she'd changed her mind. For that split second, I thought maybe she'd stay.

I looked up at her. Her green eyes had become so familiar to me, but now I didn't recognize her at all. Maybe it was the look on her face that I didn't recognize. She'd never looked at me like that. There was a hint of pity in her eyes, and I wished she wouldn't.

I couldn't stay calm enough to stop myself from crying. Tears were coming in streams. I didn't think Ava had ever seen me cry. And maybe that was because we'd never gotten to the hard stuff.

I couldn't bring myself to say another word. Even as she kissed my forehead, this long-drawn-out thing. It took everything

I had not to wrap my arms around her and beg, but I didn't. I didn't move. I didn't make a sound.

Because I knew it wouldn't make a difference. I knew her mind was already made up.

"I'm sorry." She whispered before she let go and practically ran out of the room.

I heard her say goodbye to Noah, and the front door shut, and then I was sobbing.

Ava

I regretted leaving the moment I walked out of Parker's door, standing on their landing for a minute, reconsidering, almost running back in and taking it all back. But I couldn't. I wasn't ready.

I wasn't ready for her; I wasn't ready for love. I was still so... broken. After Cam, I'd never learned how to *be* again. I'd never even wanted to try.

But Parker... she made me want to.

She made me want to figure out everything. I just didn't know how. And I didn't know how to tell Parker that. How do you tell someone who loves you that you can't be with them and heal at the same time? How do you tell them you have to leave them in order to heal?

Because that... almost didn't make sense to me.

Willow was waiting for me when I walked in the door. She was seated on the couch, but she jumped up the moment she saw the door open. Noah must have called her because she pulled me into a hug before I even said anything.

I'd cried the whole way home. I didn't really care who saw me, but I'd kept my composure, at least most of the way, so I could get home faster. I didn't allow myself to sob until I was safe at home, where being broken felt okay.

The moment Willow's arms wrapped around my shoulders; I was done for. A deep sob escaped, and once that had bubbled out, it felt like thousands came with it. We didn't make it to the couch. My knees give out, and I just let myself collapse on the living room floor.

Suddenly, I was grateful Willow was such a neat freak because at least the floor was clean.

"What happened?" Willow signed and said aloud.

I was shaking too much to sign back, and I couldn't bring the sobs to a stop enough to mouth the words. So, I shook my head instead.

I missed Mom. She'd be there when Cam and I split. Even when things were rocky between me and her, she always knew what to say, how to convince me everything would be okay again, even when she didn't know how bad they really were. Normally, she could talk me out of my bad decisions. I'd just wished she'd talked me out of dating Cam in the first place.

Maybe I didn't miss Mom. She'd probably tell me breaking it off with Parker was a bad decision.

Maybe it was. Maybe it was the worst mistake I'd ever make.

She was everything I wanted, probably everything I needed, and being with her felt right. But I couldn't open up to her, not like this. Parker loved me, and I didn't even know how to love myself. Just the idea of loving myself was so exhausting... I didn't think I'd have any love to give someone else.

I was still too broken to really feel for someone again, and as much as I'd wanted to better myself, work on getting back to the person I was before Cam, I hadn't yet. Maybe I never could. I'd avoided feeling anything real since I'd walked out Cam's door for the last time. And I'd avoided facing the reason why.

When it was undefined, we could just be, just us like that first date, and that was okay. But once labels and love were thrown into the mix, suddenly we were *something*. And that meant I needed to be *someone*.

I didn't know who I was. I just knew I wasn't who Cam had wanted me to be.

Looking at everything in clarity, seeing me and Parker for what we were, seeing what she wanted us to be, it made me realize I'd never thought that far ahead. I was too afraid to risk thinking that far ahead. And it was that fear that kept me from running back to Parker, taking it all back. No matter how much I wanted to.

Parker

"What just—" Noah started from the doorway, pausing at the sight of me. His whole face fell. "Oh. Oh, no. What—um, is there anything I can—"

I shook my head. "No," I sputtered. "There's nothing you can do."

It came out far more bitter than I meant it to.

"Right, okay." He let out a sigh. "Let me know if you need anything."

I nodded, holding in a sob until he was in the hall, my door shut behind him.

I didn't mean to push him away. He was only trying to help, but he couldn't. He couldn't fix this. I couldn't fix this. I didn't even think Ava could fix this. Even though I knew if she knocked on my door, told me she didn't mean it, I'd believe her. I'd take her back, but I'd never trust her again.

Jayde had walked out the door too many times for that.

"Hey, Nathan." I said with an achy rasp to my voice. "I'm not going to make it in today. I'm really not feeling well."

"You sound like shit." He agreed. "Okay, I'll see if Ellis can cover."

"I need a favor, too, while I've got you on the phone."

There was a beat and a shuffle.

"What is it?" He asked finally.

"I need to switch to days."

He made a choking sound. "You need to what? Are you nuts? For what?"

"It's... sort of personal."

"I don't care about your relationship problems, honestly." He sighed, like he already knew exactly where this conversation was going. He kind of did. "Ellis cannot handle the bar on nights and weekends. He's barely functional in the day."

"I know. It would only be for—"

"Parker, no. The answer is no."

"Nathan, please." I groaned. "I've been at Brickhouse three years. I've never asked you for a favor. I don't call in, I'm never late, I don't take off. I cover shifts constantly."

Another beat. And then I heard a deep sigh.

"You're going to quit if I tell you no, aren't you?"

I hadn't originally considered doing that. The thought hadn't really occurred to me, but now that it was on the table, I supposed I was willing to quit my job if it meant not having to watch Ava play every weekend. I'd changed everything else about my schedule after Jayde.

"Fine." He said before I could answer. "Fine, but you had better do some damn good prep work or we're screwed. Have you considered what will happen if Ellis says no?"

"I already asked him."

"Of course, you did. That's just great. You enjoy your sick day, Parker. I'm going to be annoyed at the sight of your face for a week."

Click.

I let out a sigh, feeling the silence in the apartment set in. I'd heard Noah leave, despite how quiet he'd tried to be. But the quiet gave me space to think of just how to remap my entire day.

I'd been seeing Ava every day, nearly every place I went, for well over a year. And in a matter of hours, I had to figure out how to avoid her in a universe that seemed to want us together. Even if she didn't.

Ava

I didn't know how I'd feel the next morning, bumping into Parker on the street. Would she try to talk to me? Would she pretend I didn't exist? I couldn't decide which I thought would hurt more. Turns out, there was a third option I hadn't thought of, and it was even worse.

Parker wasn't there.

I didn't see her at the gym. I didn't see her at the coffee shop. And she didn't show up at the diner either. That day, or the next. Or the day after that. It was like she just... didn't exist.

I was back to walking home after work at the department store, which I'd known would be the case the moment I left. I just hadn't expected the way that it would fill me with panic again, like all that time Parker had just been stopping up a well.

Willow was hassling me about therapy again. Daily. I knew she was just worried. She'd had a lot more free time that first week since she had finished school to mom me. Despite actively looking for a new job and juggling her part time stocking position, she had plenty of time to keep an eye on every single thing I did.

It was helping me to not isolate. At the very least, I had Willow to keep me accountable. She reminded me to shower, tried to help keep me on my usual schedule. But I wasn't sleeping well, and I'd lost pretty much all my motivation to do... anything.

When the weekend came around, I braced myself. Parker was dedicated to her job, if only because she was saving for her own future. I thought surely, if anywhere, that's where I'd bump into her. Or I'd catch her sneaking glances between making drinks, and it would make it hard to sing.

I wasn't about to quit the singing gig. I was actually building a following there. It was good for my online channel, as a few people had recorded live performances. Maybe that was selfish. She'd worked there first.

But I needed it. It was the first healthy thing I'd done for myself since leaving Cam. It was the first time I'd really felt... unpacked.

Parker didn't show at Brickhouse either. Ellis was working behind the bar. He was struggling, too. More than once, I caught him frantically running his fingers through his hair as he made drinks. He was nowhere near as cool and collected on a busy Friday as Parker was.

He broke two bottles.

Nathan was furious, and even with as many questioning looks Nathan cast me that first weekend, he didn't ask, and I didn't tell. But I knew he knew.

I felt lucky he didn't just fire me and call it good.

The next week, Willow started a job at a vet's office uptown. I felt like there was no warning, but she loved it immediately. It was the perfect place for her. It just meant our schedules were pretty much opposite. I saw her less and less that second week, especially when she was spending time with Noah at his house, so he didn't have to look at me like I was the devil incarnate.

I'd practically begged her not to pick sides. She deserved to be happy. And if she did, it should have been Parker's. I was the one not willing to make things work.

Out of nowhere, I was alone all the time, which felt dangerous to me. It was too much change.

"You need to go to back to the therapy group." Willow said as she gathered laundry by the door, fully expecting me to have time to wash them. "This isn't healthy. Mom agrees."

"You called Mom?" I signed back over a mug of late-night coffee.

I knew *that* wasn't good for me.

"Of course, I did! Why didn't you?"

"I wasn't ready to talk about it." I shrugged.

"You need to talk about it. You need to talk about all of it. You can't keep–"

"I know."

She let out a huff and stormed off. If I had to guess, I'd say she thought it was like talking to a brick wall. Maybe I would, too, if the roles were reversed. Maybe she just didn't want to spend what little time she had before bed arguing over my therapy.

The absence of Parker was consuming. I was amazed to find how little about my life had changed, but nothing felt the same. My normal schedule had gaps I no longer knew how to fill, and it left me feeling empty.

I never saw Parker anymore, but I saw her everywhere. Or I thought I did, at least. Every dark haired, tan skinned woman with even a few inches of height on me had her face on the first glance. I'd blink, and they'd look like someone else again.

I sent her two texts before I could think better of it. No reply. Shocker.

"Hey, Meg?" I asked in the middle of week three. "Have you heard from Parker lately? I haven't seen her around."

"Oh, well, yeah, I saw her yesterday." Meg said thoughtfully, scribbling something down in her notebook. "She said something about changing her schedule. She came in about ten minutes after you left, actually. She didn't tell you?"

I swallowed a lump in my throat and shook my head.

"Did something happen?" Meg asked, giving me that motherly look.

I nodded, letting out a shaky sigh.

"She should be in tomorrow. Want me to pass anything along?"

I shook my head, "No, that's okay. I just... wanted to make sure she was okay."

"She seems alright," Meg sighed, brushing a grey hair out of her face. "A bit melancholy lately, but otherwise—"

"Thank you." I forced a smile and grabbed my order that had just come up.

"Hey, Sugar, you know I don't pick sides in these things. I'm here for you, too."

I nodded quickly, trying to blink back tears as I exited the kitchen with a smile painted on my face.

I went by her house that night. As soon as I finished my shift at the diner, I half jogged to her side of town, hoping I wouldn't be late for my shift at the department store.

I don't know why I did it. I think a part of me just wanted to know she was okay. But a bigger part of me wasn't okay. As much as I didn't want to admit it, I thought seeing her would help.

I wanted her to know that I was going to fix it—fix me. I didn't know why I wanted that. I didn't think she'd care.

Noah answered the door.

"Is Parker here?" I asked, trying not to meet his eyes.

"No." He sighed. He crossed his arms in a really final way.

"You wouldn't tell me if she was, though, would you?"

"Probably not."

I nodded as I started to turn.

"Why are you here, Ava?" He asked.

"I was just—I don't know." I felt my eyes well up because I didn't really know. "I messed up, Noah. I went about this all wrong."

He nodded, "Yeah."

Noah didn't normally seem like the angry type. Every time he opened his mouth, everything he said came off as a joke, even when he was serious. Not this time. He was kind of scary when he was actually mad. It reminded me of my dad.

"It's actually caused a bit of a rift between me and Willow, too, just like we thought it would, so thanks for that." He scoffed. "She's your sister. She has to be on your side. And me? Well, let's just say this isn't the first time I've had to help Parker fill holes someone left behind."

I really knew Parker wasn't home then because there's no way Noah would let her hear him talking like that. Maybe she wouldn't stick up for me, but she wouldn't want Noah telling me all her business.

"I'm sorry, I didn't mean to—"

"You didn't mean to, what Ava? Shatter her? Because I'm not sure what else you thought would happen. She loves you."

"I know." I could feel two tears falling down each cheek now. "I just wanted to make sure she was okay—"

"She's not."

I shut my eyes. "Right. Got it. Don't tell her I stopped by. It probably won't help."

"You're right, it won't." He let out a grunt. "Ava, if you really care, figure your shit out before you come knocking again, okay?"

I stiffened as he slammed the door.

And then I sobbed as I headed back toward the department store, my phone dinging to let me know it was time for the therapy group. I'd been meaning to delete the reminder. Every week when it went off, I meant to, but I'd also been saying I was going to go back. Even before I left Parker, I'd known I still needed to work on myself. I'd just never taken the time.

Maybe a part of me was starting to believe in the universe.

I suddenly wished I could just go home and talk to Willow. But it was late, and she had to be up early to make it to the office in time. We hadn't talked at all in a week. Our schedules were so backwards now, and I had a feeling she was mad at me. But that could have just been in my head.

The group was pretty much all I had.

Parker

The first week reminded me a little too much of how it felt after Jayde left, but in reverse. I had a lot of free time on days. Too much free time. Because my schedule being opposite of Ava, meant it was also opposite of Noah. So, I was always alone. And instead of just wanting things to slow down like I had when Jayde left, I needed them to speed up.

Everything was always so quiet. I could think all day, and that was not what I needed in the slightest. I needed to be distracted. I should have stuck with nights, sucked it up, ignored Ava when I saw her. Honestly? That probably would have served her right, but I didn't think I could handle it.

I started going out again. I knew from that first night it was a bad idea.

Jayde spotted me the moment I walked through the doors.

"I knew you'd be back." She grinned, like I was actually there *for* her.

She'd always thought that. Everything was about her.

"I'm not." I said flatly, waving down the bartender, suddenly grateful I didn't work in a club. "Back that is."

"Sure, looks like it."

She sat down on the barstool next to me, and gave me that look, reminding me how familiar she was. I knew everything about Jayde, in depths Ava and I had never even tried to dive.

Ava was confusing. Everything was undefined with a maze of lines I couldn't cross. Jayde was always straightforward. It would be so easy to jump back into my old life, with her, where things were easy—none of the hard stuff. No work at all.

But none of it was real. Maybe Ava hadn't known all the dark details yet, but what she did know was honest–was me. The real me that wasn't made up in Jayde's twisted little mind.

"Dance with me." Jayde grinned, like a little physical contact would magically make us compatible.

"I'll pass." I replied, feeling a sense of satisfaction wash over me at her childish scowl.

She spent the rest of the night begging me to dance with her, a little needier each time, along with another drink here and there. I bumped into three other exes of mine as I avoided wherever Jayde was dancing, along with a few ex-friends of Jayde's, who I also had a history with. That's how it had always been there, though. A toxic and familiar hell hole of distraction.

I knew I'd chosen to walk into the lion's den of Jayde's world, but it was harder to think about Ava when I was around so much... The lights, the music, the alcohol—it all drowned out my thoughts.

I thought that was exactly what I needed, so I let that become my new routine.

Even when I was hung over and dead tired working behind the bar, at the very least, I couldn't think over the pounding headache. Running the bar was basically muscle memory at that point. It didn't take much thought. Especially in the day when it wasn't as busy.

Noah noticed. Nathan noticed. But none of the customers complained, and at the end of the day, that was all that mattered to Nathan. Hungover or not, so long as I was doing my job, he didn't really give a shit. It bothered him much more that Ellis was struggling to do my job.

He asked me three times in the first week how long I thought I'd need to be on days before things... mulled over.

On the weekends when Ava performed, the shifts in the bar would overlap. Which made avoiding her so much harder. She was always so damn early, which made no sense, as she was lugging a guitar from across town after working all day.

Somehow Ellis let me off the hook completely, like maybe he got it after him and Karlee split. Only Karlee had just quit and started working somewhere else. I didn't get so lucky.

I made it up to him by stocking the bar twice, cutting extra lemons in the scorching heat of the kitchen, even pre-making margarita mix, so he didn't have to work so hard when they were half off. If I could think of anything to help, I did it. So long as I didn't have to hear Ava sing.

At the end of my shift, I'd slip out the kitchen door, avoiding any contact with her completely. And then I'd go from one bar to the next until Noah ultimately picked me up or I chose to wait and walk.

It wasn't long before I got tired of the club scene, though. There was a reason I didn't go to the clubs anymore. There was a reason I'd stopped.

Apart from constantly dealing with Jayde's advances, drinking my feelings was too easy. And once you started drinking feelings, it was hard to actually feel them. Being numb? That was the real addiction.

Ava

I was running on adrenaline and spite. I had to be, because that was the only logical explanation for how I wound up bursting into the back room of the coffee shop. I hadn't been to the therapy group in months. Parker and I had decided to quit going, so it was no shock that Carmen was surprised to see me. There were people in the group I didn't recognize now. It was bigger, but somehow most of the faces were familiar, even if I couldn't remember anyone's names.

"Ava," Carmen smiled as I walked in, and she hugged me.

She was a therapist. Maybe she somehow knew that's what I needed. I was basically touch starved again. Maybe my face was blotchy from crying. I didn't know.

"I was wondering if I'd ever see your face again."

I realized the group had already started, and I felt my cheeks growing hot. Was I that late? No, just five minutes.

"Do—do you want to share?" Carmen asked, hesitantly.

I nodded, trying to will myself not to cry.

Just do it. Get it over with. Say the words out loud.

"I'm sorry," I breathed. "I didn't mean to interrupt—"

"No, honey, we were just getting started." Carmen nodded encouragingly. "Does anyone have a problem if Ava shares first?"

There were a few shrugs, shakes of the head. Nobody else seemed in a hurry to go. Therapy was hard sometimes. I wished rather suddenly that I hadn't stopped going. Maybe this would be easier. Maybe I wouldn't be in this shitty situation in the first place. Maybe if Parker and I had just listened to Noah and Willow...

"Whenever you're ready." Carmen smiled.

I tapped the back of the empty chair next to her with one hand and fiddled with the necklace Parker had given me with the other. That had been my chair once. Why had she always sat next to me?

"Hi," I breathed, trying to collect myself. Shit, it was hot in here. "For those who don't know, I'm–I'm Ava, and I know I haven't... I haven't been active in this group for a minute—well, I guess not ever if you think about it."

A couple of the girls I'd met when I attended the group those first couple of weeks let out a hesitant laugh. That helped. I smiled.

"I was scared to share." I had to blink to keep from crying again. "I was scared because I wasn't sure I'd really be welcome in LGBT spaces."

Carmen reached a hand out to mine, and I let out a shuddery breath.

"Because I'm asexual."

I closed my eyes, and I felt Carmen squeeze my hand.

I'd never actually said those words out loud to anyone. I'd told Willow, and she'd had to look it up. Parker just figured it out, and Cam... just thought I was cheating on her. I hadn't even known then, anyway. I didn't know there was a word for what I was feeling.

Suddenly, saying the words out loud made them feel more real. Like maybe I hadn't even accepted it myself. I knew that I was. I knew I was asexual. But I hadn't really embraced what that meant. I guess I'd lived in the grey area on that, too.

I felt arms around me, and when I opened my eyes, three of the girls from the original group were hugging me, and I let out a laugh and a soft sob at the same time. I think they were happy tears?

"I feel like there's more." Carmen said softly. I realized she still had a hold of my hand.

I didn't mind, but I nodded, and the girls headed back to their seats.

This was kind of the worst. I felt like I was giving a public speech. I'd never been all that fond of public speaking, especially in high school. But I was clinging to that spiteful energy that had filled my entire being after my conversation with Noah. Maybe that was the push I needed—being told I'd hurt Parker, which was the last thing I'd ever wanted to do.

I let out a deep breath. "I had an ex who used sex like a control tactic. And she convinced me that nobody would ever love me. And for the longest time, I thought it was because I'm asexual."

I let out another breath, and Carmen gave my hand another encouraging squeeze.

"I pushed away someone recently because of it. Someone I really cared about. I hurt her. B—but I'm ready now to let all that go. Because if I don't, I might lose her for good."

There was a beat. I wasn't sure what else to say.

"That..." Carmen said with a smile. "Was a good share. What advice do we have for Ava? Are you wanting advice, sweetie?"

I nodded. "Yeah, I don't exactly know how to go about getting someone back who I didn't think I was good enough for in the first place."

Carmen patted the chair. "First, we stop the negative self-talk, and we work on self-love, right everyone?"

There was a round of affirming nods.

Parker

Somehow, three weeks passed in a numb haze of a cycle of hangovers and drunken nights at the club. Some of which I didn't remember getting home, much less getting into bed.

It felt like the time I'd spent with Jayde—always hungover, never getting enough sleep, spending most of my money on alcohol and cigarettes. Except then, I'd had Jayde, not that I was even considering going down that road again. Now I had no one. It was just me, alone, all the time.

I didn't feel like me anymore.

I was trying hard to embrace this version of myself that I had only been with Jayde, for Jayde–this person who wasn't really me. Because with Ava, despite all the things that weren't healthy or right, I was more myself with her than I'd been in years.

I didn't think I could be that person without her. Because that meant sticking with the schedule I'd set, the one where I bumped into her several times a day. That meant seeing her face and hearing her voice, facing this pain head-on. And I'd never been good at that.

Being someone else, even for a while, while this pain dissipated, while I got over Ava, that was the only way I felt like I could get an ounce of peace.

I just didn't realize... that wasn't peace at all. It was chaos.

Ava

"Hey, Dad?" I called, stepping into his foyer that felt a little less familiar without Parker's shoes and coat hanging next to mine.

"Hey, pumpkin, I was wondering when you'd turn up." He grinned, poking his head around the corner. "Where's Parker at today?"

"Oh." I felt my chest grow tight. "We aren't..."

"Oh." He nodded, taking the pizza from my hands as he headed toward his kitchen. "I'm sorry to hear that. You seemed really happy with her. You want to talk about it?"

I let out a sigh. "Not really, but it kind of feels like everyone's hearts a little shattered, so it's only fair."

"She didn't—she didn't hurt you, did she?"

"What? No, Dad, Parker wouldn't—"

I realized Parker really wouldn't. But my dad knew Cam had. Maybe not to the full extent, but he knew.

"I left her. I just... wasn't ready."

"Can't put the paste back in the tube. You know that."

I scoffed as he handed me a plate. "I know. I just need to work on some things first, I think. I went back to the group."

"Yeah?" He smiled, sitting down in his living room. He didn't reach for the remote. "That's great. How'd it go?"

"It was hard." I nodded. "But, good. I think I'm going to try to do solo sessions with her. But the group was free, so I'm not sure how I'm going to—"

"I've got it."

"What?"

"If you're going to be able to smile and brighten the room like you used to again, then I've got it."

I let out a breath, looking at my dad's tired green eyes. I definitely got mine from him. My wavy hair, too.

He looked sad, but hopeful. Therapy wasn't some cure all, and I think he knew that. He knew this was a journey.

That was the first time since leaving Parker, and maybe even leaving Cam, that I didn't feel... alone.

Carmen had said something about accepting love. That in order to love myself, I had to accept that I was loved and lovable to begin with. Maybe I'd always thought love came with conditions, even with the people I knew loved me. My dad, my mom, Willow.

The next day, I got almost halfway home before I realized I'd left my phone at work. Nobody really texted me anymore. It wasn't a huge deal. But if Willow knew I was walking home from the department store without it, she'd have my head.

I ducked back into the café and into the kitchen without even glancing at the tables. With a huff, I started searching around the cubbies where we kept our stuff. It had to be around there somewhere.

"Forget something?" Meg asked, pulling my phone out of her apron.

"Oh my god, thank you!" I sighed.

"Found it in one of the booths. You're lucky I recognized it."

"You're the best!"

"Hey, your... friend is here if you want to say hi." She smiled as she grabbed a plate from the receiving area.

"My—" *Parker*. "Oh, no. Um, that's okay. I'm actually super late for my other job, so... I'll just text her."

I smiled, shaking my phone a little.

She nodded knowingly, grabbing some extra straws. Meg was a no bullshitter. She knew that was bullshit.

"Thank you, Meg." I said, quickly ducking out the door before she could hassle me.

I couldn't stop myself from glancing toward Meg's section. Sure enough, Parker was in her usual booth.

It was actually her. Not some case of mistaken identity. That was Parker. The real Parker. She was so close to me. I could just walk up and sit down, tell her all about the group and doing solo sessions like I'd wanted to that day I went to her place. A part of me didn't think she'd want to hear it.

I felt my eyes well up as I instinctively grabbed the necklace she'd given me. Why the fuck was I crying? Because I missed her. Because I wanted to run to her and hug her. Because I wanted to shout a thousand sorrys to her. Because I couldn't do any of those things, even Carmen said so.

Her head turned, and I bolted for the door, wiping the stupid tears off my stupid face.

That night on my way home, I saw her again.

My job at the department store had gotten more demanding as they got ready for a change in the seasons again. The countdown to Christmas had begun, and it wasn't even

Halloween yet. I was working longer, later, more days. And I think it was the only thing keeping me sane because I'd pretty much started using it to fill the gaps I had with the absence of Parker.

But even if I was filling my gaps with things to do, Parker was still on my mind. After seeing her at the diner, I'd thought about her my entire shift. I'd realized I didn't just miss Parker. I needed her. She made me want to be better. And a part of me was starting to believe in the universe or fate or whatever. She hadn't come into my life by happenstance.

And that was the same time I realized she didn't need me. I realized why she wasn't returning my texts. Why she wasn't home that night when I'd talked to Noah. Why I never saw her in passing anymore. Why I hadn't seen her once since I'd left.

Halfway between the department store and my apartment complex, was a club called EQ Point. I knew it was an LGBT club—the only one in town, but that was about it. I hadn't once considered going. Clubs weren't my thing–the noise I could handle, the people not so much.

I hadn't thought they were Parker's thing anymore, either. The number of times she said she wasn't into the club scene made me actually believe it. It made me think she'd really turned her life around from... whatever person she'd been before she met me. I'd realized I had no clue who that was.

My headphones had broken the week before. I wasn't surprised. They were cheap as hell, but it sucked because I had full ears of everything. A familiar laugh caught my attention, and sure enough, walking out of EQ Point with a rather wobbly Jayde, was Parker.

I stopped mid-stride. I don't know why I did it. Seeing Parker with her arms around Jayde was like watching a movie. A horror movie that you just want to look away from, but you can't.

I watched as Parker hailed a cab and helped Jayde slide in, my vision going a little blurry. I looked away. I didn't need to know how that story ended. Because either way, it didn't involve me.

I bit my lip hard, willing myself to keep moving, and I cried the rest of the way home.

I did that. Because I knew she had turned her life around. I knew she wanted nothing to do with Jayde. And the only reason she was back at the clubs, in Jayde's arms, was because of me.

Parker

I heard Ava's voice echo across the diner and turned around to find her practically running out the door. It looked like she was crying, but I couldn't be sure. And it took all my willpower not to chase after her, but I wasn't even sure why.

She was supposed to be off. She was supposed to be home or halfway across town, doing whatever it was she did these days. Ava wasn't ever late. That was my job. The whole point of coming after work was that Ava was long gone.

"Something happen between the two of you?" Meg asked as she came up to refill my drink.

I swallowed hard, trying to muster up some sort of explanation.

Meg took a seat. "You used to chat my ear off, and the two of you seemed inseparable."

"We were."

"So, what happened? You've both been depressing as hell lately."

"She left." I replied, wondering why Ava was so upset. She did the leaving.

Meg sighed. "Is that why you changed your whole schedule around? To avoid seeing her?"

I nodded.

She made a face at me, and I knew she was about to give me tough love.

"What?" I asked.

"You're going to the clubs again, aren't you? You look hungover."

I scratched the back of my neck to avoid looking at her.

"Thought you were done with all that. You said it wasn't good for you."

I sighed. "It's not."

Meg raised an eyebrow at me.

"I can't make your decisions for you." Meg sighed. "But that girl? Was good for you."

"Yeah, well," I let out a sigh. "I clearly wasn't good enough for her."

Meg gave my hand a familiar, motherly like pat. "She tell you that, or are you telling that to yourself?"

I let out a deep sigh and looked to the door Ava had just disappeared out of. I honestly hadn't gotten around to asking her. Why did she leave? Why didn't she want to stay? What had I done that was so wrong besides love her?

She'd said it wasn't me, but I couldn't imagine how it couldn't be. If there was nothing wrong with me, why did everyone always leave?

It felt like a true blessing not seeing Jayde that night. The club was packed for a Thursday, though. Must have been whatever drink special they had going on. I grabbed my usual and found a curved couch near the back that was halfway empty.

I wasn't there long before a set of long legs and a short skirt came into my vision. Lexi sat on my lap and smiled down at me.

I stifled a groan, struggling to find a way not to touch her any more than I already was.

"I heard a rumor about you, Parker Watson." She smirked as she ran her fingers through my hair.

"Oh, yeah?" I took a sip of my drink and fought the urge to smack her hand away or shove her off my lap.

"Mhmm. I heard you're single again."

She said it like she had more to say, so I looked at her expectantly. Lexi leaned in to my ear.

"I heard you haven't gotten laid in a year."

"Yeah, I'm not doing this."

I grabbed her waist, picking her up with one arm, and set her back on the couch. I downed what was left of my drink with a gulp and set it on a nearby tray. I wasn't drunk enough to be in the same building as this woman, much less for this conversation.

"I could make you forget about her." Lexi called after me.

I was not that desperate.

"I doubt it." I yelled back, heading for the bar.

She apparently wasn't done pressing her luck because she slipped onto the barstool next to me. I rolled my eyes at her as the bartender I was starting to recognize handed me a drink without my even asking.

"What do you want, Lexi?" I sighed, rubbing the bridge of my nose.

Her leg brushed mine. "You."

She said it like I was a conquest. A game. She was probably on the outs with Jayde again, which meant that's exactly what this was.

I took a deep breath and let it out before I took a sip of my drink. Why was I thinking about this? I knew I didn't want Lexi. I wanted Ava, and not even like that. I just wanted her in my life.

But toying with the idea that she didn't want me in hers was driving me to a point of no return.

"So," I sighed, turning slightly. "How exactly could you make me forget her?"

She shrugged. "I could show you better than I could tell you."

I met her eyes.

I was totally going to regret this.

EQ Point didn't have gendered bathrooms. Just two non-gendered spaces with individual, floor to ceiling, locking doors. Was hooking up in one of them glamorous? Absolutely not, but it was pretty common. I couldn't say I'd ever done it. I could say that I'd never been happy with that decision. Not once.

There was no way in hell I was bringing Lexi home. She was the last person I wanted to have my address. And I was not going to deal with whatever Noah had to say about it. Because there probably wouldn't be anything worse than what I'd say to myself once whatever was motivating me wore off.

Lexi smelled like makeup and expensive perfume. Her lips tasted like lip-gloss, and not in a good way. I got past that, ignored it, choked it down maybe. This might have been a revenge thing. Because kissing Lexi reminded me of that night, Ava's birthday, the look on her face when Lexi kept touching my arm.

I didn't have second thoughts when Lexi started kissing my neck. I didn't have them when she unbuttoned my shirt. Or lifted my bra. I didn't have second thoughts until she started whispering all the things, she wanted *me* to do to *her*.

It reminded me of Jayde, the way she'd demanded things, but wasn't really much of a giver in any aspect of life. Which reminded me of all the reasons I'd left Jayde, and all the reasons I knew Ava was the one. And suddenly, revenge wasn't worth it. Because how would Ava ever know, anyway?

I pulled away. "I'm sorry."

I let out a breath, running my fingers through my hair as I stood, causing her to stumble on her heels.

"I can't do this." I whispered, fixing the buttons on my shirt.

Lexi watched me for a minute, waiting for me to change my mind, maybe. She was slightly blocking the door like she genuinely thought she could stop me from leaving if she wanted to.

"You're an asshole." She spat at me as I pushed past her and slipped out of the stall, not even bothering to button half of my shirt.

I really needed to find a way to forget Ava. Even if only for a minute. And that's when I ran into Jayde.

"Parker!" She grinned widely, throwing her arms around my shoulders.

She was way more drunk than I was, and she was always clingier when she was drunk. She slurred her words, so I didn't quite catch what she'd said, but I had a feeling it was some sort of advance like she did any time I bumped into her these days. Just like that, I was ready to go home.

My home, my bed. Alone.

I just wasn't a big enough asshole to leave her there like that.

Ava

I went back to the group the next week. I even stuck around after the group ended, just a few minutes. Things felt different. They were talking to me like they had each other when I'd first come to the group. I felt like I was part of something.

Tate was trying hard to warm up to me, which was just as cathartic with her bright red hair as seeing the girl who worked the coffee counter in the mornings. Maybe we could have been good friends by now had I not stopped going to the group.

"I'm demisexual, actually." She said randomly as we stepped outside.

"Really?" I asked. "Why didn't you ever talk about it with the group?"

"Same reason as you, I think. It's much easier to tell people that you want to take things slow than it is to explain your sexuality. Not everybody gets it."

I nodded, letting out a sigh. Not everybody, indeed. I'd misjudged this whole group of people, all of whom were far more like me than I ever could have realized.

"Listen," Tate said in a bit of a fury because she knew I was headed to work. "I wanted to give you, my number."

She thrust a little piece of paper at me, and I looked at her hand for a second, my throat going dry. What was it with people in this group? I was not that pretty.

No negative self-talk.

"Tate, I–" I felt my cheeks growing hot.

"No, not like that!" She let out a laugh. "I know you have someone... sort of. I just mean, if you ever need somebody to talk to who isn't Carmen or your sister."

"Oh," I nodded, taking the slip of paper from her.

"No pressure though."

"Thank you."

It had been a while since anyone had wanted to be my actual friend. It made me all misty eyed as I headed toward work. I was making friends. I was going to therapy. If I could do those things, maybe there was a chance for me and Parker after all. If she'd still have me by then.

The next day, I saw Carmen solo. She gave everyone in the group discounted rates, which made me feel less guilty since my dad was insisting on paying for it, even after I told him I might be able to handle it with the discount.

I was sacrificing me time every Tuesday, but maybe this was part of me time. I needed to work on myself, not just work on sad covers to play my feelings at Brickhouse. And they'd gotten pretty sad lately, even I could admit that.

Carmen's office was ridiculously close to the coffee shop. It annoyed me, mostly because it meant that I could have gone at any time. I could have worked on this at any point, and instead, I covered all my problems with a Parker sized band aid.

When I stepped inside, I was met with the general things you usually see in a therapist's office. The desk, the chair, the couch, an array of motivational posters and frames, and a calming aroma in her diffuser. She was digging through her closet, and I caught a glimpse of a wedding photo on her desk. Of course, she was gay.

It only made me more comfortable.

"Hello, Ava, I'm so glad you came." She called over to me while she dug a bit more. "Please, have a seat. I'm just looking for a fresh notebook. Mine has apparently run out."

"Okay," I nodded, flopping down on the couch, which was ridiculously lush and comfortable.

"Here we are! So, how has your week been?"

Carmen took a seat in the red accent chair across from me and pulled out a pen. This was what I'd hated about therapy before. The note-taking, the analyzing. But that was the most important part, right? How else was she supposed to help me problem solve?

"Honestly, it was shit." I laughed. "I'm not... coping well."

"That's understandable, you've been through a rough time lately, and from what you said in group, it sounds like you had a rough past. Where would you like to start?"

I let out a shaky breath and bit my lip, fiddling with the necklace Parker had given me. It made me think about all the things I'd been through; how much I hadn't told her—hadn't told anyone. "Where's a good place to start?"

Carmen smiled at me. "Let's start at the beginning. How did you come out... the first time?"

I told Carmen about coming out, about my mom. About my first, short-lived lesbian relationship, and then... Cam. How we covered so much in one session, I didn't know. I was basically rambling, telling my whole life story because once I started, I didn't know how to stop. By the time we reached the end, I'd only grazed a little bit about Parker, leaving out her name.

I'd tell her that later. I hoped.

At the end, Carmen asked me a question that stuck with me. "What do you hope to gain out of therapy, Ava?"

"Honestly?"

She nodded.

"I want to get better." I shrugged. "Because I want to be with... her, and right now, I know I can't."

"I think you know I'm about to tell you that's not how this works." She clicked her pen and set it down. "Healing isn't something with an end goal you can see, with clearly defined steps to get there. The goal of therapy is to reach a place of acceptance with what happened and embrace, life knowing it can be good, anyway. You don't have to be healed or perfect or pieced together with your life on a shiny new track to be with someone you love. Because the right person will want to be there rooting for you as you make these changes."

A lump filled my throat and my face got hot as big tears threatened to fall down my face.

"Do you think this woman could be that person? A person who can root for you as you grow and heal?"

I nodded slowly because I knew Parker had already tried.

She gave me some homework, which mostly involved working on feeling things as they happened, in the moment. Which meant no more band aids. No more busying myself. I had to embrace life... as it was. Which sucked because I had a lot of open wounds.

Parker

I wasn't much in the habit of talking with Jayde, but she caught me outside of the club, cigarette in hand. It was pretty hard to ignore her. I'd just lit the damn thing.

"Just who I was hoping to bump into." She beamed, leaning against the wall next to me.

"I wish I could say the same." I shot back, letting out a deep sigh. I had no clue just how awful I had to be to this woman to convince her it was over. I was never letting her back in my life.

"Awe, don't be like that."

How was she already drunk?

"You're still moping, aren't you?" She continued like I wasn't slowly inching away from her and trying to smoke this cigarette faster. "All because of that one girl? I figured you'd have moved on from that by now. She did."

I felt a lump rise from my throat all the way to the pit of my stomach.

"She did what?" I asked, looking over.

"Sure, now I've got your attention." Jayde rolled her eyes, turning toward the door as she mumbled. "You didn't even compliment my dress."

I grabbed her arm. "You look hot, blue's your color, goes well with your eyes. What did Ava do?"

Jayde yanked her arm away from me with a childish squeal, which caught the attention of the guard at the door. I took a step back.

"I saw her leaving the coffee shop the other day with some redhead." She laughed. "Come to think of it, didn't she used to date a redhead? I think Lexi mentioned something about Cameron dating an Ava back in the day. Huh, you two both have a type, don't you? Clearly you're not hers."

Of course, Jayde knew Cam. Maybe. Cameron was a popular name. Maybe they weren't the same person. But I seriously doubted it.

Jayde reached up and ran her fingers through my hair. I smacked her hand away and stomped my cigarette out before throwing it away and heading inside.

I was not sober enough to deal with the thought of Ava being back with Cam. And the longer I thought about that, the more likely I was to find Ava and talk some sense into her. Maybe she didn't want to be with me, but she sure as hell shouldn't be with her.

Ava

I got off earlier than usual, which was a surprise given how much work I'd had on my plate lately. I was tired, and trying hard to just sit with that. I made it halfway home, near that stupid club, before I heard a familiar voice on the street. I needed a new route.

Parker was dancing on the sidewalk, albeit not very well, singing out of tune to a song I had mostly definitely covered a few weeks before. Between mispronounced lyrics, she was babbling about something that didn't make sense. She turned and her eyes met mine, going wide.

"Ava!" She smiled like I was her favorite person in the world. I knew she was *really* drunk then.

She ran to me, the smell of Jack on her breath, and tried to kiss me. I turned my head abruptly.

"Parker, no." I sighed. "You're drunk."

Parker pulled away, frowning. "I love you; you know?"

My eyes stung with a misty haze. What I wouldn't give for her to be saying that to me sober. But sober Parker hated me.

"I know." I nodded. "Let's go home."

She smiled, throwing an arm around me. Then she kissed my cheek four times, this gross sloppy thing. She started singing again about a half block later. We made it halfway to her apartment before she started yawning.

The last five blocks, I was basically carrying her completely. She was only coherent when I patted her cheek a few times, and even then, her feet were dragging. The biggest struggle was getting her up the stairs to their second-floor apartment. I'd never once wondered what it would be like to drag someone up a flight of stairs, but there I was. She was definitely waking up with bruises tomorrow.

I knocked on the door. "Noah?"

I waited a beat, practically gasping for breath. The weight of Parker's arm over my shoulder had caused a major cramp. I was sweating everywhere. No way was I going to the gym tomorrow.

"Noah!" I groaned, knocking again, breathless. Parker was freaking heavy. "Come on."

"Ava, I told you not—" Noah looked between me and Parker. "What the hell?"

"Listen, it was a bitch getting her up the stairs. Can you just—can you just help me get her inside and give me the third degree after?"

"Right, okay."

Noah threw her other arm over his shoulder and helped me walk Parker to her room. We got her settled on her unmade bed with little to no flare, and we were both out of breath by the time I got her shoes off and had her covered up.

"What were you doing out with Parker?" He glared.

"What? I wasn't! I just got off work. Ask Willow." I stammered. "I found her halfway between there and here, outside the club, babbling and singing wildly off key. And then—you know what? It's not important. I just wanted to make sure she got home okay."

"You could have called me, and I could have come to get her. But you walked her here instead? What is that, 20 blocks?"

I felt my cheeks grow hot. "Something like that. I guess—I guess I didn't think about it."

I let out a sigh. He was eyeing me rather pointedly, and it made me uncomfortable.

"Right, I'm gonna go." I headed for the door, and Noah followed me.

"Maybe you can convince Parker you don't feel anything because you broke her heart, but you can't convince me and Willow." He called after me.

I stopped, swallowing hard. I turned around, and I was blinking back tears. "I can't convince me either, so."

"Then why—"

"Because you were *right*, Noah."

He frowned.

"I have some shit to work through. And I've got to work through it before I—before I can even think about trying to come back." I bit my lip hard to keep from crying, and my eyes instinctively flashed to Parker's door.

I could still see her, passed out, incoherent, not listening to this conversation.

"If she'll even have me by then."

"I don't think she's moving on any time soon." He let out a big sigh. "Willow told me you're back in therapy."

I nodded.

"I'm sorry." Noah sighed. "For what I said. I was really harsh. I know you didn't tell Willow, but—"

"Thank you."

"What—"

"I needed harsh." I laughed. "Willow loves me too much to tell it like it is. She's sweet and motherly, even when she's mad. I know I hurt Parker. I know this is my fault."

He nodded slowly, thinking.

“I wasn’t ready for her, Noah. But I want to be.” I let out a long breath, eyeing the way Parker looked peaceful. “I left for me. It was selfish and stupid. But everything I’m doing now is for her.”

“You can’t just go to therapy and better yourself for someone else.” He said, but there was a hint of a smile there, that sarcastic tone he used on people he actually liked. “You know that’s not how it works.”

“I’ve never cared about myself enough to try.” I let out a big sigh. “That’s why I’m so fucked up. I don’t value me. But I value her. I love—”

I stopped myself and his eyes met mine, going wide. I looked down again, feeling my whole face grow hot.

“Don’t say anything to her, okay?” I mumbled. “If she’s going to forgive me, it should be because I earned it.”

He nodded, and I slipped out the door. I stood on the landing, letting out a shaky breath, realizing I’d just admitted that I loved Parker. Out loud. To her best friend.

Parker

I felt ice. Ice cold. Wet.

Suddenly I was awake, on the floor. I apparently didn't keep down my alcohol.

"What the fuck, Parker? I'm not cleaning that up." Noah yelled, setting down the glass he'd used to toss water on me.

My head was pounding as I pushed myself off the floor. I think I'd started liking it that way, but definitely not when Noah was yelling.

"I'm fine, Noah." I grumbled, pulling myself onto my bed.

"Have you looked in a mirror lately? Because you are the exact opposite of fine."

I tried to brush him off, but he smacked my hand. Hard, leaving a stinging feeling.

"No, you don't get to do that to me." He snapped. "Do you remember what you said the last time you were out with the party crowd? You told me going to the clubs was making it harder to stay sober at work. You said drinking was easy and living was hard. You said you wanted to *live* life, Parker. What the fuck do you call this?"

"I'm just—" I felt like I was going to be sick, so I reached for my trash can.

He scoffed. "Even Ava wouldn't want to see you like this."

"Pretty sure Ava doesn't give a shit."

"Yeah?" He crossed his arms, but I felt like he was getting less angry the more he spoke his peace.

"Yeah, Noah. She left. She knew I was in love with her, and she left. I'm pretty sure she doesn't care about me, or she'd be here, and not with—"

"You're right, she left, but if she didn't care, she wouldn't be asking about you. She wouldn't be—"

My eyes snapped up, and I groaned. Fuck, sudden movements hurt.

"I know you're hurting. I know she left, and trust me, I don't want to be the one who says this, but let's say theoretically she did want to come back, how would she go about that, when you're—" He gestured at me vaguely. "Like this."

"She knows where to find me." I rolled my eyes.

"Does she?" He scoffed. "Because lately, I don't even know where to find you half the time."

I let out a sigh.

"Go back to nights, Parker."

"I can't just—"

"Nathan would switch. I'm sure Ellis would be happy about it, too."

"What if Ava—"

"I shouldn't have brought her up. Stop thinking about Ava for five minutes and think about yourself." He motioned to my whole body. "This isn't good for you. I can't keep watching you do this to yourself."

I swallowed hard, nodding.

"If it's any consolation," Noah said before slipping out the door. "All her music at the bar has been pretty sad lately."

I groaned, laying back against my pillow. I could smell Ava's perfume. It was all over my jacket from the night before, lingering on my shirt, smelling familiar and foreign at the same time.

Suddenly memories started coming back in flashes. Ava on the sidewalk. Me trying to kiss her.

Fuck, I told her I loved her.

I absolutely did not want to switch back to nights. But if I was going to, then I needed to embrace the idea of seeing Ava again. So, I got the hell out of the apartment.

"Parker!" Carmen said cheerily. "What a surprise. How are you doing?"

I was more surprised Carmen had my number saved. I hadn't been to the group in going on eight months, and I'd only been twice. The only reason I even had her number was because, in the beginning, I really had contemplated those solo sessions.

It turned out now I needed them.

"Uh." I cleared my throat. "Not so hot. I just... went through another breakup, and I was hoping maybe I could take you up on that offer for solo sessions? My best friend's been pressing me about therapy, and after the month I've had, I think it's time."

"Absolutely!" I heard a shuffle, what sounded like pages turning. "I have a four on Tuesdays open and a ten am on Wednesdays. Would either of those work for you?"

I had to think long and hard about it. Wednesday was definitely pushing it for work. Tuesdays though. It didn't seem Ava had changed much about her schedule. She should be home most of the day.

"Tuesday works." I sighed.

"Okay, hon. I've got you down. Is there anything you need in the meantime? I have a minute if you have something you need to get off your chest."

There was a beat, during which time I considered unloading to Carmen on the phone while walking through town. I considered telling her all about Jayde and Ava. I considered telling her about my dad, how he'd fallen off the sobriety wagon, and that's what had killed him. I considered telling her how losing Ava, the way I'd turned to clubs and alcohol immediately as my means of coping had proved the apple had not fallen far from the tree.

But I didn't.

"It can wait until Tuesday." I said, far more calmly than I felt.

"Okay, I'll see you then." Carmen replied. "You know where to reach me if anything comes up."

That morning, I went into work and talked to Nathan. He practically jumped with joy. I thought he was going to hug me.

"I thought you were just going to quit, eventually." He laughed, reaching for the schedule he had happened to be working on. "Yes. Yes, you can have your nights back. Tell Ellis. I'm sure he'll be thrilled."

He was, sort of.

"When you wanna start that?" Ellis asked when he came in that night.

"Whenever works for you." I shrugged.

"Now, bro. Like yesterday. You know I'm not cut out for this dinner rush vibe." He said, his cheeks bright crimson. "I can barely tell my brands apart. I need that slow chill lunch rush where I can take breaks when I wanna."

"I think you're in the wrong profession." I laughed.

"Shh." He whispered, eyeing the sound booth where Nathan had the door open. "They don't drug test here."

He motioned to his mouth with his index finger and his thumb.

I let out a snort and clocked out for one of my last day shifts. It was bittersweet.

I knew I had to face Ava. I had to get used to seeing her again, hearing her voice, knowing I'd probably never get that feeling of holding her close again. I figured unblocking her number was a good start.

I had just a few days before she'd play again, so I had time to adjust, I thought. It took nearly all three days for my head to stop throbbing on a regular basis. I knew the hangover was gone, but it was probably the shift in sleeping schedules doing me in.

I guess I deserved that. I'd been playing a dangerous game that I knew better than to play.

Friday, I forced myself to go to the gym again, but I tried to be late on purpose. I wasn't ready yet. I didn't know if I could handle the small talk, the weather, or how we were doing. Not with Ava, not when I'd pictured our whole future together.

I saw her anyway, about halfway there just as I was walking by the park. It was like time slowed for a minute. Six weeks can change a person, and even though Ava looked... the same, she didn't.

She looked happier, or happier than when I'd seen her last, and that nearly broke me all over again. Because a small part of me had hoped she was just as broken about this as I was. Because that's what Noah had implied.

Ava didn't see me, or maybe she did, but it felt like she looked through me. We locked eyes. Or so I thought. And then she shook her head and kept going, not even saying a word.

I was pretty sure Noah was wrong. Ava had no interest in coming back to me.

Ava

Week six, I was seriously losing it.

I saw Parker twice, in the daylight, in our normal schedule, or I thought I did. I could have sworn I locked eyes with her that morning, but I knew better. I'd been seeing her in the faces of so many people, I didn't trust myself anymore. Not if I didn't have someone else to back me up. Like Meg. Or Jayde.

That night, I stepped in the back door like usual and got set up. Nathan gave me his typical thumbs up from the door of the sound booth without a word. He looked less angry than he had been, so that was nice.

I got started, strumming through what I knew was probably the most hopeful melody I'd sung in weeks. I was through the bridge of the first song when I saw her, missing a chord, and nearly forgetting the words.

I was pretty sure it wasn't my imagination this time.

She was behind the bar, making drinks, chatting and smiling with customers. It almost felt like nothing had changed, but she looked different. She looked tired, a little sad, a slump to her shoulders where I'd grown used to seeing confidence. It made me want to get off the stage and hug her, but I didn't. I kept playing and singing through the lump that was rising in my throat.

I gave a nod, and a 'thank you' to the small bit of applause that came when I finished, and then I caught her looking my way.

She looked back down, but I caught the red tint of her cheeks, anyway. I wondered how much she remembered from Tuesday night. Probably nothing. She was really drunk. But maybe?

I let out a sigh, adjusting the capo on my guitar.

"Here's something different I've been working on." I mumbled into the mic.

Parker's eyes met mine again, and I felt a flutter in my stomach. It was weird how infuriating that feeling had been in the beginning, but how much hope it gave me now.

I knew the music I'd been playing for a while was depressing as shit. It's hard to sing happy songs when all you want to do is cry. Music is emotion, and most of the time, I could only play what I was feeling.

I found it funny how easy it was to think of a song for 'I'm sorry.'

Maybe a part of me knew Parker had probably already moved on. That's why she was working the bar on nights again, right? Maybe Jayde would walk in any minute to rub it in my face. Maybe they'd leave together at the end of the night. Maybe I'd have to see them dancing at Willow and Noah's eventual wedding. And maybe Parker would not save a dance for me.

I guess I didn't care.

I couldn't look up for most of the first verse. But by the time I got to the chorus, I had to know if she was listening. I didn't know what I'd do if she wasn't. Let go, move on, pretend Parker had never come into my life? Impossible.

She was listening.

Her eyes locked with mine, and we got stuck in a deep, intense stare. And singing without crying while holding that stare was becoming increasingly difficult.

By the time I got to the part about wishing I could go back and change things, I had to look down. When I looked back up, Parker had turned around, fumbling with bottles, making more drinks, but I could have sworn I caught her wiping her cheek.

Parker

Who did Ava think she was?

She knew damn good and well I was too sentimental to work through a song like *that*. Especially when she was—why was she looking at me like that, anyway? I knew she'd sung songs basically for me before, but why in the hell would she be doing it now?

This was a terrible idea. I should have stayed on days. I wasn't ready for this. I hadn't even been to therapy with Carmen yet, for Christ's sake.

Did she really think she could apologize through *a song?*

Dinner rush came and went while she played. I tried stealing more glances at her because, despite everything, I loved watching her play. But I kept getting caught, and I hated that feeling, feeling like she knew she had a grip on me with just her freaking voice.

Slowly, the bar started dying down, too, like it always did right around the time she headed out. I knew she was about to stop. I knew she'd be heading out the back door, probably walking home alone.

God, how many nights had she just walked home alone?

I heard her final, "thank you" echo throughout the bar area. She told the tiny crowd to have a good night and stepped down from the stage. I turned toward the sink, while I heard the familiar latch of her guitar case, the click of her shoes on the floor of the stage. I didn't think I could handle watching her walk out. It would probably take everything in me not to chase after her.

Someone pulled out a chair at the bar. I didn't remember hearing the bell over the door ding, but I couldn't bring myself to turn around. Not until I heard the click of the back door. If she was already gone, maybe I could just finish my shift in peace. Maybe I could pretend I didn't want to—what? What did I want to do, exactly?

"You in the habit of ignoring your customers?" I heard her say, and I stiffened instinctively. "Terrible service. I should speak to your manager."

I turned to face her, biting the inside of my lip. "Don't do that."

"Do what?" She looked down.

"Don't joke with me like... like nothing happened." I grabbed the towel from the bar and started drying a nearby glass, if only for something to do. "You can't just laugh your way out of this."

"I'm sorry." She whispered.

"Yeah, I got that."

Why was I being an asshole? Isn't this what I wanted? Didn't I want Ava to come back? Didn't I want her to say she was sorry and beg me to take her back? Didn't I want her to be sitting here, hanging on my every word, looking at me... like that?

Didn't I?

I turned to put the glass down, and I heard a shuffle.

"Have a good night, Parker."

Shit.

"Ava, wait." The words tumbled out of my mouth, running together.

She turned really slowly. Was she already crying?

"What do you want?" I mumbled. "T-to drink. On the house."

"You don't have to do me any favors." She shook her head slowly. "It's not like you owe me anything."

"Please." I choked, grateful there was only one table.

She took a step back to the stool and sat back down with a sigh.

"I don't even want a drink." She said so softly I barely heard it. "I just thought it would be a good excuse to talk to you."

"Yeah?" I felt my eyes narrow. I didn't really know why. "If you came here to grovel, it's really beneath you."

"Look who's joking now."

A painful laugh slipped out.

Things had always been so easy with Ava, like everything always fell into place even when we didn't want them to. Why was this so hard?

The bell on the door dinged, and Ava looked at it and back at me.

"You get a break any time soon?" She asked.

I nodded, even though it would probably piss Nathan off. Just then, I looked up to find him eyeing us from the door of the sound booth with a look that screamed, "you've got to be fucking kidding me."

Ava

I waited for Parker out back, digging ruts in the gravel with my toe because I didn't know what else to do with my nervous energy. Probably ten minutes went by before the kitchen door opened and she stepped out with a long sigh.

She smiled at me, but it was forced, and it didn't quite reach her eyes. She was still defensive, I could tell. There was at least four feet of space between us, and she didn't even look at me, not really, not like she used to, not in the way I practically ached for her to.

She pulled out a pack of cigarettes and lit one. I didn't even know Parker smoked. In six months together, she'd never had a cigarette around me, not once. No smoker's breath. I'd never smelled it on her.

I didn't just send her back to Jayde. Shit, I really was toxic.

A stillness settled between us.

"I shouldn't have left like that." I said finally, realizing I had to be the one to break the silence.

She let out a puff of smoke and sighed in response.

"I'm sorry, Parker."

"I know." Parker nodded, taking another drag from the cigarette before her eyes met mine. "But I don't know if I can forgive you yet. And I don't know if I should."

I nodded, looking down, blinking back tears before they could form, even though I knew that was not embracing my feelings whatsoever. But somehow, crying in front of her felt manipulative, even if I didn't mean it that way.

I wasn't sure what I'd expected. That she'd hug me, tell me everything was okay, and it would go back to how it was? It didn't work like that. It couldn't because how it was... didn't work, either.

"Jayde left like that." She said, pulling my attention back to her, and my breath caught in my throat. "Packed up all her stuff in a rush, told me she couldn't do this anymore. Next thing I knew, she was dating some guy."

It wasn't a secret Jayde had hurt her. She'd never told me the nasty details, but I'd never asked. Maybe I should have. Maybe if I'd known... maybe what? I would have been more rational? Doubtful.

"She kept coming back though." Parker continued, brushing the cigarette against the building before putting it in the trash. "Told me everything I needed to hear to convince me she wanted me. And once she had me, she was gone again. It was a game."

A game you fell for again. I thought, thinking of the night I'd seen them together. I knew I couldn't be mad at her. It wasn't like we were ever officially together, anyway. She really didn't owe me a thing.

"So, why are you sorry, Ava? Why now?"

I didn't know how to answer that. I didn't think anything I could say would sound like anything but a broken record, especially not if Jayde had given her every sob story in the book.

I missed her. I'd missed her the moment I walked out of her apartment. There was a hole where she should have been. I shouldn't have left. I should have stayed.

I was just scared.

I didn't think any of that was good enough.

"Whenever you figure it out, let me know." Parker sighed, grabbing the handle of the door and heading inside.

"Parker—"

She didn't stop or turn around, and kicked the wall like a toddler, feeling a sharp pain shoot through my leg up to my knee.

Way to feel your feelings.

I started sobbing instead as I slid down the brick wall to the damp pavement.

I'd been right. Leaving Parker was the biggest mistake of my life.

That's what I should have said.

I started thinking about what Carmen had said, about how I needed to feel things in the moment, not bottle them up. So, I did. I let myself cry, and feel, and hurt. I let me be mad at me. For choking on my words, for leaving in the first place, for quitting the group, for not going to Carmen's one-on-one sessions sooner, for not seeing any of Cam's red flags until they were collectively slapping me in the face. I cried for every version of me that got me to that moment. And once I was done doing that... I was too tired to move.

This sucked. All of it sucked.

And I couldn't help but feel like... if I'd just never met Cam, maybe I could've loved Parker right to begin with.

Parker

I finished the night with Ava consuming the majority of my thoughts. I wanted to forgive her because a part of me still believed she was my person. Just being around her made me feel warm again. I wanted her to be serious, and want me the way I wanted her. And now I couldn't be sure if she did. Because I'd thought she had the first time.

The bar officially closed at one am, leaving straggling drinkers to finish their drinks and be out by 1:30. It gave me time to clean, stock what made sense, and wait for Noah.

By the time the end of the night rolled around, Nathan was sitting at the bar waiting for the kitchen to close, having a beer with me. It was weird, but maybe he was just grateful I was saving his weekends again.

Nathan was saying something about the game on the screen, but I was only half listening. I was trying to talk myself out of walking to Ava's house. I just wanted a hug.

"Hey," Noah whispered. That was a very hesitant 'hey.'

"What?" I asked, turning around.

I was hoping like hell he hadn't spilled something in the kitchen because he should have at least been close to done by now.

He was fidgeting with his phone.

"I hate to ask, but what happened with Ava tonight?"

"We just talked." I shrugged, trying to avoid looking at Nathan's very pointed gaze.

"Well... what did you say? Willow said she didn't come home."

I felt the blood drain from my face.

"Nothing... nothing bad, I don't think." I was reeling, grabbing my jacket from the bar, instinctively shoving my arms through the holes where they were supposed to go. There was a numbness there, somehow only overpowered by fear. "I mean, I wasn't exactly promising her the moon and stars. You think she's just late getting home from—"

"She didn't work tonight."

"Fuck." I mumbled under my breath. "Okay, let's go. Last I saw her, she was behind the kitchen door. Let's start there, and I'll see if I can think of where she'd go."

Nathan cleared his throat, and I felt my fists clinch. Ava could be in trouble, and he was going to double check we'd finished all our work first? I wasn't much of a fighter, but I just might hit him. The comradery from two minutes ago was long gone.

"Matt said she was still out back a few minutes ago." Nathan said casually, taking another sip of his beer. "I thought she was just waiting for you."

Yeah, waiting outside in the alley when she could have just sat at the bar? Logical, Nathan.

"If she's back there, we can take her home." Noah sighed. "Willow won't forgive me if I make her walk."

He smirked as he slipped back into the kitchen.

I wouldn't forgive myself.

Sure enough, when I walked around the back, I saw a figure seated in the alley. I was ready to snap at her, tell her how reckless it was to just chill out back here in the first place. She could have at least told Willow she was okay. But she was too still for that. Was she asleep?

She didn't look my way when I walked up, or move for that matter. It wasn't like I was quiet about it, in fact, I was storming up to her at first.

I wasn't even one hundred percent sure she was breathing. She was so still and quiet, just staring off into space. It felt like a mirror to the numbness I'd been drowning in for weeks.

I reached down and grabbed the guitar case, and she jumped, eyes darting to mine.

"Come on, we'll take you home." I said, trying to ignore the feeling that came when she looked up at me. The protective feeling, like all the love I had for her, had never gone away.

Her eyes were puffy, makeup smeared down her face. She'd been crying for a good minute, and it took all my willpower not to pull her into my arms and hug her.

She looked away, rubbing her hands against her knees. "It's okay. I don't think Noah would want to. He's not my biggest fan these days."

"It was his idea."

Midway through tucking her hair behind her ear, she looked up at me again.

"Willow was worried about you." I added.

She nodded, standing up mechanically, like she was stiff.

I wasn't going to feel sorry for her. I wasn't going to feel sorry for her. I wasn't going to feel sorry for her.

"I'm sorry," she whispered so low I almost didn't even hear it. "I didn't mean to—"

"It's fine." I mumbled as we reached Noah's car.

I was getting really tired of hearing apologies.

She took the guitar case, and her hand brushed mine, and my stomach twisted up in knots. It's funny how the smallest touch could do that. I guess she felt it, too, because her eyes were wide when she looked back up at me, sparkling in the streetlight. How had I forgotten how beautiful she was?

I was too close to her.

I turned, grabbing the handle to the front door. Without a word, I climbed into the front seat where I could keep my distance.

She was a little slower, maybe more hesitant, as she climbed in the back. I thought I heard her sniffle and fought the urge to look back at her. If she was crying again, I probably wouldn't be able to stop myself from hugging her.

Why was I like this?

It was so easy to let go. Forgive, without any ounce of self-preservation. It was like I only knew how to love other people more than myself.

Didn't I deserve better than that?

I could not wait for Tuesday. Maybe Carmen could help me make sense of the self-destructive way I put my heart on my sleeve for people who had already proven they would just throw it back in my face.

Ava

I didn't realize how long I'd been crying in that alley. Long enough I stopped crying and just went numb. Longer than I'd cried when I actually left Parker because at least then I thought there was a chance for us. Now I didn't know. And I was supposed to be embracing my feelings, but I didn't quite know how to do that. Instead, I stopped feeling, stopped processing. Started dissociating–doing all the things Carmen wanted me not to do.

I wanted grey area, well I fucking got it.

The only thing between me and Parker now was murky, grey space. Too much space. She felt too far away, and she was still so close, which only made it worse. It felt like there was a window between us. Look, don't touch.

Maybe we'd never get back to what we were. Maybe we'd never be better than that. How painful would that be? Going through the motions of forgiveness just to realize it's far too broken to fix. Maybe she didn't want to. Maybe she didn't even want to try. I guess I couldn't blame her. I still didn't get what she'd seen in me in the first place.

No, that was not positive self-talk. I took a deep breath and let it out.

I deserve love.

My guitar case tapped my foot, and I jumped, looking up to find Parker standing next to me.

Shit, what time was it?

She had a tired look in her eye, whether from the shift she'd just worked or something else, but something about her was less rigid now than it had been earlier. I settled for even an ounce of her guard down. Because that lit a tiny spark of hope in me.

I tried not to be hurt when she told me Willow was worried about me. Was she worried about me, too? Or was she past letting herself care? I didn't think I wanted the answer to that.

We were only waiting in the car for Noah for five minutes at most, but it felt like a lot longer. Time had never felt slow with Parker. It always seemed to fly. But Parker was stiff and silent instead of the casual and confident version of her I was used to. I tried to convince myself she was being like this because she was scared.

Just like I had been. Like I was now, but for an entirely different reason.

I did that to her. I managed to take someone who believed in soulmates and fate and the power of the universe, and I managed to make her not believe in me. Suddenly, I was crying again. I thought I caught Parker growing even more stiff.

When Noah finally came out, he was chipper, typing away on his phone. I bet he and Willow had another big date coming up or something. I was glad someone was happy. At the very least, he could cut some of the tension in the car, fill the silence, make the short ride to my apartment bearable.

I wasn't even listening to what he was saying. He wasn't talking to me, anyway. I felt like we had an understanding after

I'd walked Parker home, but that didn't mean he had to like me. He was looking out for her, and I deserved it.

I probably wouldn't have gone back to the therapy group without him.

I deserve love.

But did Parker deserve me? Or did she deserve better?

Parker

We pulled up to Ava's apartment building, and I got out. I didn't know why I felt the need to walk her to her door, but I did. Despite how painful it was just to look at her, I needed to know she was okay. Not just physically. Something about the way she was staring off into space in that alleyway worried me.

"Thank you, Noah." Ava whispered.

"Mhmm." He replied tersely.

She was tired. I could tell because she was lugging her guitar case like it weighed a thousand pounds. I took it from her as we reached the door of the building. I ignored the knots in my stomach from the brush of her skin against mine, turning my head back to the car to catch Noah shaking his head at me.

I had a feeling I was in for a talking to when we got home. He was going to make one hell of a dad one day.

When we reached the door of her apartment, she met my eyes.

"Thank you." She murmured, so hesitantly it hurt.

I leaned the guitar against the door frame, and she turned toward the door.

I let out a sigh, and caught her wrist before she could turn the knob. The look of shock on her face when I pulled her back to me was satisfying. As was the gasp she let out when I wrapped my arms around her shoulders. I'd been giving her all the control before, taking things at her pace. Almost how I'd been with Jayde, but for an entirely different reason.

Not anymore.

She was stiff for a second, like she wasn't sure how to respond, and then her arms settled on my back, and she let out a sigh. I felt her relax against me, a little puzzle piece falling into place. I should have pulled away. I shouldn't have given in to that urge to just have her close to me.

"You're not forgiven yet." I said, even though I didn't want to. "That's going to take some... time."

She nodded wordlessly against my chest.

I held on a little longer because I wanted to. Maybe because I needed to. Ava made me feel better despite the fact that she was the one who'd hurt me to begin with.

"Do you—" I heard her suck in a shaky breath, and then sigh. I thought she might have been crying again, but I didn't pull away. "Do you still want me?"

"I wouldn't be here if I didn't."

Fuck, why was I like this?

She nodded again. I pulled away before I did something stupid. I looked down at her, grabbing her face in my hands. She was crying again. I was pretty sure she was shaking, too.

"What can I do?" She asked. "How can I—"

"I just need time, Ava." I whispered, and she nodded.

I kissed her forehead. I could feel her clinging to my sides, the touch making me warm like it used to and cold with fear at the same time. This felt so different from what I'd been through with Jayde, yet there were so many ways it felt exactly the same.

Jayde had known how to throw a pity party, too.

"Goodnight, Ava." I whispered, pulling away before I made the mistake of forgiving her too easily. Before I kissed her like I wanted to. Before I went inside, curled up in her bed, and got a good night's sleep.

“Goodnight.” She replied, but I was already turning toward the stairs.

I had to put as much distance between us as I could. Or I’d risk making the same old mistakes, forgiving too easily, not asking the hard questions like Noah said I should do, letting Ava undo any progress I was attempting to make. I couldn’t do that. Not again.

Ava

We didn't talk the next day I played at Brickhouse. I caught her eye once or twice as I slowly shifted to happier music, but I could tell she was doing her best not to look in my direction. There was too much tension, and I left without a word. I was trying to give Parker space, and it was killing me.

"Morning." Parker nodded as she passed me, headed to the gym Sunday morning. She was late, as usual.

"Morning." I mumbled back. "Hey! That was really you the other day, right?"

"Huh?"

"The other day, I thought I saw you... headed to the gym... that was you, right?"

"Yeah," she nodded, frowning at me like I was nuts.

"Okay," I nodded. "Glad I'm not completely crazy. Have a good day."

I turned, walking away. Missing Parker might even be harder with her halfway back in my life.

"What'd you mean by that?" Parker asked, suddenly next to me.

"I just..." I let out a breath and shook my head, feeling my cheeks burning.

Parker did not need to know that I'd been seeing her in every face of every woman who even slightly resembled her.

"Ava, you looked right at me. Who else would it have been?"

I swallowed hard. "I'd just... I thought I saw you so many times... I wasn't sure."

"You thought you saw me where?" There was a hint of a grin on her face.

"You want me to be honest?"

She nodded.

I sighed, meeting her eyes and stopping. "Everywhere."

Her brows knitted a little closer together.

"I thought I saw you every day. Everywhere I went. Different places, different people." I bit my lip, looking down for a minute. "But it was never you. After a while, I quit letting myself believe it. I thought if I saw you, unless someone else saw you, too, I was just... seeing things. So, I didn't mean to ignore you. I just... I didn't believe it was you."

When I looked back up at her, Parker was grinning. She had that look in her eyes that she used to have in the beginning. The one I was afraid of then, and practically craved now.

"While I'm being honest." I sighed. "I missed you."

I let it hang there. I wasn't trying to just feed her what I thought she wanted to hear, but I knew it was going to come out that way.

"It wasn't just that—" I huffed. There really was no good way to fix this. "Never mind. It's not going to come out right."

I started walking again, feeling Parker next to me, keeping up with my pace.

"Ava—"

"No, you told me to think about it." I said as I stopped. "To think about what I could say to you. Well, you know what? It's all I've thought about for weeks." Fuck, I was crying again. I was so sick of crying. It felt childish and manipulative. "And I didn't realize until you asked that there's nothing, I could say that won't sound pathetic and insignificant. Because the truth just sounds like a sad sob story of an excuse. And you deserve better than that."

"I'd still like to hear it." She laughed. It was soft, barely above a whisper. But she fucking laughed.

So, I did, too.

"Your sob story of an excuse, I mean."

"Another time, maybe." I sighed, wiping my cheek. "You're already late."

She let out a sigh, and laughed for real, looking down. A frown spread across her face, and she met my eyes.

"You're still wearing that." She said breathily, nodding to my neck.

I looked down, eyeing the guitar pick necklace. Still the best gift I'd ever been given. "I never stopped."

She let out a sigh, and I eyed the street that led to the gym.

"I'll meet you at the coffee shop? If you can be on time."

"Save a spot in line for me?" She grinned, backing down the street.

I nodded, and then she was off.

Parker

The next two days were weird. Being back in the old schedule, seeing Ava every day, several times a day, even when it was tentative, it felt so odd. Because it felt natural, even when it didn't. Even when it didn't feel normal, I felt like I was in the right place, anyway.

I kept reminding myself this wasn't like it had been with Jayde. Ava wasn't Jayde.

She'd hurt me the same. Maybe even worse because I felt like myself with her, and I could still picture a future with her. But none of this felt like a game to Ava. She wasn't really the type for games. I knew that, deep down, but it didn't make it feel like any less of a risk.

"Hey," I asked Monday morning when I bumped into her on the way to the gym. "You want to get dinner tonight? After you get off."

"I can't." She sighed, and I felt my heart sink. "I have therapy."

I almost had to shake my head to be sure I'd heard her. "You went back?"

She nodded. "Yeah, I'm actually sharing now."

This definitely wasn't how things went with Jayde.

"Sharing about...?"

"Me, mostly, which is probably good. A little about you, too, but I didn't tell them who you are if that's what you're worried about."

"It's not." I smiled. "Do you... feel like it's helping?"

She nodded. "I'm learning positive self-talk and self-love."

She let out a deep sigh, looking off somewhere I couldn't make out. "Carmen says I'm the kind of person who can't let myself love someone else because I don't value myself. I don't think I'm good enough. All that 'accepting the love we think we deserve stuff.'"

My heart was racing. I'd never heard the word 'love' come out of Ava's mouth before.

"Anyway, I think it's been good for me." She looked back up at me. "At the very least, I'm learning to embrace what I feel."

"Which is?" I swallowed hard.

She smiled, letting out a soft laugh.

"Another time, maybe?" She said like she had the other day. "You're—"

"Late, yeah I know."

I looked down. It was weird not kissing her every day. I'd grown so used to—

She reached up and kissed my cheek. Fast like she had that first time in the car with Noah. I stiffened instinctively.

"I'm sorry—" she breathed, her mouth hanging open as she slowly started to back away. "I don't know why I—I shouldn't have—"

"It's okay." I sighed. "That was—it's okay."

Her cheeks flushed. "I'll see you later."

She turned fast.

“Ava...” I sighed, running to catch her, grabbing her wrist. “Come here.”

I pulled her into a hug like I had the other night. I wasn’t ready to kiss her yet, but this might even be better. Nobody had ever hugged me like Ava.

Ava

"Would you like to share, Ava?" Carmen asked. I wasn't first, thankfully.

I nodded. "Um, well update."

I let out a laugh and a couple of the people in the group leaned forward in their seats.

"She's back on the old shift, and we're talking, sort of. It's... complicated. I know it's going to be a process."

Carmen nodded. "That's progress."

I nodded back, letting out a sigh. "I apologized for leaving, but I'm realizing that might not be good enough at this point. I really hurt her, and I think she wants to forgive me, but I know it's not going to be easy. She—she has a past, too. Her ex left in a similar way, so I think it's hit a little harder than I'd realized."

"Sometimes the pain we feel can manifest itself into actions if we let it. Like you leaving because of the things your ex had done. And now her struggling to forgive because of what her ex has done. Do you believe you could deserve her forgiveness at this point?"

"I've been working on the self-love. Or trying to, it's really hard. I don't know if I deserve her forgiveness, but... I want to earn it. Right now, I'm just," I sighed. "I'm just trying to give her what she needs from me, and I'm leaving the ball in her court."

Carmen smiled. "I think that's a great place to be. Anyone have anything they'd like to add?"

Tate raised a hand tentatively, and Carmen nodded. She looked at me and smiled.

"You love her, don't you? Are you ready to admit that now?"

I nodded, my eyes instantly growing misty. "Yeah. I really love her."

"How do you feel about yourself?" Carmen asked.

I let out a sigh, nodding. "I do deserve love."

The group finished, and I stayed chatting for a minute with some of the members. I hadn't texted Tate yet, but her number was still in my purse. It was weird how quickly I was accepted by them. I could have been friends with these people from day one. All I had to do was be honest. With them, and with myself.

When everyone was dwindling, I slipped out the door and back into the coffee shop lobby. Parker was waiting for me by the door, leaning against the frame with that confident look in her eye again.

Her face lit up when she saw me. She was looking at me... like that again, like I was what she wanted, like I was hers.

"What are you doing here?" I smiled.

"Waiting for you." She said, looking between me and Tate for a moment.

"Bye, Ava," Tate grinned wide as she looked between me and Parker, dots connecting.

I felt my cheeks flush, and Parker raised an eyebrow. I looked away because her face was making my cheeks burn hotter.

"How was the group?" Parker asked when I didn't explain.

"Good," I nodded. "I think I actually made friends."

"Oh, I didn't think you knew how to do that."

I smacked her arm. Lightly, though, I wasn't sure how comfortable she was with this—with us. Were we an 'us'?

"You want to grab a coffee? Maybe talk somewhere for a bit?" Parker asked, and I heard her swallow. "Maybe tonight could be another time?"

I let out a laugh. "I don't know about all that."

"No, no, I think you owe me a sad sob story of an excuse."

I grinned, knowing just that sentence gave me far more hope than I thought I could afford in the moment.

Parker

That night, I went to the little bar I'd taken Ava for her birthday to just think. It felt weird being there without her. Maybe that's why I was there. I needed to think about Ava. I needed to think about that night, her birthday.

I needed to decide if I was going to forgive her and work on things, or if I was going to walk away. Because walking the line was killing me.

A woman walked up to my booth. A red-headed woman, maybe my age. She was pretty, with piercing blue eyes and freckles dotting her cheeks. She flashed me a tired, hesitant look.

"Parker, right?" She said, sliding into the booth across from me. I didn't ask how she knew my name. I didn't really care. I'd give her five seconds to shoot her shot and then I'd leave. "I'm Cam."

I felt a chill and set down my glass. "Yeah, I'm out of here."

"Wait," she pleaded. "Look, I know Jayde."

"And now I'm really out of here."

"Shit, no—look I hate Jayde, okay?"

"And I'm not so fond of you." I snapped back.

"I wouldn't expect you to be."

I paused halfway out of the booth, looking back at her. Was this supposed to be some revenge hook up? Because if so, I was really ready to tell her off.

She let out an exasperated breath. "I know about you and Ava. I know Jayde has been trying to get you back, so—"

"I'm really not interested in whatever you think is going to happen here." I motioned between the two of us and started to get up again.

"Whoa, no, no." She laughed. "It's not like that."

"Why are you here, Cam?"

She let out a deep sigh and her eyes got really sad, which almost made me feel sorry for her. Almost. Maybe if Ava hadn't told me anything about her, I might have.

"I'm here for Ava." She said finally, meeting my eyes.

I had to hold back a laugh, but I managed a single eyebrow raise. "I find that really hard to believe."

"I'm sure she's said some not nice things about me, and I deserve it." She tapped her glass with the ring on her finger. That finger. Shit, that was a big ring. "I hurt Ava... in more ways than one—"

"Yeah, I know, which is why I find it hard to believe that you're here for her. Why would you care about me and Ava?"

"Because Ava was the best thing that ever happened to me. And I didn't just take her for granted... look, at one point, she was my best friend. She was the person I told my deepest, darkest secrets to. Secrets I still can't tell anyone else. She loved me better than anyone else ever could."

"So, why'd you abuse her?" I wasn't going to sugarcoat it. If she really was here for Ava, she wouldn't avoid calling it what it was.

"I was really fucked up." She shrugged, her eyes getting a little glassy. "And I was young, and using any unhealthy coping mechanism I could to get past my own trauma that I really needed therapy for."

I scoffed. I didn't mean to, but I did.

"Look, I don't deserve to have Ava back in my life."

"No, you don't."

She let out a breath. "But Ava deserves someone better than me. Someone who understands her, someone who loves as deeply as she does, and I think that someone could be you."

"You don't even know me."

"You're right, I don't, but I know Jayde. I know what she put you through. I've heard all about it. And... I've seen her out with you a couple times. Ava. She's happy with you. Really happy."

She got a faraway look in her eye and turned away, wiping her cheek before she turned back toward me.

"Seen her out because you're still stalking her?"

"No, I'm not. Okay, I was. I did. But I also live here." Cam sighed. "I stopped following Ava a while ago."

"So, what do you want?" I asked.

"I want you to stop avoiding her and—"

"How did you—?"

"Stop going to the clubs and drinking your feelings." Cam continued as if I hadn't said a thing. "Ava needs reassurance. Constant reassurance that she's good enough, that she's wanted."

"And you'd know?"

"Who do you think fucked her up so badly?" Cam squeezed her drink. "I'm the reason she—"

She made a choking sound.

"I'm the reason she doesn't think she deserves to be loved. I'm the reason she uses those words." She let out a shaky breath. "Because I told her nobody would love her and no one would want her every night for eight months. This is my fault."

"Yeah, it is, but you being here, this? That's not going to fix it." I let out a huff, sliding a little closer to the edge of the booth again. "I'm not going to put in a good word for you so you can waltz back into her life."

"I don't want you to. I'm leaving—we're moving to Texas." Cam fiddled with her ring. "Ava doesn't have to worry about me anymore. She doesn't want to hear from me, and that's fine. That doesn't mean I don't think about her. That doesn't mean I don't wish good things for her. If I could have a do over, I wouldn't date her. I'd just be her friend because she's a really amazing friend."

"Well, we don't get do overs, do we?"

"I can't, but you might."

I let out a breath and downed the rest of my drink, nearly out of the booth.

"She gets bad migraines, but nap and a coffee usually do the trick." Cam said before I could walk away, and for some reason, I paused. "She really can't handle hard liquor. If she gets drunk enough, she'll do anything, *let you* do anything, but she'll regret it in the morning, so even if she begs for it, tell her no."

I tried not to scoff at her. How many times had she taken advantage of that?

"Most of the time, you can fix anything with a hug... or a kiss." She continued. "Don't go to bed angry because she won't sleep it off. She'll just stew."

"She's allergic to nutmeg, and she can't have pumpkin spice anything, ever. Since it's that time of year. Gummy candy is her period craving, but she'll tell you it's ice cream. She loves lilies, but Milo tries to eat them, and they can kill cats, so daisies are the best second choice."

She looked back at me, meeting my eyes again.

"I think she loves you." Cam said with a sad smile. "I think she deserves you."

She downed what was left of her drink like a shot and slid out of the booth.

Cam reached out and grabbed my hand, and it took all my willpower not to snatch it back. She set a tiny piece of metal in my palm.

"She should have that back. It was her grandma's." She let out a sigh, looking down at her shoes for a second and then back up at me. "I really am trying to be a better person. I can't undo what I did, and I know I don't deserve to have her back in my life. I'm okay with that. If this is the only amends I get, that's something I can live with."

The moment Cam left, I booked it to the coffee shop. The group would be done soon, and I'd already answered my own question. There was no way I could walk away from Ava. Ever.

She wasn't Jayde. This wasn't the same. It wasn't a game to her. And not just because she was going to therapy.

I didn't wait long, though I did see some familiar faces from the group making their way through the lobby long before I saw Ava. She was smiling, but when she saw me, her eyes went wide. It made my heart race until the smile returned.

She gave a pointed look to a girl I remembered from the group. Tate. Redheaded Tate, who looked nothing like Cam, as it turned out, but the buzzword of red hair had fueled jealousy in me when Jayde had said it.

Of course, she'd been lying.

Tate said goodbye, eyeing me, and I knew that meant the group would have the whole scoop now, but I didn't care. I didn't care what they knew.

I just needed to talk to her. I needed to get out my feelings, say everything I'd been afraid to say before. I could do this. I could forgive her. She was Ava. Even the universe wanted us to be together.

We stepped up to the counter, and Ava eyed it.

"I think I want something... warm, maybe fall themed. It's that season." Ava squinted, and I eyed her out of the corner of my eye, my thoughts wandering to the conversation with Cam.

She had to. She had to go for a fall drink. I was supposed to have more time to talk about this. Maybe explain myself or why I suddenly knew things about her that she'd never told me, but I didn't get the chance.

"We have our pumpkin spice latte or—" the barista said with a smile.

"Oh, she can't have Pumpkin Spice." I cut in, not even thinking, before Ava could answer. "She's allergic to... nutmeg."

I could feel her eyes on me. The reality set in.

"How did you know that?" She grinned. "I don't usually worry about it until the holidays come around."

I must have gone stiff or something, because she frowned.

"What?" she asked.

"Nothing." I forced a smile.

"I'll just take a mocha. You have that one with cinnamon and almond, right? She'd probably like that?"

I looked at her for confirmation, but she was frowning at me, not answering. There was a line forming behind us, so I handed cash to the barista. I shoved my hands in my pockets as I made my way to the receiving counter.

I knew I couldn't lie to her.

"Parker." She said flatly.

"Can we just—can we wait until we get outside?"

She let out a huff, thinking for a minute. She hadn't even said anything before our coffee came out, and I felt my throat go dry. Ava grabbed my hand and practically dragged me outside.

"What aren't you telling me?" She snapped.

"I met Cam." I said finally.

"You met Cam?" She raised an eyebrow.

"Yeah, we talked—"

"Fuck you, Parker." She snapped and turned, storming off.

"Ava, wait, it wasn't like that!" I said, trailing after her.

"Oh of course it wasn't! It never is with Cam. She would go after you, of all people."

"No, Ava," I let out a sigh, still struggling to keep up with her without wearing this coffee. Damn she was fast when she was mad. "She found me at St. Clare's, and we talked. We *just* talked. She talked about therapy and making amends—"

"Oh yeah, she's always trying to make amends. I've heard that bullshit before." Ava snapped, turning on heel and shoving her index finger in my face. "And *you* fell for it. What did she want this time? And what did you give her?"

"She didn't want anything." I said quickly. I'd never once thought Ava could be unnerving. "She didn't ask for anything. She's moving to Texas—"

"Bullshit. She always says she's leaving town when she wants me to drop my guard."

"She said she just wanted you to be happy. She gave me some advice—"

"Oh, yeah, you might as well toss out whatever she told you because she knows *nothing* about me."

I reached into my pocket and pulled out the necklace, dangling it in the air between us.

"Where did you get that?" She sucked in a breath.

"Cam said you should have it back. She said it was your grandma's."

Ava swallowed hard, reaching up with shaking fingers and took the locket from my hand, still clutching her coffee with the other.

"Three years." Ava glared up at me. "Three years, I've been begging Cam to give back this necklace, and every time, it was the same manipulative bullshit, about apologies and meeting in person, and now she just *gives it to you?*"

"She doesn't want to reach out to you. She just..." I let out a sigh as she looked back down at the locket. "She just wanted me to get my head out of my ass."

Ava looked back up at me with a sharp glare. "And did you?"

I shrugged. "I'm trying to."

Ava nodded, biting the inside of her lip.

"I didn't go looking for Cam, okay?" I sighed, stepping closer to her. "She found me, and—"

"Yeah, that's what she does."

"I wasn't having any of her bullshit, if that makes you feel any better."

"I don't know." Ava shrugged.

"Can we...can we still talk?" I swallowed. "I guess if you're mad at me, we don't have to."

"We can still talk." She smiled sadly. "I can't guarantee any groveling though, so if that's what you're after..."

I laughed, wrapping an arm around her shoulder, hoping that wasn't too forward.

Ava

I didn't know what this was, but me and Parker sat down on the steps in front of the department store to talk, anyway. I didn't really want to go inside. Work had slowed down again. The fall line was out, and I was pretty sure they were giving me busy work again.

"So, what did you want to talk about?" I asked, trying to avoid the obvious.

"Well, you know I need this sob story excuse. I've been waiting ages." She smiled at me, maybe trying to be lighthearted about the whole Cam thing, but I couldn't bring myself to return it.

Knowing she'd actually sat down and heard Cam out after what I'd told her... it made me question everything about her—about us. But when she was looking at me... like that...

I looked down, fumbling with the lid to my coffee with one hand and the necklace she'd given me with the other. I did like the stupid cinnamon drink.

"Why did you leave?" Parker asked. I realized rather quickly that her voice was shaky.

"I was scared." I met her eyes, expecting her to roll them, but she didn't. "I overheard you talking to Noah, and I just... I didn't think I was ready for all that. I had to work on me first. I didn't think I could be with you and heal at the same time."

"What about now?"

I felt my eyes well up, and she wrapped an arm around my shoulder, which somehow made me feel like I could actually get through this conversation. Why was everything easier when Parker was touching me?

"I missed you, Parker." I whispered. "I didn't just miss you, though. It was like... there was this gaping hole where you should have been. Everywhere I went, every minute of the day... nothing was right without you in it."

"That's a really good start." Parker breathed, and I let out a laugh.

"I wasn't okay." I continued because I needed to say it and she needed to hear it. "Not once, the whole time. I wasn't okay. I tried to text you a couple of times."

I felt her stiffen002E

"I figured you blocked me. It's okay."

She rubbed my back, this soft, circular motion. I didn't know if she was doing it on purpose or absent mindedly. I didn't care.

I let out a sigh.

Lay it on the table. Ball in her court. You deserve love.

"Leaving you was the biggest mistake I've ever made." I closed my eyes because, maybe I could pretend she wasn't there. I could pretend I was home, and she couldn't reject me. Maybe I could get it all out that way.

"I-I know I realized it a little too late." I stammered. I tried to blink back tears while they were forming, but it didn't work. "But I do want a future with you. In fact, there's no version of the future that makes sense without you in it."

I could hear her heart racing as I rested my cheek under her arm. Other than that, she was really still and quiet.

"I realized the other night at the bar." I sighed. "I realized there was a chance you didn't want that anymore. That maybe I'd waited too long, and hurt you too much—"

"I still want that, Ava." Parker said, though her voice was raspy.

I looked up at her, and she was crying. I reached up and wiped her cheeks.

"I'm sorry." I whispered, feeling my eyes well up again. "I'm sorry I didn't see it like you did. I'm sorry I wasn't ready to talk about the hard stuff. But I want to know what Jayde put you through. I want to know about your dad. And I want the ugly, and... I'm ready to share mine. I think I'm ready to believe in the universe now because if it can give me you, it can't be all bad."

I must have said something right.

Her lips crashed into mine in this wet, tear-filled kiss that didn't bother me much because my stomach was too busy tying in knots to let my brain process why her lips tasted like salt.

She pulled away, and I leaned my forehead against her neck.

"I love you." I said quickly before I could talk myself out of it.

"What was that?" She asked, bringing my chin up with her fingers.

"I love you." I said again, looking into her eyes, holding on to the nerve that kiss had given me.

Even with all that fear, I still managed to say it first.

Sober at least.

Parker

"It's so good to see you, Parker." Carmen smiled as I sat down on the cushy couch in her office.

I eyed the motivational quotes on the wall before responding.

"You, too." I nodded, turning my focus back to her.

"So, on the phone, you mentioned a breakup. Would you like to start there?"

I nodded, and then a laugh escaped my lips. "You know? It's funny because we actually... sort of made up?"

"Oh? Does that feel like a good thing? A healthy, made up?"

"I think so." I nodded. "She was... just scared after everything her ex put her through, so she... left. And my ex had left me, so that sort of set me off—"

Carmen dropped her pen, sputtering for a second as she picked it up off the floor. When she sat back up, it seemed like she'd only halfway regained composure. But despite not being the therapist here, I was still pretty sure it had nothing to do with dropping the pen.

"I'm sorry, your ex left, and that set you off?" She asked, but her voice had gone up an octave.

"Mhmm." I nodded. "Is everything okay?"

"Yes, of course." She said, writing something in her notebook. "So, do you think this, um, this breakup affected you more because it felt like history repeating itself?"

"Yeah, I mean, it doesn't help that my mom..." I let out a deep sigh. "My mom also left. When I was little."

"How old were you?"

"Too young. I barely remember her at all."

"Do you have trouble connecting with others?" Carmen asked, and it finally seemed like she was back to normal. "Or do you assume everyone will leave?"

"Honestly, I've never had much trouble connecting. Now, though, it feels a little like a cycle."

Carmen made another note.

"Why don't you start with your ex?"

So, I did. I told her about Jayde. I told her about my dad. I told her about the drinking. I cried. At one point, it looked like she wanted to cry.

And by the time I was done, I needed a hug from Ava more than ever.

Ava

I bumped into Parker on my way into Carmen's office Tuesday afternoon—literally. I smacked right into her chest.

"Oh, my god. I'm so sorry." I mumbled, a breath of shock escaping my lips when I looked up to find familiar eyes looking back down at me.

"We've got to stop having the same ideas." Parker smirked.

"Agreed." I looked between her and the reception area. "Are you... here seeing Carmen?"

Parker nodded. "I figured it was time I saw someone for all my stuff. You're not the only one who has issues, you know."

I smiled.

"Speaking of." She hooked her thumb over her shoulder toward the stairs. "That was really...rough, and I could use one of your hugs right about now."

I was in her arms before she could even blink. Parker never had to ask for hugs. Ever.

A sigh escaped her lips, tickling the top of my head as it ruffled my hair. "Thank you."

"Anytime." I mumbled into her shoulder.

"Okay," she sighed, pulling away. "You get in there. I'm sure you'll have some interesting conversations. I think she might have figured out I was talking about you."

My eyes went wide, and she scratched the back of my neck nervously.

“Great, okay.” I whispered.

“Text me later?”

I nodded, and she kissed my forehead before heading down the street toward the diner.

Carmen did indeed have a few things to say when I stepped foot in her office. She asked more about Parker, about our relationship and how it had ended. Though she didn’t say Parker’s name, I had a feeling she knew. We talked about how easy it was with Parker despite all the ways it was harder now.

“Rebuilding trust is definitely a long-term commitment to acting in alignment with the things you say.” Carmen said, as I commented on how hesitant Parker was. “Which may be hard for you as you’ve bottled up things for so long.”

I nodded. “I’m definitely working more on embracing what I feel. Saying what I mean instead of avoiding what I really want to say because it’s hard.”

“That’s a great start.” She set her notebook on her side table and let out a sigh. “Ava, I want to ask you something, and I don’t want you to take it the wrong way, but given your sexuality, and your past, without assuming hers, how do you see your relationship working sexually?”

Okay, we really were talking about the hard stuff.

“Well, I’m...” I ran my fingers over the guitar pick on my neck, thinking about that day I’d taken a bath with Parker. I’d been willing to have sex with her then. “I’m not sex repulsed. I mean, I am for me. I don’t want sexual acts—I don’t want them done to me. But the funny thing is, all the things Cam did, I never minded having sex with her so long as she didn't touch me."

Carmen nodded, grabbing her notebook again. She wrote something down silently, and I wondered if that was the wrong answer. Was there a way to do therapy wrong?

My shift at the department store flew by in a blur. Maybe I was just tired from therapy, or maybe I was just looking forward to a quiet night to myself. Willow was over at Noah and Parker's place.

I wished I could be there.

I knew better because we'd just worked things out. I felt like I was still on thin ice. And Carmen would probably have my head. We had to take things at a reasonable pace.

"Ava!" I heard a singsong voice call from behind me. I knew that voice.

I really needed to pick a different route home.

"Jayde." I grimaced.

"It's so good to see you!"

Fake bitch.

"I've been wanting to talk to you." She continued.

"What about?" I sighed. I wanted to go home.

"Parker, what else?"

I nodded. "Yeah, okay, what about her?"

"So, I know you two like, have this thing, or maybe you don't. She's been spending an awful lot of time with me lately."

I tried to hide my wince, but I was pretty sure Jayde would be too drunk to notice.

"Anyway, I know she's into you or whatever, and since Cam gave her some advice, I thought I'd—"

"I don't want your advice, Jayde. I'm sure there's nothing you could tell me that would be useful."

"I know Parker better than anybody." She snapped.

"Do you?" I raised an eyebrow.

She huffed. "Listen, all I was going to say is that I meant what I said that night at St. Clare's. Parker is needy, okay? So, do what you have to, moan her name a few times, pretend if you've gotta. The number of times I've faked an orgasm for Parker." She let out a laugh.

I could have gone a million lifetimes without hearing 'Parker' and 'orgasm' coming out of this woman's mouth. The mental image made me ill.

"Thanks, I'll try my best to never remember that."

"Come on, Ava. All I mean is that if you want to keep Parker, you're going to have to step up your sex game a little bit. You do want to keep her, right?"

"I don't think..."

"You need to decide, okay? Because, like, there's a line of us just waiting. I will always be here for Parker. I will always take her back. So, if you don't want her, tell her. Let her move on."

I felt a lump rising in my throat. Jayde was a little late. Parker and I were figuring things out. Things were... patchy still. But it was better than it had been a week prior.

"Alright, I gotta go, car's waiting, but we should hang out sometime! And remember what I said, *needy.*"

Jayde stumbled to the waiting car about as gracefully as a baby giraffe learning to walk and practically fell into the back seat.

I let out a huff of frustration and started home, pausing at the laughter coming from the club Jayde had just left. Her car was speeding off, probably toward whatever hellish side of town she lived in. I was suddenly grateful I had far less money than her, if only to avoid being in the same neighborhood.

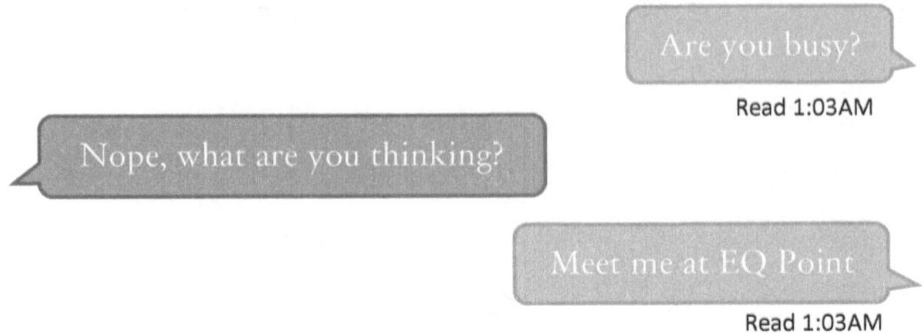

I took a deep breath and stepped inside, not waiting for her reply.

Maybe Parker and I weren't ready for this. Or maybe we were. We'd waited so long to get to any of the hard stuff, and here I was being reminded for the second time in one week that there was something entirely new I'd never given Parker—something maybe Jayde hadn't given Parker either.

But I was going to need to embrace some old feelings in order to do it.

Parker

I'll admit, Ava was different from anyone else I'd ever dated. The word asexual was new to me, and exploring intimacy without sex, while refreshing and nice, was also new. Normally, the two were pretty entwined. But despite all the newness, Ava was fairly predictable by now. She'd never once asked to hang out somewhere with lots of people. This was weird.

I'd already had a couple beers at home with Noah and Willow, but I wasn't about to ignore her, and if she was at a club, there's no way I wouldn't show up. Even if I was only there to rescue her.

I hadn't missed being there. It had only been a week since the last time I'd gotten plastered on this very dance floor.

The music was loud. It was a Thursday, half priced drinks, so they were packed. The flashing lights never made it easy to find someone. Though, normally, I wasn't looking.

I recognized a few people I knew, girls I'd hoped not to see again. But I didn't stop to chat. I grabbed a drink and eyed my phone, hoping she'd given me some clue of where to find her.

She hadn't.

Great.

I started around to the other side of the club. I didn't even know what she was wearing, but I was pretty confident I could pick out Ava anywhere.

It took less time than I thought. I spotted Ava at the rear bar. She was easy to pick out because she wasn't dressed like the other girls there. No short, flashy dress. Just a ripped pair of black jeans and a sage sweater. She took a shot and then headed back for the dance floor, swaying back and forth, her hands going up in the air to the music. I knocked back the rest of the drink in my hand and went to her.

She was drunk. I was pretty sure, because she didn't pull away when I took her hand, and she made eye contact with me. There was none of the hesitation there had been over the last few days. Instead, she smiled, pulled me closer, and started dancing with me, like none of what we'd been through had happened at all. Like it was our first date all over again. We just hadn't been dancing like *this*.

Her hands were all over me, gliding from my hair, to my chest, to my stomach and back again, somehow keeping time with the music. Or maybe she wasn't. The room felt a little hazy, so I couldn't be sure. I didn't know how long we stayed like that. I knew the song changed, but how many times?

I'd never imagined I'd be rewriting memories of this place, but there Ava was undoing some of the distaste I had for clubs. Making even EQ Point feel like something new—good.

Ava wasn't a party girl, though, and it wasn't just the clothes, which I wasn't sure how she could breathe in. She didn't go clubbing, or really go out a lot, period. I had no idea why she was even here. Or why she'd texted me asking to come hang out at one in the morning. How long had she been at this?

Her lips met mine, and I could taste tequila. She was kissing me like she did that day in my room, when we'd just gotten out of the tub. With her tongue in my mouth, her hands slipped up the back of my shirt, and suddenly the room felt very warm.

She pulled away, looking up at me with dark, fiery eyes. "Take me home?"

I was dazed, and I nodded without thinking. She barely even watched me nod before her hand was in mine, and she was leading me to the door, through the crowd, between dancing couples and groups.

Once outside, the chilly night air gave me a momentary sobering feeling while she clumsily hailed down a cab. I shouldn't be doing this.

Then she kissed me again, in that same intense way, like she wanted me, bringing back that same heat I'd felt inside.

"You ladies need a ride or what?" The driver called from the window, and Ava pulled me toward the car.

The jack was kicking in. I was about to do stupid things, and I couldn't even remember why they were stupid.

Somehow Ava was sober enough to tell the driver the address, and she kept her lips off mine on the short ride to her apartment, instead she was planting soft kisses along my collarbone while her fingers were playfully trailing back and forth along the inside of my thigh, keeping me from having any rational thoughts.

We barely made it inside her empty apartment and got the door locked before her lips were on mine again, tossing my jacket on the floor. She had the collar of my shirt in her fists, and she was backing me up toward the couch.

She'd never kissed me like this, not even that day after the bath. Then, there'd been a little hint of hesitation. That was gone, and I wasn't sure Ava had ever been so confident or clear about her intentions before.

Her fingers slowly moved to the buttons of my shirt, but her lips didn't leave mine. We were halfway across the room before I knew what to do with my hands. They rested on the bare skin of her hips where her shirt had ridden up. She didn't pull away like she had that time in her room. Something about the touch lit her up even more, if that were possible, and she started moving faster.

She shoved me onto the couch and climbed on top of me. We'd been here before, that I could remember somehow. I hadn't had *that* much Jack. How much tequila had she had?

Her lips started making trails along my jawline and toward my neck, making it hard for me to think about anything else.

"She can't handle hard liquor."

Her lips reached my collarbone.

"If she gets drunk enough, she'll do anything, but she'll regret it in the morning."

Her hands fumbled briefly with the buttons of my jeans.

"Even if she begs for it, tell her no."

"Ava, wait." I said, my heart racing more at the thought of taking advantage of her than where her hands were. "We can't. We should definitely be sober for this."

"I am sober." She whispered, eyeing me for a second. "Are you... are you not sober?"

All I could think about was the shot I'd seen her take.

When I didn't answer, she leaned it toward my neck again, and pushed her back as gently as I could.

"Remember what you said?" She asked before I could get a word out. "You said if I really wanted to, we could talk about it. Parker, I want to."

"Ava, you're drunk." I sighed, running my hand through my hair. "That's not the same."

"I'm fine."

"Oh, yeah? How much did you have?"

"I had one shot of tequila." She said, giving me a look like I'd actually hurt her feelings. "I want to."

I let out a breath. I couldn't believe I was even thinking about this. "And you're not going to regret this in the morning?"

"No, I'm not." Her voice was low, as one of her hands slid up my shirt, trailing across my abs, leaving goosebumps in their wake. "Are you?"

"Am I what?" I choked out, barely above a whisper. Her hand was now trailing circles around my belly button. She was making it dangerously hard to have any coherent thoughts.

"Are you sober? Will you regret this in the morning?"

I didn't know how to answer that without feeling like an awful person. Was she really sober? Was it really just one shot of tequila? Did she really want to do this, or was it just the tequila talking? Would she regret this in the morning? Would this be the biggest mistake of my entire life?

I'd never seen Ava drunk. I didn't know what I was looking for, how much was enough to make her do things she'd regret.

"Do you want me to stop?" She asked, her eyes looking into mine. "Be honest."

"No, but I–" I whispered back, breathily as I tried to reason why just because *I* wanted something didn't mean she needed to do it.

Her hands slid from my stomach and wrapped around my hips. Her lips met my neck in a furry, trailing down to my collarbone. A moan slipped out of my throat.

Her hands reached to the button of my jeans again when another moan escaped my throat. I really didn't know what to do with my hands. Because I kept thinking back to the boundaries she'd set before, and I couldn't be sure if those had changed just because she was definitely crossing them.

She slipped a single finger inside the hem of my boxers, which made me gasp like an idiot, and a smile spread across her lips. There was a devilish look in her eyes that made my throat go dry.

"Come with me." She whispered, standing up and pulling me toward her room.

She shut the door behind us, locking it slowly while I stood in front of her bed, practically shaking.

"Ava, we really don't have to—"

Ava wrapped her hands around my waist and kissed me again before I could say another word. She was serious about this, and she wasn't stumbling anymore. She wasn't slurring her words. Her eyes didn't look glassed over.

She wanted to do this, and I couldn't convince myself she was drunk.

I still didn't know what to do with my hands, so I cupped her face. And it might have been more romantic and less of a hot mess if she wasn't taking my pants off.

A shudder went through my body when her hands brushed across the back of my thighs. She pulled away, backing up toward the door. I thought I'd done something wrong until she shut off the light.

My eyes didn't get a chance to adjust before her hands were on my hips again, gliding up to the remaining buttons of my shirt. She started kissing my neck again while she slid my flannel off my shoulders and let it drop to the floor. It seemed really weird that I was practically naked, and she hadn't even kicked off her shoes, but I wasn't about to say so.

"What do you want me to do?" I breathed as she nibbed on my collarbone.

"Nothing." She said back in a deeper tone than I'd ever heard from her. Shit, it was basically a growl.

Nothing? I didn't know what to do with nothing. I was so used to doing everything.

"What?" I asked, hyperaware of the way my mouth was hanging open.

"What do you want me to do?" She asked, but there was a grin on her face that I could barely see from the light of her salt lamp.

"What?" I asked again, a sudden hitch in my voice that I couldn't hide, even when I not so subtly cleared my throat.

"I'll tell you what." She said as her hands slowly trailed up my sides until her fingers hooked on my sports bra and lifted it over my head. "If I start to do something you don't want, tell me to stop, and I will."

Her lips went to my neck again, and her hands were on my bare back, her shirt rubbed against my chest, and it clicked. She was fully clothed. She wanted me to do nothing. The way that felt one sided, like I really was taking advantage of her.

"Ava, you really don't have to—"

"I know," she said, pulling away and looking up at me.

It was the first time she'd given me the chance to have a seriously rational thought since we'd walked through the front door.

"I know I don't have to." She repeated. "That's why I want to."

"I don't—" I tried to say, but her teeth were on my collarbone again, so it came out more like a hiss. "I don't understand that logic. You're trying to distract me."

"No, I'd rather you be fully present, thanks." There was a sly grin on her face, and I let out a nervous laugh.

That was probably the hottest thing anyone had ever said to me.

Then she pushed me on to the bed, and I let out a not so attractive gasp.

A beat passed. I expected her to be on top of me instantly, like she had on the couch. Instead, I heard the familiar sound of clothes rustling, and I felt chills cover my entire body. Then I heard a soft click, and an old song I only faintly remembered hearing as a kid started playing.

When she did climb on top of me, I felt nothing but her. Her bare legs on mine, her stomach against my chest. She still had on a bra and underwear, and I wasn't about to question it. I didn't ask why the music was so loud either.

She kissed me again, harder this time, like she had when we'd first walked in the door. And then she was trailing kisses down my jaw, to my collarbone. She pushed me back against the bed until I was laying down, and her kisses got lower and lower.

Now I really didn't know what to do with my hands.

She hooked her fingers in the band of my boxers and started pulling them down, slowly, too slowly. She was doing that on purpose. I just knew it. I could feel my heartbeat racing faster as they fell to the floor. Her lips brushed the inside of my thigh, closer and closer.

"Fuck, Ava." I whispered, grabbing a fistful of the sheet.

Ava

When I woke the next morning, I was very much not hungover. I couldn't remember the last time I'd done anything like that and not woken up hungover. There was no dark haze, no questioning anything. I could remember the feel of Parker's body in full clarity. But I couldn't actually feel her.

Her arms weren't around me. I couldn't hear her breathing. I was completely alone.

I reached behind me, a sense of dread washing over me when I came up empty. What was worse, the bed was ice cold. Tears formed immediately.

Why was I so fucking stupid?

A clanking sound came from the kitchen.

"Shit." I heard Parker whisper.

I let out a sigh of relief, wiping my eyes. She didn't need to see me cry.

I scanned the room, looking for my robe, finding Parker's flannel first. I felt a sly grin tugging at the corners of my mouth as I slipped it on without even bothering with the buttons that likely would protest regardless and stepped into the hall.

Stifling a laugh in the back of my hand, I eyed the sight of Parker in my kitchen, fanning smoke into our tiny hood vent. She'd slipped her boxers back on along with her sports bra, but she wasn't wearing anything else. I could see the curve of every chiseled muscle in her back, and I eyed those for a good minute before I couldn't help myself.

"What are you doing?" I asked, leaning against the doorway.

She jumped and turned sharply toward me. "Oh, I was just—I mean, I... I was trying to make breakfast."

Her cheeks and neck turned bright red as she looked me up and down. I'd always hated when Cam looked at me like that, but Parker looked at me like I was art–like I was the most beautiful thing she'd ever seen.

"Willow is going to kill you." I smiled. "You've tainted her kitchen."

"Yeah, well, I think I've done worse to these pancakes."

A laugh slipped through my lips as I crossed the room to examine her handiwork. They were without a doubt the worst pancakes I'd ever seen, but I ripped off a piece and took a bite anyway, nodding and smiling with a fake sense of approval while I looked for a napkin to spit in.

"They're bad, aren't they?" She asked, but she was grinning when she did. "Oh, god I swear I didn't try to poison you."

"No, no, they're good." I forced myself to swallow. "I think you should just order delivery next time, though."

She blushed again, handing me a glass of orange juice.

Nope, not orange juice, I learned after a sip, almost spitting it back out. Mimosa. That was definitely a mimosa.

"I'm sorry!" She said frantically. "I should've—I thought maybe you might be hungover, so I thought—"

"It's okay." I laughed, setting down the drink, and pulling her closer to me by her hips. "You're a much better bartender than a cook."

“So, I’ve been told.” She smirked, leaning down to kiss me, slow and soft, the way she’d learned I liked it. “I like you like this, in my clothes, I mean.”

“This is as in your clothes as it gets. This thing would never button over my stomach.”

“I think I like it better this way.”

My cheeks burned when she slid a hand inside the flannel and around to the small of my back. That would have freaked me out before, but I knew there was nothing more to it. She kissed me again. This time, though, she didn’t pull away until the front door opened, and I heard a cry I knew beyond the shadow of a doubt came from Willow’s mouth.

Parker

"Get out of my kitchen!" Willow yelled, setting down her purse, while she ran to the living room to open the door to their tiny standing balcony and clear out what remained of the smoke.

I was lucky I hadn't set off the smoke alarms, really. Why hadn't I just ordered food?

"Whoa, what happened in here?" Noah laughed, eyeing the room while Ava tightened my flannel around her as quickly as she could before scurrying out of the room. "Oh, no, you tried to cook, didn't you?"

I grimaced.

"Get out!" Willow said again, scanning the tiny kitchen. "Did you use metal on this?"

I shook my head. I'd been really careful with her stuff, to be honest. I was just a terrible cook. She let out a sigh before she started washing the pan I'd nearly caught on fire.

Willow shoed me one more time before I decided I'd be much safer in Ava's room.

"You were right." I laughed as I shut the door behind me. "Willow is pissed."

"I told you." Ava laughed as she bounced into a pair of yoga pants. "That girl does not play when it comes to her pots and pans."

She was out of my flannel again, reaching for a t-shirt instead.

"So..." I breathed, a sudden hitch there. "About last night. I don't—"

Ava reached over and grabbed my hand, pulling me to her. She put a hand on my cheek and stretched up to kiss me.

"I don't regret it, okay?"

I felt a smile tugging at the corners of my mouth. "How much of it do you remember?"

Suddenly my cheeks were burning as she reached up to my ear like she had on the couch.

"All of it." She whispered, giving me a quick peck on the lips before she slipped out of the room.

I had chills everywhere.

"Hey Parker." Jayde sang as she walked up to the bar.

I groaned internally. I didn't think she'd ever dared show up at my work, but I wasn't going to let her ruin my good mood. "Hi Jayde."

"You're in a good mood."

She leaned across the bar far enough that her shirt lowered a bit, and I turned away.

"I am, actually." I smiled, but I knew she couldn't see it.

"I haven't seen you out lately." She sighed.

"Yeah," I nodded, turning back toward her. "And I don't think you will."

She grinned really slyly. "So, Ava took my advice then."

I felt my face fall. "What advice?"

Her eyes darted to the door. "I think maybe you should ask her yourself."

Jayde waved casually to Ava on her way back out the door like they were friends. Ava frowned at her, shaking her head.

"What was Jayde doing here?" Ava scoffed, leaning her guitar case against the bar.

"Just came to check and see if you followed the advice she gave you." I cast a glare at Ava.

"What advice?" Ava asked, straight faced, but I could tell she wasn't being completely honest.

"Don't lie to me, please. When Jayde cheated on me, she looked me in the eye and told me she did it. She has no shame. She doesn't lie. What advice did she give you? And when were you hanging out with my ex?"

Ava let out a breath, almost in a painful laugh. "I didn't hang out with your ex. And you know what? I'm not going to tell you what she told me because it would just hurt your feelings."

I let out a breath, leaning both arms on the bar so I was closer to Ava. This definitely wasn't the place for this conversation.

"When did you talk to Jayde?" I uttered each word separately.

"Last night." She sighed, and there was a look of fear in her eyes, reminding me of the first Friday I'd been back on nights.

"Was that before or after you asked me to meet you at a club you don't go to?" I scoffed, leaning back against the cooler. "What the hell were you doing at EQ Point with Jayde?"

She let out another painful laugh. "First, I really don't like the way you're talking to me, but *I* wasn't at EQ Point *with Jayde*. She was at EQ Point. I was walking home, walking past EQ Point like I have every night for the last six weeks."

We made eye contact, and I felt the color drain from my face. How many times had I found Jayde a car, called a taxi or put her in an Uber? Had Ava seen me? Had she gotten the wrong impression?

That was an issue for another day, though, because I could not get the thought of Jayde giving her any advice out of my head.

"So," I let out a breath, biting the inside of my lip to keep from tearing up. "So, last night? That was because of Jayde."

Her face softened, and all the anger that had been building faded, but she didn't deny it. She looked down instead.

"No," she whispered. "No, it wasn't."

"I don't think I believe you, Ava." I snapped, tossing my towel on the bar and heading for the kitchen. I needed an hour in the walk-in cooler.

Ava was off the barstool and in front of the bar door before I could even cross the room.

"It wasn't because of Jayde." She insisted, trying to meet my eyes, but I really couldn't look at her. "If I had listened to Jayde, last night would have been a lot different."

"But you still had to get drunk to do it."

"I wasn't—" She looked down and tapped the bar with her thumb, a wave of frustration washing over her face. "I wasn't drunk. I told you that like four times. I had one shot of tequila. I thought it would help my nerves."

She looked back up at me. She was so close I could have kissed her instead of getting angry, but it was too late for that. I was already angry. I was already hurt.

"Right." I laughed. "You know, Cam gave me some advice about you when you're drunk?"

Her eyes welled up instantly and her cheeks turned a bright red. If she'd been Jayde, she might have slapped me. I regretted the words the moment they were out of my mouth.

She let out a shudder of a breath.

"I..." I sighed. "I shouldn't have—"

"I didn't follow Jayde's advice, just so we are clear." Ava hissed, low and quiet so no one else would hear, but she might as well have been yelling at me. "Because if I had, I'd have faked an orgasm and called it a night like she apparently has hundreds of times."

I winced. Fuck Jayde if she thought I was ever talking to her again.

"Ava—"

She turned, storming off to where her guitar was sitting.

"Ava, wait." I sighed, stepping out of the bar. I could see Nathan eyeing us, so that was as far as I got.

"No." she snapped, looking at Nathan and giving him a tense smile and a wave before turning back to me. "Last night was about you. It was for you."

"Ava—"

"No, don't. I need to get this out while I'm mad, or I probably won't." She looked down, letting out a sigh. "Jayde said that if I wanted to keep you, I needed to step up my game. Specifically... in that department."

She looked up at me again, I felt my cheeks burning.

"But I realized that you and Jayde didn't work out because she thought you were needy, and you are—"

"Hey—"

"You're just needy in all the ways Jayde isn't willing to give."

I let out a sigh. Because she was right. One conversation, and she'd got our whole relationship down to a T.

"And just so we are clear," she let out another shuddery breath. "Last night wasn't so I could keep you, either." She paused, eyeing Nathan again, who looked rather annoyed. We'd be lucky if he didn't fire us both. "Sex isn't something you just use to manipulate people. Especially not to me. I just wanted to give you something that I knew I could, and it seemed like no one else had cared enough to, and I didn't regret it until just now."

I turned away from Nathan and back to Ava just in time to catch her heading for the door.

"Ava..." I sighed.

"Tell Nathan I'll be back for my set." She snapped.

Ava

What the fuck had Cam told her?

I was stalking down the boulevard with my headphones in. I just needed to think. I needed to breathe. I needed to feel... whatever this was, like Carmen was teaching me to do. I didn't want to be mad at Parker. We'd just worked things out. I'd thought so anyway.

Maybe not.

Knowing she was actually taking advice from my ex, though, that cut deep. I guess it was only fair because it looked like I was taking advice from hers.

Better communication skills. That's what we needed. How the hell did we manage that? I guessed honesty was a good start.

I could be honest. Not even honest, because I rarely lied, anyway. I could be *forthcoming*. Maybe that's what we really needed. It was hard sometimes. Hell, sometimes it was painful, but I could do it. I could do it for Parker. Maybe I could do it for myself, too.

I let out a sigh and rounded the next corner, making a circle back to Brickhouse. If I walked fast enough, I could make it back in time to apologize to Parker before I needed to set up to play.

But when I walked in, the bar was packed, more so than the average Friday normally was. Parker was swamped, and Ellis had stuck around to help instead of skipping off to do prep work. Even the dining room was a buzz. I let out a sigh and headed back for the sound booth, giving Parker a reassuring smile as I went through.

Nathan looked up from his seat in the sound booth when I walked in, almost seeming surprised I was there. He flipped a couple of switches, and nodded silently to me before shutting the door and going back to the game on his phone.

I pulled out my guitar, slipping the strap over my shoulder with a bit of resolve I hadn't had before.

"Hi, everyone." I waved.

I was starting to see familiar faces every week. This same girl had been coming for a minute, recording my performances and uploading them online. I didn't mind because she'd tag me. It was kind of cool. But now I saw more faces that I recognized. I didn't know their names. I just knew they'd been there before.

"I've been putting this off, but tonight I have something original for you."

Parker

My nerves didn't settle until I saw Ava walk back in the front door. She didn't seem mad. There was that, at the very least.

Why did it seem like we were always working through something? When would we get to where we were? When would we be able to just... be?

The bar was packed. More so than usual. It wasn't like we were some major hot spot for games, even in season. We didn't have a huge sale going on. People were just... there. I could see Ava taking the stage out of the corner of my eye. Nothing seemed different until she spoke.

My eyes snapped over to the stage when she said she had something original. I knew Ava wrote music. She was always trying new little riffs and humming tunes. I'd just never heard any of it. Nobody had as far as I knew. The only one she ever played something original around was Willow.

There was a little bit of applause, like usual. It seemed louder, though.

"I've got a few warm up songs first." Ava's eyes met mine. "There's someone special I want to make sure hears this one, so I hope that's okay."

She had four warm-up songs. All of them were love songs. I kept sneaking glances at her, catching her smiling at me, like she wanted me to know she was basically singing to me. It was growing increasingly hard to focus.

I was lucky the crowd was dwindling. Well, not really. They just weren't currently getting drinks. Most of them were standing toward the back of the dining area where the stage was, listening with their drinks in hand.

Ava was drawing a crowd.

I sent one of the servers over to her with a glass of water.

"So, I'm starting to see some familiar faces." Ava grinned, pointing to some girl in the room who had her camera out before taking a drink of the water and setting it down. "Some of you probably have noticed that my music has been really sad lately."

I swallowed a lump in my throat and leaned over the bar.

"See, I think music is emotion, so normally, I play what I feel. It's hard to play something happy when I'm down."

She looked up at me and smiled. I saw Nathan coming out of the sound booth. He crossed his arms, looking rather annoyed.

"Recently I went through a really tough time." She let out a sigh, eyeing Nathan out of the corner of her eye like he might swarm on the stage. "But I think everything's going to work out now."

I couldn't help but smile, and Nathan looked between us with a serious glare.

"So," Ava cleared her throat. "Here is a song that I wrote for someone I love."

If Ava never figured out how to say what she felt, if she never figured out how to come out and say what she needed to, I could live with that. So long as she could put it in a song and sing it to me.

I always thought her covers were good. She was incredibly talented. And a part of me knew that sometimes she was singing to me. But it was a different thing entirely when I knew not only was she singing to me, she was singing about me. Her words, not someone else's that happened to fit. This was about me; about us.

And suddenly, she wasn't just whispering 'I love you' to me on a quiet street. She was telling everyone in that room. Three and a half minutes worth of 'I love yous' out in the open, on camera, for everyone to hear.

Ava

I played six more covers, and then someone in the room asked me to re-sing my original, so I sang that, too. People were heading out when I started just strumming around with a few riffs of different songs all together. I was fighting it, but the night was over.

When I finally got off the stage and put away my guitar, Nathan came up to me.

"Ava, I've tried to tell you, the performance isn't about you. It's about entertaining the guests."

"Right," I nodded. "Sorry."

"Nath*an*." Ellis chimed, walking up and clapping Nathan on the shoulder.

I thought Ellis had gone home a while ago.

"Best night we've had in a minute." Ellis continued. "A few people said they came here just to see Ava."

He smiled at me, and I felt my cheeks burn. Then Nathan turned around, and I let my smile drop.

"Right," Nathan nodded before promptly turning around and heading back into the sound booth.

Suddenly Parker was to my left, coming at me at almost a run. She grabbed me by the waist and picked me up, spinning me in a circle. A squeal escaped my lips before she set me down.

"So, you liked it?" I grinned.

She nodded. "You got a minute?"

She hooked her thumb toward the back door.

"Do you?" I eyed the bar.

"Hey Ellis, you got this for a sec?" She called over, and I could see Nathan in the sound booth peeking his head out the tiny window.

"Yeah, I got you." Ellis gave Parker a weird little salute.

I let out a laugh as Parker and I slipped out the back door.

It was barely shut before she pushed me against the wall of the building, waiting only a second for me to pull away, and she kissed me. She kissed me like she was saying, 'I love you.' Like kissing me was music. That was her original song.

"You still mad at me?" Parker asked when she pulled away.

I shook my head, smiling up at her. "I think we need to work on our communication, though. Something about boundaries, I think."

Parker nodded, "How about we start by agreeing not to talk to our or each other's exes?"

"I think I can agree to that."

Parker grinned. "And we both stay in therapy."

"I can also agree to that." I looked down, and I felt the mood shift. "About last night,"

A space somehow grew between us.

"I don't regret it." I said, grabbing her hips and pulling her to me. "And I shouldn't have said that I did."

"We don't have to—" She swallowed, touching my cheek with her thumb. "I'm okay with us just being... like this."

"Oh, yeah?" I asked.

She nodded, and it was genuine, and I should have felt guilty when I slid my hands in the back of her shirt and planted a kiss on her neck. But I didn't. Because her breath hitched, and she leaned closer to me, and I knew that even if it was confusing to her, I made her feel like that. And the power to decide was mine.

"That's not fair." She whispered into my shoulder.

"Look at me," I replied, pulling my hands back out of her shirt and resting them on her hips.

She did, but there was an entirely different level of nervousness there.

"I had one shot of tequila." I said. "I wasn't drunk. I wasn't even buzzed. I wanted to."

"So, you just wanted me to think you were drunk?" She smirked.

"Actually," I cringed. "I hoped you hadn't seen me take that shot at all."

"But... why? Why would you want to—"

"Because I want to take care of you just as much as you want to take care of me. I want to make you blissfully happy, too. We just have different needs."

She scoffed again. "That doesn't seem fair. It feels like I'm... using you."

"That's not using me at all." I continued. "Intimacy comes in many forms. I just happen to crave it in the nonsexual forms, but that doesn't mean I can't give you something you crave. I love you, and I'm happy to give you... that. Just don't ask me to talk about it in depth."

She laughed, "Oh, you don't want me to tell you how much—
"

"Nope." I groaned, pulling away and heading back toward the door. "Sexting is off limits, too."

I heard another short laugh.

"And it has to be dark. Music is required, no working around that."

She sucked in a loud breath through her nose while I tried to lead her inside by just my fingertips.

"I can agree to those terms."

She was blushing a bright red. "Can I ask why?"

I scrunched my face.

"I'm not trying to argue," she said softly. "I just want to understand."

"Anxiety." I shrugged. "Maybe it's a sensory thing. I don't know. If I can see or hear what I'm doing, it freaks me out."

"Okay." She nodded, pulling me back to her before I could get the door open.

She leaned down and kissed me. Slowly, softly, another 'I love you.'

"I love you." She whispered when she pulled away, looking at me like she loved saying it—like she loved finally being able to say something she'd thought for so long.

And then she was trying to lead me inside.

"You're going to quit smoking, right?" I asked.

She laughed, reaching into her jacket pocket and pulling out the nearly full pack. She handed them to me.

"I just did."

Two Years Later

Ava

"Babe," I heard Parker call from our room. "Have you seen my leather jacket?"

I tucked in a bobby pin before calling back, "Last I saw, it was on the bar."

"Actually, it's on the coat rack where it belongs." Noah teased, as he and Willow headed to the living room.

Parker wrapped her arms around my waist from behind. "How many times are you going to redo your hair? You look beautiful."

"It's just this—one piece." I grunted as she kissed my cheek, making it practically impossible to touch my hair.

"It's perfect."

Her dark eyes met mine in the bathroom mirror. She was giving me that look, and I tried to match her smile.

I was nervous.

This was my first serious performance gig. I wanted to take it seriously. Even if my girlfriend was the one paying me. And here she was, brushing off my hair looking good.

"Come on, we'll be late."

I let out a sigh, eyeing that one piece of hair one more time before Parker grabbed my hand and led me to the living room where Noah and Willow were waiting on the couch, both of them dressed up despite the fact that Noah was about to spend most of the evening in the kitchen.

He must have been used to the heat, or he didn't care. I couldn't decide if he was dressed up for me or not. But we finally seemed on good terms, Noah and I. At the very least, he didn't seem worried I was going to shatter Parker's heart again.

Life got easier when Willow and I moved in, despite how unnerving that was at first. The last time I'd moved in with someone... but that didn't happen. Parker wasn't Cam.

Instead, things got better. Rent was cut in half for all of us, no more walking across town to see each other, no more swapping apartments twice a week. And by some miracle, our cats got along. Life was simpler. And our little family fit so well in that two-bedroom place.

As we all headed out toward the car, I eyed Willow and her little waddle. I hated the idea that things were about to change again. It felt like we'd just reached a nice balance.

But I'd finally learned that different didn't have to be bad. Things could change, and we could grow, and life could go on without disaster striking. And when Parker kissed the side of my head, right on my temple, I was reminded of what Carmen had drilled into me.

I deserved this.

Parker

I walked out of the kitchen to find Ava on a bar stool, leaning over into the bar area, her hand in a small jar of cherries.

"Ma'am, employees only behind the bar." I teased.

She plopped back on the barstool clumsily and pulled a cherry off its stem.

"Well, I know the owner," she said back, carefully sticking the stem in her mouth.

She walked over to me less than gracefully, sticking out her tongue where a perfectly tied knot resided.

"Here, you keep that." She put the stem in my shirt pocket, and then her hands brushed my hips and eventually settled in my back pockets.

"Do you think you get special treatment?" I raised an eyebrow.

She stretched up on her toes and pressed her lips to my ear. She smelled like coconut and sea salt. And she didn't own a single perfume that smelled like either.

I swear if someone bought her tequila...

"No, but you do." She whispered.

I sucked in a sharp breath. "That is not appropriate conversation, ma'am. We have rules."

"Yeah, but they're *my* rules." She whispered, inches from my lips. "I can break them if I want to, right?"

I thought she was going to hug me. I was ready for a hug. I was not ready for her to bite my collarbone. I had to grab the bar to steady us both because her hands were still in my pockets. I really needed to stop teasing Ava when she was drunk.

"Get a room!" I heard Noah yell from the kitchen door.

"I own the whole building." I smarted back, and he swatted his spatula in my general direction.

Ava sighed, leaning back far enough I had to grab her waist, so she didn't fall. "When can we get out of here?"

I grinned, looking up at the dwindling crowd. There were still far too many people here for me to just bow out. The kitchen wasn't even closed, and while I trusted Jax, Willow, and Noah, it wasn't their job to lock up.

"Soon," I nodded, kissing her while I led her to an empty booth. "In the meantime, you are cut off."

Her jaw dropped, and I let her fall into the cushioned booth with a squeal.

"Jax, did you hear that?" I asked the only person I trusted running my bar.

"Yes, ma'am." He nodded, grimacing at Ava, who had sat up to look at him. "Sorry, Ava. She signs my checks."

"Parker!" Ava groaned, long and loud as she fell back against the booth. She was yelling.

I knew that tone. I knew that drunken yell that meant vastly inappropriate words were about to spill out of her mouth at a high volume. I bolted back to the booth.

"All I want is to do—"

I covered her mouth, trying not to laugh. "Ava stop. You can't just yell across the bar."

"Oh, hello." She grinned, eyeing the fact that I was on top of her. She dropped into a ridiculously loud, over-exaggerated whisper. "I want to do naughty things to you."

Jax snorted, and my cheeks burned. I rubbed my eyes, letting out a sigh. Ava erupted into giggles.

So, we were at that stage. Good, she'd be asleep or sobering up soon.

I started to get up. I was nearly out of the booth.

"Wait, wait, wait, wait, wait." Ava grabbed my tie, pulling my face inches from hers. She'd gotten really serious—wide glassy eyes pouring into mine. "I love you."

I let out a laugh. "I love you. Now, can you drink some water? And maybe eat something. Because I have a feeling you're going to regret your decisions tomorrow if you break any more of your own rules. Especially if you have to see some of these people next week. You remember you work here, right?"

She buzzed her lips, right in my face. "Okaayy."

"Thank you."

She let go of my tie and went to pouting. I turned to Jax, who was biting the inside of his lip rather furiously, but his shoulders were bouncing like he was having a laughing fit.

"Could you get her some water and see if Noah will make her a burger?" I asked, and Jax nodded wordlessly as he headed to the kitchen.

I heard him bust out a laugh the moment the obviously not sound proof doors swung shut behind him, followed by, "Noah, you gotta hear this."

I looked back at Ava, who gave me an albeit glassy but sincere smile before she yawned.

A chuckle slipped out, and I made my way back to the sound booth so I could switch the playlist. I couldn't wait to hire a DJ.

When I stepped back out of the booth, Ava was hunched over the table, asleep.

"Goodnight, Parker!" A few people called as they headed out.

I nodded to them, but I didn't really take my eyes off of Ava.

Here I was, living the life I wanted. I was following my dreams. So was Noah. We had the perfect place, and I could actually afford it. Business was doing well. And despite how wildly inappropriate Ava had been that night, I couldn't have done any of it without her.

She'd worked hard for months to pay my entire half of rent so I could save it. It was crazy to me how she believed in my dreams as much as I did. And I believed in hers. I bit my lip to keep from getting teary-eyed.

"I see you." Willow said, coming up next to me. "When are you going to ask her?"

I grinned, feeling the box in my pocket. My step mom had given it to me. She even made a special trip for it. She said my dad had given it to her, and he would have wanted me to have it, especially if I was as sure as I was.

I was pretty damn sure.

Her dad was ecstatic. He basically laughed at me when I tried to ask for his blessing. He told me he didn't understand the question because I should have already known the answer. *"I see the way she looks at you. I think you're the best thing that's ever happened to her. You pulled her out of that dark place. You helped me get my little dreamer back."*

"I was going to ask her tonight, but..." I gestured to where Ava was sleeping.

Willow grinned. "She had many shots."

I let out a laugh. Someone had definitely bought her tequila.

"It's okay," Willow shrugged. "You have time. I don't think she's going anywhere."

I nodded, and Willow headed for the kitchen door. She was showing now. It wasn't ridiculously noticeable, but I could tell she was already getting the waddle. I wondered how much longer Noah and Willow would stay in the apartment before they realized it was too small for the four of us *and* a baby.

Maybe I could talk Ava into moving into the tiny place upstairs from the bar. It needed some renovations, but I didn't mind. We'd never been just the two of us. Lord knows what kind of mess that would be with no Willow or Noah to clean it up.

But I'd happily live in that mess with her.

Just then, she jumped, sitting up and looking around like she didn't know where she was. There was a red mark across her cheek where the zipper of my jacket had been sitting. Her eyes met mine, and she smiled sleepily.

Yeah, I could wake up to that face every day for the rest of my life.

Acknowledgements

I want to firstly thank Kathleen, who has been my Carmen the last year and a half. Thank you for helping me through these traumas. Thank you for helping me find the road to healing, and giving me a safe place to feel the pain that led to this book.

To my wife, Kara. You are my Parker, my muse, and the person who has inspired every love interest in every story I've written for the last six and a half years. Thank you for walking through the darkness with me when I truly believed I'd never see the light. Thank you for seeing the worst in me and still seeing someone worth loving. But most importantly, thank you for seeing who I am instead of the person I thought I had to be.

Dad, thank you for encouraging my dreams and being there for me when I needed you most.

Mom, thank you for trying your hardest to talk me out of my bad decisions. And for encouraging me to believe in love again after I undoubtedly proved I get my taste in partners from you.

Sami, Nea, and Kayln, thank you for being the little sisters I will always, until I die, give the mom treatment, at least a little.

Lainie, my best and oldest friend, thank you for sticking by my side the last fifteen years. Thank you for helping me through so many trials and tribulations. You have truly saved me from myself time and time again. Without you, Noah would not be.

To Cate and Shawna, Catawna, the OTP of the century, thank you for diving headfirst into this journey with me. Thank you for encouraging me to get help when I didn't know I needed it.

Thank you for seeing things I couldn't see. I owe so much to you.

Thank you, Melissa, for convincing me this book was not garbage. Imposter Syndrome dwells within the soul.

I'd also specifically like to thank the Hansen House Team. So, yeah, I'm thanking me, too.

About the Author

Elizabeth Jeannel is a saphhic ace author of queer stories she wishes she'd had in her yesteryears and insistent that all of them end happily. Her releases currently include *The Art of Feeling, Cursed* (the novella), and *Waking Rory*. She is the founder and ringmaster of Hansen House, an artist, a photographer, and a gamer when she can squeeze in the time. She is a massive nerd and lover of most sci-fi and fantasy, only wishing more of it had queer representation.

When not writing, she can usually be found wrangling her small farm, hyperfixating on the wrong thing, or consuming just shy of too much caffeine. She currently resides in Southwest Missouri with her wife, who she says will always be her muse.

www.ingramcontent.com/pod-product-compliance
Lightning Source LLC
Chambersburg PA
CBHW030628310726
48979CB00003B/923

* 9 7 8 1 9 5 6 0 3 7 0 0 5 *